IN TIME FOR CHRISTMAS

IN TIME FOR CHRISTMAS

Katie Flynn

**WINDSOR
PARAGON**

First published 2009
by Arrow Books
This Large Print edition published 2009
by BBC Audiobooks Ltd
by arrangement with
The Random House Group Ltd

Hardcover ISBN: 978 1 408 43135 1
Softcover   ISBN: 978 1 408 45881 5

British Library Cataloguing in Publication Data available

Printed and bound in Great Britain by
CPI Antony Rowe, Chippenham and Eastbourne

For Margaret Chamberlain, a good friend of long standing, on her becoming Mayor of Oswestry. Congratulations, Margaret!

PART I

1936–1941

CHAPTER ONE

March 1936

'Look out, Nick! Help, help, I'm slipping! Oh, dammit, look what you've made me do!'

Adelaide Fairweather pointed down at the large hessian sack upon which she was balanced, and at the steady stream of rice pouring from the tear that had resulted when she had stopped suddenly in her onward flight. She had stopped to avoid bumping into her pal Nick Bentley, who had hesitated fractionally before taking the next leap, and Addy's toe had caught in the hessian, ripping it open and allowing the rice the sack contained to escape. The three children were playing Off the Ground in the storeroom of the Fairweathers' corner shop, a game that Addy knew would have been strictly forbidden if her mother had known what they were doing. The main object was to circle the room leaping from sacks to boxes, and from boxes to stacks of tinned goods, without once touching the floor. There were two truly tricky places where, for obvious reasons, there were no goods on to which one might leap: the door leading into the yard and that which opened into the tiny back room of the shop where Nell Fairweather retreated when she had no customers. Addy, however, had foreseen the difficulty and had put 'stepping stones' across the spaces; a large tin of peaches and another of Beaulah's peas bridged the gap by the back door and Lyle's Golden Syrup and a can of Bartlett pears did a similar job for the

3

other.

And now the sack had been split and Addy's mother would be bound to find out and Addy's name would be mud. In addition, she would lose her Saturday penny for the next hundred years, she supposed gloomily, jumping down off the sack and trying to stop the steady flow of rice cascading on to the floor.

Nick turned back towards where Addy crouched, beginning to deny that he had had anything to do with the mishap, while the third member of the party, Nick's younger brother Paul, who was ten, the same age as Addy, pointed out that it had been an accident and surely Mrs Fairweather would only be a little angry, for the rice could be returned to the sack and the hole, he assumed, sewn up.

Addy, now on hands and knees trying to hold the edges of the tear together, cast him a scornful glance. 'She'll be mad as fire,' she said darkly. 'She'll say the rice on the floor has been con— con— what-chama callit and she'll chuck it all away.'

'Contaminated, you mean,' Nick said loftily. At thirteen, he was the oldest of the three of them. 'But I don't see why she should do any such thing,' he added after a thoughtful pause. 'This floor's so clean you could eat your dinner off it. Look, tell you what, you nip up to your flat, Addy, and get a needle and thread while Paul and I shovel the rice back into the sack, then you can sew up the tear and no one needn't be none the wiser. What d'you say to that, eh?'

Addy sniffed dolefully. Earlier, she had told the boys that her mother had given permission for them to play in the storeroom since it was raining

4

cats and dogs, putting an end to their usual Saturday afternoon activities. This, however, had been far from the truth, and now, with an inward shrug, she admitted she had lied. 'She thinks we're in that old woodshed at the back of Tommy Cobbler's shop,' she told them. 'She said I were to stay out until teatime, 'cos if I couldn't be helpful at least I needn't be a nuisance. Oh, dear, wharrever am I going to do?'

She and Nick stared at one another, speechless with dismay, but Paul spoke up at once. 'If you're supposed to be at Tommy Cobbler's, why not go round to his shop and get a borrow of a length of thread and one of them big curved needles he uses?' he said brightly. 'Once the rice is back in and the tear stitched, Nick 'n' me will turn the sack round so's the mend's against the wall, where no one will notice it. Only you'd better gerra move on, queen, in case your mam needs something out of here and comes bustin' in.'

'Paul Bentley, you're a bleedin' genius. Much cleverer than your big brother, old thick Nick here,' Addy said joyfully, then dodged as Nick aimed a swipe in her general direction. 'Sorry, sorry, that weren't fair. It were your idea to mend the tear to start with. Look, you take hold of the edges of the split whilst Paul keeps shovelling, and I'll go to Tommy Cobbler's. I'll run all the way—'

She stopped speaking abruptly as the door that led to the shop opened and the tins blocking it skittered across the floor, then relaxed. The figure in the doorway was not her mother but her little sister, Prudence; eight years old, blue-eyed and golden-haired and right now staring accusingly from the sack of rice to her sister. Desperately,

5

Addy tried to manoeuvre herself between Prue and the spilt grains, but her sister was no fool. Addy knew that she was well aware that the three of them should not have been in the storeroom and would guess immediately that the tear was the result of one of her sister's wild games. However, Prue glanced quickly behind her, then shut the door. 'Mam's sent me through to fetch as many tins of conny-onny as I can carry,' she said. 'But wharrever did you do to that sack, our Addy? Gracious, wait till our mam sees the mess you've made! How did you do it, any road? I bet you were playing Off the Ground and you know you aren't supposed to be in here. Our mam'll be as cross as two sticks when I tell her what you've done. She won't sell that there rice, not once it's been on the floor.'

'If you don't tell, she won't know,' Addy pointed out hopefully. 'Honest to God, Prue, Nick just said you could eat your dinner off the floor in here. We're going to shovel the stuff back in and sew up the split, and no one won't be any the wiser, or not if you keep your gob shut, anyhow.'

Prue came a little further into the room. 'Gob's rude, you know it is,' she said primly. 'You should say mouth. And as for keeping me mouth shut, it wouldn't be right. It would be tellin' a lie in a way an' nice kids don't tell lies.'

Nick smothered a laugh. 'Aw, come on, be a sport, Prue,' he wheedled. 'It weren't your sister's fault; we were all to blame. And if we put it right and sew up the tear—Addy's off to get needle and thread from Tommy Cobbler—no one need know.'

'But it's food. Someone's going to eat that rice in a pudding or something,' Prue said righteously.

6

'Mam would be afraid we'd make someone ill.'

'Well, Prudence Fairweather, fancy you not knowin' that folk rarely eat raw rice!' Paul said, his voice mocking. 'Besides, don't they say that everyone eats a peck o' dust before they die? I think it's in the Bible. So don't that make it all right?'

Prue gave him a malevolent glance, but before she could speak Addy jumped to her feet and made for the back door. 'I'm off for the needle and thread,' she said over her shoulder. 'And if you tell, Prue, you'll find slugs in your bed for a whole week, I promise you. There's a grosh o' slugs at the back of Tommy Cobbler's woodshed, hard up against the brick wall. So what'll it be? Tale-clattin' and slugs, or keepin' your gob shut—your mouth, I mean?'

Nick, holding the edges of the slit together whilst his brother scooped up the rice and returned it to the sack, twisted his head round so that he could see Prue's face as she said sulkily: 'All right, all right, there's no need to be horrible just because I try to help our mam. I wouldn't have tale-clatted anyway. Only what'll I say when I go back into the shop? She'll ask me what took me so long. And she'll mebbe have heard our voices . . .'

Addy paused, pulling the back door open and squinting hopefully up at the grey sky. 'Still rainin', but I'll run like the wind and scarce get damp,' she said philosophically. She returned her attention to her younger sister. 'The conny-onny's on the shelf, right by your hand. As for Mam hearin' our voices, that's a load of codswallop and you know it. Ta-ra, fellers, back in a tick.'

As she closed the door and set off at a fast run

7

along the jigger, heading for the back of the cobbler's shop, Addy smiled to herself. She disliked slugs just as much as Prue did, so if her sister had thought for a moment she would have realised that slugs were an empty threat tonight— but then perhaps Prue's threat to tell had been an empty one as well. Addy admitted, reluctantly, that though her sister was a proper little goody-goody, she wasn't actually a bad kid. She was certainly a nuisance, tagging along when Addy went off with her pals, but quite often, when she told tales, it was more or less by accident. Prue adored their mother and wanted to please her, and if that meant relating some doings of Addy's . . . oh well, it was no worse than what other folk's sisters did. The trouble was, other folk's sisters tended not to be as unfairly pretty and good as her own particular specimen. Addy thought that if Mam hadn't made it so clear that Prue was the apple of her eye, a long way ahead of Addy in the affection stakes, she would have found it quite easy to be nice to her little sister.

She reached the cobbler's shop, pushed open the heavy door and tumbled inside, inhaling the rich smell of leather and dirty socks with a mixture of pleasure and disgust. Mr Thomas looked up from his work, pushing his tiny spectacles further down his nose in order to examine her over the top of them. He was a kindly old man who even after years of living in the city retained a strong Welsh accent. He beamed at Addy. 'If you've come after me laddo,' he began, then stopped as Addy shook her head.

'No, I'm not after your Ned for once,' she said. 'I'm afraid I'm on the borrow . . .'

When Prue had staggered back into the shop, her arms laden with tins of condensed milk, Nell had felt quite guilty. Prue adored working in the shop and was such a real help to her mother that Nell sometimes forgot how young she was. She restocked shelves, weighed up goods and occasionally served behind the counter, which was more than Addy did. Oh, Addy could be persuaded or forced to help, but Nell declared that the sight of her elder daughter's sulky face was enough to put any customer off. So though Addy ran messages, tidied the flat and used an ancient bicycle for deliveries, she seldom appeared in the shop.

Most of the small corner shops along the Scotland Road were family run, and the Fairweathers' place was no exception. Nell herself was usually in the shop from early morning until nine or ten at night, with her own mother coming in almost daily at ten a.m. and not leaving until five or six in the evening. Nonny, as the children called her, had snapping black eyes and a dark complexion and without her Nell did not think she could possibly have taken on the shop. Indeed, when her dear Bert had died four years previously, she had been at her wit's end to know how to provide for her children and herself, and when the shop on the corner of Blenheim Street and the Scottie became vacant she had resolutely refused even to look at it. She had told her mother tearfully that she had no head for business and would be bankrupt within a twelvemonth. But

Nonny, bless her, had taken her daughter firmly in hand. 'Them shops is little goldmines, gal, and wasn't you the brightest of me kids when we lived in Blackpool?' she had said severely. 'Your brothers weren't half as clever as you, but every man jack of them's done well, and you could run a corner shop wi' both hands tied behind you. I won't deny it's a challenge, but when you consider that nice roomy flat above and the big storeroom behind I can't see how you could go wrong.'

'Oh, but Mam, I've never even worked in a shop . . . well, not since before I were married, and then it was in Bunney's Department Store, not a corner shop,' Nell had said helplessly. 'But if you're set on it, I'll go with you to take a look, though I won't make any promises. If it weren't for the Depression I'd be far happier working for someone else, but though I've been keeping my eyes open there seems to be a hundred people chasing every perishin' job.' She had glanced curiously at her mother. 'How come you know the shop's needin' a tenant when no one else has so much as mentioned it?'

Nonny had given her a gap-toothed grin and tapped the side of her large nose. She often boasted of her gypsy blood and also claimed to have second sight, though her daughter said that her mother's predictions of future events were largely guesswork, and wrong as often as they were right. 'I read it in the cards,' Nonny had said, grinning even more widely. 'Actually, me landlord owns all them houses and he told me old Mr Goldberg was looking to retire . . . well, not retire precisely. He's going to move out to Great Sutton on the Wirral, where his daughter runs the village

10

shop. She could do wi' someone to give an eye to the place from time to time and Mr Goldberg's willin', particularly as the doctor says his chest would improve away from city fogs. So we'll go this afternoon.'

They had gone, and despite her fears Nell had been enchanted by the compact little shop and the flat above. Mr Goldberg wanted her to buy his stock, and though it had cost her every penny she possessed, including Bert's insurance money, she had never regretted taking it on.

The children had loved the shop at first but Addy had soon found her duties irksome, preferring to play with her friends. Prue, scarcely four years old when her mother took on the shop, had, so to speak, grown up with it, accepting the life of a shopkeeper's daughter with a sunny smile, and promising her mother that as soon as she was old enough to leave school she would take a permanent place behind the counter.

And true to Nonny's forecast, the little business thrived despite, or perhaps because of, the Depression. Nonny refused to accept a wage in return for her assistance, though Nell made sure that her mother never had to buy anything that she stocked, and when Addy went off to the market in Great Nelson Street she always purchased enough fruit and vegetables for both Nonny and the Fairweathers; but had Nonny been forced for some reason to withdraw her help, Nell now knew a number of local women who would have been glad to take on part-time employment in the shop.

'Where do you want these put, Mam?'

Prue's plaintive voice brought Nell abruptly back to the present. 'What a good girl you are,

11

sweetheart,' she said admiringly. 'Here, let me help you. Gracious, how on earth did you manage to pick up so many tins? You must have got a dozen at least!'

'Paul did it; isn't he kind, Mammy?' Prue said, beaming. 'Nick would have helped too, but he was . . . he was . . .'

She fell silent, looking conscience-stricken, and Nell, removing the tins from her arms and placing them in a pyramid on the back shelf, sighed gustily and smoothed a hand across the tight, almost white curls on her daughter's head. 'What are those boys doing in my storeroom?' she demanded. 'I suppose Addy's there too? If they've done any damage . . .'

'No, no, they only came in to help,' Prue said wildly. 'And Addy isn't there, honest to God, Mammy, she's gone to fetch the slugs—oh, I mean she's gone to Tommy Cobbler's, 'cos that's where she were meant to be, in his woodshed wi' Ned and the Bentleys. There's nothing wrong, or there won't be soon at any rate. Oh, Mammy, I does hate slugs! Where's you going?'

Nell had been about to march through the back room and into her store to see for herself just what was going on, but at that moment the bell above the door tinkled and two customers entered. Automatically, Nell reached behind her for a packet of Player's Navy Mixture for Mr Bartholomew, a regular customer. Mrs Beech, on the other hand, had a piece of paper in one hand and a pencil in the other, which meant she was about to give her weekly order and would probably want it delivered before five that evening. The storeroom, and whatever had been going on there, would have to wait. Nell turned a bright smile

12

on her customers. 'Here's your baccy, Mr Bartholomew,' she said. 'Is there anything else I can get you?'

* * *

In bed that night Addy went over her day and decided that it hadn't been a bad one. Usually, she and her pals went to the Saturday rush at the Gaiety Cinema, a short distance along the Scottie, but today this had been impossible. Mr Bentley, father of Nick and Paul and licensee of the Vines Public House, had given Nick a list of messages and Nell Fairweather had loaded Addy's old delivery bicycle with groceries for customers who lived in the area. Addy had got through her tasks in good time, but she would have felt mean going to the pictures when Nick, her best pal, was unable to join her, so she had hung round the Vines until he returned with his messages. Then the three of them had gone to the corner shop in the driving rain and had begun the ill-fated game in the stockroom that had resulted in the torn sack.

However, she and the boys had managed to get the rice replaced, the sack sewn up and all signs of their recent game cleared away by the time her mother had come through to see for herself just what they had been up to. By then, the three of them had been tidying the stockroom, and though Mrs Fairweather had commented suspiciously on Addy's wet hair and damp clothing, it had been a simple matter to assure her that she had got wet running from Tommy Cobbler's backyard to their own premises.

'I see,' Addy's mother had said thoughtfully. 'But

13

what made you think me stockroom needed tidying?'

Addy had smiled guilelessly. 'It didn't really need it, Mam,' she had said. 'But it's powerful wet out there and we thought if we made a good job of the stockroom, you might let us go up to the flat and do a jigsaw or sort out our cigarette cards.'

Her mother had sighed but not questioned Addy further. Instead, she had looked carefully around the stockroom and had then—surprise, surprise, thought Addy—nodded almost approvingly. 'You've sorted out the tins in order of size; that'll be a real help,' she had said. 'And you've tidied away those loose boxes and folded some of the cardboard flat. But I can't believe you're thinking of doing a jigsaw! What're all these good deeds really in aid of?'

Addy had been properly flummoxed, since it would scarcely do to say they had tidied the room in the hope that by so doing they would take Mrs Fairweather's mind off sacks of rice and such. But before she could think up a more convincing explanation, Paul had burst into speech. Like Prue, he was fair-haired, blue-eyed and small for his age, so an innocent expression came more easily to him, Addy thought, than to either Nick or herself, both of whom were dark-haired, dark-eyed and—well, to be honest—plain. 'We thought you might let us make hot buttered toast, missus,' Paul had said eagerly. 'We remembered you let us do that on Christmas Eve when we tidied your stockroom, so we thought . . .'

Mrs Fairweather had laughed and rumpled Paul's smooth blond hair. 'Well, I dare say half a loaf of bread and a pat of butter won't break me,' she had

14

said and once more Addy had thought, rather wistfully, how different her mother's reply would have been if she herself had asked for buttered toast.

However, as the three of them had thundered up the stairs to the flat, Addy had thought gratefully that she would take her mother down a cup of tea as well as a round of buttered toast, just as soon as both were prepared. Why not? It would put Nell in a good mood and if she included a drink of milk and another round of buttered toast for Prue, her mother would no doubt be doubly grateful.

The children had burst into the flat's pleasant kitchen to find Prue sitting at the table reading a book and eating bread and jam. 'Mammy said I could have this bread and jam 'cos I've been helping her all mornin' and most of the afternoon,' she had said smugly. 'If you helped more, Addy, you'd get bread 'n' jam 'n' all.'

Now, Addy scowled to herself at the recollection of how all her good resolutions to be nice to her sister had fled at these provocative words. However, she had said loftily: 'Who wants bread and jam when they can have tea and hot buttered toast? You're only a kid so you ain't allowed to light the gas stove to boil the kettle, or to make toast under the grill. And we shan't let you have any 'cos you've already made a pig of yourself with bread 'n' jam.'

Prue's lower lip had jutted and she had glared at her sister. 'You're a horrible person, Adelaide Fairweather. You know I isn't allowed to use the bread knife, so Mammy cut me one slice and that's all I've had. An' I'll tell her you called me names, see if I don't.'

15

Nick had guffawed, seized the loaf and begun to cut large uneven slices. 'Slugs, slugs, slugs!' he had said teasingly and then, as Prue's blue eyes had filled with tears, he had given her a friendly shove. 'It's all right, kid, you can have a round of buttered toast, though I wouldn't tale-clat if I were you. Slugs in a bed ain't no picnic. Now dry your eyes and you shall have the first slice.'

Prue had sniffed, stopped bawling and turned to Nick. 'Thank you, Nicky,' she had said. 'But I isn't scared of the slugs no more because I 'membered Addy 'n' me shares the bed when our gran stays the night. She does stay sometimes at weekends so Addy ain't likely to go puttin' slugs on my side in case they slide across to her and march up her legs.' She had looked across at her sister with a mixture of pleading and defiance. 'Did you think of that, Addy? You don't like slugs no more'n I do.'

Addy had laughed despite herself and had felt almost fond of Prue for several minutes, though this warmer feeling had disappeared when Prue had jumped to her feet saying she would take the first round of buttered toast and a mug of tea down to the shop for her mother. 'You can bring the next lot down for Nonny; she did her marketing this morning and came in so's I could have a break,' she had said grandly. 'What's the matter, Addy? You look cross.'

'*I'm* taking a tray down for Mam and Nonny, with tea and toast for the pair of 'em,' Addy had said repressively. 'You'd only spill half before you got anywhere near the shop.'

Prue had begun to protest that she would be very careful, would not spill a drop, but Addy had told her to shut up and then hastily loaded a tray with

16

two mugs of tea and two plates of hot buttered toast. Prue had run down the stairs ahead of her to open the door which led into the shop, and to Addy's secret resentment her mother had thanked Prue for this small service far more warmly than she had thanked Addy herself for the tea and toast. Because of this Addy had banged the tray down rather hard on the counter, causing tea to jump out of both mugs. Mrs Fairweather had sighed and told Addy to be more careful, but Nonny had given Addy a grin and a secret wink and said, taking a bite of her buttered toast, that Addy were a good girl and the tea and toast had been a kindly thought.

'I thought of it first . . .' Prue had been beginning, but though Addy had longed to slap her she realised that it would scarcely endear her to her mother if she gave way to her desire. So she had ordered Prue sternly to go back upstairs and had told her mother, rather stiffly, that she would come down for the dirty crockery presently. Then of course she had returned to the flat, and whilst they crunched toast and drank tea they had started a noisy game of I Spy and what with one thing and another Addy had forgotten all about collecting the dirty crockery and had been mortified when Prue had appeared with it, having carried the whole lot up from the shop.

Addy had sighed and said she would wash up and put away, but Nick had looked at the clock that hung on the wall and said that he and Paul must be going. The Bentley boys helped at the pub in the evenings, washing glasses and delivering the sandwiches their stepmother made from the pub's large kitchen to the shelf behind the bar. Addy would have liked to help there too and perhaps earn herself a few coppers, but her mother had forbidden her daughter to enter licensed premises so she could only accompany Nick and Paul to the back door.

She had done so on this occasion, bidding them a wistful farewell and wishing that Nell had taken on a public house instead of the corner shop. It looked so jolly on winter evenings with the big log fire lit in the grate, the lights blazing out and the customers getting happier and happier as time went on. But this was a prohibition she knew she must not break, so she had waved to Nick and Paul and returned to her own home through the shop, since her mother locked and bolted the door to the yard as soon as dusk began to fall, and dusk falls early in March.

Nonny had grinned at her as she entered, but Mrs Fairweather had been serving a customer and apart from sending her daughter an incurious glance and telling her to peel a pan of spuds, she had made no comment. Nonny, however, had accompanied her across the stockroom to the foot of the stairs. 'I were the eldest in our family when I were a gal, same as you are,' she had announced as soon as they were out of her daughter's hearing. 'The eldest allus gets more cuffs than kisses, I reckon, but it don't mean to say your mam ain't fond of you, 'cos she is.' She had pinched Addy's cheek. 'Blue eyes an' golden curls is all very well, but a bright mind and a lovin' heart counts for more in the long run. And what's more, you take after meself. You'll have the second sight, same as me, and you'll be a ravin' beauty once you've growed up.' She had grinned at her granddaughter.

18

'You might think I'm an ugly old biddy now, but once I had fellers linin' up to spend money on me and tek me about.'

'Oh, Nonny, I do love you, and I think you're downright handsome,' Addy had said gratefully. 'As for second sight, I've not seen a sign of it yet, but I dare say it'll come, like the looks, when I'm grown.' She had smiled at her grandmother, but privately she had thought she would sooner not have the second sight of which the old woman was so proud. Being pretty would be enough, she told had herself. 'I do me best, but if only Prue wasn't so perishin' *good*! I mean to be a help, to make you and Mam proud of me, but somehow things go wrong. Today I had a bit of an accident . . .'

At this point the storeroom door had shot open and Mrs Fairweather's head had appeared round it. 'Oh, you've not gone up yet,' she had said sharply. 'I might have known you'd be hanging around gossiping, young Addy. When you've peeled the spuds, you'll find a pound of sausages in the meat safe. You can give me a shout, then put the sausages in the frying pan, and I'll hang a notice on the shop door sayin' we're closed for half an hour. It's still rainin' cats and dogs, so I don't reckon we'll miss many customers.'

'Right-o, Mam, I'll do that. And I'll put the kettle on and make a brew,' Addy had said. She had realised that Nonny's kind words had somehow made it easier to speak pleasantly to her mother. Had Nonny said nothing, Addy might have suggested—crossly—that Prue be asked to do something to help, but as it was she had given the soft answer which turneth away wrath, so often recommended by her grandmother, and had

19

actually received a little nod of the head before her mother had withdrawn once more.

*   *   *

Alone in the shop, Nell had emptied the till, save for the float, and cashed up. Her mother sometimes stayed overnight when they had been working late, but although this was a Saturday, usually one of the busiest days of the week, there had been so few customers once it had grown dark that Nonny had decided to go home. She had a little house in Albermarle Court off Silvester Street and had a lodger, Mr Cracknell, whose name Nonny had long ago shortened to Cracky. He was a retired seaman, and she provided him with breakfast and an evening meal when she was at home to cook it. But she and Cracky were good friends and, like most seamen, he knew how to cook and to do any number of small household tasks. So when she stayed overnight with Nell, Cracky would either buy fish and chips or cook himself a simple meal, using the ingredients that Nonny always left ready.

Nell glanced around the shop, then tucked the money bag into the large pocket of her overall, hoping as she did so that the customers who had been put off by the rain today would come in on Monday, and headed for the stairs. If Addy had done as she had asked, the meal would be pretty well prepared, and if she could get the girls comfortably settled in bed she might spare time to nip round to the Vines for a bit of a chat with her friend Maureen Bentley.

Maureen was the boys' stepmother, having

married Joshua Bentley around the time that Nell had taken on the corner shop. She was a good deal younger than both Nell and Josh, but the landlord had taken one look at her and fallen in love. His proposal had been accepted, they had wed in St Silvester's church, and Maureen Colman had changed her name to Bentley and become the pub landlord's wife.

Maureen was the prettiest thing and she and Nell had speedily become close friends. Nell had known Joshua Bentley's first wife—had attended her funeral after she had died of consumption—but the first Mrs Bentley had been a good deal older than Nell and had taken little notice of the younger woman. Maureen, on the other hand, was grateful for Nell's kindness to her stepsons and the friendship had developed from there. Fortunately, both boys were fond of her, which had made her life a good deal easier, and did away with what Joshua had once confided to Nell was his worst fear: that Nick and Paul might see his little darling as the wicked stepmother of fiction. However, this was far from the case; indeed everyone liked Maureen including Addy and Prue, Addy once remarking after a row with her mother that she wished Nell was a bit more like Maureen, who was never cross.

Now Nell only waited for both girls to fall asleep before donning her coat and scarf, letting herself out of the shop, locking the door behind her and heading for the Vines, knowing that her children would not be awoken by would-be customers. When she had first taken on the shop, she had known indignant women intending to buy some small item after she had closed for the day who

21

would hammer on the door for five minutes hoping to get her to open up, but she and Nonny had put a stop to all that when they took over. Once the shop door was shut and locked everyone knew that it would not be opened again until eight the next morning. If someone wanted baccy or a tin of conny-onny after closing time, they would have to purchase it elsewhere.

She began to make her way along the Scotland Road, which for a change was almost deserted, for the rain continued steadily. Nell found herself skirting large puddles and wishing that she had thought to wear the rubber boots she kept by the back door. However, it was only a short walk to the pub, which was on the corner of St Martin's Street, so Nell sloshed grimly on. When she reached it, she turned into the yard and hurried towards the back door, which was open, allowing golden light to spill out on to the wet cobbles.

As she entered the kitchen a delicious smell of cooking met her. Clearly, Maureen had been busy; still was in fact. The other woman turned towards her, beginning to smile, but then the smile faltered and a little frown took its place. 'Oh! It's you,' she said ungraciously as Nell took off her soaking wet coat and headscarf and hung them on the back door.

'Who were you expectin'?' Nell said, and continued without waiting for a reply. 'Sorry to mess up your kitchen floor, Reenie, but the puddles are that deep I got soaked to me ankles and the rain's still belting down, same as it's done all day.'

'Goodness, no wonder you look like a drowned rat!' Maureen remarked, pausing in her sandwich

22

making. 'The pub's been quite busy though, rain or no rain, and I'm fair wore out.'

Nell pulled a sympathetic face. 'Want a hand wi' them butties? We've had a real poor day, but you know I sometimes think it's even more tiring when scarce a soul enters the shop. You're waiting for the door to open and getting cross and upset when it don't. Do you want a hand with those butties or not?'

Maureen was buttering bread, plonking slices of ham on to rounds and adding sliced onion, tomato or pickle. At Nell's offer of help, she shook her head but said she'd be obliged if her friend would peep into the oven. 'I made three dozen Cornish pasties earlier and I reckon they're probably just about done,' she said. She wiped a hand across her brow, then blew out her cheeks in an expressive whistle. 'Gawd, I'm tired of this bleedin' pub! It's work, work, work from morning till night; clean the house, cook the meals, see to the boys, provide pub food . . . and all Josh does is just sit behind the bar, being the genial host an' doin' bugger all to help.'

'But the boys help,' Nell pointed out. 'They wash glasses until you send them off to bed.' She did not add *and that isn't ever early enough, in my opinion*, because she had no wish to antagonise the only friend she had managed to make since taking over the shop. She liked Maureen, but knew that whatever the younger woman might say she had lots of help, and had been offered even more. Nell wondered that Maureen should complain about Josh, too, for she must know that he was doing his best. Trade was down because of the Depression, and Maureen had agreed when Josh had suggested selling food as well as drink, so it was pointless to

23

object now to the extra work. Nell knew that Maureen liked holidays, expensive meals out and other such luxuries. These things might not be possible if the pub stopped serving food.

Nell walked over to the oven, opened the door and produced from its depths three trays of beautiful golden brown Cornish pasties. She turned the oven off, then began to place the pasties on a wire cooling rack, hissing in her breath as she burnt the tips of her fingers on the first one. When all the pasties were transferred, she gave Maureen a playful poke in the ribs. 'How can you say poor Josh does nothing? He's never still for a moment when the pub's busy. He gets drinks, pulls pints, takes the money, supervises the barman, passes down orders to the cellarer; why, he even interferes if a fight looks likely to start! Don't underestimate your old feller, Reenie, because I wish I had one half as good.'

Maureen turned her wide blue gaze on her friend. She was a very pretty woman with curly golden hair and a retroussé nose. She was not tall but had an enviably slim figure and was much admired in the neighbourhood, not only for her pretty looks but for her sweet nature and abilities as the landlord's wife. Now she sighed and began to cut her sandwiches cross-wise. 'Well, I suppose he could be worse,' she said grudgingly. 'And the boys aren't bad as boys go, but honest to God, Nell, I get up at eight in the morning and scarce sit down until eleven at night, and I get no help at all.'

'Oh, Maureen, what a whopper!' Nell said, half reproachfully, half admiringly; if you looked into Maureen's innocent blue eyes, you would not credit the fibs she could tell. 'You have a cleaner who comes in the mornings and does your living quarters, and Mrs Bithell who cleans the bar and tidies the stockroom, and though you've never bothered to take him up on it Josh has said over and over that he'll pay someone to help in the kitchen, evenings. Only you always say no, so really and truly you've only yourself to blame.' She picked up the bread knife and began to slice the loaf. 'Then there's me; I know I only come in when I can close the shop early, but I always give you a hand whilst we chat, and I work pretty hard myself, you know. The shop's mostly open from eight in the morning until late at night, and though Nonny's a great help . . .'

'Sorry, sorry, sorry!' Maureen said, not sounding a bit sorry, however. 'An' I've told Josh I don't want help in the kitchen in the evenings because . . .' and here she glanced slyly at her friend, 'because you ain't my only pal, Nell Fairweather. I've another who comes in during the week sometimes, what's a dab hand at butties.'

Nell felt the hot colour rise in her cheeks. 'Then if you have so much help you shouldn't grumble,' she said tartly. 'I suppose when you talk about another pal you mean Bessie Strickland; if she's a dab hand at sarnies it's because her family live on 'em, 'cos she can't cook to save her life. Still, if that's your idea of a pal . . .'

Maureen dropped the knife she was holding and ran round the table to give Nell a hug. 'No, it ain't Bessie. It's someone you've never met and I'm real sorry if I were nasty,' she said remorsefully. 'But it don't matter who my other helper is. No one could have been a better friend to me than you've been, Nell. And I'm sorry I grumbled, because you never

25

moan and I reckon you work even harder than I do.' She went over to the door which separated the kitchen from the bar, opened it and shouted: 'Sid, come and fetch the pasties, there's a good lad, whiles I bring the butties through.'

Nell had meant to stay at the pub just for half an hour, but in fact it was nearly an hour later when she left the premises and hurried back through the wet streets to her own home. She realised as she entered, locked the door behind her and went swiftly up to the flat that she was uneasy. Just what was Maureen playing at? She often grumbled that the work was hard, but never before had Nell heard her complain about Josh. Nell knew him to be an easygoing man, still very much in love with his wife even after nearly four years of marriage. He was always anxious to please her and to make her life easier. He gave way to her when they disagreed, which Nell thought was rather hard on the boys since it meant, quite often, that they had to take on tasks which their stepmother did not wish to do.

Up in her own room, Nell reminded herself that it was none of her business. Husbands and wives, she knew, quarrelled from time to time and it did not mean very much. Sometimes one turned on the nearest person, blaming him or her for whatever had gone wrong. Thinking back, she could remember instances when she had positively snarled at poor Bert for a sin he was unaware of having committed. Yes, that would be it: Josh and Maureen must have had a tiff.

As she undressed and slid between the sheets, she remembered something else. The door between the kitchen and the bar had been shut,

26

whereas normally it would have been ajar so that Josh and Sid could call to Maureen if they needed something from the kitchen. She snuggled into her pillow, smiling to herself. She could imagine sharp words and a slammed door, leaving a good deal of ill feeling, so no wonder Maureen had criticised her husband.

Satisfied that she had discovered the reason for the chilly atmosphere which had prevailed when she had first entered the kitchen, Nell settled down and slept.

CHAPTER TWO

'Oh, Mam, can't we *both* go on the school trip? They're going to New Brighton, which isn't very far . . . the charabanc takes us there and we gets us dinners and then tea and buns before we get back on board.' Addy looked pleadingly at her mother. 'We'll need a bit of money for ice creams and a teeny bit more for the funfair, but I *would* like to go. All me pals is going and I've bagged the seat next to Paul—I mean, I would be sitting next to him if you'd only say I can go!'

It was a hot and sunny day towards the end of July and Addy was trying desperately to put forward a good case so that her mother might relent. Nonny had gone off to visit her sister for a few days' break, and Nell was insisting that she could not manage the shop alone. 'And this is the first year that Prue has been old enough to go on the school trip,' she had reminded Addy when it had first been proposed. 'You've been for the last three years, Addy, so I think it's fair enough that you should stay behind and help in the shop. Surely you don't expect your little sister to miss a day at the seaside when she's had so few and you've had so many?'

That had been several days ago and Addy had agreed with seeming complacence that Prue should certainly go on the trip, even if she herself could not. The reason for such meekness had been that in her heart of hearts she thought that Nonny would agree to change her holiday dates so that both her granddaughters might go off to the seaside. This had proved impossible, however, since Aunt Dorothea was spending the month of August with one of her daughters who lived in Colwyn Bay, and could not change her plans.

Now, sitting at the table opposite her mother, with Prue beside her, all of them eating their breakfast porridge, Addy sighed and realised that the sensible thing to do would be to capitulate, but she decided to play the last card up her sleeve. 'All right, Mam, if you really need me I suppose I shall have to give it up this year,' she said, trying not to sound regretful, but not succeeding very well. 'The only thing is, if I had been going, I could have sat next to Prue on the sharra and kept an eye on her all day, made sure she didn't eat nothing what's bad for kids, stopped her climbing on the slippery rocks that lead out to the castle, made sure she didn't go too far into the sea—still, I dare say she'll be all right without me.'

Prue stopped spooning porridge, eyes widening. 'Well I never did, Addy! You said you was goin' to sit next to Paul on the charabanc and the pair of you didn't want me tagging along behind. You said

28

I'd to play with me own friends, and when I asked if you'd keep my ice cream money you said I were to keep it myself so's if it got lost it 'ud be no one's fault but me own.'

Addy watched as her mother turned away for a moment, shoulders shaking. I do hope she isn't crying because she knows now that I've been tellin' whoppers, Addy thought anxiously, but at that moment her mother turned back to the table and there were no tears in her eyes. 'Adelaide Fairweather, I've never met anyone better at digging a pit for others and then falling into it themselves,' she said roundly. 'I think you deserve to lose the school treat for being so nasty to your sister. I suppose I could employ someone, just for the one day, but I'm blowed if I see why I should. The trouble is, Addy, that I know you too well. You'll promise the earth to get your own way and then cast your promise to the four winds once you're out of my sight. So I think the fairest thing will be to let Prue choose. If you aren't there, Addy, Paul will give an eye to your sister. He's got a kind heart.' She turned to her younger daughter, who had stopped eating her porridge to stare from one face to the other, like a spectator at a tennis match. 'Well, Prue, what's it to be?'

It was unfortunate that even as Addy's lips formed the word 'slugs' her mother happened to be looking at her. She slammed both hands down on the table and leaned towards her elder daughter, her expression downright dangerous. '*What* did you say?' she hissed. 'And don't try another lie because I've had a good deal of practice in lip reading. Well, that's it! I won't ask Prue to put herself in the firing line. You shall *not*

29

go on the school trip, Adelaide Fairweather, not if you were to go down on your bended knees. You're going to stay here and do something useful for once.'

Addy would have liked to burst into tears, but she was too angry. Instead, she stuck her chin in the air, pushed her porridge plate away from her and said loftily: 'Right! If you can't afford to ask Mrs Beech to help out for the day, then I suppose I'll just have to— Ouch!'

Nell's hand, connecting with her right ear, nearly knocked Addy into Prue's porridge plate and she opened her mouth to protest, but the expression on her mother's face deterred her. Having one's ears boxed by Nell Fairweather was no joke and Addy realised, belatedly, that she had asked for trouble. Why oh why wasn't she more like Prue? But it was no use wishing. Her unruly tongue gave vent to whatever she was thinking, no matter how hard she tried to stop it. And to be honest, she didn't often try at all, but just let rip.

Now, however, rubbing her sore ear and reading in her mother's expression more retribution to come, Addy squeezed out a couple of tears and gave a loud sniff. Nell often criticised local parents for hitting their kids and if she, Addy, said she was truly sorry she might avoid further punishment, although she knew she had been both rude and unkind, as well as untruthful. Nell could well afford to pay a helper and would not have stinted either daughter when it came to ice creams and funfair money, so it behoved her to get her apology in fast. 'I'm sorry, Mammy, I'm really, really sorry,' she gabbled, trying to sound as much like Prue as possible. 'That was a horrid thing to say and I did

30

tell lies but I'll really, really try in future to be truthful, like—like . . .' she cast a look of loathing at her younger sister, 'like Prue here. I often mean to be good but somehow being good gets boring, and . . .'

'All right, all right. Try not to make promises you can't keep,' her mother said hastily. 'Now eat up your porridge.' She turned to Prue. 'The trip isn't until the day after tomorrow, but if you'll run round to the Vines—the back door, mind—and ask Paul if he'll give me ten minutes some time today, I'll arrange with him to keep an eye on you and I'll give him Addy's share of the ice cream and funfair money.'

Addy, spooning porridge, waited for an opportunity to tell Prue that Paul was *her* pal and that if she tried to pinch him off her the retribution would make slugs seem a positive pleasure, but since her mother remained in the kitchen even that revenge was denied her. And then, as Prue passed her chair, she gave Addy's shoulder a little pat. 'I'm real sorry, Addy, and if it *had* been my choice I'd have asked for you to come, honest to God I would,' she whispered. 'But if you're real good today, and clean the flat beautifully when you get back from school, Mam might easily change her mind.'

Addy was beginning to tell Prue that she wasn't such a bad kid after all when her mother turned from the stove and carried the empty porridge saucepan across to the sink. 'Off with you, Prue,' she said briskly. 'Don't forget to go to the back door. And tell Auntie Maureen that I'll see her later if I can get away.'

'I'll do that, Mammy, and then I'll go straight to

31

school,' Prue said virtuously.

Her mother turned to Addy. 'Wash up the breakfast crocks and the porridge pan and put everything away neatly,' she said briskly. 'And please come straight home this afternoon so you can tidy your bedroom and then peel a pan of spuds, scrape some carrots and chop up the onion you'll find in the vegetable rack. I'll buy a parsnip and some best end of neck, and if you put it on the stove as soon as you've done the vegetables it'll all be simmering nicely by the time we're ready for a meal.' She turned from the sink and to Addy's astonishment gave her hand a quick squeeze. 'Nonny's always telling me that I put too much on you and I'm always telling her that if I didn't nag, you'd never do a thing to help. Now's your chance to prove me wrong. If I come up to the flat this evening and find the kitchen shining and the meal simmering on the stove, then I reckon you and I will have made a good start. Nonny's away for a whole week, you know. She's never taken a holiday since we took over the shop, so if you and I, and Prue of course, can show her we can manage without her, it will be a real triumph. Does that make it easier to understand why I'd like you here, helping me, instead of being with your pals in New Brighton?'

All Addy's resentment fled and her heart swelled with pride. Her mother had confided in her, explained why she needed her. It made Addy feel grown up, sensible and trustworthy. If only she'd done this years ago instead of just scolding, I'm sure I would have been as good as Prue for ages, she told herself. And I'm going to be good now. I won't smash any china, I'll make all the beds with hospital corners and I'd peel a thousand spuds if it made Mam give me that loving look. Yes, I'm a changed person from now on!

*   *   *

The day of the school trip dawned bright and fair, and Addy tried not to feel jealous as she helped Prue to dress in the clothes which her mother thought suitable for a day at the seaside. After all, she reasoned, she had had far more exciting trips in previous years. The school had taken their pupils to Rhyl and Llandudno, whereas on this occasion they were only going to New Brighton, a stone's throw away. Furthermore, her mother had promised that when Nonny got back she would ask Mrs Beech and possibly another of their regular customers to come and work in the shop for a day so that she might take both her daughters to New Brighton.

Addy thought this was a grand scheme, though she would prefer it if Prue were left behind, not because she wished to deprive her small sister of a treat, but because it would be nice to have Nell to herself for a change.

The relationship between Nell and Addy was better than it had ever been, Addy reminded herself now, buttoning Prue into the blue gingham dress which suited her little sister so well. Ever since she had given up any hope of going on the school trip, Addy had been working really hard at being good. Only two days had elapsed since she had promised to improve, but she had truly done her best to be helpful. She had even worked in the shop, and to her own immense surprise had quite enjoyed it, especially when Nell had let her take the customers' money, use the till and hand out their change, although it was a little galling to see them smile as Nell checked this carefully, despite Addy's reminding her that arithmetic was her best subject.

'Should we plait my hair, Addy?' Prue's question brought Addy abruptly back to the present. 'Mam usually plaits it and I know it's tidier, so if you'll find my blue hair ribbons I'll go down to the kitchen and she can do it for me.'

The two girls were standing in front of the tiny mirror that stood on the chest of drawers, and now Addy seized their hairbrush and began to wield it on her sister's head. 'If you don't mind having a centre parting I can plait it for you, which will save Mam a job,' she said. 'Is Paul going to call for you? I know it won't be Nick, because his trip is going to Snowdonia to climb a mountain, and they left at six this morning.'

'Paul said he would, since you isn't going, Addy,' Prue said. 'I am sorry, truly I am. If only Nonny wasn't away, we could both have gone . . . but then Mam would never have thought of having a day off work, midweek, to take both of us to the seaside.' Through the mirror she beamed at her sister. 'Every cloud has a silver lining, as Nonny says.'

'You're right there; and it'll do Mam good to have a bit of a break,' Addy said, though rather absently. She had just noticed that her sister's left plait was thin as a piece of string, whilst the right one was thick and glossy.

She wondered whether she ought to brush out her sister's golden locks and re-plait them more evenly, but decided against it when she heard her

34

mother's voice coming up the stairwell. 'Girls! The porridge is cooling in the plates and I've just poured two mugs of tea; do get a move on, because school trips always leave dead on time.'

Prue shot across the room, threw open the bedroom door and dashed downstairs, with Addy in hot pursuit. They arrived, breathless, in the kitchen and slid on to their chairs, for though Addy was not going on the trip her mother had given her permission to walk down to the school with Prue and Paul, so that she might wave them off. Everyone in her class knew she would not be going to the seaside with them, but instead of mocking her as she had feared they were rather envious, and clearly thought that serving in the shop would be at least as much fun as paddling and building sandcastles in New Brighton.

Accordingly, the girls gobbled porridge and drank their tea, and had actually stood up to leave when Nell stopped them in their tracks. 'Prue, you look neat as a new pin apart from your plaits, which aren't perfectly . . . I think since this is a holiday, a simple ponytail would be much easier to cope with.' Addy seized her mother's comb from its place on the dresser, but Nell took it from her, shaking her head. 'No, Addy, I can manage this whilst you get your sister's coat off its peg.'

Addy did as her mother asked, then glanced at the clock. 'Shall I run down and open up the shop?' she said brightly. 'Paul may be here any minute and it's rude to leave him standing on the doorstep, ain't it, Mam?'

Her mother laughed, finished off Prue's hair with a nice big bow and pushed her daughters ahead of her to the stairs. 'No need; we're all ready,' she said reassuringly. 'But I expect he will, because I've noticed Paul and Nick are usually early rather than late. In fact I wouldn't be surprised . . . yes, someone's just knocked. Open up, Addy, and let him in.'

Addy flew to the bolts, heaved them back and flung the door wide. Her mother was right: it was Paul who tumbled into the shop. She began to tell him that she was coming to wave them off, but Paul interrupted her.

'I'm not goin' on the school trip; me dad needs me at the Vines,' he said breathlessly, turning to Nell as he spoke. 'I'm awful sorry, Mrs Fairweather, but I shan't be able to keep an eye on your Prue. Nick left before we knew anything was wrong, but I was there when Dad read the letter.'

'What on earth's happened, Paul?' Nell said, sounding as mystified as Addy felt. 'What letter? And why should a letter stop you from going on the school trip? Why, I spoke to your mam only yesterday and she said nothing about any letter. Did it come in this morning's post? If so, your post must be delivered a lot sooner than ours.'

'I dunno,' Paul mumbled and Addy thought, suddenly, that her friend looked uneasy. 'But Pa said could you go and see him as soon as possible, so's he can explain? He said as how you could leave me and Addy in the shop, just for a little while.'

Nell frowned. 'Is your mam ill? Of course I'll come, but I'll have to drop Prue off at the school first, because her name's down for the trip, and whilst I'm there I'll tell them that you won't be going, is that all right?' She waited for Paul's confirmatory nod, then continued, 'Very well,

36

that's settled. You and Addy can stay here and open up if a regular customer comes in, but I don't suppose I'll be away long.' She looked anxiously at her elder daughter. She's probably remembering times I've made a mess of things, Addy thought rather resentfully, but I'd best not remind her I'm a changed person because it might only make her mad. 'Is that clear, Addy? You're only to serve regulars. If someone you don't know comes in, tell them you aren't open yet.'

'Righty-ho,' Addy said. She grinned at Paul, then noticed for the first time how white he was, and how wretched he looked. Suppose Mrs Bentley was in hospital? Had been run over? Was dying . . . or, worse, dead? Hastily, she schooled her expression to one more in keeping with disaster. 'Is your mam really ill?' she asked tentatively. 'Oh, Paul, no wonder you can't go on the school trip!'

Paul, however, shook his head and waited until Prue and Nell had bustled out into the sunny morning. Then he lowered his voice so much that Addy had to ask him to speak up. 'I said our mam's gone,' he mumbled. 'She must have gone ever so early, even before Nick got up to go on his school trip, and his sharra left at six this mornin'. That's why our dad wants a word wi' your mam. He thinks she might know something, bein' as how the two of 'em's pals, like.'

Addy was completely mystified. If Mrs Bentley was not ill, then why shouldn't Paul go on the school trip? She asked for an explanation, and Paul said with a touch of impatience: 'Are you deaf, Addy? I said she's gone, and that's what I meant!'

Addy stared at him. 'Gone to get the messages? But if she's kept you back from the school trip, you could have done any marketing she needed. And why should my mam have to visit the Vines? *She* won't know anything!'

Paul heaved in his breath and then let it out in a long slow whistle before he spoke. 'She's gone, vamoosed, buggered off, left us,' he said wearily. 'Can't you understand English, Addy Fairweather? She left a note but Dad took it away before I could read it.' He looked wildly around the shop. 'And as soon as your mam gets back, I'm going down to Central Station and then to Lime Street to find out if anyone remembers seeing her, 'cos when grown-ups run away they goes on buses or trains. A kid might skip a lecky or hang on behind a brewer's dray or even foot it, but grown-ups have money, which makes all the difference.'

'Oh, Paul, I wish I could come with you and help you to find her, but with Nonny away on holiday Mam truly needs me in the shop,' Addy said regretfully. 'But why should your mam run away? The Vines is the loveliest pub in Liverpool and your dad's always buying her things and giving her treats. Why, I never knew anyone laugh and smile more than your mam.'

'She hasn't smiled or laughed much lately,' Paul said gloomily. 'And she an' Dad have been having awful rows—oh, not in front of us and not in front of the customers either, but late at night, when everyone else is asleep.'

'If everyone else is asleep, how come you know they quarrelled?' Addy asked curiously. 'Don't tell me you hear in your sleep, 'cos I shan't believe you.'

'They woke us up some nights, shouting at each other,' Paul said. 'Then they'd remember us and drop their voices, but you know how it is: once you're woken up it's hard to get back to sleep, especially when there's bad feeling. I told Nick it worried me, but he said married folk often quarrel and to be glad it never came to blows, because Bessie Strickland's husband knocks her about when he's had a few drinks and our dad has never laid a finger on *anyone*, norreven on me or Nick.'

'I see,' Addy said thoughtfully, though in fact she did not. Her experience of married couples was very limited, for she could barely remember her father, though she was certain that he and her mother had never quarrelled, let alone fought.

However, she did not intend to let Paul know how ignorant she was. Instead, she was beginning to say brightly that no doubt Mrs Bentley would not be gone long when the door to the shop opened and a regular customer entered. He raised his eyebrows at the sight of the two children standing behind the counter. 'Well, well, well, I've not seen you in the shop this early before,' he said cheerfully. 'I'll have me usual . . .' he grinned at them both, 'except that you won't know what me usual is, of course. Ten Woodbines, please.'

*　　　*　　　*

Nell hurried Prue along the road, meeting the curious glances of folk she met without fully understanding why they stared so. She looked down at herself and realised, with some embarrassment, that she was wearing her shop overall and had not even thought to slip a coat over it. No one commented when she dropped Prue off at school, and then she headed for the

Vines, going down the jigger, crossing the courtyard and entering the pub kitchen after announcing her arrival with a shout and a tap on the old oak door.

Josh was sitting at the kitchen table with what appeared to be a mug of cold tea in front of him and a letter propped up against half a loaf of bread. As Nell entered the room, he snatched up the piece of paper and thrust it into his pocket, looking up and giving her the travesty of a smile as he did so. 'I'll put the kettle on; this tea's cold as charity,' he said gruffly, getting to his feet. He lit the gas under the kettle, then spoke with his back to Nell. 'Where's she gone, Nell? Surely you can tell me?'

Nell stared at his broad back and the droop of his shoulders. 'Wharrever d'you mean?' she enquired. 'If your Maureen's ill . . . is she upstairs? Can I go up to her?'

The publican swung round and Nell saw that his face was blotched and red, his eyes swollen as though he had been crying. Immediately she concluded that Maureen must be very ill indeed and began to head for the stairs, but as she passed him Josh shot out a large hand and grabbed her arm. 'Are you tryin' to tell me you don't know that my Mo's left me?' he said incredulously. 'Aw, come on, pull the other one, it's got bells on! Just lately you've been round here almost every night when the pub's at its busiest, and Mo's always shut the door so's you and she could talk secrets. I admit I didn't like it; I told Mo husbands and wives should be open with one another. But she said you talked about women's things, what would only embarrass me—and the customers—if she left the door open

40

so we could hear.' His grip on her arm tightened, painfully. 'Where's she gone, damn you? I'll have the truth if I have to beat it out of you!'

Nell gave a scornful laugh. 'Joshua Bentley, if I knew what you were talking about mebbe we could untangle this mess,' she said. 'I'll make us both a drink of tea and we'll sit down quietly and you can tell me just what has happened. Paul said you wanted me to come round as soon as possible and I thought Maureen must be ill, but clearly I've got hold of the wrong end of the stick. And now if you'll kindly let go of my arm and act civilised, I'll make a brew.'

Joshua released her, looking sheepish. 'Sorry,' he mumbled. 'But you will tell me where she's gone, won't you?'

Nell sighed but began to make a pot of tea before answering. Only when she and Josh were seated at the table with mugs before them did she speak. 'Josh, Nonny is away on holiday so I've not visited the Vines once this week, and before that I've only popped in sometimes on a Saturday night to give Maureen a hand with the grub and the glasses. I gather from what you've said just now that Maureen's left you, but I'll swear on the Bible if you like that she never even hinted at such a thing to me. She did once say she was fed up with the pub and the work involved, and I remember she mentioned a pal who popped in from time to time. Since then, though, I can't say I've heard her complaining about anything; in fact she's been pretty happy. Even having to make the nibnabs—butties, I mean—didn't get her down. And now I've told you all I know, so you'd better tell me just what's been happening.'

41

Josh picked up his tea and took a long drink, then fished the piece of paper out of his pocket and handed it to Nell. 'You'd best read that,' he muttered. 'Not that it tells you much. I thought . . . I hoped that she'd have confided in you, but it seems she didn't.'

Nell took the piece of paper and began to read.

Dear Josh,
I'm fed up with the pub and the sort of life I've been living, so I'm leaving. Don't try to find me because nothing will make me come back. I've a friend who will look after me and give me the sort of life I've always wanted. He's really nice and has sworn to make me happy. I hope you will divorce me, but it don't make any difference because I really do love him, and he loves me.
Maureen.
PS I ought to have said that it weren't you or the boys what got me down. It were the pub. I'm real sorry, Josh, because I know you've done your best, but I can't help myself. I have to be with my chap. M.

Nell read the letter through three times before meeting Josh's anxious gaze. 'Josh, I knew nothing of this,' she said earnestly. 'But one thing does strike me: she hasn't once used this feller's name and that must be because you know him. Can you think of anyone who has shown her special attention these past few weeks? It must be someone who can take her away from here because she's clearly unlikely to set herself up in this area.'

Josh nodded. 'I see what you mean, queen,' he said heavily. 'But all the customers make a great

42

fuss of Maureen 'cos she's such a pretty thing, so lively and clever. I suppose it could have been any one of 'em. Oh, God, however will we go on without her? The boys will be heartbroken, and though they'll do their best to help out they can't possibly take her place. The truth is, no one can.'

'Perhaps she'll change her mind and come back,' Nell said, though without much conviction. 'The PS does give her a sort of escape route because it makes it clear that she's still fond of you and doesn't blame you for what's happened.' She rose to her feet and went round the table, handing the letter back to Josh and giving his shoulder a little pat. 'I've known you for years, Josh, and I'm sure you'll cope with everything. I wish I could be more help but I can't just abandon the shop to Nonny. The only time I was able to give Maureen a hand was on a Saturday night after we closed; the stalls in Byrom Street stay open late on Saturdays and sell stuff really cheap, so I reckon I don't lose much business by locking up early. Look, I must go, because I've left the kids in charge and I don't want to get back to find chaos and grumbling customers.'

Josh rose to his feet and walked with her to the door. 'Yes, you and me go back a long way,' he said. 'If I remember right, it were me that introduced you to your Bert.'

'Yes, I believe you did,' Nell said lightly. 'But a good deal of water has passed under the bridge since then, Josh. And now I really must go. I'll send Paul back to you as soon as I reach the shop.'

'Yes, I suppose you'd better. Tell him not to bother with the stations. I told him to check at Lime Street and Central, and to ask if anyone remembered seeing Maureen with a feller. But there ain't no point. He can give me a hand clearing things up.'

For the first time, Nell looked round the kitchen and felt a stab of guilt at the array of used glasses, plates and cutlery that was piled up on the draining board. She thought remorsefully that she should have tackled the washing up whilst they talked, but it was too late now so she just patted Josh's large hand, suggested that he might get Mrs Bithell to come in early and stepped out into the yard. 'Things aren't ever as black as they seem,' she said as cheerfully as she could. 'And if you need help in the bar this evening, I've several customers—trustable folk—who'd be glad of a few hours' work; want me to send 'em round to see you?'

Josh looked undecided, then nodded dolefully. 'Aye, I suppose you'd better. And I'll nip round to Mrs Bithell and tell her Maureen's mam has been took bad and she's gone to take care of her for a few days.'

'Good idea,' Nell called over her shoulder as she let herself out into the jigger. She did not add that everyone, including Mrs Bithell, knew very well that Maureen's mother had died many years ago and that Maureen had been brought up by an elderly aunt. She also knew that if she was not careful Josh would keep her talking for hours, and though she was sincerely sorry for him she had enough on her plate with the shop. She couldn't take on his worries as well.

When she entered the shop Paul was balanced on her short wooden stepladder, reaching down a packet of porridge oats, whilst Addy was peering hopefully into the till and asking her customer

44

whether she could possibly find another twopence, since they were short of change so early in the morning. Both children looked up as she entered, and Paul descended rather abruptly from his perch, the packet of oatmeal clasped to his bosom. 'Is me dad all right?' he enquired anxiously. 'Has me—'

'Everything's fine,' Nell said hastily, aware of two customers with stretched ears. 'Why don't you two go up and clear away the breakfast things . . .'

'Paul too?' Addy asked, her brow wrinkling. 'He said he had to go to Central and—'

Nell clapped a hand across her mouth, thinking what a poor conspirator she would make. 'Oh, yes, I'd quite forgotten. But you're to go home first, Paul, because your father wants you to run some messages for him.' She turned to Addy. 'So you nip up to the flat, dear, and see to things whilst I finish serving the customers.'

*   *   *

When Paul got back to the Vines he found his father already much more in command of himself. Mrs Bithell, wrapped in a large calico apron, was tackling the huge mound of washing up, whilst his father dried and put the clean crocks away.

The landlord turned as his son slipped into the kitchen. 'Good lad, Paul. How did you enjoy being shop manager for an hour?' he said with pretended joviality, though Paul could hear the strain behind the words. 'You can take over putting away the stuff as I dry it, save my poor old legs.'

'Righty-ho, Pa,' Paul said, reaching for a pile of clean and shining plates and carrying them over to the Welsh dresser.

He wondered what his father had told Mrs Bithell and was presently rewarded by the old lady's remarking: 'You said Mrs Bentley's mam had been took ill, but a' course I realise you meant her aunt, 'cos Mrs Bentley's ma and pa died of the influenza when your wife were only six, as I recall.'

'So they did,' Josh said resignedly. 'And now you're going to remind me that me wife went to her aunt's funeral a couple of years back.'

Mrs Bithell chuckled and wiped a soapy hand across her forehead, pushing back a lock of her limp grey hair. 'I were just wonderin' how I could say that without soundin' rude,' she remarked. 'I didn't know Mrs Bentley had any close relatives living, but I suppose . . .'

Josh heaved a sigh. 'You're right in what you're thinking,' he said. 'Mrs Bentley found the pub just too much. She's gone off for a few days' rest, but I hope she'll be back as soon as she's feeling better.'

'Oh aye?' Mrs Bithell said and there was the world of disbelief in her tone. 'Nothin' to do with that young feller she took up with then?'

There was a moment of frozen silence before Josh spoke. 'Young feller? Who would that be?' He turned to Paul. 'There's money in the big black purse and a list tucked into your mam's straw marketing bag,' he said. 'Mrs Strickland has kindly offered to come in and cut the butties tonight, and though it goes against the grain you'll find I've asked you to buy four dozen sausage rolls and two dozen pork pies from Samples. Home baking's nicest but Samples is the next best thing.' He looked anxiously at his son. 'Will you be able to manage all that lot? But you've got the whole day;

you can bring a basketful home and go back for more if necessary.'

'I'll manage fine,' Paul said. 'But I'll have to pay a visit first, if you don't mind, Dad.' He went past his father and out of the back door through which he had just entered, casting Josh a meaningful glance.

Once in the yard, he headed towards the brick-built outside privy but did not go in. Instead, he leaned against the wall, whistling under his breath and waiting for his father to join him. Presently Josh emerged from the kitchen, closing the door carefully behind him, and approached his son, eyebrows rising. 'What's up?' he asked eagerly. 'Have you seen your mam? Did you get a chance to speak to her?'

'Oh, Pa, I'm sorry. I've not seen Mam at all. I just wanted a word with you without old Ma Bithell earwiggin' every word I say,' Paul explained. 'The thing is, you never said Mam had run away with a feller. Only if it's true what Mrs Bithell said, I reckon Nick and me know who it is.'

Josh stared at his son, eyes and mouth rounding. 'Tell me his name,' he said at last. 'By God, I'll break every bone in his body, makin' up to a married woman and stealing her from her rightful family. Who is it, Paul?'

'I reckon it'll be that RAF pilot, Carruthers or whatever his name is,' Paul said confidently. 'I never thought anything of it at the time, but he's been in and out of our kitchen near on every evenin' for several weeks and I know he's met our mam in town more than once. I asked her about him and she said, quite crossly, that I were a nosy kid, but he was her cousin, Andy, who'd been

47

posted to an airfield nearby. She said he were lonely and popped in to give her a hand with the grub and talk over old times.'

Josh scowled down at his feet, clearly trying to recall the man, and then his brow cleared. 'Tall young chap? Wavy black hair and blue eyes?' he asked. 'Not more'n twenty-two or three, I'd say. But what makes you so sure it was him she went off with?'

Paul looked guilty. 'He come to the Vines a few days ago and told our mam that he were being posted; I think he said to Lincolnshire or Norfolk. And he said, "So now's your chance, Mo, to show 'em a clean pair of heels." Then they both laughed like anything 'cos Mam were wearing those daft shoes with four-inch heels, and she's always complainin' she can't run anywhere in them.'

Josh hissed in his breath between his teeth and for a moment looked so murderous and unlike himself that Paul quailed. 'And it never occurred to you to tell me that your mam were meetin' some feller on the sly?' he asked incredulously. Then his shoulders sagged. 'Not that it would have made any difference, I suppose; the landlord of a pub can't compete with a pilot, especially one twenty years younger than himself.' He took a couple of strides across the yard and patted Paul heavily on the shoulder. 'Thanks for tellin' me, son; you've took one worry off me mind, 'cos there's no point in chasin' after her or hopin' that she'll come back if the chap lets her down. By the way, Mrs Fairweather's goin' to send up one or two of her reliable customers who'd be interested in givin' a hand in the bar, evenings. So if someone comes askin' for me, take them into the snug and give me

48

a shout.'

'I'll do that, Pa,' Paul said, thinking that there was no point in reminding his father that he would be out getting the messages for the rest of the morning. Josh was clearly still not thinking straight. When Nick comes back, we'll tackle Dad together and sort out what story we're going to tell people, Paul thought, as he let himself out of the gate and strolled along the jigger. Not that there was any point in telling lies; folk would learn the truth soon enough. No point in hurrying either; the list of messages, which poor Dad had thrust into the top of the straw bag, was blank.

*   *   *

A few hours before, Maureen had been sitting demurely next to Nigel Carruthers, her eyes darting nervously to the platform outside the carriage window, though she knew there was little chance of seeing a familiar face at this time in the morning. The milk train left Liverpool in the early hours, and would deliver them to their destination before her husband and his sons had done more than turn over in their sleep.

As soon as the train began to move Maureen snuggled up to Nigel, feeling relief wash over her. She had done it! There had been times during the past couple of weeks when she had doubted her ability to strike Josh such a cruel blow, but the truth was she had never been in love with him the way she was with Nigel. She had been eighteen when she had married Josh, and if she were honest she would have to admit that she had married chiefly to escape from her aunt and a job she

49

detested. Aunt Florence had owned a small dress shop on the Scotland Road. The dresses were cheap, garish and badly made, and as soon as Maureen was old enough Aunt Flo had paid her a miserable pittance and insisted that she work there.

Her day usually began at seven o'clock, when she would tumble out of bed, dress hastily and go into the kitchen to make breakfast for herself and her aunt. Since they lived in a flat above the shop, she usually left her aunt supping tea and went down to open up at around eight o'clock. She did this because stock was delivered early, when the streets were less crowded, and also because factory workers sometimes popped in for a quick look at what they regarded as the latest modes before continuing on to their places of work.

Her aunt had always been a strict and unloving guardian, constantly reminding her niece of the debt she was owed for taking her on at all and not putting her into an orphanage. Maureen had often thought a home would have been preferable to her aunt's unloving rule, but of course she never said so. If she ever dared to criticise, it was bread and water for a whole day and Maureen, like most growing girls, enjoyed her food.

As Maureen had taken on more and more responsibility for the shop, so her aunt had done less and less. She had begun to demand that Maureen should bring her breakfast in bed and had employed a little lad to get her messages. In addition to her normal work as a sales girl, Maureen had to keep the shop clean and tidy, and though this annoyed her very much it had been, in a way, her means of escape, for she had been

50

cleaning the outside of the plate glass window when Josh had passed by.

Or, rather, had not passed by; he had stepped aside to make room for a large woman pushing a perambulator and had bumped into the ladder. Maureen had squeaked and clutched the rungs, but had been unable to stop herself from falling. She had landed pretty well on top of Josh, stammering apologies, but he had taken all the blame upon himself. He had insisted on finishing the cleaning of the window for her and had offered to take her to the nearest dining rooms for a cup of strong tea or coffee, since he said he could see she was badly shaken up.

Maureen had explained that she dared not leave the shop . . . even now, sitting in the train and thinking of that first meeting, she could remember how kind and understanding Josh had been. He had accompanied her into the shop, carried her cleaning things through to the stockroom and put them away and then gone off, saying he would be back in two ticks. And he had been as good as his word. Maureen had scarcely had time to ruefully examine her ruined stockings and to dab at the grazes on her knees before Josh had returned bearing a tray on which reposed two cups of coffee and two buttered scones. 'We'll have a little picnic,' he had told her, placing the tray carefully on the counter. 'And this evening, when you've finished work here, I'll take you out for a slap-up dinner, because it were my fault that you hit the deck the way you did.'

He was a good deal older than she, and to Maureen, browbeaten and kept close by her aunt, he had seemed dependable and worldly-wise. And when he had asked her to marry him, a mere six weeks after their initial meeting, she had accepted joyfully. He had introduced her to his sons, and despite the fact that Maureen knew nothing whatsoever about children she had had no difficulty in winning their affection. And now, she thought rather guiltily, she was being as selfish in her own way as Aunt Flo had been in hers. She could still remember, all too clearly, how her aunt had tried to forbid the marriage, had bitterly resented Josh and had endeavoured first to frighten and then to bribe Maureen into giving him up.

It had not worked, of course; they had got married and might have lived happily ever after had Nigel Carruthers not walked into the bar one evening, asked for a Guinness, and then demanded to know at what time her shift finished. 'I'll take you to the Grafton and we'll dance the night away,' he had said, only half teasing, and she had agreed to go, telling Josh that she was visiting a girlfriend, and not admitting to Nigel that she was a married woman.

It had all happened so quickly, she told herself now. It was love at first sight for both of us. Well, my aunt warned me that I was marrying in haste to repent at leisure, and though she'll never know it, she was right. Except, of course, that I shall never regret running away with Nigel, because he's the only man I'll ever love.

'Penny for your thoughts?'

Nigel's voice cut across her musings and Maureen gave a deep sigh. She had never told Nigel how she had married Josh mostly to escape from her aunt, but she supposed that she really

52

should enlighten him. She wanted him to know that Josh had been a good husband and the boys good stepsons, but it was difficult to find the words that would make him understand, yet not condemn her for leaving the family who had given her nothing but love and trust. She owed him a truthful explanation, however, and it would be best if she began at the very beginning and told him everything that had happened, right up to the moment when he had walked into the bar and their eyes had met and locked.

It was a lucky thing that their carriage was empty save for themselves. Maureen took a deep breath and began to speak.

*   *   *

By the time she had finished telling her story, Maureen had convinced herself that, in her way, she had been as much a victim as Josh and the boys. She actually ended with a little sob, and rubbed her cheek against Nigel's jacket, looking hopefully up into his face and waiting for his reaction.

It was not long in coming. 'My dear little Mo, what's done is done and cannot be undone,' he said gently. 'Do you think I would dream of blaming you for what was obviously not your fault? Josh is old enough to be your father, and slaving away behind the bar is no life for a beautiful, lively girl like you. So why did you feel you had to give me chapter and verse? It really wasn't necessary, you know.'

'But—but I wanted you to know that I married Josh for all the wrong reasons. Oh, I suppose I thought I loved him, but I realise now that I didn't really know what love was. Can you possibly understand, darling Nigel?'

'Of course I can, my angel,' Nigel said. 'I'll prove it, if you like!'

He drew her into a hard embrace, which only ended when the train began to slow. Maureen heaved a tremulous sigh. If she had had any doubts, that kiss had put an end to them. She loved Nigel to distraction, the way he loved her, so their future happiness was assured. She was beginning to tell him so when the train halted and someone tried to open the carriage door. Nigel gave her one last squeeze. 'Now, no more looking back,' he commanded. 'Don't think or speak of the past again; promise?'

'I promise,' Maureen said happily, smiling up into his eyes. 'Oh, Nigel, how did I manage to get through life without you?'

CHAPTER THREE

June 1937

Giles Frobisher waited until the house was quiet and the family all in bed, and hopefully asleep. He had been sitting on the wide window seat in his bedroom, with the window open to let in the sweet summer breeze, but now he padded across the floor and headed for the narrow back stairs. He had some thinking to do and knew that he thought best in the open air. He was an adult now, of course, but ever since he was a small boy he had taken his problems to his mother's rose garden and usually solved them there.

The trouble with the back stairs was that they creaked, and the fifth from the top, if one descended unwarily, cracked like a pistol shot. But Giles knew every inch of his home like the back of his hand, knew how to descend the back stairs as silently as a cat, so he had no worries. The flight ended in a short corridor from which doors led to kitchen, butler's pantry and housekeeper's room, though the last was now only a courtesy title—as indeed was the butler's pantry—since the days when the Manor had been run by servants were long gone. Now, Giles's mother made do with a charlady who came up two or three times a week, and did most of the cooking herself, aided by Gillian, Giles's twin sister, when she was at home.

Stealing softly along the corridor towards the side door to the garden, Giles thought it was a fortunate thing that Gillian was not home at present, for though totally dissimilar in looks and character the twins often knew what the other was up to. If Gillian had been here, she might easily have woken and come down the stairs after him, which would have been annoying since he wanted to be alone with his thoughts. However, Gillian was in Plymouth, attending a secretarial college in Millbay Road, and staying with their Aunt Gertrude out at Saltash during the week, for the old lady confessed to being lonely when both her sons were at sea. He knew Gillian intended to join the Wrens if—or rather when—war was declared but in the meantime, with her usual practical good sense, she had decided to enrol at the college.

'I shall be the most efficient and experienced

secretary—writer, I mean—the Navy has ever known,' she had told him, only half joking. 'With a name like Frobisher, and our family history, they'll probably appoint me PA to the Admiral.' At the time, Giles had just laughed and asked what she would do if war did not come after all, expecting this to stump his sister, but Gillian had merely glanced at him through her thick and curling lashes before saying promptly: 'If there isn't a war, I shall start one.'

It was typical of Gillian, that quick, half-serious answer, and all Giles had said in reply was: 'Oh, Gillian, you're so positive. Wish I was.'

And Gillian had said lightly: 'You are positive, bro.' Then she had turned the subject, neatly. 'I'm going down to the shore presently; feel like joining me for a dip?'

He had done so, of course, wandering with her down the long path that led into the wild garden which, in its turn, became the thickly wooded slopes to the edge of the cliff. And in the enjoyment of the swim, he had dismissed his own worries and doubts.

But that had been months ago and now, as he opened the side door and slipped out into the moonlight, he decided that the decision he meant to make must not be affected either by Gillian or by his parents. Sighing, for he knew already that it would give his father pain, he began to walk towards the curved wooden seat set amongst the sweetest of the roses, telling himself that his choice was already made. All he needed to decide now was how best to break the news to his parents. He knew that they, in their turn, would then inform all the myriad relatives who would feel it their duty to try to persuade him to change his mind.

But no, not all of them, he thought as he reached the seat and sank on to it. His cousin Freddie would applaud his decision, and his aunt Gertrude, who had a soft spot for both the twins, would say that it was about time someone broke with tradition.

Giles fumbled in his pocket for his packet of Players and was about to light up when a breeze stirred the roses, sending their intoxicating scent to him and making him return the cigarettes to his pocket. Why spoil perfection? Comforted for some reason by the beauty of the night and the sweetness of the blooms, he allowed his mind to tackle his present problem: how to break the news to his parents that he intended to join the Royal Air Force. Indeed, he had already applied officially, a week previously, though nothing was yet set in stone. If he were honest, however, he did not think for one moment that his application would be turned down, for he knew himself to have twenty-twenty vision and to be physically extremely fit.

His parents knew these things too, but it had never occurred to them that he would not follow the family tradition, going first to university if he insisted upon it and then joining the Navy. That he might have ambitions to become a flyer would never, he was sure, have occurred to them. The fact that the ceiling in his room was hung with model aircraft had been offset each Christmas and birthday by presents of books on the Navy with every craft imaginable represented, from submarines to enormous battleships.

But it's my life, Giles told himself rebelliously

now, and they're reasonable people. When they can see that I'd be miserable in the Navy and happy in the air force, surely they'll understand, see my point of view? After all, Cousin Freddie gets seasick even on a dinghy.

So it isn't a case of explanations and apologies, so much as choosing the right moment, Giles thought, getting to his feet. He was just down from Cambridge where he was reading modern languages, a course his parents thoroughly approved of since his father said it was always useful to be able to talk to the natives when ashore in a foreign port. But now he acknowledged that after a lengthy absence—for he had not come home for the Easter vac—it had become obvious that the upkeep of the house and gardens was getting too much for his parents.

They had married late, which was probably the reason why the couple had produced the twins and then no further offspring. For no one who knew them could ever have doubted that it was a love match, and the tenderness between them was a byword amongst their friends.

Now, however, his mother was in her mid-fifties, though she did not look it, and his father in his mid-sixties, and last night during supper his mother had talked of letting rooms or even dividing the house into flats. 'But only until you're married and can take over here,' she had assured her son. 'Goodness, Frobishers have lived at Foliat Manor since the Middle Ages; we couldn't possibly sell it, not if it were to fall down around our ears.'

Giles did not have to ask his mother why they could no longer afford to have a full-time gardener, or why the fabric of the building was

58

being allowed to deteriorate. What money they had had been invested, and they had lost most of it as the Depression deepened. Now, so far as Giles knew, their only income was his father's pension and whatever they got when they sold off antique furniture, china and even pictures, which they did with the utmost reluctance.

'We are the new poor,' his mother had said at Christmas with a rueful smile, when he noticed that the big oil painting of a long dead Frobisher relative was gone from the large entrance hall. 'I never liked that portrait anyway, sour old blighter! Your father suggested selling the picture of little Lucy Frobisher on board her pet donkey, but I put my foot down at that.' She had given his arm a quick squeeze. 'And old sourpuss is paying for a great many things, including Mr Stebbings's wages—he looks after the kitchen garden now—so the sale of the portrait was worth it, you see.'

It had been that remark which had made him realise that he really ought to be earning, helping his parents with the upkeep of the crumbling white elephant that he loved so well. But jobs for young men, halfway through a modern language course at Cambridge, were not easy to find in the Devonshire countryside, so he had made up his mind to join the forces and to send as much of his money home as he could manage. Cambridge was expensive, and though his parents never complained he guessed that his fees there must be even higher than those of his sister at her secretarial college. So by leaving Cambridge he would be helping them financially even if he could not start replenishing the family coffers straight away.

Still not having made up his mind how and when to break the news to his parents, he rose to his feet, but instead of heading for the house he turned to his left, towards the wild garden. Then he stopped short and looked around him properly for the first time. Allowing for the black and silver of the moonlight, it was as though the wild garden had actually begun to creep nearer the house, for he saw that every rosebush was surrounded by knee-high weeds. Startled, for the rose garden was his mother's pride and joy, he went a little further, seeing brambles starred with white flowers and even nettles invading what had once been neat beds. Horrified, he turned back towards the house.

He had known things were bad, but had not realised how difficult they must have become. His mother had clearly had to choose between the upkeep of her roses and helping in the walled kitchen garden, for at supper she had boasted shyly that the peas, carrots and potatoes were home grown. At the time he had not understood the remark's significance, but now he did and felt deeply ashamed. His father did what he could to help, he was sure, but Rear Admiral Frobisher suffered from bouts of arthritis. The main burden was falling on his mother, and he, Giles Frobisher, young and fit, had never so much as suggested pulling out some weeds or gathering a crop. Well, whilst he was home, that must change. He did not mean to return to Cambridge when the long vac was over, and hoped that the air force would have taken him in by then. If they had not, however, he would not accept his friend Reggie's invitation to spend time at his parents' home in London, enjoying the bright lights; he would stay here and work his heart out.

Reaching his room once more, he undressed and was climbing into bed when another thought struck him. Gillian had been at the secretarial college in Plymouth for the best part of a year. He knew she paid Aunt Gertie for her bed and board by working as a counter assistant in one of the large Plymouth departmental stores, and did not often get back to Foliat Manor, so maybe she did not know just how bad things had become. Clearly, it was his duty both to tell her the bad news and to ask her advice. He thought her much more sensitive than himself and guessed that she would know, far better than he, how and when to break the news that he was to join the air force.

Satisfied that at last he had reached a conclusion of sorts, Giles pulled the covers up over his ears, then gave an exclamation of annoyance. The moon was at the full now and shining straight through the window on to his unprotected face. Cursing himself for his forgetfulness, he got out of bed and went over to the window. He put both hands up to draw the curtains across, then froze. Below him, in the garden, there was a movement. Someone—or something—was standing beneath the large cedar tree which grew on the edge of the shaggy lawn where once Giles, his sister and a great many little friends had played cricket. Giles was just wondering why someone should simply stand there, staring up at the house, when a breeze stirred the branches of the cedar tree and the young man—he could see it was a young man now—turned away from the house, walked briskly across a corner of the lawn and disappeared in the direction of the lane.

Shrugging to himself, Giles pulled the curtains closed and was about to return to his bed when a thought struck him and he turned back to the window, a frown creasing his brow. He parted the curtains just enough to get his head through, but the intruder had disappeared. Giles remained at the window for several moments, this time examining the entire scene. Then he went back to his bed and tried to tell himself that moonlight was tricky and that his imagination, and even perhaps memory, had played him false. But the picture in his mind persisted. When the intruder had come into the full moonlight as he crossed the corner of the lawn, he had cast no shadow.

*　　　*　　　*

The first thing Giles did when he awoke next morning was to go out into the garden to see if he could find any sign of the previous night's intruder. But since the sun had been up for hours by the time he stirred, the night's dew had dried and there was nothing to show that anyone, apart from himself, had passed that way.

When, however, he examined the bed beside which the man had been standing, which he had assumed to be part of the rose garden, he realised he had been mistaken. In the moonlight he had thought it a flower bed, but now he realised that in fact it was what his mother called her herb garden. He recognised mint and sage as well as the thick hedge of parsley that surrounded the bed. The last, he saw, showed definite signs of having been well nibbled. Rabbits were everywhere, and always hungry. I'll have to tell Mother to drape net over her herbs if she wants to keep them safe, Giles thought absently, turning back towards the house.

It did not occur to him, until he was actually inside once more, to wonder why the herbs were not grown in the kitchen garden, where the high walls—and Mr Stebbings—would have kept them safe from furry marauders. Entering the kitchen, he found his mother slicing last night's left-over potatoes and tossing them into the pan where several slices of bacon and a couple of eggs were beginning to hiss and splutter. 'Morning, Mother,' he said cheerfully. 'My, that smells good. And before I forget, I went for a stroll round the garden just now and noticed that something has been eating the parsley and scuffing up the herb bed. Why don't you grow them in the kitchen garden, where they'd be safe from rabbits and such?'

'Good morning, Giles, my dear,' his mother said, adroitly turning the potatoes with a large fish slice. 'I suppose it's because some long-ago Frobisher cook wanted to be able to pop out of the side door for a sprig of mint or a few sage leaves to flavour a stew. She wouldn't have wanted to trek all the way down to the kitchen garden.' She handed Giles a well-filled plate as she spoke. 'Get some cutlery out of the drawer, there's a good fellow, while I make a pot of tea. Your father will be down in a minute and he does like to find his breakfast ready and waiting.'

Giles complied and had scarcely raised his knife and fork when both his parents joined him in the small breakfast room, each bearing a plate commensurately laden. Breakfast-time conversation always followed a similar course, for his father was not a garrulous man at the best of times, and though he was far too polite to read a paper when his wife and son were present he kept glancing to where it lay on the sideboard. As soon as he had finished eating he got creakily to his feet, carried his plate through to the kitchen and, having asked his wife, courteously, if there was anything he could do for her and receiving a negative reply, picked up his paper and hurried off to the sanctity of his study, where he would remain until lunch time.

Giles finished his own meal, returned to the kitchen to help his mother clear away and wash up and then said, rather hesitantly: 'That was a grand breakfast, Mother, but you said last night that money was tight. Porridge and toast would be a good deal cheaper and much less trouble.'

His mother, carefully arranging the clean plates on the dresser, turned to smile at him. It was a delightful smile and Giles thought that she did not look her fifty-four years, for her hair, which was cut short and curled around her small head, still showed very little grey, and she was suntanned from spending the majority of every day in her beloved garden. She crinkled her eyes at him and wagged a finger. 'Don't expect to be fed like a fighting cock every day, Sunny Jim. As you say, porridge and toast is cheaper and easier. But for one thing it was your first breakfast with us for almost a year, and for another it was all our own produce. Since you were here last, we've gone into the chicken business. Father wanted to put them in a wire run in the orchard, but I don't believe in caging birds, though of course we had to clip their wings or they might have ended up as a gypsy's Sunday dinner. Father pointed out that gypsies are not the only ones fond of a nice bird: foxes can be a menace to poultry too. So we compromised; I bought ten in-lay pullets and a young cockerel and Mr Stebbings made us a magnificent poultry house, with nesting boxes, perches, the lot. It's down in the orchard and there's the neatest little ramp leading up to a pop hole which we close every night once the birds are inside.

'So that's why you've got a fried egg, young man, and if you're wondering about the bacon, we've taken to bartering, being somewhat short of spondulicks, as you and Gillian used to say. We gave Mr Tregarth half a dozen eggs in exchange for six slices of bacon. He keeps a big old sow and a couple of fatteners. Do you remember him? He and his wife live in the cottage at the end of the lane. His sow is due to have another litter in a fortnight and I'm seriously thinking of spending some of my hard-earned money on a couple of weaners. I know we don't have pigsties, but your father and Mr Stebbings say they could convert one of the outhouses if I'm really keen on the idea.'

Giles's mouth did not drop open but he felt sure that his astonishment showed in other ways; he could imagine his brisk, efficient mother tackling two young pigs, but guessed that it would double her workload. When he said as much, however, she shook her head chidingly at him.

'Beggars can't be choosers, so a couple of pigs, which I could manage without help, is the obvious answer. A vegetarian diet is all very well, but your father loves a nice joint of pork from time to time and he's very fond of bacon as well. Sometimes I catch him giving my hens a speculative look, and I

65

suppose when they're old and no longer laying it may be necessary to—to regard them as poultry and not just as dear little egg providers. But until that day dawns, I've told him in no uncertain terms that roast chicken is off the menu.'

Giles laughed. 'I know Father will do his best to help Mr Stebbings, but I don't quite see what he *can* do when his arthritis is playing up,' he said. 'Honestly, Mother, you've got quite enough on your plate. Pigs are hard work. Cleaning them out must be a nightmare and they're big eaters, pigs. You'll end up buying food for them and treating them like pets, and when the killing day comes . . .'

His mother shuddered. 'Maybe you're right; it's more or less what your father says,' she admitted. 'The maddening thing is that we've got a glut of peas at the moment, far more than we can eat ourselves. I'd get Mr Stebbings to sell them to a stallholder on Plymouth market, but unfortunately when one person has a glut of peas, so does everyone else, which means that the price is so low it's not worth the effort of picking and packing.' She looked wistful. 'I'd planned to feed them to the pigs but I do take your point, dear. I'll forget about buying weaners, for the time being at any rate.'

She had collected the cutlery from the drainer, and as she polished it on a dry tea towel she shot another glance at her son. 'It would be awfully handy if Plymouth was your home port when you join the Navy. Oh, I know you'd be away for quite long periods, but when you were home you could be most awfully useful. You've hinted a couple of times that you might not finish your degree because of the expense, and quite frankly, dearest,

66

we need all the help we can get. There must be other ways of making money from the house and garden, but if so, I've not thought of them yet. As you know, I've considered dividing the house into flats, but we're more than five miles from the town centre and there's plenty of cheap accommodation in town. We could really only appeal to someone who owned a car—the buses are *most* unreliable—so I'm afraid we might have to put that one out of court.'

Giles opened his mouth to tell his mother that he did mean to leave Cambridge but had no intention of joining the Navy. Then he shut it again. He was the older twin by thirty minutes, but would not have dreamed of taking an important decision without consulting Gillian. So he just said that he would do whatever he could to help whilst he was at home and then asked what tasks he could perform in house or garden.

His mother smiled fondly at him. 'You *are* a good boy,' she said approvingly. 'But I know you very well indeed, my son. You'd rather consult with Gillian, and since the stables are empty of horses and the buses are somewhat erratic, you're going to have to ride into Plymouth on your old bicycle. It'll take a while, so you'd best leave as soon as you can. Gillian has a lunch hour from one to two, so that's the best time to catch her. She knows you're coming home some time this week, so she'll be expecting you.'

'Thanks, Mother. You're quite right, of course—I do want to have a chat with her just as soon as I can. But tomorrow I promise I'll be at your command and will clean chicken houses, weed the rose garden, dig potatoes or do anything else to help the fallen fortunes of the Frobishers.'

Mrs Frobisher smiled and patted his cheek. 'Thank you, dearest. Give Gillian my love when you see her and tell her we shall expect both her and Gertie for Sunday lunch.' She twinkled at him. 'I shall trot down to the village and spend some more of my portrait money on a piece of brisket. It's just about the cheapest cut of beef there is, but I know how to cook it until it tastes like the very best sirloin.'

Giles leaned over and gave her a kiss on the cheek. 'You'll do no such thing, Mother,' he said firmly. 'Remember, I had a job as a barman all through the Easter vac and Gill works weekends, so after her class is finished we'll pool our money and buy a decent joint. It'll be beef, because you make the best Yorkshire puddings in the world, so that's Sunday dinner settled. And now I'd better be off if I'm to catch my sister before her lunch hour finishes.'

*   *   *

Despite his mother's warning, Giles managed to catch a bus into town and walked straight into Gillian, who evinced no surprise at seeing her twin but gave him a peck on the cheek, handed him her briefcase to carry and suggested that they might have their talk on the Hoe, since it was such a lovely sunny day. 'There's a fellow with an old van who sells cheese rolls and bottles of lemonade,' she informed him. 'I don't usually eat at lunch time, but I know you: you keel over sideways if you aren't fed at regular intervals.'

'That's rubbish. I often miss out on lunch and

68

today Mother did a huge cooked breakfast so I'm stuffed to the gills,' Giles said indignantly, though he rather spoiled this fine flight by adding ingenuously: 'However, a couple of cheese rolls and some lemonade would go down well.'

His sister laughed, and presently the two of them were settled on the short turf of the Hoe, looking out over the sparkling blue sea towards Drake's Island, eating their cheese rolls and drinking warm lemonade. Without a word spoken, the two of them had decided to eat first and talk afterwards, and now, leaning back on the warm grass with a contented sigh, Giles marshalled his thoughts and regarded his sister through half-closed lids. She was not at all pretty, for she was dark like himself with an angular, rather bony face and what he always thought of as a commanding nose. But her expression was so lively and her glance so full of intelligence that one could be forgiven for thinking her a good-looking girl at the least. Giles, however, was so used to his sister that he seldom noticed her appearance, and when at last he broke into speech he knew that she would hear not just his words but also the thoughts behind them.

First and foremost, he told her his most pressing problem, which was that he had applied to join the RAF and wanted her advice as to how best to inform their parents. 'They'll think me a traitor to even consider wanting to fly when the family have been seamen for generations,' he said.

'As if I didn't know that,' Gillian reminded him. 'And of course I've known for ages that you wanted to fly. What really astonishes me is that you haven't seen for yourself that there's a simple solution to this insurmountable problem of yours.

69

Think of your Kipling, my dear brother!'

'Kipling?' Giles said blankly. 'What on earth do you mean?'

Gillian laughed. 'The giddy hermaphrodite, of course! If you tell the parents that you're joining the Royal Air Force, but are applying to be one of those chaps who fly to and from aircraft carriers, they'll be tickled pink, because it's not everyone who can land a plane on a ship's tiny deck in the middle of an ocean. Don't you see? No matter what you may think, they'll consider it as part of the Navy because shipping is involved. Believe me, bro, that's the answer you're seeking. And what's all this about leaving Cambridge? You said in one of your letters that you were going to approach your tutor . . .'

'You're bloody brilliant; that's the answer,' Giles said, gleefully. 'And I've spoken to my tutor,' he added. The man, like himself, was convinced that there was a war coming. He had told Giles that he could take up his course again when his country no longer needed him, and Giles had forborne to say that it was not rumours of war that had prompted his resignation from the course, but the desperate situation in which his parents found themselves.

Gillian sat up on one elbow. 'So if you're joining the RAF at once, they'll teach you to fly, and by the time hostilities break out you and I will both be useful to our country because we've prepared in advance,' she said. 'I imagine the training for a pilot who's got to land on an aircraft carrier must be even tougher than that for an ordinary pilot, which is a good reason for your leaving Cambridge and joining up immediately. Mother and Father will see your point of view—they saw mine—so you

70

needn't fret any more.' She scrambled to her feet and held out her hands to pull him up. 'Going to walk me back to my college?'

'Of course,' Giles said, falling into step beside her. He glanced at her. 'There was one other thing . . . it's going to sound daft in full daylight. You're going to think I'm off my perishin' head. I suppose I could have imagined it, the last bit at any rate . . .'

'Oh, for God's sake stop waffling on and spit it out,' Gillian advised him. 'Just tell me what's bothering you, only get a move on or I'll be late for class.'

Thus adjured, Giles broke into speech, explaining how a full moon had caused him to get out of bed to draw the curtains across, and how he had seen a man standing beneath the cedar tree.

'Poacher? No, most unlikely,' Gillian said, answering her own question. 'Someone after the vegetables and fruit, I bet. There's a fruit cage in the walled garden; Mother has promised Aunt Gertie strawberries next time she visits, though I'm afraid cream is probably beyond her. But the kitchen garden is a fair way from the house, and what's more the walls are awfully high and Mr Stebbings locks the door at nights. I know, because Mother told me. Was he carrying anything, this feller you saw?'

'No, I don't think so,' Giles said. 'I couldn't see him clearly whilst he was under the cedar tree because moonlight creates very black shadow, doesn't it? But I suppose he might have been poaching.' Giles had meant to tell his sister about the man's lack of a shadow of his own, but suddenly realised he did not want to do so; he would keep that particular item to himself.

71

Gillian merely nodded slowly. 'Poaching is a local sport,' she said. 'But you say the chap was staring up at the house. Was he there long?'

'I don't know,' Giles confessed. 'He was already standing there when I spotted him, and when he moved away I went back to bed. Then I realised— or thought I did—that something was wrong and went to the window again to check, but when I peered through the gap in the curtains the fellow had gone—no sign of him.'

'Well, there you are then. Perhaps he was just curious . . .' She stopped speaking as they reached the secretarial college, through whose wide front doors girls were streaming, then squeezed her twin's arm. 'It's one of those odd things which happen, I imagine,' she said. 'Don't worry about it; whatever it was, I'm sure there's no sinister explanation. Cheerio for now, bro; see you on Sunday.'

CHAPTER FOUR

July 1937

Ever since Maureen had fled, Nell had left the shop promptly on Saturday evenings, leaving Nonny in charge, and gone to help Josh Bentley at the Vines. If the shop was busy, she generally remained with her mother until eight, despite Nonny's assuring her that she could manage perfectly well with occasional help from Addy or Prue, but if possible she preferred to be in the pub earlier, so that she could start on the sandwiches.

Today being Saturday and the hour almost seven o'clock, she ran lightly down the stairs and joined Nonny, who was sitting on a tall stool behind the counter, crocheting a collar for Addy's one and only party dress. The older woman looked up and tightened her lips as Nell went over to the mirror that hung by the door into the storeroom, to check her appearance. She always liked to make sure that she looked neat and business-like, her mass of dark and shining hair tied into a bun on the nape of her neck, and her trim figure clad in a navy dress, with white collar and cuffs. Usually, she worked in the kitchen, swathed in a large calico apron, but if the pub grew very busy she helped behind the bar, shedding the apron because a barmaid does not wear such things. Satisfied, she swung round to face her mother, a small smile lurking, for she had read disapproval in Nonny's attitude to her pub work for several weeks now. Josh paid her generously, but the shop was busy too and she knew that doing both jobs well was becoming too much for her.

Clearly, Nonny knew it too, Nell thought, and was about to give vent to her feelings, judging by the look on her face. 'It's time you told Josh Bentley where he gets off,' Nonny said with unaccustomed sharpness. 'He's takin' advantage of you, my girl; oh, I know you say he pays you well, but I reckon you could do with some time to yourself more than that bit of extra money. When did you last take the kids to the beach, or up to Prince's Park? You ain't bein' fair to 'em, queen, if you want my honest opinion. And you're beginnin' to look drawn and tired. Tell Josh to find himself someone else to slave at the Vines. God knows

73

there's enough women who'd be glad of some extra money and wouldn't grudge the work. Tell him where to go, queen.'

Nell pulled a face and took her jacket from the hook on the door. 'I think I shall have to do just that,' she said, tying a headscarf round her ebony locks. 'Earlier in the week Prue reminded me that it was a year ago to the very day that she went off on the school trip to New Brighton, and of course that was when Maureen left Josh. Time flies, but you're right: Josh could easily find someone to help out on a Saturday evening, but why should he bother when I keep turning up? The fact is he's taking advantage of our old friendship and it's got to stop. Apart from its being too much for me, folk will start to talk, especially now that he's nagging at me to do more hours. He actually suggested that I might employ someone else in the shop—to be fair, he offered to pay, and I didn't like to snub him in front of Sid—but I'll tell him it's not on before I leave the pub tonight.'

Nonny nodded approvingly. 'Once Josh Bentley knows that you really mean what you say, then I'm sure he'll give over pesterin',' she said. 'In fact, he might easily employ some respectable woman to help out on a regular basis.'

Nell, already at the door, paused. 'I hope you're right,' she said slowly. 'He'll use all the old arguments, I expect, about only employing people he knows well, but he's known Mrs Bithell as long as he's known me and he certainly ought to know Mrs Higgins well enough after a whole year and more.'

She opened the shop door, took the umbrella from its stand, and turned back for a last word with her mother. 'It's raining cats and dogs so you aren't likely to get many customers, but if you do Addy and Prue haven't gone to bed yet so just give them a shout. Close at eight, of course, and I'll be back around the usual time, I expect.'

Nell stepped out on to the wet pavement, glad of the umbrella and wishing that she had thought to put on boots, though her shoes were sturdy enough. She hurried towards the Vines and entered the pub by the front door, as she usually did nowadays, smiling across at Josh who was serving a couple of seamen with foaming pints of Guinness. He smiled back, and for a moment the worried frown left his face. 'Evenin', lass,' he said comfortably. 'Can you start on the glasses, please? Mrs Higgins didn't turn in this afternoon; she slipped on the wet cobbles in her back yard and sprained her wrist. They say at the Stanley that she'll be out of commission for three or four weeks.' He grinned at her. 'Want some extra hours on a Saturday? Weekdays as well, come to that. And don't glare at me, young lady, 'cos I'm only joking.'

'I'm glad to hear it,' Nell said grimly. She went into the kitchen and gasped at the pile of glasses and dirty crockery heaped up on draining board and dresser, awaiting her attention. 'Glory be, I'd better get a move on or I shan't have time to make the butties.'

Josh stood in the doorway, pointing to the pantry. 'I nipped out earlier and bought half a dozen large loaves, two pounds of Cheddar, two pounds of ham and a big bag of tomatoes. Will that do you, d'you think?'

'Should do,' Nell said, nodding. 'I just hope we

shan't be left with the ham on our hands, because it's raining, you know, and that always affects trade.' She propped the umbrella against the back door where it could drip undisturbed and struggled out of her damp coat and headscarf, put on her apron and began to run hot water into the sink, thinking ruefully that the next three weeks would be tough unless Josh could get someone to stand in for Mrs Higgins.

She was no more than halfway through the glasses when Josh's head appeared in the doorway to the bar. 'Two rounds of ham and tomato and a round of cheese and pickle, please, chuck,' he said briskly, then came right into the kitchen in order to whisper conspiratorially: 'It ain't really ham, Nell, 'cos I took your advice and bought a nice piece of boiling bacon. And don't you worry about waste, 'cos if it don't all go in sandwiches me and the lads will finish off what's left for our dinners tomorrow.'

'I shan't worry about anything, Josh, because it's really none of my business,' Nell said, turning wearily away from the sink and fetching the ingredients from the pantry. Then she felt guilty because a look of dismay had crossed Josh's face.

'Sorry. I didn't mean anything by it, it were just a remark, like,' he said humbly. 'I only wanted you to know that I'd took your advice about the ham . . . eh up, customers!'

He disappeared back into the bar and Nell, still feeling guilty, continued to work, but the small scene had made her more determined than ever to have a serious talk with Josh. And when she had carried a tray, piled up with clean, polished glasses, through to the bar and was helping him to arrange them, she took the opportunity to have a quick word. 'I'd like a bit of a chat, Josh, when the pub closes,' she said quietly. 'All right?'

Josh looked wary. 'If I offended you . . .' he began, but Nell shook her head and gave his arm a quick pat.

'You've not offended me, but we need to talk,' she said, and went back into the kitchen before he could question her further.

Despite the rain, or perhaps because of it, the pub was unusually busy, and Josh, with many apologies, had to call her through to work in the bar. Nell, who had signed the pledge when she was ten years old, always felt slightly guilty pulling pints, but since they were not for her own consumption she had never refused to act as barmaid when Josh and Sid could not manage between them.

When Josh called time Nell helped him to clear the pub, but neither of them attempted to clean down since the Bentleys would have all Sunday to do that together. Then the two of them repaired to the kitchen. Nell had made some extra rounds and now she poured two large mugs of tea and set the sandwiches in the middle of the table, gesturing Josh to the chair opposite the one she had taken. For a moment there was silence while Josh devoured a sandwich and Nell sipped her tea and wondered where to start. Finally, she decided to plunge right in, even if it did mean hurting the landlord's feelings.

'Josh, I reckon you must guess what I'm going to say, but I'll say it anyway. We can't go on like this. As I've told you, my little shop is doing really well, but it *is* very hard work, even with Nonny and the girls to give a hand. Doing the pub work on top means I have no time at all to myself, because on a Sunday I'm too tired to do anything but go to church, cook the dinner and then snooze on the sofa.' She put a hand out and patted his. 'Josh, I'm trying to give you notice. I'll stay at the Vines for another three or four weeks, until Mrs Higgins is back at work, but after that you'll have to find somebody else for Saturday evenings.'

Josh's eyes rounded. 'But Nell, you can't do this to me! I need you; you know I do. Oh, it isn't just the pub work—the butties and the washing up—it's having someone to share me worries, someone who knows about business. Why, if it weren't for you, I wouldn't know what to buy for the sarnies, nor what cleaning materials was needed. Nell, I'd be lost without you.'

Nell liked Josh and felt truly sorry for him, but this was going a bit too far. 'Lost my foot!' she said scornfully. 'Don't tell me Maureen was a financial wizard, because she wasn't. She was a pretty, cheerful young girl who worked behind the bar and in the kitchen, and taught herself to cook Cornish pasties and sausage rolls for your customers. Now you buy them from Samples, charge a few pennies more, and I'll be bound you've not lost a customer. Well, have you?'

'No-o-o,' Josh admitted. 'But it's you who tells me how many pasties and sausage rolls I'm likely to need, and how much to charge. I know you say the shop's doing well, but if you would come in as my manageress . . .'

'Well, I won't,' Nell said bluntly. 'I can't seem to get it across to you that I'm happy with my own little shop.' She leaned forward and spoke earnestly, taking Josh's hands in a gentle clasp as she did so. 'What you want is a partner, Josh. A partner would be involved in the business.'

She had been watching Josh's face as she spoke, and now saw the relief and pleasure which flooded it without for a moment understanding the reason. Then Josh jumped to his feet, came to her side and put his arm round her. 'Oh, my dearest, I've been longing to ask you if you'd be my wife, ever since Maureen left, but I was afraid to chance my arm in case you didn't like the idea and turned me down. Oh, Nell, my love, we'll have a perfect partnership. I dare say you can find someone to take your place in the shop beside Nonny, or of course you can sell it. The boys have nagged me to divorce Maureen so that I can ask you to marry me, but—'

Nell wrenched herself out of Josh's arms with some difficulty. Her heart was pounding and she knew her hot cheeks must be scarlet. She said angrily: 'Don't be so ridiculous, Josh! You aren't in love with me and I'm certainly not in love with you. When I said you needed a partner I meant a business partner, someone you could rely on because he or she would have a vested interest in the success of the Vines. Well, that settles it; I'm leaving as from tonight.'

She made for the door and was struggling into her coat when Josh, to her intense embarrassment, dropped to his knees in front of her and flung his arms round her legs, effectively preventing her from moving.

'I'm sorry I offended you,' he gabbled. 'I misunderstood what you meant . . . is that such a sin? As for lovin', I'm real fond of you, honest to God I am. I reckon I'm a bit old for lovey-dovey stuff, but you're a handsome woman and I'd be good to you. The boys gerron well with you . . .'

'Let go of me!' Nell shouted. She tried to unclasp Josh's hands, but he was far too strong. 'Do you imagine that I'd marry anyone I didn't love? I've been a widow for five years and I can tell you I've no desire to become a wife again, particularly one married to a pub. Why do you think Maureen left, you great oaf? What makes you think I'm any different?'

'Oh, but Maureen was young and pretty,' Josh said, with rare tactlessness. 'And she was full of life and laughter. I never should have married her—'

But Josh's last remark had imbued Nell with unguessed-at strength. She tore herself out of his grip and gave him a push that sent him sprawling. 'How dare you!' she gasped. 'How dare you tell me that Maureen was . . . was too good for the Vines! So I assume you think I'm old and ugly and just right for a publican's wife! No, don't start back-pedalling—the truth is out at last, and so are you, Josh Bentley! I wouldn't marry you if you were the last man on earth and if you dare to lay a hand on me again I'll have you up for assault.'

Josh scrambled to his feet. His face was red and wet with perspiration and a trickle of saliva ran down his chin, and even in her fury Nell felt a little stirring of pity for him. She knew in her heart that he had not meant to insult her, but she also knew that neither of them would ever quite forget what had happened this evening. He did not attempt to touch her but went and stood by the door between the kitchen and the bar, through which she would presently depart, looking so crushed and helpless that again Nell's reluctant sympathy stirred.

'Nell? I must have been mad to say such a thing

to the best-looking girl I've ever met,' he said hoarsely. 'Please, please forgive me. Can't we pretend this conversation never happened and start again?'

For a moment, Nell was honestly tempted. After all, what he had said was true: Maureen had been twenty-two years old, as pretty and light-minded as any little butterfly. She had airy pale gold curls, big blue eyes and skin like milk and roses. Nell was in her thirties, dark-haired, dark-eyed and olive-skinned, and in her own opinion had never been pretty. So why not tell Josh that she forgave him and would resume friendly relations? But for the first time since Maureen had left, Nell hardened her heart. If she let Josh off the hook she would be forced to come back to the Vines, at least until Mrs Higgins was able to resume her work, and Nell suddenly realised that, amongst the many other emotions she had felt when Josh had spoken so frankly, there had been relief. It was an acceptable way out for which she could not possibly be blamed, since Josh would scarcely boast that he had offered marriage and been turned down, and she had no intention whatsoever of revealing either his proposal or his inadvertent insults.

Instead, she put on her headscarf and tied it under her chin, then turned to Josh. 'I'm willing to forget everything except that I have given you my notice from this moment on, and that you have accepted it,' she said coolly. 'You must acknowledge, Josh, that working together after what has been said would be impossible. However, I shall still count myself your friend, though no longer your employee.'

She picked up her umbrella and walked towards

the door, thinking with an inward giggle that she could do quite a lot of harm with a furled umbrella if he tried to stop her passing, but of course he did no such thing. As she reached the doorway, he held out a huge hand and gave her a pleading yet hopeful smile. 'Will you shake me hand, Nell, and call it quits?' he mumbled. 'I made a real mess of things, didn't I? But you're a generous woman; always were. Say you'll forgive me.'

They shook hands. 'I've said I'll forget everything but giving you my notice, and I meant it,' Nell said gently. 'But I think it's best if we don't meet for a bit. We're both going to feel uncomfortable and awkward for a while.'

She began to cross the bar, heading for the outer door, but Josh cleared his throat and spoke urgently. 'Hang on a minute, Nell. What'll we tell the kids? They're bound to notice that you don't come round any more. My two are real fond of you, you know.'

'Tell them the truth,' Nell said sharply. 'Tell them the pub work was getting me down, so I gave in my notice and you accepted it. Good night, Josh, and good luck. I'm sure you'll find someone only too eager to work at the Vines.'

*   *   *

Addy and Prue were told the news that their mother would no longer be working at the Vines on the Sunday morning after Nell had given notice. 'Since Mrs Bentley left I've been too tired to take you to the park or the seaside, but all that will change,' she assured her daughters. 'We might even run to a proper holiday. I thought perhaps a few days at some nice little seaside resort might be good for all of us. We can shut the shop for a week and I'm sure that if we ask her Nonny will get someone in to cook the lodger's meals so that she can come with us.'

They were having their breakfast in the flat's small kitchen and Prue jumped to her feet and ran to her mother, casting her arms round her neck and giving her a smacking kiss on the cheek. 'Oh, Mam, I've always wanted a proper holiday, but I didn't think we could afford it,' she said. 'Will Mr Bentley and the boys come too? Paul would really love it and so would Nick. Do you know, Paul told me that when his mother was alive they used to have a holiday every single year. The brewery sent in a substitute landlord while they were away. He said they used to have a grand time, though I don't think he could remember much really, because he was only six when she died.'

Addy, crunching toast and marmalade, stared at her sister for a moment, her face wearing a puzzled frown. Then it cleared. 'Oh, you mean the first Mrs Bentley. I wondered, because I couldn't imagine Maureen taking the boys anywhere, and of course she's still alive.'

Prue giggled. 'You are funny, Addy! Mrs Maureen Bentley *is* still alive—well, she must be, because Paul said she keeps writing to his dad, asking him to divorce her, only he won't. And they did have holidays, you know—Mr Bentley and Maureen, I mean—only she wouldn't take the boys along. She used to say it wouldn't be a proper holiday for her if she had to keep an eye out for Nick and Paul.'

'But the boys always used to go away in August,'

83

Addy said. 'If they didn't go with their mam and dad, where did they go?'

'They used to go to a cousin of Mr Bentley's what's gorra farm in Wales,' Prue said vaguely. 'You must have known, Addy; you're older than me.'

'Ye-es, I think I did know. Anyway, they've not been away recently.'

'We were talking about our own holiday,' Nell said rather reproachfully. 'And the Bentleys won't be coming with us. I haven't mentioned it, but Mrs Higgins has had a fall and sprained her wrist. Mr Bentley says it's twice its usual size and purple as a plum, and she won't be working again for three to four weeks, so I can't see him even thinking of a holiday.'

'Good,' Addy said decidedly. Catching her mother's eye, she added hastily: 'Oh, I like the Bentleys all right—Nick's me bezzie—but we see quite enough of 'em as it is, and now that Nick's got a job he sneers at some of the games we play, says they're for kids. He won't play Relievio no more, and when we said we were going to the Saturday rush last week he wouldn't come to the Commy because they were showin' Shirley Temple in *Captain January*. He wanted to see Boris Karloff in *Frankenstein*.' She shuddered expressively. 'I'd be too scared to see that and I reckon he knew it, so in a way he was gettin' rid of me so's he could go wi' pals of his own age.'

Nell nodded. 'Yes, you're right. Paul and you are the same age, and still like the same things, but it's different for Nick now he's working. It makes an enormous difference; he's in a factory with other apprentices, and no doubt next year, when he's entitled to holiday, he'll go away with his mates. Oh, don't look so downcast, chuck,' she added kindly, seeing Addy's face fall. 'It'll happen to you in a year or two—you won't want to see the same films as Prue does, and probably you won't want to play the games Paul plays, because girls mature— that's just another word for grow up—quicker than boys.'

'I don't want to see the same films as Prue now,' Addy muttered. 'Well, not always, anyhow. But tell us about this holiday, Mam! Can it be the seaside? Prue would like that best, I'm sure.'

'We'll see,' Nell said rather guardedly. For some time now she had been putting her wages from the pub into her Post Office book and she had amassed a tidy sum, quite sufficient to take the three of them and Nonny for a week in Rhyl. If she arranged it for the first week in August, then by the time they returned Josh would have appointed her successor and the boys, she hoped, would have accepted the fact that she no longer visited the Vines.

She finished her cup of tea, dusted toast crumbs off her thin summer dress and reached for the smart brown overall which she wore in the shop. 'Addy, clear the table and wash up. I'll dry and put away, then you and I will make the beds and sweep the living room carpets whilst Prue dusts,' she said. 'After that it will be time to change for church. It's Nonny's turn to cook Sunday dinner, which means you two can play out this afternoon.' She glanced at Addy, who was still eating toast while appearing to read the back of the cereal packet. 'Addy? Were you listening to a word I've just said?'

Addy gave a martyred sigh, finished her toast and

85

got to her feet. 'No, I wasn't,' she admitted. 'But I bet you said what you always say on a Sunday, Ma. I'm to wash up, help you make the beds and clean the flat, peel the spuds, scrape the carrots and clean the cabbage, put the joint in the oven and then change for church, whilst goody-goody Prudence does a little light dusting and brushes out her beautiful golden curls.'

Nell interrupted swiftly, feeling her cheeks grow warm. 'I knew you weren't listening,' she remarked, but could not help a smile curving her lips. 'I said that since it's Nonny's turn to cook Sunday dinner this week you two could play out when you've finished your chores.'

Addy grinned. 'I did *tell* you I wasn't listening,' she reminded her mother. 'But honestly, Mam, Prue doesn't even get to make her own bed, whilst I—'

'But don't forget Prue's only nine, and a bed made by a nine-year-old can't possibly be as neat and tidy as one made by an eleven-year-old.'

Addy, carrying dirty plates and cutlery to the sink, muttered something beneath her breath and Nell rounded on her at once. '*What* did you say? I want no back answers from you, young lady.'

Addy turned and stuck out her lower lip and for a moment Nell thought she wouldn't answer, but when she did speak it was quite politely. 'I just said that when I was nine, you made me make beds,' she remarked. 'Honestly, Mam, if you'd let Prue give me a hand, we'd get the work done in half the time, and I could teach her things like hospital corners and how to push the mop under the beds to get all the dust off the linoleum, not just where it shows.'

Nell sighed. She knew Addy was right really, and that it was time Prue did her fair share of the chores, so instead of snubbing her daughter she went across to her and patted her shoulder. 'Perhaps you're right and the work should be more evenly divided now that Prue is older,' she said. 'Prue, you help your sister with her housework, and I'm sure you'll get through it in no time. Come to think of it, we might all catch a bus to Prince's Park this afternoon, since the weather's brilliant and I could do with a break.'

'Prince's Park!' Prue squeaked. 'We haven't been there for ages, Mam. We could call for Paul and Nick and all go together, even Mr Bentley if he wanted to come, though he usually has a sleep on a Sunday afternoon.'

'No, I don't think we'll trouble Mr Bentley,' Nell said firmly, feeling the heat rush into her cheeks. 'I'd better explain that Mr Bentley was very upset when I gave in my notice, so I think we'd best keep away from the Vines for a while.'

She had half expected a great many questions, but instead Addy clattered plates on to the draining board and then nodded wisely. 'Yes, he would have been upset. He wants you to be his manageress, doesn't he?' She looked slyly at her mother. 'Nick once said that if his dad were free he'd marry you, only I told him you wouldn't do anything so daft and he got really cross, so I shut up.' She raised her eyebrows. 'I were right, weren't I, Mam? You wouldn't marry old Mr Bentley and move into the Vines? Well, how could you? You've told us over and over how you signed the pledge when you were ten and you're always repeating that song they sang . . . *Lips that touch liquor*

87

shall never touch mine . . . so you couldn't marry Mr Bentley, could you?' Here a thought obviously occurred to her and she cocked her head on one side. 'Did our dad sign the pledge too? Only I seem to remember him going down to the Throstle's Nest sometimes to wet his whistle, and I don't think they sell lemonade.'

Nell turned a snort of amusement into a cough. 'It's different for men,' she said vaguely. 'Your father sometimes had a drink but he didn't spend half his life in public houses the way some men do. He was a good man, and he worked hard.'

Prue, who had been listening wide-eyed to this exchange, put in her two penn'orth. 'I expect Mam made him wash his mouth before he kissed her,' she said thoughtfully to Addy. 'Only after he'd had a beer, of course.' She turned a serious gaze upon her mother's face. 'But it wouldn't work with Mr Bentley, would it? He'd have to spend half his life washing.'

Nell laughed. 'That song is as daft as you are,' she said affectionately, rumpling her daughter's curls, 'and since I don't intend to marry anyone, you will please forget it.' She seized a clean tea towel from the drawer and began to dry the dishes. 'So we'll go to Prince's Park this afternoon; just us and Nonny. I'll make a picnic and if the ice cream cart comes round we'll have a penny cornet apiece. And we won't invite the Bentleys, is that clear?'

The girls chorused that it was indeed clear and as soon as the washing up was finished Addy and Prue began to make beds and clean the flat. Nell announced that she would be a lady of leisure for once and lay on the sofa intending to supervise. She fell asleep in seconds, not waking until the wielder of the carpet sweeper got it stuck under the sofa and woke her trying to haul it out.

Feeling greatly refreshed, Nell stretched and yawned, then glanced at the clock on the mantel and gave a squeak of dismay. 'Oh, dear Lord, look at the time! The service starts in ten minutes and I'm still in my working dress.' She raised her voice to a shout. 'Addy, where are you? You have five minutes to get ready and then we shall have to run all the way to the church.'

Addy, entering the living room at that moment, looked smug. She was already in the tight cream linen suit and fawn strap shoes which she wore for best. 'I've laid Prue's pink dress and cardigan out on her bed, and passed a duster over her patent leather shoes,' she said. 'Leave the carpet sweeper, you silly little noodle, it'll come out easily enough when Mam gets off the sofa. I'll brush your hair for you whilst Mam puts on her church things, then we'll run like blazes and be in good time after all.'

Prue hastily dropped the carpet sweeper and scampered out of the room, to return moments later with the pink dress on but unbuttoned, the cardigan drooping from one hand and her strap shoes unfastened. Nell, returning from her own hasty change of garb, tutted and began on the buttons while Addy, scolding, did up the shoes. 'Nine years old!' she said, taking her sister's cardigan and throwing it on the sofa. 'You won't need that, 'cos it's a lovely warm day. Here, your jacket and hat's hanging on the kitchen door, so the sooner we go the better.'

She pushed Prue into the kitchen, helped her into her jacket and slammed her white straw hat down on her head. Prue tried to snatch it off,

89

complaining that her sister had not brushed out her curls, but Addy would have none of it. 'No one can see your hair under that hat, any more than they can see mine,' she said briskly. 'Do stop whining, Prue, and get a move on.'

CHAPTER FIVE

Addy was not particularly surprised, when she looked around the church, not to see either Nick and Paul or their father. Even when Maureen had been with them they had not been good attenders, but now that Mr Bentley was running the pub virtually alone he claimed that he needed the boys at home, and though they sometimes turned up late for the service, even this had grown rarer. In fact now that Nick was working, they hardly ever came to church at all.

While they were singing the last hymn and then collecting their belongings, Addy kept casting furtive glances behind her at the church door, but could see no sign of them. She gave a resigned sigh. She had intended to collar Nick and Paul and tell them of her mother's plan to visit Prince's Park. Since her mother had forbidden it, she could not invite them to join them, but Prince's Park was free to everyone and if the boys turned up there and came over to chat, Addy guessed that Nell would accept their presence as a coincidence, and might even suggest that they share the picnic.

Outside the church once more, Addy and Prue watched as Nell greeted friends and customers and had a word with the Reverend James concerning a bring and buy sale that would be held some time in the next few weeks. Then she told the children that they might play with their friends for half an hour but to remember to keep their Sunday clothes neat and tidy.

'Why don't we go home, Mam, and change out of our nice things so's we're ready for the picnic?' Prue asked. 'It wouldn't take us long, and by the time we got back to Nonny's house dinner would be ready.'

Addy aimed a vicious kick at her sister's ankle but fortunately missed, though Prue was well aware that she had erred in some way. Her blue eyes rounded and her lips quivered. 'What's wrong wi' getting ourselves changed before dinner?' she asked plaintively. 'I thought you'd be pleased, Addy, but you look real cross.'

Addy immediately changed her ferocious scowl to a look of sugary sweetness. 'Of course I'm not cross. It's a really good idea,' she cooed, but as soon as her mother had handed over the front door key and hurried away in the direction of Albermarle Court, she seized her sister by the shoulders and gave her an admonitory shake. 'Don't you have no brain under all that yaller hair?' she hissed. 'I were goin' to rush round to the Vines and tell the fellers we'd be havin' a picnic and ices in Prince's Park around tea time; then they could join us, on the quiet like.' She gave her sister another scornful glare. '*They've* got more sense than to go spilling the beans. They'd pretend they'd come up to feed the ducks or have a row on the lake, and I bet Mam would have invited them to share our butties. I'm sure she wouldn't be mean to Nick and Paul because their dad was cross when she give in her notice.' She grabbed Prue's hand as she spoke and began to tow her towards the shop. 'And now you've ruined everything,' she concluded crossly.

Prue began to snivel. 'You're a bad girl, Addy Fairweather,' she whined. 'You know very well Mam don't want us to tell the boys we're going to Prince's Park. And anyway, we're not supposed to go to the Vines. What if she asks where we've been? She'll probably guess if she sees the boys in the park. I'd get into trouble just as much as you, even if it was your idea and I had to go along with it.' She began to gasp and to cry in earnest as Addy broke into a run. 'Oh, you are a bad girl, and now you're going to make me bad too!'

Addy loosed her hold on her sister's hand for a moment to give her a pinch. 'I'm doing nothing of the sort, because you spoiled it,' she said. 'All right, I meant to go round to the Vines and ask the boys to join us, but you put a stop to all that, didn't you? Now we've got to go back home to change before going to Nonny's for our Sunday dinner, so if we don't see the boys at all today it'll be all—your—fault!'

As she said each word she gave Prue an unkind jerk, and then, as they reached the shop, she swung her sister into the doorway so hard that Prue's white straw hat fell off and went bowling along the pavement.

Addy, inserting the key in the lock, ignored it, but just as Prue was about to set off in pursuit a passer-by grabbed it and handed it to Prue, saying rather sternly to Addy: 'You want to take better care of your little sister, chuck. You jerked her into the doorway that roughly, she near on lost her hat for good.'

The speaker was a handsome young man in his twenties and Prue, taking her hat and perching it on her curls, fluttered her eyelashes and thanked him profusely. Addy, on the other hand, scowled at him before saying grudgingly: 'Ta, mister. But she ain't a baby, you know. She's quite old enough to hang on to her own hat.'

The man began to speak, but Addy had unlocked the door and now she pushed her sister inside and followed her in, saying rather more politely: 'I'm sorry, mister, but we're in a real hurry. Me gran's been took ill and Mam's sent us to fetch her medicine.'

Before he could reply she had slammed the door and locked it, then turned on Prue. 'I know what you're going to say, you're going to say I were rude to that feller and told him a lie, but he don't know us from Adam, so it could easily have been the truth. Now get up them stairs, Prue, 'cos if we really gerra move on we might still be able to tell the boys about Prince's Park on our way to Nonny's. I'll give you a hand if you need it and I'll brush your hair and plait it if you promise not to tell Mam we've seen them.'

The two girls rushed into their room and began to take off their Sunday clothes. Prue selected a brown cotton dress which had been Addy's a couple of years before, and her old plimsolls, then gave her sister a tentative smile. 'D'you think this'll be all right for Prince's Park, Addy? And there weren't no need to get so cross wi' me, because I like Nick and Paul just as much as you do. If you'd explained instead of losin' your temper, we could have been at the Vines by now.'

Addy saw the justice of this but also remembered the sequence of events. 'You butted in, saying we should go straight home and change our clothes before I could so much as open my mouth,' she explained. 'I do know what you mean, though, Prue, and I'm sorry I snarled at you. I didn't have a chance to whisper what I meant us to do before you'd opened your big gob.'

Prue began to say that she did not have a big gob but at this point Addy, who had already changed into her own old clothes, picked up the hairbrush. 'Plaits or loose?' she asked briskly. 'I don't know why you haven't had it cut by now; honest to God, Prue, short hair is so much easier and you've got lovely curls.' She glanced ruefully at herself in the mirror. 'Mine just hangs there like wet string whether I have it long or short, but since Mam cut it so it just covers my ears it's much easier to deal with.'

'I'll have it loose, since that will be quicker,' Prue said. 'Here, give me the brush. It won't take me two minutes, an' if you could get a couple of slides off the dressing table I'll use them to keep it out of me face.' She giggled. 'Nonny gets real cross when me hair dangles in me food.'

Presently the two girls, about to turn into the jigger behind the Vines, saw Paul sauntering along, bouncing a very old tennis ball as high as he could, and then leaping up to catch it. 'Eh up!' he said cheerfully upon seeing them. 'Come round for a game of Relievio? Only there ain't many playin' out today, despite the sunshine, an' Nick's gone off somewhere, I dunno where. It took us most of the morning to clear and clean the bar and the snug, to say nothing of the Jug and Bottle.' He heaved an

94

exaggerated sigh. 'I reckon more drink gets spilled in that room than in the whole of the rest of the pub.' He wrinkled his nose distastefully. 'I hate the smell of stale beer, I does. Still an' all, the work's finished now. Pa's makin' us a dinner and then the afternoon's our own. I thought we might go down to the Mersey when Nick comes back and see what we can find in the mud.'

'You don't want to do that,' Addy said hastily. 'Our mam's taking us to Prince's Park for a picnic. If you happened along, she might easily invite you to join us.'

'Yes, she might,' Prue said eagerly. 'Only she give in her notice last night, Paul—to your dad, I mean—and told us we'd best steer clear of the Vines for a bit, 'cos your dad were real upset.'

Paul stared from one face to the other, then nodded slowly. 'So *that* was it!' he said. 'Nick took him a cup of tea at around nine o'clock this morning. He usually takes it at ten, but he thought it ought to be earlier today because Mrs Higgins wouldn't be coming in, and she does a lot of the work on a Sunday. And Nick said Dad were already dressed but sittin' on his bed, starin' in front of him. Nick thought he looked—oh, not ill exactly, but different. He said his face were all hot an' red and his eyes were shiny, and when Nick asked him what were the matter he stood up, snatched the tea so that it slopped over the edge of the mug, and said that he meant to go chasin' up to Burlington Street to see Mrs Chambers about working at the pub until Mrs Higgins is fit again, and would Nick kindly clear off and leave him alone.'

'That were rude,' Prue said primly, making Paul

95

give a rueful grin. 'And when poor Nick had taken him a cup of tea, too!'

Paul, however, shook his head. 'Hang on a minute. That weren't all. When he came down Nick had made some toast and Dad grabbed it, took a big bite, and then he said he'd forgot to mention that Mrs Fairweather wouldn't be coming in for a bit, either, so he'd visit Mrs Bruton at the same time, see how she's fixed for Saturday nights. And then he grabbed his coat off the peg, jammed the rest of the toast in his mouth and disappeared, leaving us to start the cleaning down without him.'

'Gosh,' Prue said, sounding awestruck. 'So what happened next? Has he come home yet?'

'Oh, yeah. He was back within the hour an' I heard him tellin' Nick that both ladies would start work this week. He seemed a lot calmer, but then Nick went and put the cat among the pigeons. We were cleaning down in the bar and so on when suddenly Nick turned to Dad and asked why didn't he write to Maureen and say she could have a divorce, 'cos then he'd be able to marry someone and wouldn't have to pay them. I thought it were quite sensible meself, but Dad picked him up and shook him like a terrier shakes a rat. He said that as a matter of fact he had written to Maureen, but a man marries a woman because he has a special feeling for her, not because he wants her to wash glasses or work behind the bar. And then he said, all sarcastic like, that he didn't fancy being tied for life to fat old Mrs Chambers or scrawny old Mrs Bruton. And that made Nick cross too, 'cos of course he hadn't suggested no such thing. He'd started to say they weren't the only women in the world when Pa clacked him round the head and told him to get on with his work and stop acting the fool.'

'What did Nick do?' asked Addy, for she could not imagine Nick sitting down under such treatment. She knew he considered himself to be a working man now, but doubted he would stand up to his father, whom he greatly admired. 'Go on, Paul. What happened next?'

Paul chuckled. 'Nick had been wiping the bar down with one of them big wet dishcloths and he flung it straight at Dad. It were a smashin' shot, I'm tellin' you. It wrapped itself right round Dad's head and whilst he was getting untangled Nick flew out of the back door and disappeared.'

'Well I'm bleedin' well blowed!' Addy said, ignoring her sister's gasp at the swear word. 'D'you think he's run away for good? Did he take a bag with his clothes and that?'

Paul laughed again. 'No, course he didn't,' he said derisively. 'He knows which side his bread is buttered. I bet he's back in time for dinner. Dad's cooking it now—it's the rest of the boiled bacon, a pan of potatoes and some carrots. But did you say your mam has given notice to my dad? If so, no wonder he had such a cob on! He's real fond of your mam, you know, and relies on her in all sorts of ways.'

'Well, he won't be able to rely on her any longer,' Addy said firmly. 'Two jobs is one too many, Nonny says. But your dad will soon find someone else—well, he already has—so once they get going we can all be friends again.'

*   *   *

97

Nonny's dinners were always splendid and this one was no exception. Roast beef, Yorkshire pudding and roast potatoes were flanked by leeks in a white sauce and carrots and swedes mashed with butter and black pepper, the whole surrounded by a sea of gravy. Mr Cracknell told the girls that but for his advanced age—he was seventy—he would have proposed to their grandmother years ago and carried her off to live by the seaside and cook him a roast meal every day. But since he made this joke regularly it was rewarded with only the most perfunctory of smiles though Nell, as usual, pretended to be hurt and to ask what was wrong with her own dinners, for on alternate Sundays Mr Cracknell joined them at the flat above the shop and always ate a hearty meal.

When they had eaten, Nonny and Nell cleared away and washed up, and then Nell outlined her plan for the afternoon. She said she must hurry home to cut butties, but Nonny vetoed the idea. 'I've a nice farmhouse fruitcake, just longing to be eaten, a full loaf of me own-baked bread and a jar of plum jam,' she told the girls. 'Your mam and me will have a cuppa from the little café and you kids can have ginger beer. Well, well. It'll be like old times to have a picnic in the park.'

At first, the afternoon went according to plan. Nonny had brought a bag of oddments—bread, broken biscuits and cake crumbs—so that they might feed the ducks. Prue had brought along an old tennis ball and an even older tennis racquet with half the strings missing, and the four of them played French cricket, speedily attracting a number of other children, who gleefully joined in the game.

Addy was just thinking, sadly, that Nick and Paul must have decided to go mud-raking in the Mersey when she saw two familiar figures approaching. Grinning to herself—but only inwardly—she nudged Prue. 'Well, look who's here!' she said, trying to sound surprised. She turned to Nell, lowering her voice. 'Mam, what'll I say if they want to join in the game?'

Nell frowned, looking puzzled. 'What d'you mean? Anyone can join in the game, though we've already got far too many for everyone to have a go with the bat.' She peered at the approaching boys, then turned a suspicious look upon her elder daughter. 'How very strange, it's Nick and Paul! And it's no use you saying they always visit the park on a Sunday because I know very well they don't. However, this is a public park and they're good friends of yours, so . . .' She raised her voice as Nick and Paul drew near. 'Hello, you two! Fancy a game of French cricket?'

Nick said he would act as umpire, but when Nell produced her basket of food and Nonny returned from the café bearing bottles of ginger beer and two mugs of tea, the other children melted away and it was only Nonny, the Fairweathers and the Bentleys who began to eat.

Prue was the first to hear the tinkling of the ice cream cart, but it was Nick who got to his feet. 'I'll mug everyone to a penny cornet,' he said gruffly, 'and I've money to hire a rowboat for a go on the lake.' He turned to Nell. 'It's a sort of thank you, Mrs Fairweather, for our share in the picnic. We'll go when we've eaten the ices, if that's all right with you?'

Nell smiled at him. 'That's a very kind thought,'

she said appreciatively. 'I expect Mrs Hammond and myself will sit here quietly enjoying the sunshine whilst the four of you play at sailors. Only don't let Addy or Prue row, will you, because though it looks easy I know it isn't, and we don't want any accidents.'

'I wouldn't want to row,' Prue said righteously. 'Girls shouldn't row; it's a boy's thing, isn't it, Mam?'

Nell laughed, but agreed that her daughter was probably right, though Addy said rebelliously that she was sure she could row as well as any lad, given the opportunity. Nell sighed. 'Addy, I want you to give me your word that you won't touch the oars. Promise?'

Addy promised. In fact she had no intention of making a fool of herself by trying to take the oars, and very soon the four of them were climbing into one of the hire boats. Nick was sculling, but after a few minutes he pulled in to the bank and shipped his oars. 'I want a word with you, Addy,' he said quietly, 'but I didn't want your mam to hear, so I suggested this 'cos I guessed she wouldn't relish a boat trip.' He turned to Prue and Paul. 'This is a private matter between Addy and meself, so I'm going to give you two a penny each and drop you off here. The ice cream cart's only a step away, so buy yourselves another cornet and then wait on the bank. By the time you've finished your ices, I'll have said all I want to say to Addy and we'll pick you up and row back to Mrs Fairweather and your gran. Is that clear?'

Paul and Prue said at once that this would be fine and scrambled out of the boat whilst Addy thought, rather apprehensively, that it sounded suspiciously as though she were in for a ticking off. However, she reminded herself that even though Nick was working now and earning a wage, he was still just a lad really, and her friend, of course. So she raised no objection when the two younger ones were put ashore, and when Nick reached the middle of the lake once more she glanced enquiringly at him. 'What's up?' she said bluntly. 'I can't think why you want secrets from Prue and Paul, but if you do, now's your chance to spill the beans.'

Nick grinned at her. 'It was something Paul said,' he explained. 'I reckon he probably gorrit wrong, but . . . oh, well, I thought you'd likely know the truth of it and could set me mind at rest. Paul said Mrs Hammond thought two jobs were one too many for Mrs Fairweather, and then . . . and then . . .'

'Then what?' Addy said impatiently, when Nick's voice faded into silence. 'Is that all you wanted to say? Because if so, all I can tell you is that I agree with Nonny. Or was there something else?'

Nick heaved a huge sigh and rubbed a hand through his hair. 'I dunno how much Paul told you about the row me and Dad had this morning,' he said. 'But after I'd stormed off out, Paul decided to clear off as well for a bit. He saw you and Prue and you told him about your mam giving my dad notice that she meant to leave, and then Paul went back home to get his dinner and see if I'd come back. I hadn't, and Paul said Dad was looking so miserable that he went and gave him a hug and asked him wharrever was the matter, 'cos he couldn't see why your mam giving notice should 'ave purrim in such a tweak. And then Dad said it weren't just that. He

101

said he'd asked Mrs Fairweather to marry him and she'd turned him down.'

'Oh!' Addy said. 'Well, what's wrong with that? There's no rule that says everyone's got to say yes, is there?'

Nick flushed and his eyes began to sparkle angrily. 'Honest to God, Addy, you've got no more sense than your silly little sister. My dad pays your mam the biggest compliment there is and she don't say she'll think about it or talk it over with Mrs Hammond, or anything like that. She just said no, and to make matters worse she handed in her notice.'

'Did she?' Addy said, enlightened. 'That explains a lot. Mam's been saying for a while now that she was always tired and she mentioned that your dad wanted her to do more hours, but if he really asked her to marry him and she said no she'd pretty well have to give in her notice, wouldn't she? You think I'm stupid, but how could they go on working together after that?'

Nick looked surprised. 'Why not?' he asked. 'A man pays a woman a compliment—'cos it is a compliment to ask someone to marry you, whatever you may think, Addy Fairweather—and just because she says no you think everything's got to change. But why the devil should it? And *why* won't she marry him? Folk are always saying the Vines is the best pub in Liverpool and my dad is real kind and generous, so why couldn't your mam make us all happy and marry my dad, just as soon as his divorce comes through?'

'Because she likes the shop and the flat and she doesn't like the pub,' Addy said bluntly. Then, seeing the angry look on her pal's face, she added hastily: 'I'm sure she don't want to marry *anyone*, Nick, but can't you see it's *her* choice? There's—there's rules about that sort of thing which grown-ups know. I mean, no woman asks a man to marry her, does she? So he gets to choose who he wants to ask, and she gets to choose whether to say yes or no. And my mam chose to say no, so that's that.'

Nick began to mutter that it wasn't as simple as that, and then blazed out with what he had obviously been thinking. 'Your mother's a bleedin' snob,' he said loudly. 'She thinks she's too good to be a publican's wife, but she's only a perishin' gypsy when all's said and done. She ought to be grateful that my dad even let her work in the pub, lerralone proposed . . .'

Addy was so angry that she completely forgot they were in a boat. She jumped to her feet and slapped Nick's face as hard as she could, screaming that he was a rude, horrible boy and she would tell her mam what he had just said. Nick rocked backwards, shouted a warning, and the next thing Addy knew was that something caught her behind the knees and she found herself struggling in the water.

As the cold and the shock hit her, she took an enormous breath, intending to scream for help—for she had never learned to swim—and sank like a stone. Terror seized her. She was going to drown, to be smothered in the thick black mud at the bottom of the lake, and they would have to get divers out to fetch up her body for burial. Oh, she was going to die; already bubbles of air were escaping from her mouth and her chest felt as though a giant hand were squeezing it like a sponge.

103

When her head broke the surface she was so surprised that she nearly forgot to breathe in again. Then her feet found the lake bottom and she clutched at the side of the boat. Even as she did so, a hand seized her by the back of her dress and heaved her out of the water. It was Nick.

Getting Addy back on board the boat was no easy matter, but Nick managed it somehow, and in complete silence too. Then, again without a word, he rowed them to the bank where Paul and Prue, round-eyed and horrified, had watched every stage of the drama. Nick pulled the boat up alongside them and spoke before either had a chance to ask what had happened. 'Gerrin, you two,' he said roughly. 'I won't row back until we've decided what we'll tell Mrs Fairweather.'

Addy was about to snap that they should tell her the truth when Paul, settling himself on one of the benches, spoke up. 'You won't have to tell her nothing just yet,' he observed. 'She came down to tell us they've gone to Mrs Hammond's house to make a cold supper. She asked us to go along an' all, Nick, but I said I didn't think we should 'cos Dad don't know where we are and anyway I think she were just being polite.'

Nick had been frowning heavily, but now his brow cleared. 'That's good; then we shan't have to explain anything, not really.' He turned to Addy. 'Just tell your mam you tripped over one of the oars and fell into the water,' he said gruffly. 'No need to say we had a quarrel.' Addy compressed her lips but said nothing, and Nick stared enquiringly at her. 'Well? Do you want to tell your mam what we were quarrelling about?'

Addy was shivering with cold, but fury still

104

gripped her. She hated Nick Bentley and intended to let him know it, but instead of speaking to him she turned to address Paul. 'Please tell your brother that I wouldn't dream of repeating the terrible things he said about my mother,' she said in tones of stiff formality. And then, descending to a more human level, she added: 'And you can tell him that I won't ever speak to him again, not if I live to be a hundred; he's a rude, horrible pig and my mam is worth ten of him, even if she is a gypsy.'

Prue's hands flew to her mouth, but Nick spoke before she could do so. 'If you never speak to me again that will suit me just fine, because I never mean to speak to you,' he said wrathfully. 'I always knew you were a nasty piece of work, Adelaide Fairweather, but to call me names when I've just saved your life . . .'

Addy gave him one of her best scowls, then turned back to address Paul. 'You may tell your brother that if he hadn't pushed me into the water he wouldn't have had to pull me out of it.' She began to rub her arms vigorously. 'And you may tell him to row us straight back to the landing stage now, because I think I ought to get out of these wet clothes just as soon as I can.'

Poor Paul looked helplessly from one to the other, clearly wondering whether he was supposed to repeat Addy's words, although this seemed unnecessary since the combatants were sitting within a couple of feet of one another. However, Nick said nothing but merely began to row back towards the landing stage. When they reached it, he made fast and climbed out, closely followed by Paul. Then he lifted Prue out and after a second's hesitation held out a hand to Addy.

105

Abruptly Addy realised what she must look like. Dripping hair, mud-streaked arms and soaked clothing, yet with her nose in the air and her lips clamped tightly shut . . . if she had laughed, if she had admitted what she knew to be the truth—that she had stepped back against the seat, knocking herself into the water—then all might yet have been well, but Nick's words still reverberated in her mind, refusing to be forgotten. He had insulted her . . . but pals insulted each other often with no hard feelings to follow. But then he had insulted her mother, called her a gypsy. Even the recollection of his words and the tone he had used were like a knife in Addy's breast. She was often cross with her mother, hurt by Nell's obvious preference for her younger daughter, but she both loved and admired her, and bitterly resented any criticism from outsiders. Furthermore, she had been delighted to learn that her mother had refused the landlord's offer of marriage and given in her notice at the pub, so why pretend? The friendship which had existed between herself and Nick would probably not have survived the gulf that had come between them now that Nick was working and she was still in school. She had other friends—Paul was one of them, and she was certain that *he* would continue to be her friend, even though she and his brother were now enemies.

So when Nick said, to the world in general, that he would accompany the Fairweathers back to the shop, Addy told Paul that this would not be necessary. 'I've still got the key so I can let us in,' she said loftily. 'I'll rinse my clothes and put newspaper in my sandals, and perhaps Mam won't realise that I've been in the lake.' She was about to threaten Prue with a horrible revenge if she told anyone about the accident when it occurred to her that making an enemy of her sister as well as of Nick was not sensible. Instead of threatening, therefore, she gave the younger girl her friendliest smile. 'Don't tell anyone what happened, Prue, 'cos it would only upset them,' she said. 'Oh, look, there's a tram. I wonder if anyone has money for a tram fare?'

CHAPTER SIX

October 1937

'Well? Any luck?' Paul had hung around at the end of the jigger which led to the back of the Fairweathers' shop, having said he would meet Prue there after school, and now he was disappointed when Prue shook her head glumly.

'No, no luck at all, really. I got Addy to myself and did what you said. I told her that over three months had passed since she and Nick had fallen out and that's a long time. I said you were sure that Nick would speak to her if he knew she wanted to make up, but she just said she was quite happy with things as they are.'

Paul sighed heavily. 'Your sister bears a grudge for longer than anyone else I know,' he said regretfully. 'And I'm just about sick of it, I am. There's Christmas coming up, so we'll want to start earning money, and Addy won't even let Nick get near enough to her to apologise.'

'Does he want to apologise?' Prue asked eagerly.

'If he wants to say he's sorry for the horrible thing he said about our mother, then I think she might . . .'

Paul pulled a face. 'I think they should both say they're sorry,' he announced. 'The trouble is, the minute Nick opens his mouth Addy will walk away from him, or say something so cutting that he'll walk away from her.'

'That's true,' Prue said. 'Oh, Paul, we simply must get them together before we start preparing for Christmas.'

'I've got a plan,' Paul said slowly, 'though of course I don't know if it'll work. The trouble is, Prue, Addy's as stubborn as one mule and Nick's as obstinate as another. But I'm hopeful that my plan may work because they know very well that the four of us working together, when Nick isn't at the factory, can make quite a bit of money for Christmas presents, if we start fairly soon. And everyone needs a bit of extra money at Christmas.'

They were about to enter the yard at the back of the shop but Prue grabbed Paul's arm, bringing him to a halt. 'What is it?' she asked eagerly. 'Your plan, I mean?'

Paul shuffled his feet. 'I'm going to tell her that if she won't speak to my brother then I won't speak to her,' he said firmly. 'I know it'll be difficult and I know she'll be mad as fire, but I don't care; I've had enough. I'll speak to you, but if she tries to get in on our conversation I shall just ignore her. I won't come into the shop, nor I won't join in a game if she's playing, and we'll see how she likes that!'

Prue stared at him aghast. 'Oh, but Paul, she was saying only yesterday that you're her bezzie now

108

that Nick's too old and snooty to play Tip and Run or footie. She really likes you, you know. And you're right about her being mad as fire, only I expect she'll blame me. But if your plan works, and I do think it might . . .'

'Fingers crossed,' Paul said. 'So if we're agreed, I'll tell Addy what we've decided tomorrow morning, before school starts.'

Prue gasped. 'Don't say *we*, please, Paul,' she said urgently. 'I know I'm an awful coward, but I have to live with Addy—we even share the same bed when Nonny stays over—and she can be so horrible. And it really is *your* plan; *I* don't come into it at all.'

Paul laughed. 'You aren't a coward, Prue,' he said kindly. 'If Addy were my sister, me knees would never stop knocking. I won't say anything about you, I promise. And now let's go in to your mam's shop 'cos I promised Dad I'd buy a quarter of tea and he gave me an extra penny for a toffee stick. We'll share it if you'll walk back to the Vines with me.'

*   *   *

To Paul's pleasure and Prue's astonishment, Paul's threat did the trick. Neither he nor Addy herself ever told Prue what had passed between them and Prue, tactful for once, did not comment on her sister's swollen red eyes or unusual quietness. She longed to know just what Paul had said but next day, when she asked him, he told her that for all their sakes he did not intend to repeat his words.

'The only thing you need to know is that it worked a treat,' he said exultantly. 'I thought it

109

would take her a couple of days to come round, but I was wrong. There's a lot of generosity in Addy and she's pretty brave too. She listened to every word I said, nodded, and then turned and marched off. Later she came into our kitchen at the Vines, looked Nick straight in the eye and asked if she could have a word in private. They went into the yard for about twenty minutes and then Nick came back in again, grinnin' all over his face, and said peace had been declared. So I said wharrabout startin' to collect orange boxes to chop up for kindling and Nick said the four of us would have a council of war—so much for peace—on Saturday morning, so we could plan our pre-Christmas campaign.'

When Addy mentioned casually to her mother that they intended to go to the Forum on Saturday morning, because the film they were showing was more suitable than the childish one at the Commodore, Prue saw her mother smile and guessed that Nell was aware that the quarrel was over and was as pleased as her daughters. When she added an extra sixpence to what they called their picture money, Prue was certain that Nell knew all about it and hoped desperately that, in future, she and Paul between them would be able to prevent any further serious disagreements.

*   *   *

The foursome emerged from the cinema, discussing the film they had just seen. Nick admired Charlie Chan greatly, though he always claimed to have discovered the murderer well before the detective did so, and now he was

110

dissecting the plot and making Addy laugh because the film was *Charlie Chan at the Circus* and he was pretending to believe that the gorilla was a real one and not, as Addy maintained, a feller in a monkey suit.

The two of them strolled along the pavement, laughing and bickering quite in the old way, whilst Paul and Prue followed, and presently Addy asked Nick whether they should take a bus into the country that afternoon to search for holly.

'Holly? But it's far too early for anyone to be buying the stuff,' Nick objected. 'It won't be Christmas for almost eight weeks, and folk won't put up holly until just before the holiday because it goes all crinkly.'

'I didn't mean to cut holly, I meant to mark down the best trees,' Addy explained. Once, she would have added 'you great fool', but she had realised, when she and Nick had made up their quarrel, that she would have to watch her words for a bit. 'Otherwise I suppose we could see if anyone in the courts wants messages run, only it don't pay all that well.'

However, Nick was shaking his head. 'Can't come out this afternoon,' he said. 'The brewery's given Dad permission to close the pub for three days, and we're redecorating so it will be all smart for Christmas. That means we really do have to work fast. You know Miss Bird? She's coming in this afternoon to give a hand with holding ladders and such so I can't let Dad down, you see, 'cos I've promised to whitewash the ceilings. Dad ain't too keen on heights so he'll do the walls, and young Paul there will do the skirting boards.'

'Oh, you lucky beggar!' Addy said enviously.

111

'How I wish I could come along and give a hand too. I might chance it, only Miss Bird helps out in the shop whenever Nonny can't or the shop's too busy, and she'd be bound to tell Mam she'd seen me in the Vines.'

'I know you aren't allowed to come into the Vines during opening hours,' Nick objected, 'but surely it would be all right if you were helping us to decorate? When Maureen was with us, you and your mother came to tea at the pub more than once. Suppose you just ask her—your mam, I mean—if she'll allow you. That's no skin off anyone's nose, and it's my belief she'll let you come.'

'Well, I will ask,' Addy said, having thought the matter over. 'Only don't be surprised if we don't turn up, because you know what grown-ups are: they see what they want to see and they believe what they want to believe, and because she signed the pledge when she was a kid Mam still thinks that pubs are—are . . .'

'. . . dens of iniquity,' Nick finished for her, grinning. 'She's right in a way. Some fellers spend their wives' housekeeping, the rent money, even the few pennies their kids earn on buying drink. But the majority of our customers have a pint or two on pay day and are respectable citizens for the rest of the week.'

'I know, Nick. If I can come this afternoon, I will, only I'll do as you say and ask Mam first. If she says yes, shall I bring Baby Prue along, or would she just get in the way?'

Nick turned and frowned at her, then wagged a warning finger. 'Stop it, Addy! Prue's not a baby, she's a good kid, and of course you must bring her if your mother agrees.'

'Sorry, Nick; I forgot,' Addy said and saw her friend turn his head to hide a lurking grin. 'But I've just thought—you said Birdie was helping your father this afternoon, so of course she won't be in the shop. Oh, damn! I bet Mam will need us stocking shelves and serving customers, because Saturdays are often busy.' She glanced up at the sky where despite its being October there were patches of blue sky showing between the clouds. 'It's a waste of a nice day, but since we've had the morning off it's only fair to help Mam for the afternoon, if she needs us.'

'Yes, of course,' Nick said regretfully. By now, they had reached the corner of St Martin's Street. 'We might see you later, then. We can't cook while we're decorating downstairs, but Dad will probably send me for fish and chips.' He smacked his lips. 'Bet you wish you were going home to a nice plate of cod and fried taters.'

Addy waved Nick and Paul off, then grabbed Prue's hand. 'Will you ask Mam if we can help the Bentleys to decorate?' she asked urgently. 'She's much more likely to say yes to you than to me.'

'All right,' Prue said readily. 'Paul told me about the decorating and I said we'd love to help, but of course Mam may need us, it being Saturday.'

'Thank you, Prue,' Addy said, then gave her sister's hand a squeeze. 'Race you to the shop!'

Despite Addy's hopes, however, not even Prue's gentle request to be allowed to help decorate the Vines brought a satisfactory response. 'Nonny has said she'll come in at three o'clock and stay until we close, so I should be able to manage without you after that,' Nell said. 'But I'm afraid you'll have to find some way of amusing yourselves other than redecorating the Vines. My dears, life has been a good deal pleasanter for all of us since I stopped working for Mr Bentley, and you know why, don't you? It wasn't just a worker he wanted, but a wife. And you're old enough now, the pair of you, to realise that marriage only works when two people both love and respect one another. Unfortunately, Mr Bentley doesn't seem to understand that. Don't ever say this to Nick or Paul, but the only thing that concerns Mr Bentley is replacing Maureen. So I'd rather keep a—a distance between our two families until he realises that I shall never change my mind.'

'Right, Mam; we understand,' Addy said. She was thrilled to be treated to a proper grown-up explanation. 'And we'll work in the shop until Nonny arrives.'

As was usual on a Saturday, they had a picnic lunch in the storeroom behind the shop, taking it in turns to nip behind the counter whenever the shop doorbell jangled as a customer entered. By three o'clock, when Nonny came bustling in, they were really busy. Prue was darting between the shop and the stockroom, filling shelves, Nell was serving the customers who had long lists, and Addy was dealing with the rest, and with any children who came in for two penn'orth of sweets or a toffee stick.

Because they could not go to the Vines, Addy suggested that they should go upstairs and start preparations for supper, but though Nell laughed she also shook her head. 'There's no need for such a sacrifice,' she said. 'You go off out and play hopscotch or skipping, or something like that. It's very cold and it'll be dark by five o'clock, so make sure you come home before then and start the supper. Put your coats on and be off with you; Nonny and I can manage.'

The children obeyed with alacrity, for the shop grew stuffy when it was full of customers, and though there was a sign on the door asking folk not to smoke in the shop itself the request was not always treated seriously, though Nell would pointedly open the door if the air became blue with fumes.

So the girls emerged on to the frosty pavement and took deep breaths of the cold air. 'I love working in the shop but it's horrid when people smoke,' Prue said, adjusting her pixie hood over her flaxen curls. 'What'll we do, Addy?' She looked around her. 'We could go down the courts; there's bound to be kids playin' out around there.'

Addy, however, had other ideas. 'Let's go to the swings and that, on Silvester Street,' she said eagerly. 'Usually there's queues of kids waiting their turn but it's getting dusk and it's mortal cold, so we might get a go without having to hang around.'

'Oh, that's a grand idea,' Prue said enthusiastically. 'If we can bag two swings side by side we'll have a race; see who can get highest first.'

Alight with anticipation, the sisters set out for the recreation ground.

*   *   *

Giles had arrived in Liverpool that afternoon. As planned, he had joined the Royal Air Force with

115

the intention of becoming a pilot aboard aircraft carriers. He had enjoyed the rigorous training and now he had come to Liverpool to meet his cousin Mark who, following family tradition, was an officer aboard the frigate *Hyperion* whose home port was Liverpool. Mark had recently got engaged to a local girl and her parents were hosting an engagement party that evening so Giles, who had never visited Liverpool before, was exploring.

He had started out by finding his way to the Adelphi Hotel, where the party was to be held, and booking himself a room for the night, though the price took him aback. After that he made for what, to him, was the most important street in the city— Scotland Road. No one with a naval upbringing could fail to know that the main passageway in any British ship was always known as either 'the Scottie' or 'the Scotland Road', and when he came across it at last he was not disappointed. It was a very cold day—his breath misted before him as he walked—but even so the pavements were crowded and the shop windows both fascinating and beginning to be lit, for dusk was not far distant.

He found Paddy's Market—he knew it well by repute—and wandered round, astonished by the low prices and the variety of goods on offer. Most of the stuff was second hand, of course, but worth a look at least. Presently, he returned to the main road and found a little antique shop where, after much thought, he purchased a pretty ivory figurine to give to the happy couple as an engagement present. It was very old, the ivory deep yellow and smooth as silk, and he thought Mark would appreciate it, even if his wife to be did not. Then he chided himself. Mark was a good bloke and would have chosen a nice girl to be his life partner. She, too, would appreciate the ivory figurine. However, the gift had not been cheap, so Giles decided that he would move to less expensive accommodation on the morrow. He hesitated on the pavement, wondering what his next move should be.

The owner of the shop had wrapped the figurine in pink tissue paper and placed it in a bag, but even so Giles found it a nuisance. He had to be careful that he did not knock it and had almost decided to return to the hotel and leave it in his room when it occurred to him that if he was to find a less expensive hotel, or even a lodging house, he might as well do so before the party, which was to start at seven o'clock.

Accordingly he walked along the pavement, examining each side street as he passed, and after a few minutes he saw a sign swinging from a nearby house front which announced that it was a guesthouse and that it had vacancies. Giles turned towards it, but decided that though its rooms might be cheap, it was too near the Scotland Road. He had no desire to find himself sharing the facilities with a number of drunken seamen, so he moved further along. Ahead of him he could see a large building which might well be a hotel.

Hurrying, for it was now definitely dusk—stars were pricking out in the dark sky overhead—he was about to climb the steps to the front door when an excited shriek made him look round, and he saw that a park or recreation ground lay to his left. There were a number of swings, a slide and a roundabout, and the shriek had come from a child—a girl, presumably—on one of the swings.

Giles glanced back at the bulk of the building behind him and felt foolish. This was no hotel, for even in the fading light he could see the brass plate by the door. It was a presbytery and it was attached to a church, which he now recognised as such. He sighed and was about to turn back towards the main road when it occurred to him that the kids playing on the swings—there were two of them— might be able to suggest a hotel or guest house where he could spend Sunday night.

He crossed the road and stood within a few feet of the children, grinning to himself. The girls were about to have a race: that was obvious. They started off sitting on the heavy wooden seats of the swings, grasping the even heavier metal chains, and then, at a word of command—'Ready, steady, go!'—the smaller of the two started to push her swing into action. When it was moving smoothly, she shouted: 'Come on then, Addy, see if you can catch me up before I goes right over the top and wins the race!' She began to scoop at the air with her legs and leaned so far back that her body was almost horizontal.

'Watch out then, Prue, here I come!' the girl called Addy shrieked, and presently both children were straining every nerve to go higher, whilst the swings creaked and the chains clashed.

Giles waited patiently and was not unduly surprised when the girl called Prue suddenly seemed to realise not only that they were neck and neck, but that it was almost dark. She did not cease her vigorous swinging, but shouted to the other: 'Oh, Addy, our mam said to be home before dark, and it's dark now. Anyway, I've won 'cos I just saw my toes over the top of the church roof and no one

118

can't go higher than that!'

'My toes is over the church roof an' all,' her sister—for they had to be sisters—replied. 'It can't be five o'clock yet . . . and I'm so high I reckon I should be able to see—'

She twisted round as she spoke and Giles shouted a warning, but it was too late: the big heavy swings lurched towards one another and collided, and the smaller of the two girls flew from her seat and crashed heavily to the ground.

Giles dropped the figurine and ran forward, narrowly escaping decapitation as Prue's swing, relieved of her weight, came back fast and furious. But he managed to duck in time, then saw, with horror, that Addy had not been so lucky. The loosened swing had caught her across the head and he saw her limp body hit the ground, only feet from where her sister lay.

Giles went straight to the older child who must, he judged, be twelve or thirteen. The swing seat had managed to hit her twice, once across the forehead and once full in the mouth, and he saw that her lips were swelling almost as he watched, while blood trickled down from the blow on her forehead. Her eyes were closed and he thought, thankfully, that she was unconscious.

He ran to the other child, but could see no obvious damage from her fall. He looked round him wildly; surely someone else must have heard the crash and would come running to help? But it was dark. Workers would not be returning to their homes so early, while mothers would be indoors preparing the evening meal and their children would be keeping out of the cold. He would have to fetch help . . . but where would he find it? There

119

were no lights on in the presbytery or in the church, so there was no chance there. There were houses on the opposite side of the street, however, and several had lighted windows.

Poor Giles hesitated. He hated to leave the children, both obviously injured, though the little one did not seem too bad, but he could not possibly cope alone. He did not even know where he would find a telephone box. No, he must get help at once. He dashed across the road and hammered on the nearest door and then, since no one came, was about to try the next house when he heard shuffling footsteps approaching. The woman who answered the door was middle-aged with sandy hair and a round pink face, and when she grinned at him she revealed only a couple of teeth.

'Evenin', wack,' she said cheerfully. 'If you're selling I ain't buyin', an' if you're buyin' I ain't sellin', 'cos I ain't got a stick o' furniture nor a single pot 'n' pan what anyone would give tuppence for.'

She began to shut the door but Giles, desperate for help, prevented her by jamming his foot in the rapidly narrowing gap. 'Hang on, madam; I came for help, not to buy or to sell. There's two children fallen off the swings. One's badly hurt—the seat caught her in the mouth and she's covered in blood—and the other's unconscious. D'you have a telephone? Could you ring the ambulance for me? I'm a stranger here myself.'

The woman opened the door again and began to unfasten the strings of the canvas apron she was wearing, Giles saw, over a shabby black dress. She dropped the apron on the floor and joined Giles on the pavement. 'A tellyphone?' she said

120

derisively. 'Who d'you think I am, Lady Muck? There ain't no one round here what owns a tellyphone 'cept Father O'Donaghue at the presbytery, and I don't reckon as he's home. He's gorra housekeeper though, sour old beggar, what might let you have a borry of it, but norrif she sees me. So you go acrost an' ring for an ambulance an' I'll go to the reccy and see if there's owt I can do for them kids.'

'Thank you,' Giles said humbly. She was an unprepossessing sort of woman but he suddenly felt sure he could trust her to do the right thing. 'I—I don't think we ought to move them, but if you could get a wet cloth and bathe the bigger girl's face—I heard the little one call her Addy, and I'm sure they're sisters—that might bring her round.'

'I'll do that,' the woman said comfortably. 'I'm Mrs Piggott, by the way, and in me far-off youth—and it bleedin' well is far off, young feller—I was a member of the St John's Ambulance, so you don't have to tell me I mustn't move either of 'em. See you in half a mo, when you've made that there tellyphone call.'

CHAPTER SEVEN

Addy clawed her way up out of impenetrable darkness to where she could see a tiny speck of light. The trouble was, she could not reach it, and this was because, no matter how hard she climbed, the speck of light climbed faster. Sometimes she thought she heard someone calling her name, and even in her black pit she was sure that it was Prue

121

needing her help and knew she must go to her sister's rescue.

She was about to try to climb up to the light again—she had lost all sense of time and felt sure she had been in this pit for hours—when something cold and wet touched her face and a voice spoke. It was a very odd voice, hollow and echoing, and Addy wondered, muzzily, whether it was the voice of an angel who had come to help her out of the pit, or the voice of the devil, who would drag her back down again.

She was still wondering, for she could make no sense of the words, when another voice spoke and this time she recognised at least one of the words being uttered above her head. 'Hospital-al-al,' the voice said. 'Hospital-al-al.'

Addy hated hospitals though she was, alas, no stranger to them. She had once gashed her leg on a loose tile when sliding down the outhouse roof at a friend's house. They had taken her to the Stanley, where her leg had been stitched and a cruel nurse had rubbed stuff which stung horribly on to the wound, saying that it was dirty and that it was better to be safe than sorry. Then there had been the occasion when she had fallen out of a tree in Prince's Park and broken her arm. A doctor at the Stanley had had to straighten the bone before they could plaster it up, and Addy had called him rude names and bitten his hand when he had told her to stop using language unsuitable for a child of eight. In fact the mere threat of hospital now was enough to make her struggle with even more effort towards that elusive speck of light.

And this time she made it, or at least she became aware that she was no longer alone, nor in complete darkness. Someone was lifting her, with infinite care, from the hard surface on which she had lain onto something softer. Now she could hear voices properly; men's voices, telling each other to go careful, keep her steady.

Then she felt someone take her hand and wag it gently back and forth. 'What's your name, queen?' It was a woman's voice, though so far as she could judge not the voice of anyone she knew. Addy struggled to lift her incredibly heavy lids and managed a quick glance beneath her lashes before her eyes closed once more. A woman's face hung over her, round and pink and topped with dry-looking sandy hair. Not a nurse then, Addy thought, relieved. She dared another glance and this time saw a young man with a worried expression. He, too, was a total stranger. Addy heard herself give a little whimper, and even as she did so the woman repeated her question. 'What's your name, chuck?' she asked urgently. 'We wants to get in touch wi' your mam, else she'll be worried sick when you don't get home. Your little sister can't tell us nothin'; she had a bump on the head an' ain't come round yet. If you can tell us your name and where you live, this here young feller will find your mam and tell her what happened.'

Addy knew the woman was talking good sense. She opened her eyes—it was much easier this time—but as she moved her head a sickening pain shot through her and she gave another involuntary moan before trying to speak. It hurt most horribly, but Addy was no coward and tried to ignore the feeling, though her voice when it emerged was scarcely above a whisper. 'I'm Addy Fairweather and me sister's Prue . . .' she began, but the woman interrupted, though she was not speaking to Addy.

'Here, young fellow, what with me bein' a bit hard of hearing and the gal's mouth mashed up, it puzzles me what she's a-saying. I think she's tryin' to tell us who she is. You have a listen.'

Addy opened her eyes and focused on the young man's face. It was lean, with high cheekbones and a jutting chin, and he had eyes so dark they were almost black. A lock of equally dark hair hung over his brow. He must have seen her peeping, however, for he grinned suddenly, a flash of very white teeth in his tanned face, and spoke reassuringly.

'It's all right, Addy, we just want to know your name and address so we can get in touch with your parents. They'll worry when you aren't home before dark; I heard your sister saying so when the pair of you were on the swings.'

The swings! So that was what she and Prue had been doing: trying to see who could get highest, first. She supposed something must have happened, but she could not remember what it had been. Instead, she began to concentrate on what the young man had said. They wanted to know her name and address, not in order to shut her up in some bleedin' hospital, but so that they could get in touch with Nell. And suddenly Addy wanted her mother very badly indeed, so badly that her eyes filled with tears and she put out a trembling hand towards the young man.

'I'm Addy Fairweather,' she whispered painfully, and saw him bend close to hear better, but for the life of her she could not have raised her voice. 'My mam runs the corner shop on the Scottie and Blenheim Street. Oh, I wish she were here! I hates hospitals, I does.'

The young man took her hand in a warm clasp. 'I'm afraid we're about to get you and your sister into the ambulance to be taken along to the nearest one,' he admitted. 'But I don't think you'll be in there very long. The ambulance man says you've not broken any bones, though you've had a nasty bump on the head and I'm afraid your mouth has taken some punishment too. Your sister's skinned her knees and bumped her head as well, but I'm sure she'll be right as rain in a couple of days.'

He had been bending over her, and now Addy realised that she was lying on a stretcher which was about to be manoeuvred into an ambulance standing nearby. She clutched wildly at the young man's hand, feeling that he was her only friend in this suddenly strange world. 'Don't go, don't leave us,' she said urgently. 'I won't go to hospital. Can't you make them take us straight home?'

The young man shook his head regretfully and detached himself from her grasp. 'I'm afraid not, my love,' he said gently. 'Someone has to tell your mother and it'll have to be me. But never fear, I'll bring her right to your bedside and be back in no time.'

'It weren't my fault, were it?' Addy whispered as the stretcher was tilted through the doorway of the ambulance and then slotted into position. The young man disappeared and an attendant, smelling horribly of disinfectant and hospitals, tucked Addy in so tightly that her first frightened impulse, to roll off the stretcher and run for it, was out of the question. Then, glancing sideways, she saw that Prue was already in the ambulance and her heart gave a little clutch of fear. Her sister's face was as

125

white as a sheet and her mouth drooped sadly. But then the ambulance jolted into movement and all Addy's various hurts began to make themselves felt. She clutched desperately at the edge of the stretcher and for the first time in her life was actually glad when the vehicle swung into the entrance to the Stanley Hospital and skidded to a halt. Moments later, the doors of both the hospital and the ambulance shot open and she was carried, rapidly but smoothly, inside the dread portals.

As the ambulance men handed her stretcher over to two porters, Addy made a desperate effort to sit up. 'There's a young feller comin' in presently,' she mumbled to the man nearest her. 'I dunno his name but he were there when the accident happened. He'll know whose fault it were.'

The porter grinned at her. He was a short, square man with a cheerful smile and an enormous moustache. 'What were that?' he asked. 'Don't try to talk, queen. I reckon that swing caught you straight in the gob, so the less gabbing you do, the better.'

'Oh, but I must know his name,' Addy began, but the porter just shook his head.

'Now look what you've done,' he said reprovingly. 'You've spluttered blood all over me nice clean blanket. Now just you lie still until you're on the ward. When Casualty have cleaned you up and put in some stitches, you'll be good as new.'

'Stitches?' Addy said. 'I won't, I can't . . .'

'Shurrup. You're makin' it worse,' the porter said, not unkindly.

The two men swung to their left and a nurse with a face like a horse and hands like shovels hurried towards them, tutting as she saw Addy surreptitiously wiping the blood and saliva from her chin with the blanket. 'Stop that!' she said severely. 'You'll only make it worse. Where's your mother?'

Addy began to try to answer, but the porter with the big moustache cut her short. 'Someone's gone to fetch the parents,' he said shortly.

*   *   *

Giles hurried along the Scotland Road, thanking heaven for Mrs Piggott. Although she had not been able to understand Addy's mumbles, when he had asked her the whereabouts of Blenheim Street she had given him instructions so concise that there was no possibility of his arriving at the wrong corner shop.

Indeed, as soon as he entered the place he knew that he had made no mistake, for the two women who faced him across the counter looked worried half to death. He realised, as the bell jangled and they looked across at him, that they were expecting to see two small girls and not an unknown man, so he hurried across to the counter and spoke before they could ask the question which was so obviously hovering on their lips.

'Mrs Fairweather? Don't worry, nothing truly awful has happened to your daughters, but they have had a bit of an accident.'

The younger woman's hands flew to her mouth, but the older woman only said soberly: 'Aye, I reckon we guessed summat had gone wrong. Where are they?'

'Um—they're in hospital, but I'm sure taking

127

them there was just a precaution,' Giles said quickly, his eyes on Mrs Fairweather. He thought her a beautiful woman, even in her distress. 'The girls were playing on the swings at the recreation ground opposite the church. I happened to be passing and paused for a moment to watch them. One of them spoke, the other turned towards her, and the swings collided. They fell quite a way. Addy—if she's the older of the two, and I think she must be—got hit in the face by her sister's swing, but the ambulance attendants said she'd be as good as new once they'd cleaned her up. The little one landed on her back and had a bang on the head, but no other injuries that I could see.'

He was going to add that the accident had been nobody's fault, but the younger woman was already turning away from him. 'I'll just run up to the flat and get our coats and hats,' she said. 'You close the shop, Nonny, and come with me up to the Stanley. You know what poor Addy's like about hospitals. If she's not too badly hurt, it'll take you an' me both to persuade her to stay on the ward. And this will be Prue's first time in hospital, so she'll be wanting us there.' She turned to Giles. 'Thank you so much for coming to tell us what's happened and where the girls are now. I'm sorry, I haven't even asked you your name.' Even as she spoke, she was hurrying out from behind the counter, closely accompanied by the older woman.

'My name's Giles,' Giles said. 'Your daughter was most insistent that I accompany you back to the hospital. I think the poor kid wants a witness to say that it wasn't her fault, which it wasn't, but since I promised her I'd return I'm afraid you'll have to put up with my company for a bit.'

128

The three of them left the shop together. Giles hailed a taxi and bundled the women into it, and soon they were in the Stanley Hospital and approaching the reception desk.

*   *   *

Giles had expected they would be led straight to the young Fairweathers, but this did not prove to be the case. Both girls were still in Casualty, Addy having her various wounds cleaned, stitched and dressed and Prue, who had still not regained consciousness, tucked up warmly on a trolley. He sat with the two women in the waiting area and, glancing at his watch, realised that he wasn't going to make Mark's engagement party, or not until it was half over, at any rate. He suddenly remembered the ivory figurine, abandoned at the recreation ground, and hoped it would be found by someone who would like it and not throw it away. He had not told either Mrs Fairweather or Mrs Hammond why he was visiting Liverpool, or what he had been doing down Silvester Street, but as the minutes went by and conversation lapsed it seemed only natural to explain his presence.

'Well, it were a lucky thing for our girls that you did mistake the church for a hotel and come along the street for a closer look,' Mrs Hammond said decidedly, when he had finished. 'God knows what might have happened if you'd not been near at hand.' Giles started to disclaim, but Nonny interrupted him. 'There's a great many folk, particularly young men, what wouldn't want to get involved and would have passed by on the other side,' she said frankly. 'What's that thing in the

Bible? Think how long it were and how many folk ignored the poor bugger what fell among thieves before the good Samaritan came along.'

Giles laughed and started to say that anyone who had seen the accident would have fetched help, but Mrs Fairweather cut in. 'The thing is, two minutes after the accident happened, a passer-by wouldn't have seen anything but a couple of swings gradually slowing to a stop. And they wouldn't have heard anything because at that stage you said Addy and Prue were both unconscious. If Addy had come round to find herself alone in the dark . . .' She shuddered expressively. 'All I can say is, I thank the good Lord things panned out the way they did, Mr Giles.'

Just then the nurse popped her head round the door.

'We've got both children into beds side by side on Lucie Attwell Ward and you may come and see them now,' she said brightly. 'You'll find Adelaide is a bit muzzy and sleepy—she had to have an anaesthetic before the doctor could work on her mouth and see to the wound on her forehead. You may be shocked by her appearance, but the doctor says she'll be as good as new in a few days.'

'And Prue? How is Prue?' Nell asked quickly.

'Prudence has regained consciousness. She has asked for a drink of milk and has taken several sips, though naturally enough she too is sleepy and a little confused.' She saw the anxious look which crossed the two women's faces and added: 'Don't worry. The bang on the head was superficial; she's bright as a button and not affected at all mentally, so you have no cause for anxiety. We've told the children you are here, and they are very anxious to see you, so if you wouldn't mind following me . . .'

Giles, feeling rather awkward, tagged along behind, and presently they were ushered into a brightly lit children's ward and over to the beds in which Addy and Prue lay. Prue was propped up on her pillows and someone had brushed her hair and cleaned her up, but poor Addy still looked a mess, her head a mass of tangled hair, sticking plaster and bandages and her lips, though stitched, still raw and bleeding.

Giles was rather shocked when Mrs Fairweather rushed straight to her younger daughter, saying anxiously: 'Prue darling, you poor child! Oh, there's a bump on your head the size of an egg and I expect you ache all over. But never mind. I'm sure they won't keep you in here for more than a couple of days.'

Mrs Hammond, however, made her way to Addy's bed and bent over to give her granddaughter a kiss. 'My poor little love, you really are in the wars,' she said tenderly. 'Still, things could have been a lot worse if Mr Giles hadn't happened along. I'm afraid you're going to be perishin' uncomfortable for a while, but your mam and meself will see you tek it easy until you're better.' She sank her voice to a whisper and added a rider which Giles, overhearing willy-nilly, thought was one of the saddest things he had ever heard. 'Mam'll come over in a minute and say how sorry she feels for you, but you know how it is, love. I've told you a hundred times how the youngest gets all the kisses and the oldest gets all the clacks.'

The child in the bed nodded feebly, then turned her eyes towards Giles, and he realised that she was trying to smile at him. Clearly, though, even the slightest movement of her mouth hurt and tugged against the restraining stitches. 'Thanks, mister,' she mumbled. 'Will you tell me mam what happened? Tell her it weren't me fault, like. I can't say much 'cos I don't 'member . . .'

'Of course I'll tell her,' Giles said quickly, anxious to spare her the pain of having to say any more. 'I don't suppose your sister remembers anything either. Now just you rest and don't try to talk.'

Addy leaned back against her pillows with a tired little sigh and Giles moved over to the other bed just as Mrs Fairweather gave her younger daughter a quick kiss and then turned to Addy. 'Oh, Addy, darling, your poor little face!' she said. 'I'm so sorry, and I'm sure it was no one's fault. But really, darling, playing in the dark isn't sensible, is it? I don't want you to worry, because it's over and the doctor says you'll be as good as new once the stitches come out, but if it hadn't been for Mr Giles here—'

Giles intervened quickly. 'Either someone else would have come along or you would have somehow made your way to the nearest house and got help for yourself,' he said reassuringly. He turned back to Mrs Fairweather. 'It's painful for Addy to talk or I'm sure she'd tell you herself, but it truly was no one's fault. Both girls turned towards each other when they realised, at the same moment, how dark it was getting. The swings collided and they fell to the ground. So you see it was just a horrible accident and no one can possibly be blamed.'

He saw Mrs Hammond give an approving little

nod just as Mrs Fairweather leaned over Addy's bed and kissed her. 'Nurse told us that you were both very tired still, so just you cuddle down, love, and go to sleep. In the morning you'll be feeling a lot better and I'll come in as soon as the staff will allow me to do so. Then I can talk to the doctor about taking you both home.'

She glanced towards Prue and smiled, for Prue, her head pillowed on her hand, was already sound asleep. She turned back to her elder daughter. 'Is there anything you'd like me to bring in tomorrow? I know how you love to read, so if there's a book at home which you would like . . .'

Addy shook her head but mumbled her thanks and Mrs Hammond patted Prue's shoulder gently so as not to disturb the sleeping child, then bent and kissed Addy once more. 'I'll bring you some comics . . .' she was beginning when the doors at the end of the ward swung open and the horse-faced nurse appeared.

'Time all my patients were asleep,' she said, ushering the visitors out, and Giles thought that her loud voice had probably woken any child who had already dozed off. As he reached the swing doors at the end of the ward he turned back briefly, just in time to see Addy give a tiny wave, and he returned it before following Mrs Fairweather and her mother into the corridor.

Outside on the pavement once more, he hailed another taxi and ushered the women into it, telling them that he would drop them off at the shop and then continue to the hotel in which the party was being held. 'I'm booked in there for tonight, but as I explained I mean to choose a less expensive hotel for tomorrow.' He turned to his companions. 'I suppose you couldn't suggest somewhere?'

'There's the Washington on St George's Place; that will be less expensive than the Adelphi and it's a nice clean hotel, as well as being right handy for the station,' Mrs Fairweather said at once. She sighed deeply, then smiled anxiously at Giles. 'I'm afraid we've ruined your evening,' she said apologetically. 'I wish there was something we could do to make amends, but—'

'Nonsense, you've ruined nothing,' Giles said robustly. 'Fortunately, since I'm staying at the Adelphi, all I have to do is change into my evening clothes and go to the room where the party is being held. I'll explain to my cousin what happened and enjoy the rest of the evening.' He glanced at his wristwatch in the flickering light of the street lamps as they passed beneath them. 'There, it's not yet nine o'clock, which is when they will serve the buffet supper, so I shall be in good time for the best part.'

As he spoke, the taxi drew up outside Mrs Fairweather's corner shop. Giles jumped out and went round to assist the two women to alight. Then he bade them farewell and would have returned to the taxicab had Mrs Fairweather not put a detaining hand on his arm. 'Thank you again,' she said urgently. 'And if you've no plans for tomorrow, we'd be delighted if you would share our Sunday dinner. If you come to the door of the shop at noon and knock very loudly, we'll let you in.'

'That's most awfully kind of you, but I suspect that my cousin Mark may have other plans for me,' Giles said apologetically. He wondered if it was his duty to visit the hospital again and say goodbye properly to the two girls, but decided that it was not. He liked children, intended to have a family of his own at some future date, but had only one day to spend in Liverpool. Being introduced to Mark's fiancée's family and meeting up with old friends from the party would preclude any possibility of revisiting the hospital. He intended to take a good look at the docks, too, because he was naturally interested in shipping.

He reached the Adelphi Hotel, scrambled into his evening clothes and hurried downstairs, where he had to explain his late arrival to a grinning Mark and his fiancée Deborah.

'I hope you've made no plans for tomorrow,' Mark said, 'because I'm taking a few chaps down to the docks to take a look at the old *Hyperion*. Care to join us?'

Giles agreed eagerly, but decided that he would write a note to Addy and Prue when he got back to his airfield, wishing them all the best. Then he put the whole incident out of his mind.

*   *   *

On the Monday following the accident, Nell came to the hospital as promised, with some books and a couple of jigsaws. The previous day, both girls had been languid, Addy complaining that her mouth hurt most dreadfully and Prue saying that she was sure she was well enough to go home, though her legs felt funny and kept jumping when she had not told them to do so.

Nell went straight to the ward, but was approached by a senior member of staff before she had spoken more than a few words to her children.

135

The nurse told her, quietly, that the doctor wanted to speak to her. Twenty minutes later, Nell emerged from his office, her eyes reddened with weeping. At first she had tried to say that it must be a mistake, that the doctor had misread the signs, but in the end acceptance had been forced upon her. The doctor thought that Prue had cracked something in her spine and was paralysed from the waist down. He had said her younger daughter would never walk again.

CHAPTER EIGHT

Once they had accustomed themselves to the dreadful news, it was a case of all hands to the pump, for there were things that Prue would need which had to be thought of, and arrangements to be made to enable her to carry on as normally as possible.

Poor Addy, very pale and subdued, told herself a hundred times a day that it had not been her fault, that no one would blame her for her little sister's condition, but in her heart she did not believe it. She racked her brain over and over, replaying the scene in her mind. Parts of it she could see clearly: her feet and Prue's black against the night sky, the tips of their toes straining ever higher, then the wonderful downward whooshes which had ended so tragically. But which of them had spoken first seemed to be different every time. Sometimes she was sure it was Prue who had said that it was getting dark, that they would be in trouble for playing out so late; sometimes it was she who had commented on the failing light. She was pretty sure, now, that they had turned towards each other, both of them causing the evenness of their motion to falter.

She longed to see Mr Giles again, because if anyone knew it would be he, but he had told her mother that he meant to leave Liverpool on the Monday following the accident. By the time she realised she needed to speak to him, he must have been long gone.

On the morning when her mother, white-faced and red-eyed, had come on the ward with a doctor and nurse in attendance to break the news to Prue that she would not be able to walk for some time, both sisters had believed that the condition would be of short duration, days rather than weeks. Then, when Nell thought the moment was right, she had told Addy quietly that the accident was more serious than she had let Prue suppose, and admitted that her youngest child might not walk for years rather than months. Addy had been shocked and horrified and had longed for Mr Giles to return so that she could ask him exactly what had happened in the recreation ground that fateful night. Nell had reminded her, however, that Mr Giles had only come to Liverpool for some sort of party and had left first thing on the Monday morning. 'I'll ask at the Washington whether they had a Mr Giles staying there, and whether he left an address,' she had said rather doubtfully. 'But why do you want to get in touch with him anyway? He made it pretty clear that he saw the whole thing and it was no one's fault.'

Addy had sighed, but had not been able to help herself asking eagerly next day whether her mother had discovered any news of Mr Giles. Nell had smiled at her and pressed her hand. 'I went to the Washington, queen, but they had no record of any Mr Giles staying there. I imagine someone at the party offered him a bed for Sunday night, so he didn't have to go to the hotel at all.'

Addy had accepted failure but went on hoping that some sort of communication might come from the young man. If it did, she would write back at once, in her neatest hand, and beg him to set down every single thing that had happened.

After some days, a truly beautiful card had arrived, with a picture of a little girl sitting in a garden, her lap full of kittens. The sender hoped both girls would soon be out of hospital so that they might enjoy a really lovely Christmas. He had enclosed a postal order for five shillings—riches indeed to Addy and Prue—which they might spend on toys, books or sweets, and had signed off: *With all best wishes, from your friend Giles.* There had been no address on the card and the postmark on the envelope had been so blurred as to be unreadable, so it had not been possible for Addy to write back.

Now, however, at home once more, Addy eyed her reflection in their dressing table mirror with revulsion. A kindly nurse had cut her hair into a fringe to hide the wound on her forehead, but she was not a hairdresser, and the fringe gave Addy a queer, lopsided look. The tip of her nose was still sore and scarlet, and of course there was her mouth. That was the worst thing of all, for despite the fact that the stitches had been out for some while her lips were still puckered and uneven, a front tooth was chipped and poor Addy, who had always known herself to be no beauty, now considered herself downright hideous.

From behind her a small voice said crossly: 'Why are you staring in the mirror, Addy? The doctor said your mouth would heal up just like new if you gave it time.' Prue giggled. 'Your nose looks just like that clown's in the circus Mam took us to see last year. D'you remember? His nose looked as though someone had stuck a cherry on the end of it. But I expect yours will go ordinary again, probably before my legs are better.'

Addy turned and gave her little sister, sitting up in the special bed that had been purchased for her, a rather restrained smile. She knew she looked a figure of fun and thought it would serve her right if her cherry nose remained for ever. Then she chided herself for stupidity. Prue's paralysis was not my fault, she told herself for the millionth time. Nonny says I should stop punishing myself, but I'm not, not really. I'm simply wishing I could take some of the burden from Prue. Then, hastily, in case God was listening, she added a more truthful thought. I don't want to be paralysed, though; not even a little bit . . . oh, dear, I'm being stupid again. All I can truly do for Prue is help to take care of her and not grumble because I can't play out so much, nor even help out in the shop, unless Mam wants to spend time with Prue.

'Addy? D'you remember that clown? Didn't the circus come quite soon after Christmas? I'm sure it did, and if so it's due in Liverpool any time now. D'you think we might go? I know my legs won't be completely better but Mam says I can use a wheelchair when she can get hold of one, and you don't know how sick I am of this bleedin' horrible flat.'

Addy turned round and stared almost unbelievingly at her sister. Prue never swore and very rarely grumbled, so this was the clearest sign yet that she was beginning to resent what had happened to her. And of course she still didn't know the full truth. They had decided not to break it to her until after the memorable and magical Christmas which Nell had planned. But somehow this had not happened. Addy's face had still been extremely painful and her appetite almost non-existent, and Prue had also eyed the treats which Nell had provided without enthusiasm. Prue's presents, too, though chosen with loving care, had not come up to expectations. She had wanted a scooter, had even chosen the model that she preferred, and when on Christmas morning it had failed to materialise, she had burst in to tears.

Nell did not know, though Addy did, that Prue had twice got out of bed and collapsed on the floor, staring at her legs and having to allow Addy to lift her back and tuck her up beneath the covers. Addy had wondered whether she should say something to Nell, but Nonny thought it would be a mistake. 'Your mam can't face up to the tragedy, not yet,' she had said. 'She's still hoping that the doctors were wrong or that a miracle might happen.'

'But I don't think it's fair on Prue to let her go on believing she'll be walking again quite soon,' Addy had said. 'If it were me, I'd rather know. Surely there must be exercises or something Prue could do to help herself?'

Nonny had shrugged rather helplessly. 'Maybe, maybe. Anyway, your mam will tell her when the moment is right.'

'Addy? What about the circus? D'you think my legs will be better by then?'

Brought abruptly back to the present, Addy turned from the mirror and spoke without thinking. 'No. The circus is next week and the doctor told Mam you might never—' She clapped a hand to her mouth. 'Oh, Prue, he might be wrong . . .'

'Never? Did you say I might never walk again, Addy Fairweather? Oh, you wicked, spiteful girl; you've said that to upset me! You've always hated me because Mam likes me best and now you're taking the most hateful revenge in the world. Get out of my room and send Mam up here at once! I'll tell her what you said and you'll get into the most awful trouble, and serve you bloody well right. I'd like to slap your ugly face—and it is ugly, all over scars—and I would if I could only get out of bed.'

Addy, appalled by her sister's words, headed for the door. She was shaking with fright and reaction, but even as her hand touched the doorknob she changed her mind and went back to her sister's bed. She knelt down beside it and bowed her head. 'Hit me as hard as you like, Prue. I'm sure your legs will work one day, no matter what anyone says, it'll just take a little longer than we thought,' she said humbly. 'You're right, I am wicked, and I've always been jealous because Mam loves you best, so go on, give me a good whack and we'll both feel better.'

She looked hopefully at Prue, waiting for the blow to fall, but Prue's hands never moved, though her expression was grim. 'Fetch Mam up at once,' she said between gritted teeth. 'Everyone's been

141

lying to me, haven't they? Mam said she couldn't afford the scooter because of the doctor's bills, but that wasn't true, was it? She—she knew I'd never be able to use it, so it would have been a waste of money. Go on, I told you to fetch Mam, and everyone does as I tell them while I'm so poorly.'

Addy took a deep, quivering breath. 'No one lied, they just didn't tell the whole truth,' she said and then, as her sister's face began to turn from white to scarlet, she scrambled hastily to her feet, ran out of the room and thundered down the stairs.

It was the work of a moment to tell her mother how she had spilled the beans without at all intending to, and to her immense relief Nell neither flew into a rage nor berated her elder daughter. It was a slow morning with only one customer, an elderly woman, in the shop and Nell simply said quietly: 'Finish serving Mrs Stubbs, Addy, while I see to your sister.' And with that she was gone.

Twenty minutes later she returned to the shop, where several people were waiting to be served. 'I think you'd better go up and sit with Prue for a bit,' she whispered. 'She blames me for not telling her how things stood and I'm afraid she blames you for the accident. She's—she's in an awful state, so don't hold anything she says against her. It's shock and dismay speaking, not my little Prue.'

Addy hurried up to the flat, crossed the small landing and went into the bedroom she shared with her sister. She sat down on the bed and tried to take Prue's hand, but it was snatched away. 'Whose idea was it to go to the reccy when the afternoon was half over?' Prue asked accusingly. 'I never even thought of it. It was all your idea. And who suggested we should have a race to see who could go the highest? I don't think it was me! And who suddenly realised it were getting dark . . . ?'

'It was probably me,' Addy said in a small, tired voice. 'I'm as sorry as I can be, Prue.'

'Being sorry isn't much good,' Prue said flatly. Then she turned her face up to her sister and all in a moment, Addy read the fear in Prue's large blue eyes and knew that her little sister was trying to face up to a terrible future, a future in which she might never again enjoy the simple pleasures of walking along the Scottie, a trip to New Brighton, or a visit to the circus.

Impulsively, Addy flung her arms round her. 'Now that you know, there are all sorts of things we can do,' she said. 'The Red Cross has wheelchairs that they lend to people who need them. Mam could borrow one of them and carry you downstairs dressed in your new red coat and hat and off we could go, with you riding in the wheelchair like a queen in a golden coach and me pushing.'

Very, very slowly, a tiny smile appeared on Prue's face, but then she frowned. 'I haven't got a red coat and hat,' she objected. 'I wanted the one we saw in Lewis's children's department, but Mam said navy or black were more serviceable.'

'Yes, I know, but when I tell her you'll need something really special to wear for your first trip out since the accident, I just know she'll buy you the red ones,' Addy said recklessly. 'An' if she won't—only I know she will—then I shall go round all our friends collecting money until I've enough to buy them myself.'

143

'Thank you, Addy,' Prue said rather stiffly. 'Will—will Mam take me to the circus, do you think? And what about school? If the teachers see me at the circus, I suppose they'll want me to start school again, and I don't want to do that. I'd rather have lessons at home, because they'll laugh at me in school and be horrible.' To Addy's consternation, tears filled Prue's big blue eyes and trickled down her cheeks. 'Oh, Addy, if I had to go back to school it would kill me, I'm sure it would. Do say I needn't go back to school.'

'I'll do my best, but I suppose it will be up to the doctor and the teacher,' Addy said doubtfully. 'I've never seen a child in a wheelchair at our school, but I believe there are special ones—'

Prue's cheeks had grown pink and she interrupted her sister at once. 'I will *not* go to a special school! The children who go to them are what Nonny calls tenpence short of a shilling and they have to board there because they're miles and miles from the city centre. Oh, Addy, tell them you'll bring my lessons home each evening so I can do them the following day. Don't let them send me to a special school!'

Oh, dammit, I've put me bleedin' foot in it again, Addy thought, hastily telling her sister that she was sure Nell would never send her youngest away. 'But you know me, Prue, I never think before I speak,' she said apologetically. 'If you want to go back to school I'm sure the teachers could manage something, but if you'd rather do your school work at home, then I'm equally sure that could be arranged.'

Prue heaved a deep sigh and leaned her head back on her pillows. 'Thank you, Addy. If you really mean to help me as much as you say, then I'll try to forgive you for what you've done to me. Because it really was your fault, wasn't it? You're older than me and ever so much bossier. If I'd said I didn't want to go to the reccy you'd have made me, you know you would. You'd have grabbed my hand and dragged me along behind you, and if I'd started to cry you'd have called me horrible names and made me go anyway.'

Addy began to protest, but there was just enough truth in her sister's remark to make the objection a pretty feeble one. Instead she said, trying to keep her voice friendly: 'Look, Prue, I've already agreed it was my idea to go the reccy. I mean to help you in every way I can, but if you're going to keep reminding me that the whole thing was my fault, I'm afraid I may end up trying to avoid you. And that won't help either of us, will it?'

'No-o-o,' Prue said thoughtfully. 'Addy, do you remember that book I was reading a few months ago? It was about a girl called Katy . . .'

'*What Katy Did,*' Addy said. 'It was by Susan Coolidge, and it was all about a girl called Katy who was crippled in a fall from a swing. She'd been an awfully naughty girl—not a bit like you—but the accident changed her and she became very, very good.' Addy did not add, as she might have done, that she had never finished the book, finding Katy's sudden change from devilment to saintliness too much to take.

'Well, you've got the right book, but what I was really thinking of was how Katy got well again and was able to do all sorts; anything she wanted to do, in fact,' Prue said. 'The doctor and the grown-ups told her she'd never walk again, but her cousin

145

Helen—I did like Cousin Helen—said she must keep on hoping and praying and she was sure Katy would get better. So I shall be like Katy and never stop believing that it will all come right in the end.'

'Well, good for you,' Addy said, rising to her feet. 'And now I'm going downstairs to tell Mam that she can send me round to the Red Cross headquarters with a letter about a wheelchair. I'll mention the red coat and hat at the same time. Is there anything I can get you before I go off?'

'I'd like a cup of cocoa and some chocolate biscuits,' Prue said.

Addy was astonished, for her sister's appetite had not been good since the accident, and only that morning she had refused breakfast. The doctor had said she must be persuaded to eat as she would need all her strength in the days to come, so Addy took her request as a very good sign. 'Right you are; cocoa and biccies coming up,' she said joyfully. 'I'll bring them up on a tray as soon as the kettle boils.'

*   *   *

'For heaven's sake, girl, if I've told you once I've told you a hundred times, what happened to Prue was just one of them awful things which no power on earth could have prevented. First you kept takin' all the blame on yourself, and now you won't go nowhere unless she can go as well.'

'Oh, Nick, that's not true,' Addy said, dismayed by his words. 'When Mam or Nonny are able to give an eye to Prue I do go off wi' me pals. Only—only if Prue hears we're going somewhere exciting like what you've just suggested, where we can't possibly take the wheelchair, then she gets very down and I get told off for upsetting her.'

'But I keep telling you, it isn't your fault, and you shouldn't stop having ordinary sorts of fun just because your sister can't,' Nick said positively. 'She's only got to say jump and you're six foot up in the air. What good does it do either of you if you won't come for a day out with meself and Paul? That bleedin' accident were six months ago, and you're still acting as though she'll die if you ain't with her. An' let's face it, Prue's a real misery, always grumbling and complaining. She ought to make the best of things, but she'd rather moan. Use that tatty 'ead of yours and leave her wi' your mam and Nonny while you come out for a day on the sands with us. The pub's doin' real well and me an' Paul work like perishin' slaves when it's busy, so Dad give us ten bob to cover the ferry, the funfair and grub. That's plenty for three of us.'

Addy and Nick were walking back to the shop on a Friday evening, Nick having sent a message by Paul to say that if she would come up towards his factory they could meet for a bit of a chat. Addy was not only willing but eager. Prue had become more and more dependent on her; the wheelchair had arrived a couple of months before and it needed someone to push it.

When Addy was at school life went on as normal, but the moment she got home she was at her sister's beck and call until bedtime. In the past Prue had enjoyed working in the shop and Nell had confidently predicted that when the wheelchair arrived she would be a great help again, wheeling up and down behind the counter, packing up goods, taking money and chatting to the

147

customers. What she had not anticipated was that Prue would become easily bored, and would begin to whine that her back ached, her arm muscles hurt and she wanted to go back to bed.

She had thought things would be easier when the Easter holidays arrived and indeed for Nell and Nonny, who supervised Prue's home schooling under the watchful eye of the teacher who came in from time to time, this had certainly been true, but for Addy, patiently pushing the wheelchair up and down the Scotland Road, there had seemed little to choose between termtime and holiday. Pavements were uneven, kerbs were high, and many of the places Prue wanted to visit had to be approached by a number of steps.

Sometimes, seeing the two children standing wistfully outside the Walker Art Gallery or the museum, a friendly passer-by would offer to carry Prue up the steps and then return for the wheelchair, but Prue would never allow this. She told Addy that a stranger would not be careful enough and might drop her, and Addy was forced to agree that the choice must be her sister's. She could well imagine the blame that would be heaped on her head if such a thing were to happen. Even Paddy's Market was denied them since Prue detested crowds and feared that she might be injured in the crush of customers.

'Well?' Nick's voice jerked Addy back to the present. 'Are you going to pluck up courage, explain to your mam that Dad's offered to treat the three of us to a real good day out and ask her to look after Prue for the whole day tomorrer? Or are you going to be a proper little goody two-shoes and let Paul and meself down? And don't you expect

148

me to invite your sister to come along because she'd spoil it for the lot of us, you know she would.'

Addy sighed. She knew this was true but thought, ruefully, that Prue could not be blamed for wanting to do the same things her companions enjoyed. It was impossible to push the wheelchair through the soft sand at New Brighton beach and equally impossible for someone in a wheelchair to enjoy the funfair, because even if Nick lifted Prue on to one of the painted ponies which graced the carousel the proprietor would lift her off again, saying it was too dangerous to allow her to use the ride.

It was not as if she had not already been to New Brighton, because Nonny, Nell and Addy had taken her only a matter of weeks previously. Despite their best efforts, Prue had not enjoyed her day out and consequently nor had Addy. It had been frustrating for all of them to be unable to enjoy the beach or paddle in the sea, let alone try the rides on the funfair, though they had all tucked into fried fish and chips before returning to Liverpool on a far earlier ferry than they had planned.

'Well?' Nick repeated impatiently. 'Are you going to be a martyr and spend a lovely sunny Saturday playing snap or snakes and ladders with your sister when you could be havin' a grand time wi' your mates?'

Addy made a lightning decision. 'I'll ask Mam to give an eye to Prue so's I can have a day out,' she said breathlessly.

*   *   *

149

Addy, Paul and Nick had a wonderful day out, perhaps all the better, for Addy at least, because a day without the responsibility of caring for her sister was so rare. And she suffered no pangs of conscience for a very simple reason. She had decided to play down the fun they had had when she returned to the flat above the shop, but to her astonishment and delight Prue wanted to hear every detail, and showed none of the envy and misery that was her usual reaction to a pleasure in which she could not share.

As they ate their meal, therefore, Prue listened to Addy's description of her day out, and when Addy's recital was finished she announced that whilst her sister had been absent she herself had had her first visit from a lady called Miss Duckett. 'She's going to come every week for a while to teach me how to get my legs better,' Prue said excitedly. 'That's why I didn't mind you leaving me, Addy. She wasn't sure if she could fit me in, which was why we didn't know anything about it, so wasn't it lucky that I didn't make you take me to New Brighton?'

'Very lucky,' Addy said faintly. So *that* was the reason why her sister had not envied her the treat. She looked across at Nell and Nonny, both of whom were beaming encouragement, their eyes fixed on Prue.

'And d'you know what, Addy?' Prue went on. 'After she'd massaged my legs and explained the exercises, and talked and talked, I twitched the big toe on my left foot and Miss Duckett was so excited, she went quite pink. When Mam came up to make her a cup of tea, she said—Miss Duckett I mean—that my muscles were not dead and useless

150

like we thought, but just flabby and weak. She says it will be a slow process and sometimes I may get discouraged, but one day she's convinced I shall walk again. She wants me to get out more as well, and not spend so much time in the flat, because she thinks it's bad for me not to be with children of my own age.'

Addy promptly dropped her knife and fork, jumped to her feet and rushed round the table to give her sister an exuberant hug. 'Oh, Prue, that's the best news I've ever heard in my whole life,' she said. 'No wonder you've been looking so happy since I got back. I can't wait to tell everyone that you aren't going to be stuck in that bleedin' chair for ever!' As she spoke, she glanced at Nonny and Nell and almost burst out laughing, for they were shaking their heads in unison, like a couple of twin pendulums on an old grandfather clock. Addy clapped her hand to her mouth, thinking that she was being reproved for using a swear word, but her mother speedily disabused her.

'Addy, love, didn't you hear what your sister said? It could be months, or even years, before Prue and the wheelchair part company, so Miss Duckett advised us to tell only our own family. You must promise me that you won't say a word to anyone, not even your dearest friends.'

Addy could see the sense of this, though her nod was reluctant. She was still secretly convinced that a lot of people blamed her, as the older sister, for what had happened to Prue. It would have been nice to be able to explain that Prue was not, as they had believed, paralysed for life, but might one day walk again. However, she realised that if folk were told, their expectations might actually slow Prue's

151

progress. Old ladies in particular, Addy thought, could question a youngster in a manner that many would consider rude. No, Miss Duckett was right. Once her sister began to improve, they could boast of every step forward, no matter how tiny. But until that time came, they should say nothing.

'Addy?'

Smiling, Addy answered her mother's unspoken question. 'Of course I agree it'll be best to keep the news to ourselves, so I won't say a word to anyone, norreven the Bentley boys. But did Miss Duckett say anything about school, Mam? If Miss Duckett wants Prue to be with other children, surely going back to school's the answer?'

'But who will push me chair?' Prue asked plaintively, her face beginning to flush. 'Norra perishin' teacher! I won't be pushed by a perishin' teacher; I won't, I won't!'

Addy giggled. 'Oh, Prue, you really are daft: there'll be a queue of kids a mile long, all begging to be allowed to push you in your chair, anywhere you want to go. I'd do it myself only I doubt they'll let me since I'm two years ahead of you. I know you won't let strangers or children push your chair when we're out and about in the streets, but school's different. It's all on the flat, and at playtime someone really responsible can take care of you.'

'Oh well, I was getting pretty bored doing lessons all by myself,' Prue acknowledged rather guiltily, for Addy had made the suggestion that she should return to school several times and been soundly snubbed for her pains. 'Well, perhaps I could try going back next Monday. In fact that would be a good idea because it's not long to the summer hols, so if I hated it . . .'

'You'll love it,' Addy said positively. She knew that Prue was not clever, or not in the academic sense, at any rate. But she had talents which Addy often thought were a lot more useful than the ability to do sums, remember dates or understand and appreciate the beauties of English literature, a subject at which she herself excelled without effort. Prue could draw and paint, could knit and crochet as well as her mother and Nonny, could embroider without needing a printed design and had, only weeks before the accident, made a most beautiful baby's dress for one of the teachers, who had insisted upon paying her a whole shilling for her work.

During the course of the meal, and as Addy helped Prue to prepare for bed, they talked constantly of the things Prue wanted to do when she was mobile once more. Since the accident, she had refused to draw, sew, embroider or knit, saying fretfully that such employment made her arms, hands and fingers ache, but now she admitted quite cheerfully that since she had never tried to use her skills, she had no idea whether doing so would be painful or pleasant.

Addy, lifting her sister from chair to bed, asked just why Prue had, deliberately it seemed, restricted her life in such an unnecessary way. Prue shrugged. 'I wasn't telling lies, you know,' she said rather reproachfully. 'Other things hurt my hands and arms: cutting up my meat, drying up the cutlery after you washed it; things like that. But I suppose the truth is, I was so miserable that I wanted to make other people miserable too. Daft, wasn't it? 'Cos in the end, it was only me who was

153

hurt by it. But it's all going to be different now. Miss Duckett said I should do anything I possibly can to let my body know that I'm still here and determined to get better.'

'I like the sound of your Miss Duckett,' Addy said, arranging her sister's pillows the way she liked them and then pulling sheet and blankets up to her waist so that her arms were not confined by the bedding. 'I wish in a way we could tell Nick and Paul what she said, but with the best will in the world they'd let it out. Oh, they wouldn't mean to, but I'm afraid they'd do it.'

'It'll be hard for us as well,' Prue said, cuddling her face into the pillow. 'But we've got more to lose by talking about it, haven't we, Addy? Think of old Ma Buttermilk; if she knew, she'd ask in that sneery sort of way why I wasn't out playin' hopscotch, or jumping rope. And if I tried to explain, she'd just blow out her cheeks the way she does, and walk away, and I'd know she was telling people I'd never get better and was just a helpless cripple.'

Addy nodded, but laughed at the same time. Old Ma Buttermilk—so called because of her passion for the stuff—was always in and out of the shop, almost never paying the full price for anything, but wheedling Nonny or Nell into reducing any item which caught her eye by a penny or two. Ma Buttermilk was not a popular customer, for she had a spiteful tongue and rejoiced in the sort of gossip which neither Nell nor Nonny encouraged. 'Well, there you are; Miss Duckett was probably thinking about folk like old Ma Buttermilk when she said we should keep our hopes to ourselves.' She leaned over the bed and patted Prue's cheek.

'Nonny will have left by now, so I'll go and dry the dishes for Mam and make the bedtime drinks. What'll you have? Cocoa? Bournvita? Bovril?'

* * *

'Hey, you idle beggar! It's gerrin' on for seven o'clock and I'm already washed and dressed; you'll miss breakfast if you don't gerra move on!'

Nick opened his eyes and scowled across the bedroom at Paul, who was peering at his reflection in the small mirror that stood on the washstand, and running a comb through his curly hair. Nick heaved a sigh, but sat up and glanced towards the window. The leaves on the plane tree outside were thinning, but the sun was shining and the sky blue; it looked as though his day off was going to be a fine one.

'Nick? Oh, gee, I'm sorry, you're off today, aren't you? Still, as I recall you're taking Prue out this mornin', ain't you? So you'd best gerrup. I'll tell Dad that you'll be down in ten minutes, shall I?'

Nick looked across at the alarm clock which stood on the small table between their beds. 'Make it quarter of an hour,' he said. 'Mrs Hammond is off to Rhyl, and of course Addy's standin' in for her, which would leave Prue at a bit of a loose end. The coach leaves at nine o'clock, so if I get there round a quarter to nine that should be plenty early enough.'

'Why's Mrs Hammond going to Rhyl?' Paul said. He reached for the navy jacket that he wore when he was delivering greengroceries for a shop further along the Scottie. 'Her sister don't live in Rhyl, does she?'

155

'I dunno, but this is an outing, you goof,' Nick said. 'She's going with the other ladies from the church; I think it's what they call the Mothers' Union. Mrs Fairweather and Mrs Hammond take it in turns to go on the outings.' As he spoke, he got out of bed, crossed to the washstand, pushed his brother aside, smeared his face with soap and began to shave.

'Hey!' Paul said indignantly. 'I can't see me reflection wi' you takin' up all the space, and that's my dirty water you're shavin' in. If you go down to the kitchen, you could get fresh, and it 'ud be hot.'

'And you could have the room all to yourself,' Nick said indistinctly, vigorously rinsing. Mr Bentley had begun to let rooms, so his sons had to share. 'Oh, my God, you haven't cleaned your teeth in this water, have you?'

Paul giggled but nodded. 'Course I have . . .' he began and then, seeing vengeance on his brother's face, hastily fended him off whilst shaking his head. 'No, no, only kiddin'. I have cleaned 'em, but I spat straight into the slop bucket.' He headed across the bedroom. 'I'll tell Dad fifteen minutes, but I reckon it'll be more like five, the way you're carryin' on.' He half opened the door, then paused to stare back curiously at his brother. 'You and Addy have always been friends, but you used to curse Prue up hill and down dale, 'cos you said she was always whining. You didn't even like going round to the shop if she was there, yet here you are, takin' her for a day out. What's happened to change you?'

'Oh, I'm doing it to oblige Addy,' Nick said. 'But Prue isn't too bad with me, provided I give her plenty of attention.' He had been let into the secret of what Miss Duckett had said about Prue's one day regaining the use of her legs. He sometimes thought, privately, that all the woman had really done was to give Prue hope; but that hope had improved the child's outlook somewhat. She was still whiny, grumbling that life was cruel and unfair, but she did admit that one day she might get better. But of course he could not tell Paul how hard she worked at the exercises she had been given, and how even the faint hope of a cure had made her more positive.

'Oh, if you're doing it to oblige Addy, all I can say is good for you, because Addy gets the rough end of the stick when things go wrong for Prue, or when her mother's in a mood,' Paul said, letting himself out of the room. He began to whistle a popular melody as he clattered down the stairs and Nick, attacking his neck, decided that he would see if he could get Prue's permission to tell Paul that she might really improve one day. He knew his brother would keep the secret, especially once he understood the reason for it, for Nick remembered all too clearly how miserable Prue had been when she had heard one of their elderly customers remark: 'Eh, there goes that poor little cripple, what won't ever walk again.' It was things like that, he knew, which had made the Fairweathers, and Mrs Hammond, decide not to share their hopes.

But he must, as his brother had remarked, get a move on. He finished washing, dried himself, and dressed quickly in a clean white shirt and his best kecks, for he knew that Mrs Fairweather would see that Prue was impeccably turned out. Despite the fact that her younger daughter was in a wheelchair, Nell was proud of the child's prettiness, and Addy was as well, so between the two of them Prue would be her usual immaculate self.

*   *   *

'Well, well, well, if it ain't young Mr Nicholas Bentley, bright and early as usual and no doubt raring to go!' Mrs Hammond, already dressed in her best black coat and a hat trimmed with violets, came bustling across the shop to greet Nick as he entered. 'I'll just give 'em a shout, chuck, so's they'll know you've arrived. Then they'll bring Prue down and you can be off.' She smiled indulgently. 'Prue's as excited as though it were she goin' to Rhyl instead of me. She says you won't tell her where you're takin' her or what you're goin' to do, 'cos it's to be a surprise. I'd ask you meself, only I know she's lookin' forward to us swappin' stories when I get home tonight, so I won't pester you with questions.'

She hurried back across the shop to the foot of the stairs where she bawled, at the top of her voice, the news that Nick had arrived. As soon as she had done so, Addy shouted to Nick to come up. Prue awaited him on the top landing, sitting in the wheelchair and already dressed in the famous scarlet coat and matching hat. She greeted Nick with a beaming smile and wrapped her arms round his neck when he picked her up, being careful to support the skinny, useless legs. 'Oh, Nick, I'm so excited,' she said as they descended. 'Addy checked the wheelchair last night and everything's working the way it ought. And Mam's given me ten bob to pay for us dinners.'

'That's nice. We'll be swimming in gelt, because

158

my dad give me two half-crowns and your gran shelled out the same when I told her you and me was going to have a day out,' Nick said rather breathlessly.

Prue was not heavy, but carrying her downstairs was fraught with peril. If one were to trip . . . but Nick's mind veered away from such horror. He reached the foot of the stairs and sat Prue carefully down on the chair which Mrs Hammond had brought forward, then returned to the flat. He took the wheelchair from Addy, patting her cheek in a lordly manner and saying as he did so: 'Little girls shouldn't try to do men's work. Stand aside!'

Addy giggled. 'So you're a man, are you?' she asked derisively. 'Let me remind you that I lug this bleedin' wheelchair up and down the stairs two or three times every day, sometimes more. But go ahead, Mr Clever!'

Nick complied and presently Prue, her grandmother and himself bade Nell and Addy farewell and set off into the bright morning. Because it was early, Nick and Prue accompanied Mrs Hammond to the church where the Mothers' Union members were to board the coach. They knew most of the waiting women and Prue told everyone within hearing how very smart they looked.

'You're lookin' good yourself, chuck,' Mrs Davies, who lived almost next door to the Vines, said comfortably. 'What d'you think of me new hat?'

'It's lovely,' Prue said sincerely. 'I do like the feathers; is it a pigeon's wing?'

'Well, it's flappin' enough to cross the bleedin' Mersey on its own,' Mrs Davies said chirpily, clutching at her blue hat, decorated with a grey wing of feathers. 'Ah, here comes our cherrybang; last one aboard's a sissy!'

Nick and Prue derived considerable amusement from watching the women get aboard their charabanc, for there was much chatter and laughter, much chaffing of the driver and much swapping of seats as the women decided whether they preferred the front or the back, and with whom they would sit. Nonny and Mrs Davies had bagged the front seat, and waved merrily as the vehicle started up at last and swung out into the moving traffic.

'They'll be going through the tunnel, won't they?' Prue said excitedly. 'I've never been through it, because when we used to go to New Brighton we took the ferry. But I expect I will one day—go through the tunnel, I mean—because Mam's saving up so we can have a holiday when she's got enough money.'

'That'll be grand,' Nick said breathlessly. 'What would you like to do now? The surprise doesn't start till two o'clock and it isn't even ten yet. How about going along to the Walker Art Gallery? I know you love looking at pictures, and if I fetch an attendant the two of us can get you and the wheelchair up to the gallery; no trouble.'

Prue pulled a face, however, and shook her head. 'It ain't only the steps outside, you know,' she said, rather reproachfully. 'Most of the best pictures are up on the first floor, and to get up there you have to climb a huge curved staircase. I suppose we could go and take a look at the big stores, Lewis's or Blackler's . . . no, I've had a better idea! I'd really like to go to Lime Street Station and watch the trains coming in and out, and see the people shouting for porters and lugging their suitcases.' Her tone changed to the whining one that Nick dreaded. 'Addy never takes me to the station because she enjoys the shops more. She says trains are a thing for lads.' Prue twisted round in her chair to stare anxiously up into Nick's face. 'Would it bore you to go to the station, Nick, and watch the trains? Before I had the accident, Paul and me used to go along there because he collected train numbers. I always loved it—what do you say? If you don't like the idea . . .'

'I do like it; it sounds fun,' Nick said heartily. 'I've never been too keen on shopping meself, particularly the sort of shopping you girls go in for, which is mainly lookin', when all's said and done. Off we go then!'

As usual, the station was bustling with people and the two youngsters spent some time simply watching what went on. Then they decided to take a look at St George's Hall, or rather the square before it, since Nick had heard that there was an old woman who begged unwanted scraps of bread, corn and the like from the local shops and fed it to the pigeons there.

They crossed the busy road, heading for the lions on their tall plinths, but there was no sign of the pigeon feeder. However, there was definitely something going on because there seemed to be children everywhere, many of whom had shinned up the plinths and were sitting on the lions' broad stone backs. Nick pushed his way through the crowd of youngsters until he could see the reason for the crowd.

A small man, with a face like a monkey's and

161

tightly curling black hair, stood behind a tripod upon which was perched an extremely large camera. He was gesturing at the children to give him room, pointing first at one and then at another. But all this seemed to get him was children surging back and forth, saying that they wanted to be in the picture, mister, and almost knocking the camera over in their efforts to be first in front of the lens.

Suddenly, the little man seemed to decide to control the situation. He swung his camera round and pointed the lens upwards towards the children on the stone lions. Then he produced what looked like a walking stick and shook it threateningly at the children milling around him. 'Bugger off, you little devils, or you'll feel the sting of my stick!' he shouted. His voice was surprisingly strong and commanding for someone so small, and the children moved back at once, gathering in groups, but leaving a cleared space of paving between the photographer and the lions. The little man nodded his satisfaction and must have caught sight of Nick and Prue, standing almost at his elbow, in the corner of his eye, for he turned furiously towards them, a scowl descending on his wrinkled brow. 'Didn't you hear what I said . . .' he began, then stopped short.

He must have seen the wheelchair and known that they could not move as swiftly as the others, Nick thought, but then he realised his mistake, for the little man was gazing at Prue as though seeing a heavenly vision. 'If I give you a leg up, little one, could you climb on to the lion's nose and smile down at me?' he said. 'I'm doing an article for—' He stopped short, and Nick saw that he had noticed the wheelchair. 'Ah, I see that will not be possible.' He turned to Nick. 'I'll just get a picture of the kids on the lion and then I'd like one of you and your little sister, so don't run away.'

Prue laughed. 'I can't and he won't—run away, I mean,' she said cheerfully. 'Carry on, Mr Photographer.'

The little man grinned: a flash of very white teeth in his dark face. 'A lassie with a sense of humour,' he said approvingly. 'Give me five minutes and I'll explain.'

Nick looked at the children on the lions, none of whom seemed capable of remaining still for more than a few seconds. He thought it would take considerably more than five minutes simply to persuade them to stop bounding about, but the little man clearly knew his job. 'When I shout "Penny", you will remain as still as the stone lions for a count of three,' he instructed them. 'Everyone who remains still will be paid a penny, but those who move will get nothing. Is that clear?'

The ragged urchins poised on the lion would have done a good deal for a penny, so were happy to oblige when the photographer ducked under the black cloth, adjusted his instrument, and shouted, 'Penny!' They froze and in fact allowed him to take a number of shots, only breaking into violent movement again when he emerged from under the cloth and produced a handful of coppers, which he rattled enticingly. The kids swarmed down from the plinth and lined up to receive the money.

The photographer dismantled his equipment, which folded up neatly into a large black bag, obviously made for the purpose. He slung this across his back, then picked up two sticks which,

Nick realised, were in fact crutches and settled them in his armpits. Now that the camera had disappeared, the other children had lost interest and made off to find alternative sources of amusement, so the photographer was able to lead Nick and Prue to an empty bench where he and Nick sat down with Prue beside them. Then he produced a bag of bull's eyes, gave them one each and took one himself.

When the three of them were sucking happily, he explained that he was a journalist from a well-known glossy magazine and had been commissioned to write six articles on children living in big cities, which he was to illustrate with photographs. He was also employed by the magazine as a photographer and often worked as a freelance when he could see that a particular piece would be easy to sell.

Nick nodded and murmured, trying to sound as though he understood every word the little man was saying, but in fact, 'freelance' meant nothing to him. He felt, however, that some response should be forthcoming, so he said: 'That's real interestin', mister, but what do you want me an' Prue here for? And she ain't my sister, by the way, she's just a friend.'

The little man began to speak, then clapped a hand to his forehead. 'What a fool I am, gabbling on when you don't even know my name. I am Eduardo.'

He shot out a hand which Nick gripped, realising uneasily that their companion thought they ought to recognise the name. He opened his mouth to admit his ignorance, but was saved by Prue who said, as she shook the photographer's hand:

164

'Eduardo what?' Then, smiling broadly, '*I* know; you took a photograph of the new queen at the coronation and she said it was the one she liked most of all. And she asked what your name was, Eduardo what?—like I did—and you said just Eduardo, which made her laugh. I remember reading it in one of the magazines that the Mothers' Union pass round.'

Eduardo beamed. 'You have a very clever little friend,' he told Nick, 'but I must get to the point. For the cover of my magazine I need a pretty child, beautifully dressed and obviously of good family. But because it will be the cover picture, I shall have to have permission from the child's parents.' He turned to Prue. 'Do you live far from here, my dear? I will hail a taxi cab to take us to your home and then your mother can be present when I photograph you.'

Nick began to say that they both lived quite near, but Prue leaned out of the wheelchair and gave his shoulder a shake. 'I won't go home before we've had us dinners,' she said crossly. 'And what about my surprise?' She then spoke directly to Eduardo. 'Go and find someone else to photograph. I hate sitting still—you have enough of that when you're in a wheelchair—and this is my special day out. If you want to take my picture, come back tomorrow.'

Nick began to apologise, but Eduardo shook his head. He was laughing. 'This little lady knows her own mind,' he said approvingly. 'But I can't come back tomorrow, because tomorrow I shall be in Glasgow, taking photographs of the children there. Suppose I treat you both to dinner and *then* we go back to little Miss—Miss . . .'

'She's Miss Prue Fairweather and I'm Nick Bentley,' Nick said. 'And we both live quite near here; it won't take more than five minutes in a taxi.' He turned to Prue. 'That would be all right, wouldn't it? You'd have your nice dinner, like we planned, and then Mr Eduardo could take your picture and—'

'No,' Prue said firmly, before he could continue. 'Wharrabout me treat, eh? It ain't fair, Nick; you've been teasing me with this surprise and now you seem to think it's not important any more, but it is.'

Eduardo turned to Nick. 'What is this surprise?' he asked curiously. 'Will it take long? Could I perhaps photograph Miss Prue here afterwards?'

Nick heaved a sigh and gave up. 'There's a puppet show in Clayton Square this afternoon and I've bought two tickets for the first performance,' he said, and smiled as Prue gave a squeal of joy. 'They're doing Snow White and the Seven Dwarfs and I believe they're really good. So you see, neither of us wants to risk missing even a part of the performance.'

Eduardo's monkey face creased into a smile. 'A puppet show!' he exclaimed. 'There's nothing a photographer likes more, when taking children, than a chance to see their faces when they are absorbed not in the camera but in something else. I shall accompany you to this square . . . it is not far? Then when the show is over we will take a taxi cab to Miss Prue's home and you, my dear, shall introduce me, to your parents—'

'I've only got one parent; that's my mam, Mrs Fairweather,' Prue interrupted. 'But if you come back to the shop with me you'll meet my sister

166

Addy as well.'

'The shop?' Eduardo said. He sounded puzzled, so Nick explained that the Fairweathers lived in a flat above their shop. This seemed to satisfy the photographer, and they set out to find a restaurant where they might get a good meal. Nick and Prue had meant to go to the Kardomah café on Church Street, but instead they ate in a restaurant in a hotel, which had starched white tablecloths and glittering silver cutlery, and the most wonderful food that Nick had ever tasted.

During the course of the meal, Eduardo asked Prue why she was in a wheelchair, and when she had explained she asked him why he could only walk with the aid of crutches. He smiled at her, seeming not to resent the question, and Nick was rather surprised, for he knew all too well that many grown-ups are curious about children but dislike a child's curiosity's being turned on them.

'Like you, I was involved in an accident when I was about eight,' he told her. 'I lived in an apartment at the top of a very tall building, reached by flight after flight of wooden stairs. It was an old building—many of the buildings are old in Italy—and one of the stairs suddenly gave way. I pitched forward and felt a bang on the front of my head, and then nothing, nothing for weeks and weeks.'

'Gosh,' Prue breathed. 'That's even worse than what happened to me. How did you bear it, Mr Eduardo?'

The little man grimaced. 'Badly, at first; I thought my life was finished, that it would never amount to anything. I was one of eleven children, you understand, and lire—that is the money of

167

Italy—were scarce. I did not start school until I was ten years old, but I was fortunate. One of the teachers began to take an interest in the little stories I wrote to amuse myself, and told my mother I had a gift for the written word. Gradually, he built up my self-confidence, my faith in my own abilities. But now, I think it is time we left here and went to this Clayton Square so that I can explain to the puppeteers what I want to do, and get their permission to photograph their audience, and their theatre.'

The show was supposed to start at two, but the proprietor told them that nothing would happen until every seat was filled, so it was half past two before the rather shabby red velvet curtains jerked apart to reveal Snow White's wicked stepmother staring into the magic mirror and demanding that it should tell her who was the fairest in the land.

Nick had expected Eduardo to sit beside him on the wobbly wooden bench and he did so at first, but once the performance got under way he got up unobtrusively, balanced himself carefully on his crutches, and took up a position alongside the booth.

Nick glanced towards Prue, whose wheelchair had been pulled up alongside the bench, and understood at once why Eduardo had been so eager to photograph the children whilst they watched the show. Every emotion chased itself across Prue's face: dismay when Snow White was lost in the wood, delight when she found safety in the home of the seven dwarfs, horror when the queen dressed up as an old woman and gave her the poisoned apple. He guessed that every child in the audience would be reacting as Prue was, and

168

when Snow White finished it was followed by a comedy that had the audience screaming with excitement and laughter. Then the puppets led the singing of many familiar old songs. They invited children to come up to the front and sing a duet with one of the characters, and though their seats had already cost the children sixpence a head, a man dressed all in black appeared from behind the theatre and took a hat round, which was speedily rattling with pennies and ha'pennies.

Nick heard the unrestrained laughter at all the little jokes with which the puppeteers enlivened the story and heard the constant click of the camera, and thought to himself that Eduardo would be able to charge what he liked for this story, for the photographs would be superb.

When at last the strangely assorted trio abandoned Clayton Square and headed for the Scottie, they felt as though they had known one another for years. Eduardo told them how he had come to England a dozen years before when the editor of a famous magazine had offered him a job. That had been his first step on the road to success, for other editors began to offer him work and because his photographs and articles were so popular he was paid well, despite the Depression.

He explained what 'freelance' meant and the children gazed at him with awe. Fancy being able to pick and choose which job you accepted and which you turned down, Nick thought. It must be wonderful to have a real talent like Eduardo's.

By the time they reached the shop, Prue was clearly beginning to wilt and Nick could see that she was very tired indeed. He knew her outings with Addy were never longer than a couple of hours, but today she had been out from a quarter to nine in the morning, and not only had it been a long day, it had also been an exciting one. He thought he would tell Mrs Fairweather that her daughter should go straight to bed, and when they entered the shop he suggested it.

Prue began to sob loudly and to say that no one thought her anything but a burden. Addy rushed forward at once and tried to put her arms round her sister, but was sharply repulsed. 'Gerroff me, you nasty girl! When you take me out, we goes where *you* want to go. If *you* had been wheeling my chair this morning, I'd never have met Eduardo, or seen the trains in Lime Street station, or watched the wonderful puppet show,' she whined. 'As for going to bed, I shan't, I shan't, I shan't! Mr Eduardo don't want to photograph your ugly old face, he wants to photograph *me*! So just you mind your own business!' She turned to her mother, who was looking flushed and embarrassed. 'You tell her, Mam; she's tryin' to push me out, like she always does.'

Nick, knowing how very tired Prue must be, was nevertheless appalled by this display of spite and temper, for he knew very well that Addy bent over backwards to please her sister, seldom having five minutes she could call her own. and received little thanks for it. Even now Mrs Fairweather only reproved Prue gently before turning to Addy and saying sharply: 'Take off your sister's coat and hat and then run up and fetch her down a glass of milk, whilst Nick here introduces me to this gentleman.' She turned back to Eduardo. 'How do you do?'

'I am Eduardo and I've come to ask your permission to photograph your daughter—' he

170

began, but was interrupted by Prue, very cross and pink in the face.

'He means me, Mam, not perishin' Addy,' she said triumphantly. 'But Nick had better explain.' She turned to Nick, giving him her most appealing smile. 'Go on, Nick, tell my mam what happened, right from the moment we came out of Lime Street Station and saw the kids on the lions.'

*   *   *

Eduardo was not surprised by Mrs Fairweather's immediate acceptance of the suggestion that he should photograph her younger daughter, but she said firmly that it would not be possible for him to do so this evening.

'I know you need to be in Scotland some time tomorrow, but Prue is beginning to look downright haggard.' She lowered her voice, despite the fact that both girls had gone up to the flat some ten minutes earlier. 'And though she still blames her sister sometimes for the accident which paralysed her, she isn't usually so rude and ungrateful, honest to God she isn't, sir. If you want your photograph to show Prue at her best, come round here at eight in the morning. Addy and I will have her down here in her best dress, waiting for you.'

'That would seem the ideal solution,' Eduardo admitted. 'But I had not intended to remain in the city for a further night, so have not booked a room in a hotel. However, I am sure there will no difficulty . . .'

'My father lets rooms in the Vines public house,' Nick said eagerly. 'They aren't posh, but they're clean and cheap and you can get a good meal at

171

the canny house just up the road; or you can have sandwiches in the pub. I ain't sayin' it's anything special and you'd have to climb a flight of stairs, but me dad would make you very welcome.'

Eduardo, who was probably accustomed to staying in the best hotels and eating at expensive restaurants, grinned gratefully at Nick. 'That would suit me down to the ground,' he said heartily. 'And I can manage one flight of stairs; I take it breakfast is provided?'

'Porridge, tea and toast,' Nick said promptly. He turned to Mrs Fairweather. 'We'll be back here on the dot of eight o'clock. Now we'd best be getting back so Mr Eduardo here can take possession of the best front bedroom.'

*   *   *

All went according to plan. Because Eduardo wanted an outdoor setting for the photograph, Prue consented to Addy's taking her in her wheelchair to the nearest gardens. Prue was in a delightful mood, eager to please. The photographs were soon taken and Eduardo was able to pack up his equipment, reward both girls with a half-crown, and set off for Glasgow.

They reached Lime Street Station and Addy wandered off to take a closer look at the trains whilst Eduardo sat down on a bench and pulled Prue's wheelchair round so that they were facing one another.

'Did you enjoy having your photograph taken, little one?' Eduardo said, once Addy was out of earshot. 'I wanted a chat with you because it seems to me that you and I are in a similar position. Oh, my legs are by no means useless; around my own home I scarcely need my crutches, but there was a time when I was stuck in a wheelchair, as you are yourself.'

'Were you?' Prue said, eyes widening. Then her face clouded. 'Oh, but it's different for you. You were special, even at school. I'm not clever at all and I can't do games or gymnastics, or any of the things other girls do. I can't skip a rope, or play marbles, or hopscotch. Addy's starting to play rounders in the summer, but because of these wretched legs which simply won't get strong, I can't do anything like that.'

Eduardo laughed. 'Anyone would think that legs were the only things that mattered,' he said. 'Oh, if you want to be a ballerina, or a footballer, then legs *are* important. But before I left your mother's shop last night, she told me that you have a—a teacher, I cannot think of the right word, who gives you exercises which will strengthen your poor legs; so I'm sure that one day you will walk again, even play rounders. But just suppose this should not be the case, then you must remember that if you want to be a happy and successful person, you can become one, in or out of a wheelchair. Decide what you enjoy doing most and concentrate on getting better and better at it. In the meantime, do as I did, and make the best of what you have. Everyone has natural talents. I discovered mine through doing what I enjoyed most and you can do the same, if you will only try hard.'

He looked at Prue and saw that her face was alight with enthusiasm as Addy came panting up to tell him that his train had just arrived alongside its platform. Eduardo got to his feet, adjusted his crutches, then shook hands with both girls before bending to give Prue a kiss on the forehead. 'Don't forget my words of wisdom, young lady,' he adjured her. 'Tell your mother I shall be in touch as soon as my editor approves your picture for the cover of his magazine. And be nice to your sister because in your heart you know very well that an accident is just that. No blame should be attached to anyone.'

He patted Addy's shoulder and saw the gratitude in her big brown eyes before giving the girls a last wave and making his way towards the waiting train.

*   *   *

'Money for jam!' Nell Fairweather said reverently, when the promised letter from Eduardo arrived. It contained a cheque for three guineas as well as four photographs. One was of Prue in her best dress, sitting beneath a tree. The second was also of Prue as she watched the puppet show. The third was of Nick gazing up at the children on the lion's back and the fourth, to the gratification and astonishment of the subject, was of Addy. Eduardo had taken her likeness whilst he was photographing Prue in the gardens, and to Addy's delight—and surprise—the scars on her face were scarcely visible. 'He's made me look pretty!' she told Nonny, when her grandmother had seen and admired the photographs, but though Nonny laughed, she also shook her head.

'No one can't make you look pretty if you ain't, not even Mr Oh-So-Clever Eduardo,' she said. 'You *are* pretty, Adelaide Fairweather, and I won't have you sayin' no different, 'cos you're as like

174

meself when I were younger as two peas in a pod. Can I have that picture for me bedroom wall—no, for me sittin' room—because your mam don't need it. She's got you in person, if you understand me.'

Addy agreed to this, though Nell said she would like a copy as well, but Eduardo must have guessed that there would be competition for his work since just before the magazine came out—it was a monthly—a fat padded envelope arrived containing half a dozen copies of all four photographs.

Mr Bentley had Nick's picture framed and hung in his room, and then, because Paul had not been included in the photographic expedition, he sent the boy down to Debrons in Bold Street. They took a very good portrait of Paul and this was also framed and hung in Mr Bentley's room, beside Nick's.

Eduardo's descent on Liverpool had certainly left its mark. Prue tried harder than ever at her leg exercises and began to be nicer to Addy, and not only to appreciate what was done for her but to acknowledge it with smiles and thanks. She also started to pay more attention to her favourite hobbies. She was a good little needlewoman and began to embroider baby clothing for a nearby shop, earning herself small but respectable sums of money.

Addy stopped trying to shrink into the background, ashamed of what she thought of as her scarred face, for both Eduardo's kindness and the beautiful photograph gave her self-confidence.

For his part, Nick began to take Prue out when he was free to do so, no longer simply to give Addy a rest, but also because he enjoyed Prue's company. She didn't whine or complain now, but appreciated everything he did for her, so it became a pleasure to take her about.

CHAPTER NINE

September 1939

'But Mam, I'm too *old* to be evacuated! In a few more months I'll be fourteen and now that war has been declared there will be lots and lots of jobs in Liverpool for girls of my age.'

Addy and Nell were alone in the shop, Nonny having volunteered to get Prue dressed and ready for the day ahead, since Nell wanted to talk to Addy, she said, while Prue was not present. Addy had felt quite flattered that her mother should, it appeared, treat her as an adult. She imagined Nell was going to consult her over the vexed business of evacuation, for although it was only a couple of weeks since the declaration of war with Germany, most of the children had already left the city for the country. Addy had assumed that she and Prue were to remain with their mother, though Nell had pointed out the previous day that this would be awkward since teachers had been evacuated with their classes, and schools were being either shut down or used for other purposes.

Now, however, it seemed that Nell had consulted the authorities and they had insisted that a child in a wheelchair would be far too vulnerable if the enemy bombed the city. Addy quite agreed with this, for she could see the sense of it: a wheelchair would have to be carried up and down the air raid shelter steps, and if such a place received a hit and had to be abandoned quickly, it might easily prevent escape.

Nell, looking rather nervous, said she was glad Addy understood, and then explained the full situation. Disabled children were to be taken to a special house that had been converted for their use, and in order to get Prue accepted Nell had had to agree that her older daughter would accompany the younger one.

'But why?' Addy raged when she realised that Nell intended her to go too. 'Don't tell me all the other children have older brothers or sisters to go with them.'

The two of them were sitting behind the counter but Nell had not yet opened up and now she looked miserably across at her daughter. 'It's Prue; she says she won't go alone and if I try to make her she'll run away,' she said. 'You needn't tell me she can't run far in a wheelchair because I know it, but the fact is she'd have a jolly good try and might get into some terrible sort of trouble. I know it's hard on you, queen, but Prue has had to face so much disappointment. She does her exercises morning and evening, but you know as well as I do that there's been very little improvement. Oh, she is a bit better, but in her heart I'm sure she thought she'd be walking by now and as you know, she can't even stand. Her legs just buckle and won't support her weight. Just imagine, queen, if she was pushing her wheelchair along a country road and an army convoy swept round the corner . . .'

Addy shuddered. She could imagine all too well what might happen to Prue, and glancing across at

177

her mother she saw that Nell's brown eyes had filled with tears. 'It's all right, Mam, I'll go with her, for a while at least,' she said quickly. She could not bear to see her mother, who never cried, mopping the tears from her cheeks. 'After all, you know what Prue's like; give her a couple of weeks and she'll probably be everyone's pet, and if that's the case she'll wave me off happily enough.'

Nell blew her nose loudly and turned a rather watery smile on her elder daughter. 'Thank you, Addy dear,' she said huskily. 'And it isn't just Prue; I want to think of you safe in the country as well.'

Addy bit her lip, thinking of a thousand things she would have liked to have said, but not uttering any of them. It was the usual story: whatever Prue wanted she must have; Addy's own wants—needs even—came a long way behind. Sighing, she got to her feet and headed for the stairs. 'I'll just nip up and give Nonny a hand and tell Prue I'll go with her.' Reaching the stairs, she turned back to her mother for a moment. 'When do we leave?'

'Tomorrow, early,' Nell said ruefully.

Addy suppressed a groan and compressed her lips. But she had made a promise to herself that she would stick with Prue until her sister no longer needed her, and she intended to keep it, so she just said: 'Tomorrow morning? Then we'd best start packing,' and continued on her way up to the flat.

*   *   *

It was a large party which assembled on the station platform, compounded by the fact that there were so many helpers, for the home to which they were going would need experienced staff and it seemed

178

sensible to employ people who had already worked with the children in Liverpool.

Unfortunately, experienced though they might be in the care of the young, they were not equally experienced as travellers. Their charges were hauled out of their wheelchairs and carried on to the train, where it was speedily realised that the chairs would get hopelessly mixed up in transit unless they were labelled in some way. Addy, Nell and Nonny tutted in a superior manner, since they had labelled Prue's wheelchair, her suitcase and the child herself. But then Nonny had the bright idea of trundling the wheelchairs one by one along the platform, under the anxious gaze of their owners, who would point triumphantly to their own conveyance. She produced a handful of blank luggage labels and by dint of shouting instructions to the staff already aboard managed to get each chair labelled and in the luggage van next to its owner's suitcase before the guard, his patience sorely tried, slammed the last door, blew a blast on his whistle and signalled to the driver to set the train in motion.

Addy, leaning out of the window and waving furiously, was pulled back in by an extremely cross teacher, and saw both her mother and her grandmother rub tears from their cheeks before they turned and hurried out of sight. Only then did she return to her seat next to Prue. For the first time, she looked around the compartment at their fellow travellers. A thin, pale-faced boy with a sulky expression, a girl of about her own age looking equally fed up, two over-excited children who kept shouting at the tops of their voices and a couple of adults—teachers or nurses, she

179

supposed—who gave peremptory commands to 'keep the noise down, please!' and then buried their noses in books.

She and Prue exchanged rueful glances; it was clear this journey was not to be a joyride. Then Addy produced the bag of humbugs Nonny had given her and a couple of comics. Sucking, more or less contentedly, the sisters settled down to read.

*   *   *

As the train chugged along, Addy realised that she had prepared herself for a lot of things, but not for beauty. They were travelling through glorious countryside, and the breath caught in her throat as she pressed closer to the train window, the better to admire the scene. Sadly, the other occupants of the carriage seemed not to notice the gentle hills and valleys, or the way the sunshine was reflected in the water of rivers and streams, chattering seawards over their rocky—or reedy—beds.

Prue was as fascinated as Addy was herself, and nudged her sister to draw her attention to each new vista opening up before them. After many hours, they reached a busy and bustling station where they were told to disembark. They were all helped off the train, with varying degrees of solicitude, and on to a very ancient bus which took them what seemed like several miles through deep country lanes, until at last it swung into a neglected drive and drew up before what the most senior of the teachers told them was Foliat Manor, where they would be living, presumably, until this wretched war was over.

Addy sorted Prue's wheelchair out from amongst

the rest and the bus driver lifted her down and into it. Then, for a moment, the sisters just stopped where they were and gazed. The house was huge and built of creamy stone and though it was dusk Addy thought that it had a friendly, lived-in look. They entered the house through the big front door to find themselves in a huge hall, the floor of which was covered in black and white tiles and the walls with what, in the dim light, Addy guessed to be family portraits. They had been warned that in future they would probably be told to use the side or even the back door, which led directly from the kitchen into a small cobbled courtyard, so Addy took a good long look at the hall, in case she and the others were forbidden to pass through it again. It was lofty, the ceiling so high above that it was almost impossible to see it clearly in the shadows. A variety of doors, all unfortunately shut, led to who knew what wonderful rooms. They did not visit the kitchen, though in answer to Addy's enquiries they were told that the courtyard was almost surrounded by outbuildings and that they would have a proper tour of the property next morning. Addy was thrilled, but did not think her pleasure was shared by the adults present, who looked resigned rather than delighted. She had already decided that most of the helpers were not here of their own volition and hoped they would leave as soon as they had settled the children into their new quarters.

Everyone had their meal in a big and rather gloomy dining room with panelled walls and a wood block floor. It was extremely cold, for no one had thought to light the fire, though the fireplace itself was piled up with logs, and there was no other means of heating that Addy could see. They were all tired after their journey and the supper consisted of shepherd's pie and stewed apple, which was gobbled up eagerly whilst everyone, Addy thought, looked surreptitiously around them, as she certainly did. The ceiling was covered in wonderful fruit and flowers made, she supposed, out of plaster. She glanced hopefully towards the windows, but it was impossible to see even their shape since they were closely curtained, no doubt because of the blackout. But the chairs drawn up to the table had embroidered seats and lion's feet and the table itself shone like dark water, so that she found herself wincing when one of the younger children swept an arm round to indicate something to his neighbour and shot the milk in his glass all over the wonderful gloss. She waited for the nearest adult to tell the little boy to be more careful but instead the woman just shrugged, helped the child to change his place for one which was not covered in milk, and when she saw Addy staring said indifferently: 'They're rich. If they don't like milk stains they'll just have to buy another table.'

For a moment Addy was too astonished to say a word; then she fixed the woman with a reproachful gaze and to her own surprise heard her voice answering quite hotly. 'They aren't rich; I'm sure if they were, they wouldn't hand their beautiful house over to—to kids from the 'Pool. And my mam would say you should take extra special care of other people's things.'

The woman gave her a look so full of cold dislike that Addy knew, with a sinking heart, that she had been marked out by that particular teacher as a troublemaker. But all the woman said was: 'If you feel like that you'd best gerralong to the kitchen and fetch a cloth and some polish and clean it up yourself, because I'm certainly not goin' to.'

Not a teacher, Addy thought, noting the careless speech. She got up with what dignity she could muster and left the room, nose in the air. She did not know where the kitchen was, but made a good guess—it would be close to the dining room, surely?—and struck lucky at her first attempt. The room was large, a good deal warmer than the dining room, and furnished with all the usual impedimenta of cooking. Addy looked round contentedly, then asked the fat grey-haired woman presiding over the big, old-fashioned stove if she might have a cloth, since one of the kids had spilt some milk.

The woman smiled at her, then tutted. 'I telled the fambly how it would be, my handsome, but would they listen to old Buffy? Course not; I's only reared five kids of me own, *and* seven grandchildren! Here, you go back to your grub and I'll bring a cloth and a bit o' polish to mek all right.'

Addy returned to her place and when the older woman—*not* a teacher—glared at her said placidly that someone was coming to clear the milk away in a minute. The woman began to say angrily that she had told Addy to clean the milk up herself, not to find someone else to do it, but just then the grey-haired woman called Buffy came bustling in and Addy's enemy contented herself with another glare before turning back to begin shovelling food into her mouth once more.

Soon after the meal was finished they were

ushered to their rooms, and Addy realised that the words 'adapted for disabled children and young people' had been frankly untrue. Some of the children could manage stairs but a dozen could not, and though there was a sort of sling in which one person could sit and be manhandled up the stairs by two hefty adults, it was an uncomfortable and time-consuming conveyance. A wheelchair was taken up to the first floor and used to ferry people from the landing to their rooms, where perfectly ordinary beds and chairs awaited them.

'I'm so glad you're wi' me, Addy,' Prue whispered as her sister helped her to prepare for bed. 'And aren't we lucky to have a room to ourselves? Some of the others have one of them helpers to sleep in the same room—imagine!'

'I can,' Addy said drily. She looked around the small room, at the shabby linoleum on the floor, the walls, pockmarked where posters or pictures had once hung, and the little bookcase with the books still in place; she knew already that the chest of drawers, the dressing table and the wardrobe were empty. 'This was a boy's room, don't you think? Only I expect he's a man now, because the books are awful old and worn. Oh, Prue, I do like this place!'

'Me too,' Prue said, but there was doubt in her voice. 'Only . . . I don't much like the people in charge, do you?'

'No. They're horrid. But I heard them grumbling that they didn't like the country and would be driven mad by all that dark.' She giggled. 'As if it would creep up and strangle them or something! So maybe the nasty ones will leave and some nicer ones will come in their place.'

'I hope you're right,' Prue said, but her voice was already growing heavy with sleep. 'Night night, Addy. See you in the mornin'.'

*   *   *

'There's two letters!' Nell said excitedly, bursting into the kitchen and clutching two white envelopes and a couple of small brown ones. She beamed at her mother, then gave Nonny an exuberant hug. 'They're addressed to both of us, one from each girl—they're the "proper letters" Addy promised on her safe-arrival postcard. Oh, I can't wait to hear what they really think of this manor place!'

'Now, now, take it easy,' Nonny said, grinning. 'You open Prue's and I'll open Addy's and we'll read them aloud to each other. And I bet Addy's is three times as long and a lot more interesting than our Prue's.'

'Addy's two years older; of course her letter is bound to be . . . but what does it matter?' Nell slit the envelope open with an impatient hand, skimmed the page it contained, then proceeded to read it aloud.

'Dear Mam and Nonny,
'You would like this place, though it is rather grand. It doesn't have a garden . . . well, it does, only it's huge and it's called the grounds. There is flowers, roses and that, though an old feller who comes to do the work most days says there'll be a grosh more come the summer. The food is sometimes good and sometimes not and some of the staff are nice to us but others are horrible. Oh, well. The school is a long way off,

185

three miles, so there's a very old bus which takes us to classes each day. Addy has explored everywhere and tells me about it after lights out at eight. She says the sea is quite near and when I can walk, and it's summer, we'll do all sorts. There are woods, I can see them, but no use for the wheelchair, the ground is too soft. There is streams and a river, Addy says.

'Must go now, lots of love and kisses,
'Your little Prue.'

'Well, well, not much to worry about there,' Nonny observed. 'If that little madam wasn't happy she'd be the first to tell you and demand to be brung back here just as soon as could be. Satisfied, Nell my dear?'

'Ye-es,' Nell said slowly. 'I want them to be happy, of course, but I want them to miss us, and Liverpool, and the Scottie, and their old school pals . . . does it sound awfully selfish, Ma, if I say I don't want them to like this manor better than their own old home?'

'No, it's natural,' Nonny said comfortably. It was breakfast time and she reached out for the loaf, cut a couple of slices, and buttered them. 'But you know kids: show them acres of grass and a river and the sea . . . well, what would you have preferred when you was a kid, eh? City streets, the odd trip to one of the parks, a nose round the stalls in Paddy's Market wi' tuppence to spend and most stuff costin' threepence?'

Nell laughed, then sighed. 'I know what you mean. Read Addy's letter now, and then I'll have to open up.'

'Right you are,' Nonny said, perching her

186

spectacles on her nose and frowning down at the pages in her hand. 'I could wish her writing was bigger . . . but here goes!'

'Dear Mam and Nonny,

'This place is like something out of a book. The house is huge, built of stone with what Mr Stebbings, who works in the grounds, tells us are "mullioned windows", which seems to mean they are made of stone and pointed at the top . . . oh dear, that isn't a very good explanation but perhaps, Mam, you know what a mullioned window looks like? A bit churchy, sort of. The stone is a pretty colour, goldy-grey, but a good deal of it has stuff called Virginia creeper or wisteria growing up it, so that it looks sort of shaggy. But beautiful, honest to God it is. The house was probably grand once, but now it's— well, I suppose you could say it's neglected. The curtains and carpets and stuff like that are threadbare, faded, some are falling to pieces, and some of the furniture is dusty and even broken, though the dining room table is absolutely marvellous—you can see your face in it. There is a little room called "the Admiral's study" where we aren't allowed to go—the door is kept locked—but Prue and me looked through the window, and the walls are lined with lovely books and pictures and there's a big desk which gleams with polish and two big armchairs. The housekeeper, the one who was here when it wasn't a children's home, told us she comes in two or three times a week to "redd that room up", as she puts it. We like her, Prue and me.

'Then there is the rose garden, and the scent and the colours are so glorious that I can't describe them. And there is a herb garden, lovely, lovely interesting smells there, and a walled kitchen garden which we've not seen yet. There are two doors and both are locked but Mr Stebbings says he will take us round one day, when he's not too busy. And the shore is so close! The people who belong to the house always call it "the shore" and never the seaside, but that's what they mean. Woods run down to the edge of the cliff, and there's a stream, and at the bottom of the cliff there's a river, broadening out . . . can't think what it's called . . . oh, yes, I think it's an estuary. There are rocks on the shore, and big pools, big enough to swim in if you could swim. We're going to learn, Prue and me, because I'm certain sure she'll get better in a place like this.

'There's lots more, because this is the very heart of the country, so there are meadows and streams and ponds all waiting to be explored. There are all sorts of different trees. I want to learn all about them: pines and beeches, and along by the river willows and alders. The headmistress, Miss Robinson, knows the names of every tree and flower for miles around and says she will teach me to identify them when spring comes. The leaves are turning colour as the gales blow them from the trees. They are piled up in heaps and I love crunching through them. The beech ones are gold, like cornflakes, and they're crisp because we've not had much rain; imagine me pushing the wheelchair through the biggest box of cornflakes in the world!

'The village school only has children until

they're fourteen. Then, if you want to go on to what Miss Robinson calls further education, you have to catch a bus into Plymouth, and that's expensive. I told Miss Robinson I'd be fourteen in a few months and she suggested that I might like to apply to become a pupil teacher. You get paid for doing it and it would be useful because she doesn't think the helpers at the manor will want to stay. Some of them are trained nurses and they will be needed when wounded soldiers have to go into hospital. Then there are real teachers who will want to take up other jobs. Miss Robinson thinks I could earn a little extra money as a helper when there's a vacancy. She didn't say "if", Mam, she said "when"! I'd love to do it, if it's all right with you. What do you think? Let me know as soon as you can.

'*Lots and lots of love to you both,*
'*Addy.*'

Nonny folded the pages carefully and pushed them back into the envelope, then helped herself to one of the rounds of bread which she had cut and buttered. She spread marmalade on it, remarking as she did so that reading aloud had made her feel quite hoarse.

'If that's a hint for another cuppa, I'll join you,' Nell said. 'Well, ain't that letter a turn-up for the books! Addy's always been a bright 'un so I reckon she'll end up as a proper teacher . . . a headmistress even. You'd best write back to her today and tell her we're all in favour of her plan. I'll write back to Prue as well. She's clever in her own way, is Prue.' She caught the sparkle of

189

annoyance in her mother's eyes and raised both hands in a gesture of defeat. 'Sorry, sorry, sorry! You're quite right; Addy must certainly grab this chance and naturally I'm very proud that this Miss Robinson thinks her good enough. I'll write straight away.' She glanced at the clock on the mantel and rose hurriedly to her feet. 'Good Lord, look at the time! If I don't open up now I'll miss the early morning factory workers. Be an angel, Ma, and bring a cuppa down to the shop when the kettle boils.'

'I'll do that,' Nonny said. 'You ain't a bad girl, Nell Fairweather. You're beginning to appreciate our Addy at long last.'

* * *

By early November, the children and their helpers had settled into their new life. The weather had started sunny and pleasant, but then the gentle breeze became first a strong wind and then a gale. Leaves whirled from the trees, a tall and skinny poplar was blown down and crashed through the roof of a greenhouse, and the children found the three-mile journey in the ancient and draughty bus from the manor to the village school—and the return trip—far less enjoyable than it had been at first, now that the wintry weather had arrived.

In December, the staff began to leave. The strong winds had been bad enough, but when it got steadily colder and colder and they awoke each morning to white frosts and icy blasts, then the excuses began. So-called helpers went home for a weekend and did not return. Soon, the staff was reduced to Mr Mason, who suffered from asthma so badly that he was judged unfit for military service, Mr Bland, a retired schoolmaster who was too old to fight, and the two spinster teachers from the local school, Miss Rose and Miss Rachel Harkness, sisters in their fifties, who had agreed to move into the manor for the 'duration', as people put it. Other than those four, there were a couple of rosy-faced girls from the village who did not stay on the premises overnight but turned up at seven each morning, made breakfast, helped the children to dress and accompanied them to school.

'If we could get Mam to send us some thick jerseys it would be a big help,' Prue said wistfully one day, as the two girls were getting ready to leave. 'What we brought with us was fine for September, but I don't believe there's a door that fits or a window that doesn't rattle in the whole of this perishin' house, and school's not much better. Them tortoise stoves sends out a good heat, but it only reaches as far as the first two rows of desks!'

Addy laughed. 'But you sit in the front row,' she pointed out. 'So you shouldn't need extra woollies. Still, I suppose we could ask Mam to look out for some warmer clothing and send it to us.'

Prue, buttoning her cardigan, wagged an admonitory finger at her sister. 'Wharrabout playtime? They drive us out into the schoolyard as if we were silly sheep. They never take into account when they're telling us to run about and keep warm that you can't run about if you're in a wheelchair. And it's not only playtime; we get put in groups for certain lessons. I'm in the top group for art and we're right at the back of the room. I'm telling you, Addy, what with the draught that comes under the door and near on cuts me feet off at the ankles, and the draught from the window, which has icicles formin' on me ear lobes, I reckon I'll jolly nearly freeze to death if you don't do something about it.'

Addy sighed. The school was a very old Victorian building, without radiators or electricity. The tortoise stoves, temperamental beasts, were coke-fired and there was one to each classroom and one for the staffroom. The children were divided into three classes: ages four to six were Standard I and were taught by Miss Rose; her sister, Miss Rachel, taught Standard II, the seven- to ten-year-olds; and Miss Robinson took the older children.

When Addy and Prue had first started at the school, they had thought themselves fortunate indeed. Because the ancient bus sometimes broke down, Addy occasionally had to walk pushing the wheelchair so no one scolded if they were late arriving. The classrooms, with their nature tables to which anyone could contribute, were pleasant, and in good weather the playground, which included a large stretch of grass upon which games could be played and a coke pile which made a marvellous site for Relievio—though in fact this was forbidden ground—was a popular place.

However, as the cold increased, the city children began to think wistfully of their warm and crowded classrooms back home.

Now, Prue had finished buttoning her cardigan and Addy helped her into her winter coat and wrapped a thin scarf round her neck before covering her curls with her red pixie hood. 'I'll write to Mam tonight,' she said. 'She can pop into Paddy's Market, leaving Nonny in charge of the shop, and pick up a better coat for you, because this is too small and tight clothing isn't as warm as loose. But you really shouldn't go out at playtime now that it's so cold. If you explain to Miss Rachel about not being able to exercise, I'm sure she'll let you stay indoors. Come to think of it, there's more than one kid in your class who can't run around. What do they do?'

'They stay in the classroom,' Prue said gloomily. 'But oh, Addy, I do hate being different! None o' me pals are in wheelchairs, and I'd rather be with them and get cold than be stuck indoors. Do Phyllis and Arnold go out, or do they stay in the classroom?'

'Sometimes they come out, but mostly I think they stay indoors and read books,' Addy said rather doubtfully. She had never become friendly with either Phyllis or Arnold, who were always grumbling about something. 'Look, I'll tell you what, Prue. Miss Robinson's a good sort, so at break time I'll write a letter to Mam, asking for warmer clothes. I don't have an envelope, but I'm sure if I explain to Miss Robinson she'll lend me one, and post it off for me this very day. Then when Saturday comes I can pay her back, and probably, next week, Mam will send us some nice warm clothes.'

Addy did as she had promised, which was as well since the weather grew even colder. When the girls awoke on the morning following the arrival of a parcel from Nell, which included a blue serge coat and some lovely warm mittens, they could not see out of their bedroom window for the flower frost covering the panes, and the water in the jug on the washstand had a coating of ice. When Addy told Prue to stay in bed whilst she ran downstairs and begged a kettle of hot water from the kitchen staff, her sister was only too glad to obey. Down in the kitchen, Sally and Flora, the girls from the village, had stoked up the fire so that the room was beautifully warm.

'I'll come up and carry your sister down here to wash and dress,' Flora said comfortably. 'It's bitter out. Prue showed me the warm clothing your mam sent, but even that won't keep the cold out altogether. It's hard for the kids in wheelchairs.'

Sally, stirring porridge, snorted. 'The rest of 'em won't even get up unless we make 'em,' she observed. 'They miss more school than you'd credit . . . you and that pretty little sister of yours are the only ones what attend regular.'

'Oh, well, we've got each other, and anyway school's good fun, if only it weren't so cold,' Addy said. 'Have you seen what our Prue's made for Mam for a Christmas present? She's very good at making things is Prue.'

Both Flora and Sally nodded. Prue had collected a number of dead leaves, the ones with the most dramatic colours, and stuck them on to a large sheet of white paper. Then she had varnished them, framed the paper with pieces of wood which she had trimmed and polished, and now her only problem was how to get the picture back to Nan and Nonny without spoiling its colourful beauty.

'Oh ah, 'tes a marvel,' Sally said, beginning to dole out the porridge. 'Are you goin' home for Christmas? If so, you could carry it, careful like.'

'We'd like to go home, but we don't know yet if we'll be allowed,' Addy said rather wistfully. 'What will Christmas be like here, Sal? I suppose you and the other grown-ups will all go home?'

'Well, for the day itself I reckon we will, but for the rest of the holiday it will depend on how many kids are still livin' here,' Sally said. 'You know the old couple who own this yur house? Well, I 'spec someone told you they'd moved into a little house in Plymouth. It's an end of terrace and a deal easier to keep warm than this great barrack of a place. The Ministry what took over the house offered to let the old couple stay on, but they didn't fancy it. Once petrol were rationed, the old feller said he could see what was to come and the manor's just too far from everywhere, if you understand me. So they've rented a house for what they call a peppercorn rent, and they've settled in right happily. They've got a son and a daughter, both in the forces, who've got leave over Christmas, so the old folk will have company, which will be nice for them.'

Flora had clumped off up the back stairs to fetch Prue and now they both appeared, Prue clutching her clothing in her arms. Flora plonked her down on the nearest chair with a gasp. 'We're feedin' this little 'un too well,' she said breathlessly. 'But it takes two to use the sling, and anyway the back stairs is too narrow for it.' She went over to the sink and poured hot water from the kettle into the bowl, added some cold, and put it on the table beside Prue's chair, along with soap, flannel and towel. 'Give yourself a nice wash, lover, then I'll help ee to dress while your sister uses the sink,' she said.

Sally had filled two porridge dishes and fetched spoons and sugar from the drawer just as the kitchen door opened and Mr Bland popped his head round it. 'Any chance of some hot water?' he asked hopefully. 'We're doing our best to get the kids up, but there's a minor rebellion brewing and I can't say I blame them. The little ones are dressing—they can wash when they come home from school and the place is a bit warmer—but the older children have demanded hot water.'

There were several kettles simmering on the stove and Sally seized one and handed it to the former teacher. 'Go careful, 'cos it's real hot,' she warned him. 'And tell them kids if they aren't down and tackling their breakfasts in twenty minutes, then they won't get none.'

Mr Bland grinned. 'They won't get any or they will get none,' he said. 'Right you are, Sally. They'll be down in time for their grub, you can be sure of that.'

Later, with her stomach full of porridge and toast, Addy pushed Prue's wheelchair carefully down the drive to where the bus picked them up. Prue was endeavouring to knit and cursing every time the wheelchair lurched, which left Addy to indulge in her own thoughts. At some time during the night, she had awoken and found the full moon shining straight on to her face. She had got out of bed to pull the blackout blind down, for she and Prue usually dispensed with the blind as soon as they blew out their candle. Padding across the icy linoleum, she had reached up to the blind cord and then stopped abruptly, staring out into the black and silver of the moonlight. She had seen a movement and for a moment had wondered if it was the wind stirring the gaunt and leafless bushes in the rose garden. Then she had seen that it was a man, tall with dark hair. Addy had stared harder, then had blinked and rubbed her eyes; there was no one out there . . . no young man staring up at the house. Addy had leaned forward, trying to see round the corner of the house, her breath coming out as clouds of steam. What on earth could have happened? She had been so sure that a man had been standing there, looking up at the house. But then she realised she must have been dreaming, for the view from the window had been completely obscured by the flowers painted by Jack Frost on the cold glass.

Addy had returned to bed, both shaken and puzzled, suddenly wondering whether what she had just seen had been an example of the second sight Nonny had spoken of. If so, she did not like it one bit; thought it weird and frightening. But when she awoke next morning, she decided she had dreamed the whole episode.

'Addy? When will they tell us if we can go home for Christmas? I love it here, of course, but . . . oh, home's the best place at Christmas!'

Addy, brought back to the present with a start, wondered whether to tell Prue about thinking she had seen someone in the rose garden the previous night, then decided against it. It might worry Prue, or she could tell someone else who might deride Addy for imagining things. No, she would keep her own counsel. Doggedly, she pushed on, telling her sister rather breathlessly that she would have a word with Miss Robinson about the Christmas holiday that very day.

'Well, don't let her send us back before we've done the nativity play,' Prue said anxiously; she was to take the part of Mary, and there would be a real donkey! 'Only I *would* like to see Mam and Nonny and the shop again, just for a little while,

197

and I'm sure you would too, wouldn't you, Addy?'

Addy thought about it and was suddenly overcome by a rush of longing and homesickness. She loved the manor, the grounds and the countryside surrounding it, but there was no one here who had known her all her life, no one to give her the love she craved. Oh, she knew Prue was their mother's favourite, but she had never doubted for an instant that Nell loved her very much as well. Then there was Nonny, who loved both her grandchildren, but had made sure that Addy knew she loved her best.

When the bus stopped by the school, Addy could see Standard II already in line and preparing to enter the building. 'Addy? Don't push me in yet! When you see Miss Robinson, tell her that everyone is hoping to go home for Christmas and it might be a trifle awkward if we were the only ones still here.'

Addy spoke to Miss Robinson, as she had promised, and was told at once that arrangements had already been made, rail fares booked and parents informed. 'The folk who take care of you at the manor should have told you,' she said rather reprovingly. 'We do the nativity play three times, on the afternoons of the nineteenth and twentieth and the evening of the twenty-first, and the following day you'll go off on an early train. I expect you'll get a letter in the post, tomorrow or the next day, confirming that your mother will either meet the train herself or arrange for someone you know to do so.'

Now that it was an established fact, Addy and Prue became wild with excitement. They were going home! They loved the manor and were fond of their teachers and the old-fashioned, chilly little school, but it was not their home and, as Prue had said, home was the best possible place to be at Christmas. Feverishly, they searched woods and grounds for anything that could be given as Christmas presents to Nell or Nonny. Prue crocheted a pretty white collar and cuffs to replace the ones on her mother's navy-blue dress, and Addy cut some small, still well-foliaged twigs from a beech, because Miss Robinson had told her that if she stood them in a vase with some glycerine at the bottom, the glorious golden-brown leaves would stay that way all through the winter and would make a delightful table decoration.

*   *   *

Addy and Prue had a wonderful Christmas Day. 'It wasn't just the food and the lovely presents,' Prue said contentedly as they cuddled down in the bed they shared when Nonny was staying over. 'It was seeing the cousins and Nick and Paul after such ages—and being with Mam and Nonny, of course.'

Addy agreed that it had indeed been grand. It appeared that Mr Bentley and their mother had managed to resolve their differences, and were on friendly terms once more. So the boys and their father had been invited to Christmas tea and Mr Bentley had managed to acquire a big box of crackers and a chocolate-covered Yuletide log, which was just as well, since the cousins, aunts and uncles, who only had a get-together once a year, had turned out in force. Nonny had made the biggest Christmas cake she could fit into the oven and Nell had done her bit with an enormous trifle.

Other aunts had provided mince pies, fairy cakes and sandwiches, and a seaman uncle, who had just come back from crossing the Atlantic, had brought a large supply of colourful and unusual sweets, which he divided amongst all the young people present.

'It's daft, really, that we only see our relatives once a year,' Prue said now. 'They're real nice, but as our mam says, we've all got our own lives to lead. They like coming to our flat though, don't they, Addy? Last year the party was held at Uncle Jack's place on the Wirral, and though it's a real smart house, half the cousins didn't come.'

'No, because it's a good way out and Aunt Effie had quarrelled with just about everyone, though she was all right today,' Addy said. 'And isn't it nice that our mam and Mr Bentley are pals again? It'll make life a lot easier when we're back living on the Scottie.'

'You're right there,' Prue mumbled. 'I asked Paul what had brought them together again, but he just shrugged and said my guess was as good as his. I say, Addy, you know the cousins were all evacuated, same as us? Well, most of 'em aren't going back to the country. It's odd, because the things we like most, they really seem to hate. They don't like the quiet or the animals or the schools. They don't like the food either, and of course things will change when food rationing really gets going. Uncle Lionel was saying that folk in the country will really suffer 'cos they don't have as many shops as we do in the city, but Mam doesn't agree, and she knows more about it. She says they're issuing ration books, which will mean everyone getting exactly the same. It'll be a lot of extra work for her in the shop, but our mam's a knowing one, you know, and she doesn't agree that folk in towns will get more food, especially fruit and vegetables. She's been talking to Nonny about the Great War and Nonny remembers that folk in the country were much better off then. She says it'll be the same this time and country people will be laughing because they've got proper gardens and orchards and things. They'll be able to grow stuff, and they'll only let the shops have what they don't need themselves.' She giggled. 'And I can't see Uncle Lionel digging up the paving in the court to plant potatoes, or Aunt Sadie trying to grow cabbages in her gutter.'

The two girls were still giggling over the thought of Aunt Sadie, a tiny wisp of a woman who spent most of her life prowling the shops in search of bargains, scattering cabbage seed in the gutter outside her tiny home when the door opened and Nonny stole quietly in to the room, stopping short and tutting disapprovingly. 'Still awake? I were comin' in quiet as a mouse so as not to disturb you, and here you are gigglin' away as though you were George Formby and the Marx Brothers rolled into one. Well, you can just avert your eyes while I shed me best dress and reveal me perfect body. Go on, eyes to the wall.'

The two children obeyed instantly, Addy assuring her grandmother that even the thought of seeing Nonny in the buff was enough to turn not only her eyes to the wall but her stomach in its moorings. Nonny chuckled and Addy could hear her grandmother's clothing being neatly removed, hung on a hanger and put away in the rickety wardrobe. 'Good girls,' Nonny said, her voice

201

coming out muffled as she pulled her nightgown over her head. 'Come on, what were you laughing at? It's been a grand Christmas, one of the best, but I'd rather end the day with a good giggle than with tears. Your Auntie Ethel is saying her farewells and prophesying that this will be our last Christmas together.'

'But that's Aunt Ethel all over when she's had a couple of pints of Guinness,' Addy pointed out. 'If we don't all die from a surfeit of Christmas pudding, then she reckons the traffic will get us or we'll freeze in our beds. The war must be a real treat for her. And now I'll tell you what we were laughing at.'

When she had done so, Nonny laughed too. 'Aye, that 'ud be right comical,' she agreed. 'But who's to say it's only poor folk what will be growin' their own veg? Will that there rose garden you've talked about be allowed to stay where it is? And you've said there are big lawns; I reckon they'll be dug up come the spring. They could hold a lot of spuds and sprouts, and rows and rows of peas, an' them gorgeous runner beans, an' even if they don't smell as good as roses they'll taste a deal better.'

'I never thought of that,' Addy said rather dolefully, then brightened. 'But we shan't miss the roses or the lawns, not if it means lots of extra food, because everyone has to do their bit, and when the war's over they'll put the roses back.'

'Ooh, I'd plant the peas myself because peas is one of my favourite things,' Prue said dreamily. 'We *are* going back, are we, Nonny? Only I do love it here, with you and our Mam, and it doesn't seem as though there are going to be bombs.'

'You're going back, just as we'd planned,' Nonny

said firmly. 'For goodness' sake, child, we've not been at war with Germany four months and you can't get much nearer the docks than we are here. I know there are shelters which folk will take to if air raids start, but the best place for young 'uns is the country.'

*　　*　　*

Addy awoke because she was cold, and also because the little alarm clock, which had been her Christmas present from Nonny, was tinkling out the message that it was time to rise. Shivering, she sat up, grabbed the alarm and depressed the button, hoping that the sound had not woken Prue, for she was certain that they would not be going to school today, any more than they had for the past fortnight. In fact they had been lucky to reach the manor before the snow began in earnest, for within a couple of days the roads had become blocked and now drifts higher than Addy's shoulder had formed in all the lanes leading to and from the village.

Things had changed at the manor, too. Because other disabled children and their helpers had not returned after the holiday, a small private boarding school for boys had been billeted on them. Several of the downstairs rooms had been ruthlessly turned into dormitories and the boys, aged from eight to thirteen, had rather taken over. They were nice lads, Addy thought now, wriggling round to see if Prue's eyes were open, but nice or not, a good deal of the attention which had been given to the disabled children now went to the boys. However, Addy thought this fair enough since there were now only three of the original evacuees left at the manor. The others, having returned to Liverpool for the Christmas holiday, had elected either to remain there or to go to a large house on the Wirral, which was judged far enough from the city for safety.

'Addy?' The alarm had not appeared to rouse Prue but perhaps it had been Addy's own scrutiny that had caused Prue's eyes to pop open. 'Oh, Addy, that *bloody* alarm clock! You didn't set it last night, did you? And I was having such a nice dream. Do we really have to get up?'

Addy glanced at the alarm clock's small face and shook her head. 'No, because we'll do what we did yesterday, and the day before, and the day before that. We'll have our breakfast in the kitchen and then go along to the dining room and join in whatever classes the teacher is giving.' She smiled at her sister. 'I quite like it, actually, but isn't it odd having to call the teachers sir instead of miss?'

'It's even odder that they call them masters and not teachers,' Prue pointed out. 'Who's taking today's classes anyway, Addy? It's all writ up on the big cork board by the kitchen door, but I never remember to look.'

'I think it's Mr Sullivan doing maths in the main hall and Mr Barnaby taking geography or history—can't remember which—in the dining room,' Addy said. 'I think I'll come into bed with you to unfreeze before we get up. I tell you one thing though, Prue—when we start lessons at the village school again with Miss Rose and Miss Rachel, we'll be streets ahead of the rest of the class. I'd never even heard of geometry until we started having lessons with the boys!'

She climbed out of bed as she spoke and would have hopped in beside Prue, except that her sister shrieked: 'Bring your own blanket!'

Addy grabbed her bedding, hauled it over to Prue's bed, and climbed in beside her. She thrust her cold feet as far down the sheet as she could reach and then the most amazing thing happened.

'Mind me legs!' Prue squeaked. 'Your perishin' feet are like ice!'

Addy, in the act of snuggling down, shot upright. 'Prue!' she said, her voice rising. 'Oh, Prue! You felt my feet touch your leg! You're not fooling; you actually felt it! Oh, Prue, you're getting better!'

CHAPTER TEN

March 1940

'All right, Neville? I'd like to get back to the *Sparrowhawk* before dark and it's getting dusk already.' Giles had spoken into the intercom because the plane had open cockpits, so pilot and navigator, one seated behind the other, could not otherwise have exchanged a word.

Now, Giles turned his head to give his observer—the navigator's official title—a grin. The two men had been working together since before the start of the war, and trusted one another completely. Neville had been heard to remark that he flew with the best pilot aboard the *Sparrowhawk*, which carried sixty Swordfish, and Giles, not to be outdone, had responded that for his part he was sure that he would have disappeared in to the ocean months ago save for the fact that his observer appeared to have second sight, possessing the ability to find the parent ship for which they searched in the very worst of conditions.

Flying a Swordfish for the RNAS was no sinecure, but having complete confidence in one's navigator, Giles thought, was the most important part of the job. Neville Brown was a highly trained and extremely skilful observer, and after working together for so long the two men had developed an understanding that was practically telepathic.

Now, Neville reached for his bundle of maps and papers, then cursed as he cracked his elbow against the side of the fuselage. The Swordfishes, which the men referred to as 'stringbags', were not large or commodious aircraft. Because they were fitted with long-range fuel tanks they were unable to carry a rear gunner, and it was fortunate that Neville was short, since the space allowed him for his work was minuscule.

'Damn!' Neville rubbed his elbow vigorously. 'You're right, though: the light's fading and the sea's quite rough. But we'll be back in good time if you stick to the course I've plotted.'

Giles grinned again and made a Victory sign over one shoulder; as if he would dream of questioning Neville's navigational skills. 'Good,' he bawled. 'It seems a long time since we ate those stale sandwiches.'

'It is,' Neville shouted back. 'I could do with a hot toddy, too. Me perishin' plates are like ice.'

'What d'you mean to do with a hot toddy? Paddle in it?' Giles shouted. Neville was a cockney, born, he claimed, within the sound of Bow Bells, and Giles had soon become an expert in rhyming slang. 'Well that's something we can be sure of—getting our rum ration, I mean. That's one custom the Navy never stints on. Apart from your feet, are you OK otherwise?'

'Apart from my fingers, the tip of my I suppose and the aforementioned plates, I'm doing fine,' Neville bellowed. 'What about you, mate?'

'I'm OK,' Giles replied laconically. They had been searching for a convoy of enemy shipping thought to be in the area, and had actually seen a U-boat and dive-bombed it, using the torpedo they carried to good effect, though neither man thought they could claim a hit; the Jerry had gone down but there had been no patch of oil to indicate a hit. 'Ah, there she is, the old *Sparrowhawk*, right where you said she would be. Now all we need is a good bats officer to guide us in.'

*　　*　　*

Addy woke early and peered hopefully towards the window, then smiled blissfully. Outside, the June sun was shining from a clear blue sky, which meant that today would be a holiday because the farmers were cutting their hay and every man, woman and child would be helping the war effort by working on the land.

Prue of course could only give very limited help, for though she now had feeling in her legs they still could not support her weight. However, the farmer's wife had said she might give a hand with the preparation of the harvest tea, so Addy planned to take her sister to the farmhouse early and then go to the meadow herself. The farmer's wife said she would push the wheelchair down to the field and Prue could not only help with buttering bread, slicing cake and similar tasks, but also carry some of the boxes of food on her lap.

Addy got carefully out of bed and crossed to the open window, sticking her head and shoulders out and turning her face sideways so that she might bury her nose in the silky petals of the climbing rose, which was in full bloom and free with its fragrance. Glancing down, she remembered what Nonny had said about the rose garden and smiled to herself. When the man from the Min. of Ag. called on them to discuss with Mr Stebbings what should be planted where, he had said that the rich soil in the rose garden must not be allowed to go to waste. 'We'll leave the herbs, they're not taking up much space, and the kitchen garden couldn't be bettered,' the official had said. 'But the lawns will have to be dug over, and that rose garden.'

Mr Stebbings had agreed and, to Addy's joy, had diligently dug and weeded between the rose bushes and planted peas, beans, beetroot and lettuce in long rows, carrots and parsnips round the edges and spinach and sprouts wherever there was a space, leaving every single rose bush undisturbed. 'They can't blame I for misunderstandin' his instructions; I'm just a simple countryman, I am,' he had said, grinning toothlessly at Addy. 'No need to move so much as one bush, let alone the whole lot. Only I'll put some wire nettin' round 'em to keep them durned chickens off or they'll be scrattin' half of 'em out afore they've had a chance to come to anything.' So now Addy drank in the beauty of the roses every morning when she awoke, breathed in the wonderful perfume, and felt privileged.

'Addy?' Prue, awake and leaning up on one elbow, gave Addy the benefit of her most appealing smile. 'I can see it's going to be a beautiful day, but I'm desperate for a wee and a cup of tea. Could you help me on to the po, do you think?'

Addy withdrew reluctantly from her perch. 'Of course I can,' she said, reaching out a long arm and pulling the chamber pot out from its hiding place under the bed. 'Then we'd both better get dressed and downstairs, so we can have our breakfast and get going.'

Presently, after dressing, Addy made their beds, and tidied the room, and then both girls headed for the back stairs that led straight into the kitchen. Prue had grown a good deal in the last six months and she weighed too much now for Addy to carry her downstairs. But Prue had learned to come down on her bottom with her sister's help, though ascending was not so simple. She despised the sling, had done so ever since her legs had begun to improve, but could not as yet manage without it, manned by a couple of sturdy helpers.

Now she reached the end of the flight, saying dreamily as she did so: 'Wish me legs was stronger, so's I could get to the shore. I know the harvest's the most important thing right now, what wi' the war and all, but if I could walk we could go down this evening, when the hay's in.'

Addy went and got the wheelchair. 'It's strange you saying that, because I dreamed about the sea last night . . . just before we woke up, I reckon it was.'

'Tell,' Prue said. 'I love your dreams; they're

always much more fun than mine.'

Addy laughed. 'It was only a short dream, no fun at all really,' she protested. 'I was floating in the sky, looking down on a vast ocean, covered in ships, and then someone called out to me and the ocean disappeared and I was in the hayfield.'

Prue giggled. 'What a daft dream,' she said. 'You know, dreams are meant to have a meaning, if you know how to look for it. I wonder what that one means?'

'It means you and your soppy sister are both round the bend,' Edgar, one of the evacuees, said tauntingly. He was a pompous fifteen-year-old which made him easily the oldest of the boys. He had a shock of untidy red hair and a large Roman nose around which clustered a crop of oozing and disgusting spots that he squeezed whenever he saw a mirror, a habit both sisters thought revolting.

He was heartily disliked by both Addy and Prue; Addy because his first remark upon meeting her was to enquire what the devil she had done to her face, and Prue because he had told her she was just lazy and could walk if she wanted to. Now they shouted, 'Shut your gob!' in unison, having discovered that entering into conversation with Edgar simply laid one open to further and nastier insults.

'Shan't,' Edgar said. 'Why isn't our bloody breakfast on the table, Flora? It's haymaking, you know . . .' He put on a whining, heavily accented voice: 'Oh, we all want to do our bit for our country, don't we? Even little sluts of maidservants . . . ouch!'

Flora's hand had caught the boy neatly around the ear, turning that member scarlet and making

Edgar threaten reprisals, but before he could do anything the kitchen door opened and one of the masters came into the room. 'Good morning, everyone,' he said politely. 'I see you've got the porridge on the go, Flora, and the loaf sliced. Does that mean I can send in the troops?'

Addy looked at Edgar, wondering how much of his last remark the teacher had heard, but Edgar, looking as though butter wouldn't melt in his mouth, was laying the long wooden trestle table at which all the residents of the manor took their meals and Flora, Addy knew, would never tell on anyone, not even the disgusting Edgar.

Flora smiled at the teacher. 'That's right, we'm ready so you can send 'em in,' she said. 'Then you can all be off to help get in the hay.' She tilted her head to look through the kitchen window into the sunny yard. 'That'll be a nice change for Sally an' myself to be out of doors for a whole day.'

As soon as breakfast was finished, Addy and Prue set off for Mrs Simpson's farmhouse, going via the rose garden so that they might enjoy the scents. 'When I've got time I'm going to make labels for each bush so that we know the names of the ones we like best,' Addy said as they lingered by a rose covered in dark red, velvety blooms. 'I used to want to be a teacher when I was old enough, but now I think I'd rather be a gardener.'

'You wouldn't say that in the winter,' Prue observed. 'And you do like teaching, you've said so often.'

'True,' Addy said. She helped in the village school now that her fourteenth birthday had passed, and did enjoy it. But she knew she would have to go to college to get her teaching certificate,

211

and every now and then she thought of the hundreds of other jobs—perhaps thousands—that she might prefer to do and wondered whether she would regret her impulsive agreement to Miss Robinson's scheme for her. For one thing, the idea of joining one of the forces still beckoned, though she hoped that the war would be over before she was old enough to join up.

'If you didn't go for teaching, there are heaps of other jobs in wartime,' Prue said. 'They say if you work in munitions, they pay you lots and lots. Or you could make uniforms, or parts for planes, or parachutes even.'

Addy gave a derisive snort. 'I haven't seen many factories springing up around here,' she pointed out. 'I suppose I could go home to Liverpool; there are lots of factories there and heaps of work, but you couldn't come, Prue. It would be far too dangerous.'

'Then you'll have to stay here and be a teacher, because I won't be left here with only one other girl and lots of spotty boys,' Prue said resentfully. 'Don't you dare leave me, Addy Fairweather. You promised, remember?'

They had traversed the rose garden and were swerving across the big lawn, heading for the drive. As they passed, Addy's skirt brushed against a rosemary bush, adding yet another aroma to that of the roses. 'I won't leave you until you can walk, and when you can you'll be able to come with me wherever I go if you want,' Addy said. She sniffed luxuriously as she continued to push the wheelchair, rather jerkily, across the lawn. 'I can smell the sea! Now summer's here we've really got to find a way to get you down to the shore.

Mr Sullivan was saying that this June is predicted by weather forecasters to be the hottest and driest for years. Which is fair enough when you think how long winter lasted. That Miss Duckett of yours said that swimming would do more for your legs than any other sort of exercise. If only the cliff path wasn't so steep and dangerous, one of the boys, or one of the masters, could teach us both to swim; wouldn't that be wonderful?'

Prue looked suspiciously at her sister from under her lashes. 'You've already been down two or three times,' she said accusingly. 'You wait until I'm in bed and you think I'm asleep, but I've woken up several times to find the blackout blind lowered again and no one in your bed. At first I thought you wanted to use the lav and had gone along to the one up the corridor, but now I believe you go down to the shore.' She twisted in her wheelchair so that she could look her sister in the eye. 'Go on, admit it! I bet someone's teaching you to swim, only you don't like to tell me. As if I'd grudge you something just because I can't do it as well!'

Addy remembered when Prue had in fact grudged her sister any pleasure in which she herself could not share, but that time was now past, so instead of mentioning it she said placatingly: 'Fancy you noticing! I did go down to the shore once when the boys had a midnight feast on the sand and invited me to go along. I had a bit of a paddle, but that was about it, because I was certainly not going to strip, like the boys did, and go right in. I tell you what, Prue: if we could find someone local who really knew the area and enjoyed swimming, we might be able to discover an easier path further along the coast. The trouble is,

213

when we go into the village, we're either shopping or attending school. The local kids all swim, though, so we could ask them where they go.'

Prue shook her head. 'They don't go any more because the bay they used to use has been land-mined and barb-wired in case of invasion. They go all the way to the swimming pool in Plymouth on the bus, but Miss Duckett said it's the salt in the sea which would make swimming possible for me, so a pool isn't any good.'

'I see,' Addy said thoughtfully. 'Well, we'll ask around. I'm sure there must be some way of reaching the shore which isn't as dangerous as the cliff path.'

At this point they entered the farmyard. Addy banged on the back door before wheeling her sister inside. 'Morning, Mrs Simpson, ladies,' she shouted. 'Prue's come to help to make butties and I'm off to the hayfield.'

She was just in time to hear one of Mrs Simpson's helpers say: 'Butties? Do ee mean sandwiches, my heart?'

Prue laughed. 'Aye, that she does, chuck! See you later, Addy.'

*   *   *

Giles and Neville were on the deck of the *Sparrowhawk*, having just tucked their Swordfish up for the night. As the war progressed and they came into contact more often with enemy aircraft, they were beginning to appreciate the stringbags' many good qualities. They were old-fashioned—no one was building biplanes any more—and this meant they were also slow. Modern planes found it downright impossible to fly slowly, so when the enemy got a stringbag in their sights they had whizzed past it before they were able to fire off their guns. Then they could be used for a multitude of purposes, and they were by far the easiest aircraft for a pilot to fly. They had played their part in the evacuation of troops from the beaches of Dunkirk, lumbering overhead and keeping enemy aircraft at bay as the little ships came as close to the shore as they dared to pick up the troops waiting patiently up to their waists in water. The stringbags' top speed was nothing compared with other military aircraft, yet even so their reactions were swift and immediate. Giles remembered doing a landing during his training when he thought he had slowed far too much and would stall any minute. But the little biplane had landed as smoothly as silk at what seemed no more than walking speed, a feat Giles could not imagine any other aircraft matching.

'Penny for your thoughts, Giles?'

'Nosy parker,' Giles said, but as he was beginning to tell Neville what he had been thinking he stopped suddenly, raised his head and sniffed the air. 'Roses!' he said wonderingly. 'Can you smell 'em, Neville? There's a wonderful dark red one in the garden at home and another with pale yellow blooms which climbs up beside my bedroom window; I don't know their names but I can smell the scent as plainly as I can smell the salt on the breeze.'

'No you can't, because we're abaht two hundred miles from the nearest land, and if you can smell roses, you're off your rocker,' Neville said frankly. 'Unless someone's smuggled a leggy blonde aboard, o' course. Or mebbe it's my good self. They say some folk come up out of the you-know-what smelling of roses.'

Giles laughed a trifle unwillingly. 'But I *can* smell roses,' he insisted, then shook his head at himself. 'Well, I thought I could,' he amended. 'It's gone now, worse luck. Nicest scent in the world, roses. Glory, how it takes me back! Just for a moment I could see the house, the grounds, even the rose garden, though God alone knows whether they'll have been allowed to keep it. Dig for victory and all that, I mean,' he finished.

'Well, if they've rooted it up they'll surely replant it when the war's over,' Neville said. 'Your people let the army take it over, didn't they?'

'No fear, not the forces,' Giles said at once. 'Kids . . . disabled ones at first and then, after most of 'em went back home, a private school for boys; you know the kind of thing. My mother reckoned they'd take better care of it than soldiers or sailors—or airmen, come to that. She and my father moved into Plymouth. He's in some sort of official post at the Admiralty and my mother virtually runs the WVS . . . but I've told you all this before, I bet.'

Neville grinned. 'Oh, not more than a dozen times,' he said airily. 'So when you get leave, where will you go? To your parents' little house, or to the manor with the rose garden? You've no girlfriend to shack up with, I do know that.'

'Chance would be a fine thing, stuck out here . . .' Giles said rather wistfully. 'But I shouldn't grumble, and when we do get leave I reckon I'll be fighting the girls off, if only because of the uniform. And I suppose I'll stay with my parents

216

and take the opportunity to visit the manor and have a look round; if it's allowed, that is. I'm not too sure of the rules governing requisitioned houses. But I intend to visit my sister whilst I'm home. We were always very close—I told you she's my twin—and letters aren't the same as a face-to-face encounter. Besides, she's got a feller, and I want to see if he's worthy of her.'

'I don't suppose she'll care whether you like her chap or not, but trust you to poke your nose in,' Neville said. Getting his own back for being called a nosy parker, Giles thought. 'But I don't think you'll need permission to visit your own home, even if it has been requisitioned,' Neville added, turning towards the nearest companionway. 'Come on, it's time for grub and I smell liver and onions!'

*   *   *

Addy was one of the first from the manor to arrive at the hayfield, but after she had strolled around, admiring the deep pink of the wild roses and drinking in the scent of the newly mown hay, the boys began to arrive. Most of the people there she knew, but some were strangers, members of the forces carefully taking off battledress to hang over the gate and rolling up their shirtsleeves in a very determined manner.

When Mr Simpson arrived, leading a big shire horse that would pull one of the wagons when it was laden with hay, pitchforks were handed out. This was not a random business; each pitchfork was a different size and had to be given to a person of suitable height, since it was no use giving an enormous pitchfork to Addy, or a small neat one to a farmhand six feet tall.

After that, the work began in earnest. A week previously, the meadow had been mown and the cut grass left to dry out for two very sunny days. Then the workforce had come back and turned the grass so that the underside could also have its drying time. Today, some of the workers would rake the hay into mounds whilst others would use their pitchforks to lift it on to the wagons. Then it would be taken back to the farmyard and the more experienced men would stack it and thatch each stack so that the hay would be protected from the weather. Since it would have to last all winter, the job of making the stacks was most important and only the farmhands were allowed to undertake that particular task.

Addy thought getting the hay in was great fun, but by the time they paused for dinner she was glad of the rest and sank down beside a flush-faced girl who was the Simpsons' youngest daughter. They knew each other slightly, but Emma Simpson was in her late teens and waiting to be called up, having put her name down to become a Wren, so Addy had not often come in contact with her. However, she was a friendly and forthcoming girl, round-faced and twinkly-eyed, her dark brown hair rolled round a ribbon in the popular style. She settled herself on one of the straw bales that her father had put at the edge of the field, in the shade of a mighty oak, and turned to Addy, holding out a tin full of delicious-looking sandwiches. 'Want one, lover?' she asked. 'It's cold pork and apple sauce, and my mother's home-made bread.' She eyed Addy up and down, though without malice. 'You could do with a bit more flesh on them bones.

Take a couple of these yur sandwiches, 'cos once the fellers get their hands on 'em they'll likely be gone in a trice.'

'Thanks, I will,' Addy said, helping herself. It occurred to her as she began to eat that this plump and friendly girl, having spent her entire life on her father's farm, might well be able to tell her if there was another way down to the shore. She would have to explain that though the boys, herself, and almost everyone else from Foliat Manor had no difficulty in reaching the beach, her sister, confined to a wheelchair, was unable to do so.

As soon as she finished her mouthful, she turned to her companion. 'Emma, you must know this area better than anyone else in the whole world. You know I've got a sister who can't walk . . .'

She told her story simply, but stressed the importance of Prue's needing salt water if she was to learn to swim; stressed also how the lady in Liverpool had thought that swimming would greatly increase Prue's ability to use her legs, not only in the water, but eventually on land as well.

Emma gazed placidly ahead of her, then nodded slowly. 'There *is* another beach, o' course, but 't won't do you no good, lover, because it's been mined. *You* can get down the cliff path on to the Foliat shore, I take it? If you put your sister in one of them things, a harness like, couldn't you get her down that cliff path too? There's plenty of young fellers livin' at Foliat what 'ud give you a hand, I'm sure.'

Addy had begun to say that Prue was frightened of heights when the other girl suddenly slapped her knee, her eyes brightening. 'Of course! The person you should really ask is Miss Gillian, because she

219

spent all her life at the manor and mebbe she'll know a thing or two what us village kids never learned. Why don't you ask her?'

Addy stared at her blankly. 'Who's Miss Gillian?' she asked.

Emma looked astonished, clearly believing that the whole world knew Miss Gillian. 'She'm Gillian Frobisher, the daughter of the folk who own the house you're living in,' she explained. 'When we were kids I used to wonder how they got down to the beach before us, so mebbe there is another path what only the Frobishers knew.'

'Gosh, a secret path!' Addy said, awed. 'But how can I get to meet Miss Gillian? I've never even seen her parents . . .'

Emma laughed and dug Addy quite painfully in the ribs. 'She'm come to help with the haymaking, you daft girl, else I'd not have mentioned her name. She's the tall skinny one, pouring tea from the flask into her mug. Want me to introduce you? Only if there is another way—a secret way—down to the shore, she'll mebbe not want to talk about it in front of me.'

'Right you are,' Addy said, getting purposefully to her feet. 'I'll explain about Prue and how important it is for her to learn to swim in salt water. Thanks ever so much, Emma. You're a brick.'

She was still holding her tin mug when she reached the tall slim girl with the neat pageboy of dark hair, and automatically held it out. The tall girl immediately poured tea into it. Addy thanked her and then asked if she were Miss Gillian Frobisher, whose parents owned Foliat Manor.

'That's me,' the girl said cheerfully. 'Only now I

think of myself as Leading Wren Frobisher and not
"Miss". You must be one of the evacuees living at
my old home. How do you like it? My brother and
I thought it was paradise when we were your age.'

'It is paradise,' Addy said fervently. 'There's only
one thing wrong with it, and that isn't exactly
wrong . . .' As quickly and succinctly as she could,
she explained about Prue, sea bathing and the cliff
path, whilst the former resident of Foliat Manor
('call me Gillian, everyone else does') listened
intently, never taking her large brown eyes from
Addy's face.

When the tale was over, she nodded
understandingly. 'I see; clever of Emma to have
realised that Giles and myself had found a quicker
route. It's down through the pinewoods. It's a good
path, on a gentle slope, but it would be hard work
pushing a wheelchair back up it, I'm afraid.' She
looked thoughtfully at Addy, then lowered her
voice until it was almost a whisper. 'Look, when
the hay's in, will you be free to come out for an
hour after you've had your supper? You might
bring your sister's wheelchair and we'll see whether
our secret way will be any good to you.' She gave
Addy an impish grin which made her look much
younger, less like Leading Wren Frobisher and
more like the Gillian who had once lived at Foliat
Manor, Addy thought.

'Yes, I'm sure no one will notice if I slip out, only
I don't know about bringing the wheelchair,' Addy
said. 'Oh . . . *I* know. If you don't mind Prue
coming along as well, we could pretend we were
just out for a last stroll before bed. They aren't
nearly as strict with us as they are with the boys,
because the teachers who came to look after us at

221

first have gone back to Liverpool. The girls from the village leave as soon as they've served supper and Miss Harkness, who looks after Prue and me, goes to her room immediately after the meal.'

She waited for her new friend to object, to say that Prue in the wheelchair would slow them down, but instead Gillian nodded at once. 'Yes, that's a very good idea. We'd best meet where the pine trees come almost down to the edge of the drive. There's a big old rhododendron . . . d'you know where I mean?'

Addy nodded at once. 'Yes, I know exactly where you mean; shall we say eight o'clock?'

Gillian agreed and then, as the others began to start work again, they followed suit. This time, however, they worked side by side and Addy told Gillian about her home in Liverpool, the difficulties of running a corner shop in wartime, and how wonderful all the evacuees thought Foliat Manor. 'I didn't know anything about the country until we came here, but now I can't even imagine wanting to live in a city again,' she told Gillian.

For her part, Gillian talked mostly about the Wrens. At one point she sighed and for a moment, as she looked down at Addy, the younger girl thought that Gillian reminded her of someone, though she had no idea of whom. When her new friend turned back to her work, Addy took a long look at her thin brown face, with its winged brows and dark eyes that were tilted a little, like a cat's. Who *does* she remind me of, Addy thought. Or perhaps she looks familiar because I've seen her working on the hay without realising who she was. Oh . . . I know! She used to live at Foliat Manor; I bet I've seen her photograph. There's lots of photos in the study, though we don't look through the window much now that the boys are into everything. And then there are the portraits. Sally said once that one could trace a family likeness from the lady with the white ruff up to her chin, and her husband, with his little pointed beard, right down to the Frobishers of the twentieth century. When we get back to the manor, I'll have a good look in the portrait gallery and if Sally's right I'm sure I'll spot the likeness.

Because she had worked so hard, Addy was allowed to ride Ginger, the biggest of the Clydesdales, on his last trip from hayfield to farmyard. She sat up proudly, enjoying the feel of the muscles moving in the big horse's back. When she collected Prue she told her about the planned trip down to the shore that evening and explained about Gillian. Prue was delighted with the thought of a secret expedition and was thrilled at the idea of meeting one of the Frobisher family.

After their evening meal in the manor kitchen the girls, with ostentatious casualness, said that they felt like a breath of air before bed and would go for a stroll in the grounds. The boys had been packed off to bed and Miss Rose and Miss Rachel had retired to their rooms, so Addy was addressing herself only to Mr Sullivan and Mr Bland. Mr Sullivan grunted, but Mr Bland looked up and said, with some surprise, that he would have thought a day haymaking was fresh air enough for anyone.

'But I didn't haymake. I made sandwiches and flasks of tea and it was jolly hot in that kitchen because we baked another dozen loaves and a harvest cake for tomorrow,' Prue said. 'We shan't

223

be long, I don't suppose, and we won't disturb anybody when we come in because we always use the back stairs.'

Addy wondered, a trifle apprehensively, how she would get her sister up those same back stairs on her own, but knew she would manage it somehow. The girls said their good nights and headed, purposefully, for their rendezvous with Gillian.

'I hope she comes,' Prue said as Addy pushed the wheelchair towards the big rhododendron, but before Addy could even begin to reassure her a figure in a dark jumper and trousers came into view, beckoning them to hurry into the shelter of the pine trees.

Addy introduced the two, and Gillian shook Prue's hand and said she hoped that they would be able to reach the shore that very evening. 'But one thing you must promise me,' she said, 'this really *is* a secret path, as you'll see presently, so I want your word that you won't tell anyone else about it.'

Both girls agreed to tell no one and followed Gillian into the pinewood, Addy breathless with anticipation and Prue very solemn and round-eyed. At first, they could see no reason for secrecy, for they merely wended their way amongst the trees, Addy finding it easy to push the chair over the pine needles underfoot, particularly as they were going gently downhill. But presently they came to a chain-link fence more than six feet high and firmly rooted; it would have been impossible for so much as a rabbit to wriggle under it. They stopped short, dismayed, but Gillian turned to them, smiling.

'Looks pretty impassable, doesn't it?' she said. 'Years ago, when Giles and I were quite young, Father sold off the land from here'—she tapped the mighty fence—'to the water's edge, and our nice easy access to the shore was stopped until Giles took it into his head to make us a sort of gate . . .' She tapped the fence again and then wiggled it, pushed, and a section swung back. 'Like this; see? He came down here at midnight with wire cutters and a sort of rasp thing and some pieces of wire, and though we didn't use it too often we soon realised that we were unlikely to be caught. The land was bought by the Admiralty, who wanted to build some sort of secret station, or laboratory; we never did know what. It was awfully hush-hush and no one ever used this path at all, and I bet they still don't. So if you're careful, there's no reason why you can't still get to the shore by our secret way.' She beamed at them. 'What d'you think?'

'I think you're brilliant, you and your brother,' Addy said. 'But what would happen if we *were* caught? We don't want to end up in prison.'

Gillian laughed. 'If you were caught, you'd just have to say you'd come through a big hole in the fence since someone had told you that you could get the wheelchair to the shore this way. But if you're afraid . . .'

Both girls replied indignantly that they were certainly not afraid, though Addy guessed that Prue, like herself, felt some apprehension. However, Gillian told them that now she was in the Navy herself she had made enquiries about the hush-hush station and had been told that it was no longer in use. 'I think it was too small once the war started, and of course the only access to it was by boat and then a scramble up a very rough path, far too narrow for motorised vehicles. And just in case you're worried, it's on the estuary and not the sea,

225

so even if it were still in use, no one would come up or go down by the path I'm going to show you.'

It was not really a path as such, since no one had used it for several years, but Gillian, saying that Addy and Prue might not be able to remember the way, made a mark on each tree with a penknife. 'Coming back, you two will be the guides, and I'll follow your lead,' she said. 'If you get lost, or if you find it too hard to push the wheelchair uphill, then I'm afraid this way will be closed to you.'

The two girls exchanged a quick glance and Addy said, fervently, that she was sure they would remember every inch of the way, even without the trail their new friend had blazed, and presently they emerged on to a tiny narrow bit of beach, with the cliff towering above them. They rounded it and there in front of Addy was the beautiful familiarity of the Foliat shore, with its enormous rocks and deep-sea pools exposed by the low tide.

Prue clapped her hands with joy. 'It's even more beautiful than I imagined,' she breathed. 'I'm sure I'll learn to swim in no time. Oh, Gillian, you are so kind. Thank you!'

Gillian smiled. 'Don't thank me too soon,' she said. 'The most difficult part will be getting you up the path again. I know it's a fairly gentle slope, but there are one or two places which are pretty rough. If it takes Addy and myself to negotiate the steep bits, I'm not too sure how you will go on. Still, no point in meeting trouble halfway; let's get going before you two are missed.'

There were only a couple of places where Addy had real difficulty, but she managed it. Prue sat well forward, keeping an eye cocked for the white marks on the trees, and somehow or other, though not easily, they ascended the path and went through the 'gate' in the fence, closing it carefully behind them and emerging cautiously on to the drive. Then they bade Gillian farewell, thanked her again, and renewed their promise not to tell of the secret path.

They were almost back at the manor when a most disturbing incident occurred. As they wended their way towards the rose garden, heading for the side door that would, they knew, not be locked, a gruff voice sounded behind them and something jabbed Addy in the back.

'Stand and bloody well deliver, you sneaky kid,' the voice said. 'Roamin' the grounds after lights out . . . everyone else thinkin' you're in bed and snorin' fit to deafen the rest of us and here you are, cool as cucumbers, marchin' across the garden as though you had a special right!'

Addy froze, thinking that it was a gun she felt between her shoulder blades, but then she recognised the voice. She swung round, snatched the stick from Edgar's hand and tried to hit him with it. 'Sneaky yourself!' she said hotly. 'Where did you spring from, you horrible spy?'

Edgar grinned nastily. 'Saw you scuttlin' down the drive from my window, when the rest of us were gettin' ready for bed,' he said. 'You aren't the only ones who wait till the masters are out of the way and then have a bit of a look round. I thought you'd be after the radishes or the peas, so I followed you down, only you went straight and into the pinewood. You met up with some feller so of course I followed you, wondering what you were up to.'

Addy stared at him, feeling a cold clutch of

dismay. Of all the people in the world she most wanted to avoid becoming involved with, Edgar Wilkinson came top of the list. 'How—how far did you follow us?' she faltered.

'All the way down to the shore,' Edgar said triumphantly. 'I'm the last of the Mohicans, I am, silent as a shadow and as swift as an arrow from a bow . . .'

'Sneaky and nosy and sly,' Addy said furiously. 'Whatever shall we do now? We promised Gillian we'd never tell a soul and she'll think we broke our word. She'll be so upset . . . oh, Edgar, you're the most hateful—'

'You mean it was a girl?' he said wonderingly. 'A girl in a black jersey and trousers? Huh, funny friends you have!'

'There's nothing funny about Gillian. She and her parents—'

Addy had been about to spill the beans when Prue interrupted. 'Edgar, I think it was pretty bright of you to spot us and follow us all the way down to the shore. I know we left the gap open when we went down, but we shut it behind us when we came back and Gillian fastened it with two bits of wire. Did you have an awful job to get it undone again? Gillian had some sort of pincher thing to wind the wire and close the gap.'

'No, it was easy,' Edgar said. 'And if you were to ask me nicely, I dare say I'd promise not to tell anyone else. After all, why should those spoilt little sissies know another way down to the shore?'

Addy realised that Prue had said exactly the right thing and hastened to back her sister up. 'Oh, Edgar, if you really would promise not to tell, we'd be eternally grateful,' she said. 'You see, Prue has

228

been told that if she could find a deep salt water pool she might be able to swim even though her legs don't work properly, so this path is truly important to us.'

'I can swim; I could teach the pair of you,' Edgar said eagerly. 'I'll let you in to *my* secret, if you like. You know I'm older than the rest? Well, when I was eleven, I got rheumatic fever. I missed school for two whole years, so that's why I'm in class with fellers so much younger'n me. They're tryin' to help me catch up—the masters, I mean—but it makes me a bit of an odd man out, like.'

'Oh, I see,' Addy said, enlightened. She had often wondered why Edgar was so much older than his companions; now she had the answer. But the information would not affect his knowledge of the secret path if he chose to tell, perhaps in an effort to curry favour. 'But won't the other boys wonder how you reach the shore if you use the secret path? If one of them were to follow you . . . look, I don't mean to be nasty, but us knowing why you're older than the rest needn't stop you telling on us. Quite the opposite, in fact.'

'They won't find out about the secret path; I'll make sure of that,' Edgar said. 'And if I did split on you, you could tell the fellers I was a sneak and a liar, and they'd be even more horrible to me than they are already. Say, why don't the three of us have a pact? We could mingle our blood like the Indians used to do and call ourselves the Mohicans. No, I know—the Mohican gang! And we'll swear only to visit the shore by our path when no one else is down there. Gee, think of their faces if they knew!'

'It sounds OK,' Addy said rather dubiously. 'But

you know what you're like, Edgar. You don't like me or Prue, and sooner or later . . .'

'I like you all right, it's you who don't like me,' Edgar said, quite indignantly, Addy thought. 'You say horrible things about my spots, and you poke fun because my hair is ginger, and—'

'We will like you if you'll keep our secret and be our pal the way you said just now,' Prue cut in. 'Come on, agree! And I'll tell you something else. I'm going to call you Ed, or Eddie if you'd rather, instead of Edgar. What d'you say?'

Edgar grinned at them. He looked rather nice when he grinned, Addy thought, surprised that she had never noticed it before. But then she remembered that he hardly ever smiled, let alone grinned. For the first time it occurred to her that perhaps Edgar had become unpleasant because of the way he was treated and not the other way around.

'I'd like to be called Ed,' he said. 'It's easier to say than Edgar and nicer than Eddie, which sounds too like Addy, anyway.' By now they had reached the side door and he opened it for them, then rumpled Prue's hair as she was pushed past him. 'See you in the morning, girls!' He lowered his voice to a conspiratorial murmur. 'And we'll have you swimming in no time, young Prue, see if we don't!'

*   *   *

When autumn came, Nell left Nonny in charge of the shop and paid a visit to the manor. Because it was such a long and tedious journey, she hadn't been able to make the trip before, though the girls

230

had returned home the previous Christmas and meant to do so this year as well.

The big disappointment during Nell's visit to the manor, so far as Addy and Prue were concerned, was that they could only show Nell her daughters' aquatic abilities in the swimming pool in town. They had promised Gillian to share their secret with no one, which meant they could not tell Nell about their private path down to the shore. Prue had become quite tearful after they had taken their mother to the swimming pool, because she knew she had not appeared to advantage in the water. Her legs refused to function properly, and when others swam across her path, or bumped into her, she panicked and began to sink. Maddeningly, she could not even hint how much better she swam in the saltwater pools with only Addy and Ed for company, because Nell would naturally want to know how she reached the shore. They had shown her the cliff path, but Nell, who was terrified of heights, had not gone within half a dozen yards of the edge, and had been obviously glad to turn her back on what must have seemed a giddying drop, though in fact, as Addy had tried to point out, the path zig-zagged and was nowhere near as dangerous as her mother imagined.

In every other way, however, Nell's visit was a great success. She told the girls that though she herself was not a countrywoman, and found several aspects of the manor downright frightening, she envied the way they had adjusted to an entirely different sort of life.

Addy was frankly puzzled by her mother's fears. Nell disliked the quiet and the complete darkness. She hated being woken at the crack of dawn by cockerels announcing the new day and, even worse, the hooting of the owls in the pinewood and the triumphant shriek of a hunting bird as it fell upon its prey.

'Don't you miss *people*?' Nell asked Addy, when they had walked into the village to buy toffees with Nell's sweet coupons. 'Oh, I know there aren't many folk about at night, even on the Scottie, but there's always someone. Air raid wardens, civil defence people, fire watchers . . . and then there are all the cinemas and theatres, the pubs, and folk catching the early tram to work and coming home on the late one . . . that's what I'd miss if I were you.'

Addy laughed. 'I suppose you could say we miss it all right, the way you miss a bad cold in the head, or a teacher who's got it in for you,' she said. 'Though it was lovely to come back to the city last Christmas, to meet old friends and ask the customers what they're doing now. I used to think I would envy the girls working in factories because they earn good money and are all friendly with each other, but now I think differently. D'you know, Mam, some of the girls making components for aircraft—radios and the like—told me that they get into trouble if they chat, and the bosses don't much like it if they even need to go to the lavvy during a shift. I know the war effort is enormously important, but I tell myself I'm doing my bit as a pupil teacher. So even though the money isn't very good at all, I still wouldn't swap with any of my pals back in Liverpool.'

CHAPTER ELEVEN

Addy had thought that the time between her mother's visit and their going home to Liverpool for Christmas would drag on leaden feet, but in fact it passed like lightning and was not without events which brought the war home even to the inhabitants of the manor.

At the end of November, the children were in their rooms getting ready for bed when the siren sounded and sent them scuttling for the cellar, which had been made into a splendid underground shelter and supplied with everything the staff considered necessary for a fair number of people who might have to spend many hours confined there.

As soon as she heard the air raid warning Addy bundled Prue into her warm dressing gown and slippers, and slung an extra blanket round her sister's shoulders. She was trying to carry Prue down the stairs when Edgar appeared and took her burden from her.

'I'll take her down to the cellar while you go back and get something warm on yourself,' he said roughly. 'Not that it's likely to affect us—the raid, I mean—because I reckon they'll be aiming for the docks again.'

'Thanks, Ed,' Addy said breathlessly, happy to release her sister into stronger and safer hands. 'I hate the noise the planes make going over, and I still can't tell friend from enemy just by the sound of the engine. But you're right, I'd best get my dressing gown and slippers.'

Addy scampered up the stairs again and went to peer out of her bedroom window whilst she buttoned her dressing gown and scuffed her feet into her worn old slippers. The night was clear and sparkling cold; every tree was rimed with frost so that the garden gleamed like a beautiful Christmas decoration, glittering as brightly as the stars in the dark sky above.

The heavy door at the top of the cellar steps was closed, but she tugged it open and stepped inside, to be met by the smell of damp wood, mould and candles. Carefully, Addy closed the door behind her and fumbled her way down the stone steps. Mr Sullivan stood at the foot of them and wagged a finger at her in admonition. 'You're late, young lady,' he said reprovingly. 'What's happening out there? There was one heck of an explosion a few minutes ago and I wondered if they'd hit an ammunitions dump or one of the big warships anchored in the dock.'

'I don't know what it was they hit, but it lit up the whole sky in the direction of Plymouth. Showers of sparks were going up when I looked out of my bedroom window,' Addy told him.

'I'll just nip up for a moment and take a look,' Mr Sullivan murmured as Addy took her place on the bench between Prue and Edgar. They smiled sleepily at her, both now well wrapped in blankets they had taken off the bunk beds which had been erected in the cellar. Addy settled down and pulled her own blanket more tightly round her. She had almost nodded off, though she was still sitting up, when Mr Sullivan returned and told them all to get into the bunks. 'We'll spend the night here and find out what's happened to poor old Plymouth when daylight comes,' he said.

*   *   *

Although Plymouth had suffered several air raids since the phoney war had ended, the raid in which the Admiralty oil fuel depot had been destroyed was easily the worst. The fires lasted for four days and Turnchapel railway station was put out of action. When Prue heard that the people of Turnchapel had been evacuated to Plympton and that no trains could run until massive repair work had been carried out, she burst into tears, convinced that they would be unable to return to Liverpool and would lose their Christmas at home, for which they had planned for weeks now.

However, Mr Sullivan reminded them that Plymouth North Road, which was the main station, was still functioning. Also, the town was an important port for many ships, which meant that in order to get the seamen to and from their homes and vessels rail links were essential, and sure enough, once the fires were out, gangs of workmen were drafted in to tackle the necessary repairs.

So the girls continued to make their plans for Christmas and in due course set off for Liverpool with a friendly fellow passenger who had offered to keep an eye on them. It was a long and tedious journey, and they arrived in Lime Street in total darkness. The entrances and exits were dimly lit, casting a ghostly blue light on the faces of passers-by. So strange did people look that Addy very nearly pushed Prue past Nell and her companion; indeed she did not recognise the latter until, greetings over, her mother said rather

235

reproachfully: 'Aren't you going to say hello to Mr Bentley? He was kind enough to say he would carry your suitcase and push the wheelchair too, if necessary.'

Addy turned round, astonished eyes on the man standing next to her mother. He looked completely different in a cloth cap, check scarf and thick winter coat, and Addy realised that though she had seen him often in the past it had always been in the pub. They had met out of doors in summertime, of course, but never in winter. She was surprised when she held out her hand and he ignored it, taking her shoulders in his large capable hands and kissing her cheek instead. 'Hello, love; nice to see you and your sister after so long,' he said.

He bent over and gave Prue a kiss too and Addy noticed, with some dismay, that as soon as he straightened up her sister scrubbed vigorously at her cheek. Oh, dear, Addy thought, I do hope Prue isn't going to be difficult. She's always been very possessive over Mam, but things were much easier last Christmas because Mam and Mr Bentley were friends again. I'll remind her of that as soon as we get home and Mr Bentley has left. Aloud, she said: 'Thanks, Mr Bentley. That case is really heavy. But who have you left in charge of the Vines? I s'pose Nick's at work.'

'That's right,' Mr Bentley said. 'Paul's working too, of course, but Mrs Bithell is there to keep an eye on things and I reckon I'll be back before opening time.'

'I've asked Josh—Mr Bentley, I should say—to come back to the flat and have high tea with us,' Nell said. 'Nonny will have everything ready and she'll shut the shop early. To tell you the truth,

236

what with rationing and all these coupons and points, we close at five o'clock two or three days a week now. The amount of red tape which rationing has brought to small shopkeepers means I spend as much time filling in forms and clipping out coupons and points as I do serving our customers.'

'It's the same at the Vines,' Mr Bentley said, a trifle breathlessly, for he had insisted on pushing the wheelchair *and* carrying the suitcase; no mean feat. When Addy had been managing alone she had put the suitcase on Prue's lap, but Mr Bentley had scoffed at the idea, saying that he could manage both easily, with one hand tied behind him if necessary.

So Addy, unburdened for once save for her shabby handbag, was able to look about her as they walked. She knew Liverpool had suffered several bombing raids, but there was little sign of it here, though of course the blackout could hide all sorts, she supposed. She said as much to Nell, who told her that at the end of November the city had had two nights of intensive raids. 'They got the Technical School in Durning Road that first night,' she told her daughter, 'and did more damage the second night. They don't say much on the news because they don't want the Germans to know how successful they've been, but they reckon near on two hundred people were killed when that school collapsed, 'cos they were in a big old shelter under the building. When it's light, you'll see devastation everywhere.' She patted Addy's hand. 'But you're not that far from Plymouth, and they took a real pasting!'

Addy nodded sagely. 'Yes, and it'll get worse; everyone says so. They're just getting our measure.

237

But I'm hoping they'll give it a rest over Christmas because the Luftwaffe pilots must want to be in their own homes then, the same as our boys do. Prue and me want to go shopping; I hope Paddy's Market is still functioning?'

Nell said it was and Addy hoped that she and Prue might have time the following day to visit it, for though they had done their best, they had not managed to buy anything really pretty for their mother in Plymouth. Prue had knitted her a bright pink beret and matching scarf and had made something similar for Nonny, only in blue, but Addy, unable to so much as hem a handkerchief, had had to be satisfied with a small brooch for Nonny in the shape of a maple leaf and some cheap little earrings for her mother.

Back at the flat, they were greeted with cries of pleasure and kisses from Nonny. Addy thought her grandmother looked worn and tired. Her face seemed thinner and her black hair was streaked with white. When the meal was over and they were washing up, however, Nonny told her that she had run out of hair dye and meant to spend the following day searching every shop for a supply. Addy, drying up the cutlery whilst Nonny washed, gave her grandmother an exuberant hug. 'You old cheat! You and your gypsy blood! Why, I remember you telling Prue and me that gypsy men never went bald and gypsy women never went white, so you can take your choice, Mrs Hammond: either you ain't a gypsy, or gypsies go white just like everyone else.'

Nonny gave a gurgle of amusement. 'You've got me there,' she admitted. 'At a guess I'd say gypsies are just like other folk. Only the men use badger

238

grease on their hair and mebbe it's true that the stinking stuff acts like fertiliser and keeps the hair on their heads where it belongs.' She finished washing the crockery and crossed to the small mirror hanging beside the kitchen door, examined her reflection critically for a moment and then turned back to her granddaughter. 'There isn't much white in my hair, it just looks worse because the rest is so black,' she announced. 'And now let's join your mam and Prue in the sitting room. We could have a hand of cards, if you'll enjoy that.'

She would have left the room, but Addy put a restraining hand on her arm. 'Hang on a minute, Nonny. I know Mr Bentley popped in and said goodbye when we began the washing up, but just what *is* going on? And don't say nothing because we're neither of us blind. Last Christmas it was "Mr Bentley" and "Mrs Fairweather"; now it's "Josh" and "Nell" and—and Mr Bentley knows where everything's kept, because he laid the table for tea, so it's pretty clear this was by no means his first visit. Is he going to become our stepfather, and if so, do you think it's a good thing?'

Nonny sighed deeply. 'I knew you'd notice; you're a couple of bright kids, you and Prue. Yes, he's become very friendly with your mother, though he's not pushing it, if you understand me. He seems quite content to let your mother set the pace, which is a good thing . . . oh, Addy, I wouldn't tell anyone except you, but I've a bad feeling about the whole business. I know you laugh at me, but when I get a premonition of danger or trouble I heed it, and whenever I see Josh Bentley making sheep's eyes at your mother there's a cold feeling inside me.'

Addy had opened her mouth to ask Nonny what made her distrust Mr Bentley when the kitchen door opened and Prue wheeled herself slowly into the room. 'Mam's nipped down to the shop. She thought it might be fun to play cards, so she's gone to get a box of matches to use as money, and some sweeties as well,' she said in a breathy whisper. 'So I thought I'd come and ask you what's going on, Nonny. Between Mr Bentley and Mam, I mean.'

'Well, they're good friends, and we all need every friend we can get in wartime,' Nonny said cautiously.

Prue sniffed. 'Oh, well, p'raps it's nothing,' she said hopefully. 'I like Mr Bentley, but I don't like Josh!'

Addy and Nonny both laughed and Nonny, hearing her daughter's footsteps on the stairs, hastily changed the subject. Addy knew that though her grandmother was deeply worried, she would do nothing to interfere. She would say that Nell was old enough to make her own decisions, that Mr Bentley was a good man and that his sons would doubtless approve of his marrying someone they had known and liked all their lives. She would not voice the fears that she had shared with Addy.

Sighing, Addy joined the rest of the family in the living room. No point in worrying over something that might never happen. She sat down on the sofa next to Prue and began to deal the cards.

*   *   *

It was a good thing that Addy and Prue had decided that it was important to attack the shops as soon as possible, since within a very few days of

240

their return the raids began again. However, though the Luftwaffe were undoubtedly aiming for the docks, Scotland Road remained relatively undamaged, and despite rationing and shortages both girls thoroughly enjoyed their Christmas at home. Because of war work, the usual family party was not possible, and they spent Christmas Day at home in the flat with only the Bentleys and Nonny for company. Boxing Day was spent at the Vines and they went round to Uncle Lionel's for high tea on another day, finishing up at Aunt Sadie's, where Prue pretended to search the gutter for cabbages.

*　　　*　　　*

'There she blows! By Christ, Neville, this isn't going to be a piece of cake by a long chalk! Hold on to your hat, feller!'

Giles, tired and drained after six hours in the air, had privately wondered when and even if they would sight the parent ship, but good old Neville, calmly plotting their course and adding on the number of sea miles the *Sparrowhawk* would have travelled since they had taken off early that morning, had had no such doubts. 'Told you so,' he said laconically. 'Be a bit of a bumpy landing, though. Oh, damn it, here comes a Messerschmitt. We'll give it a quick burst with the guns and then try to ignore it whilst we position ourselves for landing.'

The enemy aircraft was above them but levelling out to attack as it passed, and Giles breathed a silent prayer that the pilot would not have realised yet that the plane he was attacking had no great speed but could turn on a sixpence. Let the Jerry

241

be inexperienced . . .

He must have been, since he passed them at high speed, his gunner firing all the time. If he had known anything at all about the stringbags he would have lowered his flaps and his undercarriage and reduced his speed as much as he possibly could without stalling the engine, but this chap came on at full throttle, guns beginning to blaze a good twenty yards in front of the British craft, and then turned to repeat the manoeuvre—and stalled. The Messerschmitt staggered, then went into a steep dive. Giles saw the parachutes blossom but doubted whether the men would be picked up with the sea running so dangerously high.

'One for us,' Neville bawled. 'Now let's get this crate down before anything else happens.'

Giles nodded and lined up for his landing and presently he touched the deck, bounced a good six feet in the air, and just managed to bring the stringbag to a halt before he nearly mowed down the small figure waving them in. Stiffly, he and Neville climbed out of the plane and Giles grinned ruefully at the white-faced bats officer. 'Sorry about that,' he said. 'But the sea's too rough for a normal landing. And we downed a Messerschmitt. Did you see?'

'I did,' the bats officer said, recovering his poise. 'You're the last home today, thank God. And it's bully beef stew and spuds for supper, so if you want a share, best get below.'

Still tired and stiff, the two men made for the mess deck. When the meal was finished, Giles found a quiet spot—not easy on such an enormous and busy ship—fished a letter out of his pocket and felt a warm glow as he turned to the first page. It was from Gillian and had been written the previous summer. He had received many since, but had kept this one because it dealt with his twin's visit to their old home and drew a comforting picture both of Foliat Manor and of his parents' odd little house in Plymouth. It even mentioned the evacuees.

Gillian had been posted to the north of Scotland recently, as secretary to an important member of the Admiralty, and the long, newsy letters that she used to send to him had almost ceased. Giles knew that she no longer had time to write at great length to him because, as he had told Neville some time ago, she had a boyfriend, a war artist of all things, and though he tried not to resent the slackening of her interest in himself he could not always help feeling bitterly jealous of this Dominic Cranshaw. Giles and Gillian had had little time for others when they had been growing up. Now he had to acknowledge that someone else meant more to her than he did, and, like a dog who dislikes its dinner, he tried to bury it, to ignore it, to deny it, in fact.

Now he turned to the letter. He had been amused and enchanted by her account of her meeting with the two little evacuees living at Foliat Manor, particularly since she had admitted revealing the secret of their own private path down to the beach, explaining that the younger girl was paralysed from the waist down and could not otherwise have visited the shore.

They're a couple of nice kids, Gillian had written. *And I made them promise not to tell another soul. They promised, of course, because when they lived at home—they hail from*

Liverpool—they were told that the thing most likely to help the younger girl's legs to regain some strength was learning to swim in saltwater. After they told me that, I didn't have the heart to keep the secret of our own special way to the shore from them.

A couple of days later, I went up to the manor to have a look around. The staff were quite happy for me to do so and honestly, Giles, you wouldn't recognise some of the rooms because they've been turned into dormitories and classrooms. They've done their best to see that it's not ruined by the changes, but the dining table has disappeared and the room is full of desks. They eat their meals in the kitchen, just as we did, but oh, Giles, the garden! They've dug up the croquet lawn and planted potatoes and the side lawn under the cedar tree is cabbages and cauliflowers. The rose garden isn't so bad because clever old Mr Stebbings has planted between the rose bushes: salad stuff, peas, broad beans, beetroot, radishes—oh, you know the sort of thing. I was so glad he'd managed to keep the roses because some of those big bushes must be nigh on a hundred years old.

Anyway, when I left, the older of the two girls, the one not in a wheelchair, came belting down the drive after me and said she had a confession to make. Apparently, one of the schoolboys had followed us down to the shore. Addy—that's her name—assured me that the boy had sworn never to tell another soul, so I suppose that was all right. Probably there's no need for all this secrecy now that the hush-hush station has been *abandoned anyway, but in any case it was fun to revisit the old place and to see it being put to good use.*

The letter had gone on to explain that she had regaled her parents with the description of the manor and its grounds, which had greatly relieved their minds. Her father had said they were lucky that the army or Navy had not taken the place over, since the chaos left by the forces after the Great War ended had been legendary.

Giles had replied, of course, saying that when he got some decent leave he, too, would visit the manor and see for himself how things went on. But for the moment, leave seemed an impossible dream.

Oddly enough, when he had first received Gillian's letter regarding the two sisters who had been evacuated to his old home, the coincidence of the older child's being called Addy, the name of the girl he himself had met whilst in Liverpool, had not occurred to him, but it did so now. It must be simply a coincidence; from what he remembered, Liverpudlians were fond of nicknames and probably there were a dozen or more girls named Addy living in the area he had visited.

Despite Gillian's own backsliding in the matter of letters, he still wrote to her whenever he had the time, so now he went and fetched writing materials from his locker and settled down to tell her what had been happening to him lately. After describing the downing of the Messerschmitt, he raised the point that the elder of her two evacuees had the same name as the child he had taken to hospital after her accident.

It's strange that I didn't notice the coincidence of the name when you first mentioned the sisters, he wrote. *Of course, they couldn't possibly be the same ones because the younger girl came out of it pretty well unscathed; it was the older one—Addy—whose face was such a mess, though the doctor swore she would be good as new once the stitches came out.*

Giles chewed the end of his pencil and frowned. He knew the family had lived above a shop, and he even remembered that their mother's name was Nell, but he only remembered that because he had once owned a border collie with the same name. He regretted that he had not kept in touch with the family, but after all, why should he? A chance meeting with a couple of kids scarcely merited a correspondence between the parties, but now of course, when he was so dependent upon letters, he rather wished that he had given them his name and address. He was pretty sure that, had he done so, Addy would have written to him. Ah well, he had done nothing about it at the time and it was much too late now. If only he could remember their surname! It had been written in faded gold lettering above the shop, but for the life of him he could not bring it to mind. Perhaps one day, when the war was over, he would revisit the city and try to find the shop.

Picking up his pencil again, he tried to remember the contents of his twin's last letter, but his mind refused to co-operate; it was still fretting at that name above the shop window and wondering what had become of the little family. Nell something or other and an old grandmother whose name began with an H. Harris? Holland? Hammond? But the memory eluded him. He was only sure of the name Nell, which wouldn't get him far. Giving up, he pulled the paper towards him and began, laboriously, to write.

*   *   *

Nell sat at the big table in the kitchen of the Vines public house, reflecting that the letter she was trying to write was the most difficult of her life. It was addressed, of course, to Addy and Prue and would break news which she rather feared would be unwelcome to them, though some would have thought it a matter for rejoicing rather than the weeping and wailing she anticipated.

It was now several weeks since the Luftwaffe had targeted Liverpool and the town had been almost destroyed in the Blitz. The fires had been put out, however, and things were beginning to return to normal, but Nell thought that the enemy must know they had achieved their objective. The destruction was unbelievable; the approaches to the docks were full of sunken ships and the docks themselves a shambles. Warehouses and offices had been flattened, and the corner shop of which Nell had been so proud was no more. Nonny's home, too, had been destroyed, though fortunately her lodger had been on ARP duty at the time, and Nonny herself in the shelter with Nell. She knew how lucky they were, however, compared to some of their neighbours. Old Mr and Mrs Foggit had been killed, along with their elderly spaniel, Floss, who was the reason they had not gone to the

247

nearest shelter. The warden in charge, a cross-grained greengrocer constantly grumbling about the effect the war was having on his business, disliked dogs and refused to allow them in his shelter. So poor Floss and her elderly owners had made themselves a bed under their dining table and had been killed on the third day of the raids.

'How are you getting on, queen?' Nonny came into the kitchen and tutted disapprovingly when she peered over Nell's shoulder and saw the almost blank sheet of paper. 'Now this isn't like you, Nell my girl. Do you want me to break the news to them? I hope you ain't tempted to keep them in the dark because it won't do; they deserve better from us than that.'

'I know,' Nell said miserably. She lowered her voice. 'It was comparatively easy telling them that the shop and the flat had received a direct hit and that Mr Bentley had invited us to move into the Vines to work in the bar. But telling them Josh and I are going to get wed . . .'

'It's never too late to change your mind,' Nonny observed. She went over to the sink and began to wash up the breakfast dishes. 'It's been good of Mr Bentley to take us in, but I know you, Nell. You'll work every hour God sends to pay him back for his hospitality. I'm telling you straight, love, that there's no need to marry him as well. Believe me, he should be grateful that you're working for him for the sort of money most women would sniff at now that factory work is so well paid. If you marry 'im, I dare say he'll not pay you a penny.'

Nell laughed. 'Husbands don't pay wives,' she observed. 'And it *is* too late to change my mind. After all, I turned him down once; to do it twice would be unforgivable.'

Nonny shrugged and turned back to her work. 'Please yerself,' she said crossly. 'I minded me own business when he began to make his intentions clear, but I'm telling you straight, queen, that you're makin' the biggest mistake of your life.'

*　　　*　　　*

It was a glorious June day and Addy and Prue were having breakfast when the letter from their mother arrived. Around them, the boys were eating toast with rhubarb and ginger jam, and drinking weak tea sweetened with saccharin. Some of them had had letters from home too, which they were reading eagerly, though Addy noticed that the younger boys were finding it hard work to keep back tears. Letters were wonderful—everyone looked forward to receiving them—but sometimes they brought it home to the recipients how much they missed their parents and families.

Prue read Nell's letter first, uttering squeaks of dismay as she completed each page and handed it to Addy. When she had read the last word, right down to *Your loving mother*, she turned a horrified gaze on her sister. 'Oh, Addy, can you believe it? Mr Bentley's divorce is absolute and our mam's going to marry him on the twenty-eighth and wants us to go home to be bridal attendants, whatever that may mean. Well I bloody well won't! I don't want to live in a pub and come to that I don't want to live with Mr Bentley either, nor I don't want Paul and Nick to be my brothers. They're OK as pals, but being brothers would make them think they could boss us about. I bet I'll spend me life washing up and cleaning, and then there's that awful smell of stale beer, and the sandwiches he'll expect us to make. I'm going to write back to Mam and tell her I can't leave school now because of exams and haymaking, and you can't possibly go either, Addy. They pay you to be a pupil teacher, even if it isn't much, and if you just walk out on them they might take your job away.' She looked anxiously up into her sister's face. 'We won't go back for the wedding, will we? It isn't as if Mr Bentley were young and handsome; he's got a big belly and a big nose and little eyes. I don't see why our mam wants to marry him . . . he's old, too, a lot older than our mam.'

'I reckon Mam's marrying him because, what with the shop and Nonny's flat both gone, she's got nothing to do and nowhere to go,' Addy said, quickly scanning the last page of the letter for herself. 'I know she says she's working at the Vines, but it's not the same, is it? If she marries Mr Bentley, then the Vines will be half her business . . . at least I suppose it will. As for going back for the wedding, we'll simply have to, chuck. It would be an awful insult, both to Mr Bentley and to our mam, if we weren't there, because I'm sure Nick and Paul will be.' Addy pushed aside her plate of half-eaten toast, stood up and seized the wheelchair handles. 'I'll get permission from Miss Robinson to let us both go home for a few days. No, don't scowl and pout; although I'm fifteen and working, so far as Mam and Nonny are concerned—and Mr Bentley, of course—we're just a couple of kids. Oh, how I hate the horrible Nazis! If it wasn't for them, we'd never have to call Mr Bentley Uncle Josh, as Mam suggests, and things could go on just as before.'

*   *   *

Although Nell would never have admitted it, she was not at all sure that by marrying Josh Bentley she was doing the right thing. She knew of course that she did not love him, but had accepted his declaration that he had love enough for two. He had certainly shown every good intention and had promised every effort to make their marriage work. He had welcomed Nonny into his household and was paying her a very good wage, though Nell thought her mother earned every penny. He had also promised to pay Nell, even after their marriage. He said he would call it a housekeeping allowance, but it was a very generous one and Nell, knowing how shortages had affected the Vines, as they had affected her own little shop, hoped he was not digging into his savings in order to pay her, but thought it quite possible.

He had been the perfect gentleman as regards their relationship, and the fact that they were living under the same roof. When they parted at the end of each day, he would squeeze her hand and give her a chaste kiss on the brow or the cheek, but he never took advantage of their proximity, not even after he had bought her the most beautiful engagement ring. She had told him it was not necessary, that she still wore her wedding band and the little ring Bert had given her, but Josh had suggested that she might wear his ring on her right hand until she was, at last, Mrs Bentley. He agreed that it would be perfectly permissible for her to continue to wear the wedding band she and Bert had bought together since, in any event, she could not get if off.

Now, making beds, whilst the cleaners tackled the bar and the kitchen, Nell thought about her wedding. It would not be a white one, of course, but she had a very smart navy suit, and as soon as she had heard that the girls were able to come back for the day itself she had combed the city for a couple of pretty dresses for them to wear. Everything, in fact, was going according to plan. She had appealed to all her relatives to bring food instead of wedding presents, and she and Nonny had searched the shops for anything off ration that they could purchase for the wedding reception.

Nell and Nonny had one night off a week, when they ventured out to a nearby church hall for a whist drive, but on the Thursday before the wedding they thought they would have to give cards a miss, since Addy and Prue were arriving from Devon.

Josh, determined that the girls should know they were welcome as flowers in spring, had arranged for them to sleep in the large bedroom on the first floor, next to the one which he and Nell would occupy as soon as they were married. At present Nell shared the third bedroom on the first floor with Nonny, and the boys had been relegated to the attic, though only Paul lived permanently at home, since Nick had joined the air force some time before.

Getting Prue up the stairs would not be as difficult, Addy had written, as it had once been. Prue could haul herself from tread to tread, for her legs had improved with the sea bathing. She could even stand for a few seconds, though so far she had not taken even one step. Addy had said in her last letter that she thought her sister suffered from a lack of confidence and a fear of falling and making herself worse, but she truly thought that Prue was on the road to recovery at last.

The girls arrived and were polite to Josh, though Nell noticed that they tried not to address him directly. When Paul returned they were somewhat cool towards him, but Nell hoped that they would resume their old friendship after a day or two in one another's company, for Addy and Prue were to stay from Thursday until the following Tuesday. This would enable them to give Nonny, Mrs Chambers and Mrs Bithell such help as they needed whilst Josh and herself were on a short honeymoon in Blackpool. They intended to catch a train before the reception was over on the Saturday, and would return on the Wednesday.

Now, supper over, Nonny asked the girls what they would like to do and was not particularly surprised when they opted for bed. Paul too said he could do with an early night since he was starting work at the crack of dawn the next day. 'If Prue and I could have a bath first that would be lovely,' Addy said wistfully. 'I don't know why it is, but travelling by train makes me feel grimy all over.' She turned, politely, to her host. 'Would that be all right, Mr—I mean Uncle Josh? I know there are rules about hot water, but if Prue and I share the tub . . .'

'That will be fine,' Josh said heartily. He turned to Nell. 'If the children are going early to bed, you and Nonny can have your evening off after all. No, don't be foolish. It's your night off and I see no reason why you shouldn't both enjoy your usual

253

game of whist. I'll hold the fort here, so you can leave as soon as they're all in bed.'

Nell demurred, but Nonny shook her head chidingly at her. 'Don't be silly, Nell. Half the whist club have bought little wedding presents which they plan to hand over this evening; I know that for a fact. Don't deny them the pleasure of giving.'

Nell smiled fondly at her mother. 'As if I would! I enjoy our evenings at the whist club, so we'll go as usual and I'll invite them all to come to the reception on Saturday.' She turned as though to give Josh an impetuous hug, but instead simply squeezed his hand and told him not to wait up for them. 'We're bound to be later than usual because I shall have to thank everyone individually for their wedding present, and I can't do that whilst we're actually playing cards,' she said. 'I do hope there'll be enough food to go round, though—at the reception, I mean—with the extra people from the whist drive.'

'I'll buy another chicken from that spiv who hangs around outside the station,' Josh said reassuringly. 'The black market has its uses. Now go and get your glad rags on and I'll go through to the bar and give Mrs Bithell a hand with the customers.'

*　　　*　　　*

Josh did not know it was raining until a customer came in, shaking the drops off his black cap and remarking that it were brass monkey weather out there tonight. Only then did he realise that the floor near the door was wet and probably slippery. There was a bag of sawdust in the corner of the

254

outhouse, with a large dipper stuck in the top, so Josh went out, filled the dipper and came back to scatter the sawdust in the doorway. Once, the dipper had been used for hen food, and it would be so used again when Josh got round to buying a few nice pullets. In his youth, his father had kept poultry, pigs and goats on his smallholding, but it had been a hard life with little material reward and Josh, a sociable animal, had been glad to exchange it for that of landlord of a thriving public house. Now, however, returning the dipper to the sack of sawdust, he visualised it filled with corn, could almost hear the clucks and squawks of the hens which came flying the moment they saw him, dipper in hand, approaching them.

Josh pulled a face. The life of a landlord in wartime was no joke. If he were given the choice now, would he really consider the Vines a better proposition than his father's smallholding? But then he remembered cutting sprouts whilst snowflakes whirled and his hands and feet got colder and colder, and the mud sucked at his rubber boots. No, he might have been born a country boy, but now he was a Liverpudlian through and through.

He returned to the warm kitchen, glancing at the clock as he did so. Soon he could call time and start the cleaning-up process, which he carried out every night with the help of his staff. Then, when they had gone, he would pour himself a pint of Guinness and settle down by the range to drink it and eat any unsold sandwiches.

Everything went according to plan and at eleven o'clock, when someone knocked on the door of the pub, he got reluctantly to his feet to cross the

255

darkened bar. He hoped it was not some kid playing tricks, or a drunk trying to wheedle an out-of-hours drink from him. Of course it might be Nell, if she had forgotten her key, but he thought that very unlikely; Nell was organised. He unlocked the door, opened it a few inches and looked out. He did not think he knew the person standing on the threshold, muffled in a mackintosh and rain hood, but it was difficult to be sure in the gloom.

'Yes? We're closed, you know.'

'I know; but—but can I come in, just for a moment? I'm—I'm looking for work.'

Josh could tell from the voice that it was a woman and began to say he was fully staffed, then relented and opened the door wider so that his uninvited guest could enter. He closed the door carefully behind her, pulled the blackout curtain across and switched on the light. The girl ducked her head, then pushed back her rain hood and looked him squarely in the face. There was a livid bruise across one cheek and she had a black eye, but Josh recognised her instantly. For two long seconds, he could only stare unbelievingly at the woman before him. Then he held out his arms and she collapsed against his chest, beginning to weep with great shuddering sobs that shook her small frame.

'Maureen!' Josh uttered. 'Dear God, what's happened to you? Oh, my poor little love, what has that brute . . .'

'I found him with another woman,' Maureen said in a tiny tired voice. 'It wasn't the first time; there have been—oh, four or five, I suppose. It didn't matter while I kept my mouth shut, but when I said

I'd not stand for it, he beat me up. The first time he said he was sorry, told me he'd been drunk and not responsible for his actions. But this time he wasn't drunk. I think he wanted rid of me. Oh, Josh, I thought he was going to kill me, so as soon as I was able to move I ran away.' She gave a bitter laugh. 'Well, that isn't quite true: I limped away. And I came to you because the biggest mistake I ever made, and I've made an awful lot, was leaving you all them years ago. Oh, Josh, I know you won't want to marry me again, but if you'd just let me work in the bar . . .'

Josh put his arm round her waist and half carried her into the kitchen, where he removed her mackintosh and rain hood, sat her down in a cosy armchair and turned to pull the kettle over the flame. 'I'm supposed to be getting married on Saturday,' he said heavily, turning back towards her. 'But the truth is, there never was any question of its being a love match. I didn't know it, mind, until I saw your little face, but a landlord needs a wife and Nell Fairweather needs a home. So we're going to tie the knot the day after tomorrow.'

Maureen sighed. 'Then that's me finished,' she said dully. 'No one else won't take me in.' She began to struggle out of the chair, wincing as she did so, and Josh saw black bruises round the base of her neck, saw also that she held one arm stiffly, as though even the thought of moving it was painful to her.

'Sit down, Mo. We've got to talk about this,' he said gently. 'This Carruthers chap—did you marry him when our divorce came through?'

Maureen shook her head and her yellow curls bobbed, sending a stab of painful recollection through Josh. He had loved her desperately once. He had told Nell that love had died when she left him, but now he knew he had lied. Maureen had treated him abominably, but she was scarcely more than a child after all, and had been under the spell of a ruthless and self-willed young man who had swept her off her feet.

The kettle boiled and Josh made tea for them both, then sat down in the chair opposite Maureen. 'We haven't got long,' he said urgently. 'Nell's shop was bombed, so she and her mother have moved in here. They're out right now, but they could be back at any minute. We've got to sort this mess out before they return.'

Maureen looked around her, her glance reminding Josh of that of a hunted animal. 'Where are the boys?' she quavered. 'And Nell's little girls?'

'They're all in bed,' Josh said. He leaned across the small space that separated them and took Maureen's hand. Once it had been smooth and strong; now it was fragile as a bird's claw. 'You're to stop worrying, because no matter what, I'll see you right,' he said. 'Now drink your tea and I'll tell you what I mean to do.'

*   *   *

Nell was not at all surprised when she and Nonny crossed the darkened bar to find the kitchen also in darkness. Normally, they would have turned on the lights and made themselves a cup of tea before going to bed, but tonight the folk at the whist drive had arranged a little party. There had been sandwiches, fairy cakes and of course the inevitable cups of tea, so neither woman even suggested turning on a light, and instead they headed straight for the stairs. Once in their own room they discussed the wedding arrangements yet again, keeping their voices low in order not to disturb either Josh or the children.

'I meant them to try on the dresses I bought before they went up to bed,' Nell said. 'Addy's grown taller since I saw her last and she's getting a proper figure. I'm afraid hers won't fit.'

'You've got all Friday to either add a panel at the back or take it down to Paddy's Market and see if you can exchange it for something else,' Nonny said, ever practical. 'You aren't working tomorrow, I take it?

'I expect I'll be cooking,' Nell said ruefully. 'But never mind, Addy's quite capable of changing the dress herself if it doesn't fit. And now let's get to bed, because it's awful late and we've a busy day tomorrow.'

*   *   *

Addy and Prue woke early, got dressed and went downstairs, arriving in the kitchen just ahead of Nell, who entered yawning hugely and explaining that she and Nonny had not arrived back from the whist drive until after midnight. 'Paul was on the early shift,' she told them when Prue asked, 'so knowing him he'll have stayed in bed till the last minute and gone to work without a bite or a sup. But that's lads for you.'

'Where's Mr Ben— I mean where's Uncle Josh?' Prue asked.

'Oh, I expect he tried to wait up for Nonny and

meself to return from our evening off and tired himself out,' Nell said, going over to the window and pulling up the blackout blind to let in a ray of bright sunshine. 'He'll be down in a minute. Addy, could you lay the table, queen? It's only porridge and toast and tea of course, but we've a busy day ahead.'

Addy had already begun to get out the porridge dishes, but as she put them round the table she spotted a letter propped against the marmalade pot. She picked it up and turned to her mother. 'Letter for you, Mam,' she said cheerfully.

'A letter?' Nell said without much interest. She laughed. 'Perhaps it's from my daughters! What's the postmark? Local, I suppose.'

'There isn't one,' Addy said. 'It must have been hand-delivered, because it just says *Nell Fairweather*. You'd best open it.'

Nell sighed, then came over to the table, took the letter from Addy's hand, slit open the envelope and pulled out the page it contained. Addy, watching her face, saw her mother begin to flush. Nell tightened her lips, then banged a fist down on the kitchen table. 'Well of all the . . . how *dare* he! Addy, fetch Nonny down! I've got to . . .'

Addy began to ask who the letter was from and what it was all about, but before she could utter a word Nell had dashed across the kitchen and through the darkened bar and was almost at the door when she fell heavily. For a moment she did not move, and Addy ran towards her. But then, to Addy's complete astonishment, Prue, who had not walked a step for the best part of four long years, ran—actually ran—past her. She threw herself down beside her mother and began to try to lift

260

Nell from her sprawled position. 'Mam, oh, Mam! What's happened? Has someone been cruel to you?' she cried wildly. 'Don't die, Mam, please don't die.'

On the floor, Nell stirred, then sat up, her hand going to her head. Then, as Addy pulled up the blackout blinds, she put both arms round Prue and began to pat her reassuringly. 'It's all right, love, it's quite all right, I've not gone mad, I'm just blazingly angry,' she said. 'But Prue, my love, your wheelchair's still in the kitchen! It's the miracle we've all been praying for! So sometimes something good does comes out of something bad.' She turned to Addy. 'Did you help her to walk through into here?'

'I didn't have to; she ran like a deer, faster than I could, when she saw you fall,' Addy explained. 'I think she thought you'd fainted, but I think you slipped on all the loose sawdust someone's scattered across the floor.'

'That's right, I did,' Nell said, getting rather stiffly to her feet. 'Oh, what a fool I've been! I thought I could catch him, make him see reason, but of course he must be long gone.'

'Mam, we don't know what you're talking about,' Addy said gently. But when her mother bent to pick Prue up, Addy pushed her away. 'No, I think we must let Prue walk back to the kitchen herself, without help.' She turned to her sister, who was making no attempt to get up from the floor. 'Come along now, Prue; you've proved your legs can not only walk, but run. Now you must come slowly and carefully back to the kitchen, and then Mam will tell us what this is all about.'

'I can't get up, I can't, I can't,' Prue was wailing,

and Addy was about to help her to her feet when she realised there was another course open to her.

'Right, Prue, you stay here while Mam and I return to the kitchen and she explains about the letter,' she said. 'If you aren't interested enough to come through, then you'll have to go without breakfast as well.'

Prue looked up at her. Her big blue eyes were brimming with tears, but there was a glint of amusement in them as well and for the first time it occurred to Addy to wonder whether Prue had been practising walking whenever she was alone. After all, it was undoubtedly much easier to let others run back and forth whilst one sat at one's ease and did only the tasks that one chose to admit one could manage. Addy Fairweather, you really can think horrible things sometimes, she told herself. Feeling guilty, she heaved Prue to her feet. 'Mam, you take one hand and I'll take the other, just in case she does fall, only I'm sure she won't,' she said. 'Then when we're back in the kitchen you can tell us what's going on. Ah, here comes Nonny—or is it Uncle Josh? I can hear someone coming downstairs, anyhow.'

'Well, it won't be Josh,' Nell said grimly as they settled themselves at the table, Prue having walked slowly but steadily right across the bar and into the kitchen. 'Ah, Nonny! Come and sit down . . . I've got good news and bad. Prue just walked right across the bar and back, which is the good news. And the bad news is in the letter which Addy is going to read to you . . . but it speaks for itself.'

She handed Addy the letter, which her daughter read aloud.

'*Dear Nell,*

'*This evening Maureen came back. That bloke beat her up. Nell, I'm real sorry, but I have to take care of her. I can't simply let her get on with it. She's not strong, like you; she needs me. You can have the Vines; she and myself will set up somewhere else, don't know where yet. I've written to the brewery saying you've virtually run the place for years, so I'm sure they'll let you have it. I expect you think I've let you down. I suppose I have. I'm real sorry, but I can't let Maureen struggle; she'd do something desperate, I know she would. Tell the boys I'll be in touch when we're settled. I'm telling myself you won't be angry once you get used to the idea but that won't be for a while yet.*

'*All the best,*
'*Josh.*'

For a moment, Addy was too astonished to say another word and guessed that her grandmother and Prue felt the same. Then Nonny burst into speech.

'To be honest, Nell me love, I wouldn't call that bad news. I ain't gonna say I told you so, because it won't be no manner o' use, but there's no denying that I knew Josh weren't the man for you. However, I do admit he's let you down and you'll have a struggle to clear up the mess he's left behind him. I don't just mean cancelling the church and breaking the news that there's to be no wedding, but more practical things. For instance, the brewery won't appoint you as landlady, no matter what Josh may think. He's left you in a real bad position because you'll have no roof over your

263

head once the brewery discover Josh has flitted. Why, when I think of that fluffy little piece of nothing, simply walking in after all those years and snatching Mr Bentley back two days before his wedding, I tell you I could swing for her, and him. What do you think, girls?'

Prue began to say that she had never liked the idea of living in a pub, but Addy shushed her. She had glanced up at her mother's face when she finished reading the letter and had seen the flush of anger fade and a sickly pallor take its place. With more experience than her sister, she realised that Nonny was right and that what lay ahead for her mother was going to be a very difficult time indeed. She would have to cancel the register office and get in touch with all the wedding guests. Fortunately, they were catering for the reception themselves, but though some of the food could be kept, quite a lot would have to be eaten within a couple of days. Then there was the honeymoon to be cancelled, the wedding presents to be returned and the brewery to be informed that Josh had simply abandoned the Vines and did not intend to return. All these things would fall upon her mother's shoulders, for though Nonny, Mrs Chambers and Mrs Bithell would do their best to help, they could do little without her mother's guidance.

Addy took a deep breath. 'What would happen, Mam, if we just moved out and put up the shutters? Now that Prue can walk, I'm free to do— oh, no end of things. I could take a job in a factory, and when I'm a bit older I could join the forces. Come to that, Mam, so could you. Nonny and Prue could look after each other, and you and I would be earning good money, so they needn't go short.'

Prue began to say that she wanted to return to Foliat Manor and would need her sister, but Addy shook her head, interrupting her without compunction. When she had seen Prue running and later walking so steadily, she had felt as if an almost impossible burden had slid from her shoulders, turning her from an anxious and responsible adult into the young girl who had wanted to do something for her country, as other girls her age did. 'No, Prue, you've got to learn that you can't have it all ways,' she said. 'When you were paralysed and couldn't move, I did everything that you needed, helped you in every way I could, but now, queen, it's my turn. You could probably go back to Foliat Manor, but I don't believe you'd enjoy it much, with just the boys. I think we shall both have to give Mam and Nonny all the support we can until they can manage without us.' She turned to her mother and grandmother. 'Don't you agree, you two? I'm sure I can be released from pupil teaching once the authorities hear what's happened.'

Nell beamed at her daughter and Addy saw her mother's deathly pallor give way to her more normal colouring. It occurred to her that Nell was a very pretty woman, and at only thirty-nine years old she was indeed eligible for the forces if she decided to join up. 'I wouldn't let the brewery down, even if in the end they refuse to let us stay,' Nell said. 'However, as for finding somewhere else to live, that's just about impossible, in Liverpool at any rate. And what about the boys? It's all very well for Josh to say he'll write to them when he and Maureen are settled, but I know breweries; he'll never get another pub, not after walking out of this one. Besides, there's Nick to consider; when he comes home on leave, he'll need a roof over his head. If we stay here, the boys can remain with us, for the time being at any rate.' She looked sadly at her daughters. 'I suppose you'd far rather go back to Foliat Manor and maybe you will, in the fullness of time, but for a while we shall need you here.'

Seeing that Prue was looking woebegone at the thought of staying in Liverpool, Addy leaned over and took her sister's hand. 'Don't be sad because we won't be going back to the manor, queen,' she said gently. 'We *will* go back there one day; I feel it in my bones.'

*   *   *

Despite Josh Bentley's promise, it was many weeks before the boys got a letter from him, and then it was only to say that he had got himself a job as a porter on a London railway station, where Maureen was working as a part-time kitchen assistant in the station's buffet. They had found themselves a tiny room but did not expect to be there for long since London was targeted virtually every night and poor little Maureen was so nervous that she seldom managed to get any sleep at all.

'Serve her right,' Paul said callously when he read the letter. 'I really liked Maureen and I thought she liked us, but she couldn't have, could she? I mean, first she deserts us, leaving our dad in an awful state, and then she comes back at dead of night and steals him away, the same as you might steal an old dog from its place by the fire.'

Nick laughed and turned away from the mirror,

266

where he was trying to part his unruly light brown hair, to grin at his brother. The boys were in their bedroom at the Vines, both getting ready for the day ahead. 'Trust you to call our dad an old dog, though I think you hit the nail on the head,' he said. 'Of course it really doesn't concern me now that I'm in the RAF, but I shall still need somewhere to spend my leaves and it seems a bit of a cheek to expect the Fairweathers to put me up. However, since Dad didn't think to give us his address, we can't write back, and even if we could, I wouldn't fancy living in London. They're getting a terrible pasting. A pal of mine at the factory had a week off and went to visit his uncle who lives in Pimlico. He says he didn't get one undisturbed night, but spent most of his time down the underground, sharing an old eiderdown with two of his cousins, and longing for the morning.'

'Sounds hellish,' Paul agreed. 'I'd rather stay here, only I'm not sure it's fair on Auntie Nell and the girls. I know you shell out every penny you can afford, but I've only got my wages from the factory and I'm not earning much. It seems to me bus fares and canteen dinners take up all my gelt.'

Nick finished parting his hair and reached for the Brylcreem to slick it down. 'If you didn't smoke you'd be better off,' he commented. 'But the time to worry is when the new landlord arrives to find that the bedrooms he's supposed to let out to bring in more money are occupied by us.'

'But we pay what we can afford,' Paul said, reaching for his jacket. Addy had got a job in his factory, though in a different department, and when they were on the same shift the two of them set out for work together. 'See you later, old feller.

I'll give Addy's door a knock on my way down to brekker.'

*   *   *

Some time later, however, Josh Bentley wrote again and at more length, and this time he included his address. He and Maureen had taken over a tiny run-down café in a small Yorkshire village. The owner was recently widowed and unable to cope with all the difficulties of rationing, so had advertised the property for rent. A friend had forwarded the advertisement to Josh, knowing that he had had considerable experience in the licensing trade and thinking that his old friend might be glad of a job which would employ both Josh himself and Maureen.

The friend had been right. Josh and Maureen had hurried to the village for a brief interview with Mrs Haggarty, who had been delighted to offer them not just the job, but also the little flat above the café.

She's going to help us for the first few weeks, until we know the ropes and don't make a mess of things, Josh had written. Whilst we're learning the trade, she'll live in the flat and we've taken a room at the local pub, but as soon as she sees we're competent, she'll go to her married daughter in York and we'll start paying the rent for the café and the flat, which is very reasonable. It isn't a large flat, but there are two bedrooms, so you boys will be able to come to us for your leaves, which will mean that Nell will be able to let your room at the Vines.

268

It will be good to see you again; indeed, I dare say I shall scarcely recognise you! Let me know when you get leave, Nick, so we can kill the fatted calf!

Give my best to the Fairweathers. Maureen sends love.

Regards,
Dad.

PART II

1944–1946

CHAPTER TWELVE

May 1944

Prue finished packing her last parachute and turned to her friend Maisie, who worked beside her at the long bench. 'Done!' she said triumphantly. 'I can't wait to get home today, because I've two letters which I didn't have time to read before I left for work this morning. One's from my sister Addy, and the other's from Nick, a feller I've known since way back.'

'Way back!' Maisie scoffed, turning away from their workbench to head for the cloakroom and linking arms with Prue. 'You're only a kid now . . . how old are you?'

'Sixteen,' Prue admitted. 'But I've been friendly with Nick since I was thirteen. He was Addy's friend really but they seem to have drifted apart, while he and I get on pretty well now we're older. He's in the air force now, in one of them big bombers.' She lowered her voice. 'He's hoping for leave when the invasion they're talking about is over. He's promised to come back to Liverpool so we can go on the town, but I dare say it'll come to nothing.' She sighed and, as they reached the cloakroom, began to unbutton her overall, slipping out of it and reaching for her jacket. 'This bloody war spoils everything,' she concluded.

When the girls emerged from the factory, it was into a truly beautiful evening. The sun shone and a gentle breeze stroked Prue's cheek, and when a tram drew up alongside them and her friend

273

hopped aboard, holding out a hand to help Prue up the step, Prue shook her head. 'It's a lovely evening and I'd rather walk,' she said, and watched the tram trundle down the road without regret. In her jacket pocket, the two letters rustled, but she did not mean to read them just yet. That pleasure would come later, she told herself virtuously, because she had a good deal of thinking to do, and thinking was best done while she was alone.

When she and Addy had first moved back to live at the Vines, her ability to walk had been so new and so precious that she guarded it as a miser guards gold. She had refused to take on war work, terrified that she might over-exert herself and bring back the weakness which had haunted her for so long, or even the terrible paralysis. Everyone knew that Addy, on the other hand, wanted to become a real part of the war effort and join the Wrens, but she had still been too young, so it was no surprise when she had applied for work at a factory where radios for aircraft were assembled. She had got the job and was soon working shifts and proud of her ability, becoming a fast and accurate assembler within a couple of months.

Prue had not been envious at first because her life at the Vines was so pleasant. Nell, who had shared Prue's fear that she might do too much and suffer a relapse, had insisted that her daughter should not even try to work in the bar or help in the kitchen. So Prue had spent her days knitting or sewing by the kitchen fire when the weather was bad, or taking short walks around the shops, keeping an eye out for anything not on ration and returning home as soon as she felt even slightly tired.

This idyllic life had lasted for six months, but after that Prue had begun to realise what she was missing. Addy was having such fun! At work, the girls talked and joked and discussed everything under the sun, and when she was not working Addy and her pals went to cinemas and theatres, visited dance halls and went out with any young man who asked them.

Prue, who seldom met anyone, not even the customers at the Vines, since Nell would not let her serve in the bar, had begun to be bored. She had hunted out a length of rope and begun to practise skipping. She had run up the stairs of the Vines a dozen times a day and had rejoiced in her new strength. Then, ignoring Nell's pleas not to overdo it, she had applied for a job packing parachutes and had soon been truly happy with her lot, though Nell frequently criticised the accent and words she picked up from her workmates. Prue had assured her, however, that it did not pay to be different.

Now, Prue slowed outside the small shop run by her Auntie Effie and stopped to poke her head round the door. 'Lovely day, Aunt Effie. Have you got any wool for me?' she asked hopefully, but her aunt, though she smiled, shook her head.

'Norreven an inch, queen,' she said regretfully. 'Try again tomorrer.'

'Okey-dokey,' Prue said cheerfully and continued on her way, letting her thoughts return to the early days, when Mr Bentley had first flitted, leaving them all in limbo, though of course she herself, suddenly able to walk once more, was less affected by his leaving than her mother and grandmother.

But it had been an anxious time nevertheless,

though Nell, suddenly freed by Josh Bentley's desertion, had rallied wonderfully. She had handled the cancellation of the register office, the reception and the honeymoon swiftly and efficiently, and had then returned every single wedding present with a letter of explanation and apology. After that, she had insisted on an interview at the brewery's headquarters, explaining the situation and telling them that she had no desire to become the landlady of the Vines but would, if sufficiently well paid, run the business for them until they could find a replacement for her former fiancé. She had expected resistance, blustering, even rudeness, but instead met understanding, a rise in her salary and the promise of action to find a new landlord as soon as possible.

Now, Prue smiled to herself at the strangeness of fate. It had clearly been impossible for the brewery to employ a young man, because all fit young men were in the forces, but three months after Josh Bentley had abandoned both Nell and the pub, Josh's replacement had arrived. He had previously worked for the brewery in a quiet little pub in a tiny rural village, and had trebled sales in the year that he had been acting landlord. The reason he himself had not been called up was because he was a chronic asthmatic; when he had gone for his medical he had been turned down even for deskwork.

Nell had told Prue that when he had presented himself at the Vines, looking anxiously at the woman he was to replace, he had been so shy and diffident that she had taken him for a customer and had explained that she could not serve him for another half an hour, but that he was welcome to sit in the bar and have a cup of tea and a sandwich until opening time.

Prue had met the new landlord, Jamie Finch, that very evening and had immediately liked him. He was tall and willowy, with soft golden-brown hair that flopped over his brow and shy blue eyes. However, Nell had told her daughters that she doubted his ability to run a busy pub like the Vines, and Prue had wondered whether he would take the credit whilst her mother did all the work. But very soon she realised she had wronged him. His quiet, unassuming manners hid an iron will, and when he called time, woe betide any drinker who hung around the bar or tried to wheedle a member of staff to sell him another pint. Mr Finch might look weak, but in fact he was nothing of the sort. He could, and did, put a stop to fights and eject troublemakers, though occasionally he had to call for help from the cellar man.

It had never occurred to Prue that the Vines under Mr Bentley had not been a particularly happy pub, but now she realised that in the old days it had merely been a workplace so far as the staff were concerned. But Nell and Jamie Finch had changed the entire atmosphere, largely because neither wanted to rule the roost, so each was able to work with the other in harmony. Now the staff actively enjoyed themselves at the Vines and guarded their jobs jealously, knowing they were valued and proud that both Mr Finch and Mrs Fairweather appreciated them and were not slow to say so.

Nell and Jamie, Prue reflected as she hurried along the pavement, were two of a kind. They

277

never quarrelled, never disagreed, and always consulted one another, so it had been no surprise to either Prue or Addy when, at Christmas, Jamie had proposed marriage. At first, Nell had been doubtful, pointing out that she was half a dozen years older than he, but Jamie had thought that was rubbish and had said so.

Prue had written to Addy at once, for Addy had joined the Wrens only a matter of weeks before so had been unable to get leave to attend the ceremony. However, she had been delighted with the news and had congratulated the happy couple with obvious sincerity, telling Prue that it would be an ideal match. Even Nonny, always cautious, had said that her daughter was doing the right thing and would not regret her decision. So the wedding had gone ahead and the couple were happier than anyone had a right to be in these anxious times.

Prue paused in her walk to admire a tiny garden, whose proud owner had nurtured a couple of magnificent rose bushes. One had crimson blossoms, the other flourished golden-yellow flowers, and the scent, wafted on the breeze, reminded Prue, nostalgically, of the rose garden at Foliat Manor. She and Addy had loved that rose garden, vegetables and all, but recently Prue had heard from Trixie, a friend from the village school, that the whole garden was a wilderness now.

Trixie had told her that the school had left the manor around the time Addy had joined the Wrens, and the army had moved in. Trixie had taken a quick look from the driveway and one glance had been enough to convince her that the army had no time for gardens; the lawns were hayfields, the flowerbeds overrun with enormous weeds and the drive ridged and potholed by army traffic.

But as Prue bent over the rose bush and took a deep breath of the sweet scent, the rose garden at Foliat Manor still bloomed in her mind, as it had done years before, without so much as a weed in the beds to spoil its perfection.

Now, Prue turned on to Scotland Road and began to hurry. As soon as she got in, she would go to the room she had once shared with Addy and enjoy the luxury of reading her letters. She would read Nick's first because his letters were usually short and mainly concerned with life on his RAF station and in his Lancaster bomber. Then she would read Addy's. Her sister was stationed in Scotland, billeted in a big old house right on the edge of the sea, only Addy had said it wasn't exactly sea but what they called a 'firth', which seemed to be a long finger of water stretching inland between hills that were purple and gold in autumn with heather and gorse. Addy was a messenger in the Navy, but seemed to have plenty of time off during which she and a friend would explore the hills and glens and even fish in the lochs, though Addy had told Prue that fishing meant too much hanging around for her liking; she preferred a more active sport.

Knowing that opening time was not for another half-hour, Prue did not approach the big doorway of the Vines but dived down St Martin's Street and into the jigger, then across the yard and through the door into the kitchen. Nell was sitting at the table, shelling peas. She looked up and smiled as her daughter entered the room, waving the colander of peas as she did so. 'I want to finish

279

these because they're for our supper, but the kettle's just come to the boil and there's a new loaf on the pantry shelf, alongside the jar of jam. Help yourself,' she said briskly. 'You can make me a cup as well; I'm really dry. Jamie and Nonny have gone to the shops for stuff to make sandwiches, but I expect you'll want to change and have a wash before you're ready to give a hand down here.'

Prue laughed and rumpled her mother's hair affectionately, then went to the stove and began to make the tea. 'You're forgetting that packing parachutes isn't the same as assembling radios,' she pointed out. 'Addy often came home in dire need of a good wash, but we have to keep pretty clean so we don't get oil or anything on the 'chutes.'

She handed her mother a large mug of tea, picked up the second one and headed for the hall and stairs. As she began to mount them, she shouted over her shoulder that she had not read her letters but would do so before she came down again.

'Of course; I forgot we both had letters this morning,' Nell called up after her. 'I'll read you mine if you'll read me yours.'

Prue laughed but made no rejoinder. She knew Nell thought that Nick Bentley was her boyfriend and probably imagined that their letters were lovey-dovey. Prue wanted her mother to think this, and one way of making sure that she had the right idea was to keep the letters from her and smile, coyly, when asked to share the contents. Because Prue was so young, her mother was happy to believe she was conducting a romance only on paper; if she had suspected her daughter was

280

fancy-free she would have watched her a good deal more closely. That would not have suited Prue, who enjoyed trips to the cinema and attending the dances that were held somewhere most nights of the week. She always went with a crowd of girls from her factory and had made it a rule never to dance more than once with the same man, for she was not yet in the least interested in having any sort of romantic relationship.

Reaching her room, Prue changed into an old cotton dress and cardigan and sat down on the edge of her bed, slitting Nick's envelope open and scanning the pages within. As usual, he talked mainly about life in the RAF, his friends and the weather which, when he had written the letter, had been distinctly unpleasant. He ended by telling Prue he missed her, adding, as he always did, that as soon as he got enough leave he would come and see her.

We'll paint the town red, dance all night and eat at the best restaurants, he had written exuberantly, if untruthfully, for neither of them was exactly rolling in wealth. Prue, however, appreciated the sentiment behind the words and guessed that life in his Lancaster must be both frightening and boring at times. Imagining the fun that he and Prue would enjoy together was one way of dispelling the depression which, he had once or twice admitted, sometimes attacked him.

Prue laid the letter down with a sigh. Even though she knew they were just pals, she guessed how important it was for Nick to be able to claim he had a girlfriend.

Now Prue slit open Addy's envelope and was surprised to find it contained only a couple of sheets, though both were closely covered with Addy's fine sloping hand. Prue read a few sentences and then gave a squeak of excitement, jumped off the bed and hurried down the stairs, clutching the letter. She burst into the kitchen, making her mother and Nonny, who was just emptying her shopping bag, jump as she hurtled through the doorway.

'Mam, Nonny! I've just begun to read Addy's letter and you'll never guess where she's writing from, never in a thousand years!'

'Yes we shall; she's writing from Scotland,' Nell said placidly, continuing to pod peas, but Nonny shook her head.

'No she ain't; she's on her way . . . south,' the old lady said in a sepulchral voice. 'I sees her havin' a long train journey. She's going to somewhere on the coast where there's already a deal of men and ships.' She pressed the tips of her fingers against her forehead and Nell, glancing across at Prue, fluttered her dark lashes in an enormous wink.

'When you're stationed in the north of Scotland, you've pretty well got to come south,' she pointed out. 'And of course the best way to travel all that distance is by train. As for being on the coast, you would scarcely find Wrens billeted anywhere else. So if you're trying to convince us that this is your second sight at work, Ma, you'll have to do better than that.'

'Oh, Mam, I think she's doing jolly well; keep it up, Nonny,' Prue said, though seeing that Nonny had her eyes shut she returned her mother's wink. 'What else can you see?'

Nonny frowned. 'Just because I've got me eyes shut don't mean I can't see you two nudgin' and gigglin',' she said reproachfully. 'I see a big old house with a lot of girls goin' to an' fro, wearin' them saucy little sailor hats our Addy has . . .'

'Well, Nonny, you've near as dammit said what Addy says in her letter,' Prue admitted. 'She's back in Devon! It's to do with invasion plans, I guess, though she doesn't actually say so, and she's hoping to be billeted at Foliat Manor, though not until the army move out, of course. I've not read all of her letter, only the first page, but she's tremendously happy and excited. Here, I'll read the whole letter aloud, shall I?'

'Yes, dear. And you can make your grandmother a cup of tea while you do so,' Nell said. 'Jamie's setting up in the bar, but I dare say he'd be glad of a cup as well.' She popped the last pod and held out a hand. 'Here, I'll read it now I've finished the peas.'

It was not a long letter but, as Nell remarked, it had been written some days after the one addressed to herself, though both had arrived at the same time. Addy was full of the delight of returning to Devon, eager to remind Prue of how happy they had been and how well they had grown to know Plymouth. In fact, it was a letter largely filled with nostalgia for the past, a past in which Prue shared.

And you'll never guess who I met walking along from the station, her letter went on. *Gillian Frobisher, the girl who showed us her secret way down to the shore. She's a writer in the Navy now to someone frightfully important at Naval HQ but she recognised me at once and was as nice as anything. We had a long chat and it really is on the cards that after a certain date we Wrens might actually be billeted at Foliat Manor.*

The letter had been written within hours of her arrival at Plymouth and finished abruptly with a promise to write again as soon as she had the leisure. Nell laid the pages down on the table and smiled at Prue. 'Nice that she's gone back to Plymouth,' she said, then turned to her mother. 'Well, you weren't far wrong when you described where our Addy's gone,' she said. 'Any more second sightings, Ma?'

'No, and if there were I wouldn't tell you,' Nonny said crossly. She finished emptying her shopping bag on to the table and turned towards the stairs. 'I'm goin' to get me pinny on and then I'll start on them butties.'

She was pushing rather rudely past Prue when she stopped suddenly and raised her nose in the air. 'Roses,' she said. 'I smell roses!'

Prue was still staring as her grandmother left the room, closing the door rather sharply behind her.

*　　　*　　　*

Addy had been truly happy in Scotland for several reasons, and loved the countryside in which she was stationed. In summer, the girls had bathed in the firth, fished in the streams and gone for long walks over the heather-clad hills. In winter they sledged, caught the trundling twice-a-week country bus into the nearest town and went to the cinema, or simply made their way to the nearest woodland to collect fuel for the large wood-burning stove which kept their living accommodation warm.

When she had arrived in Scotland, having done a crash course on both cars and motorcycles, she had had considerable difficulty in finding her way from one place to another along what were scarcely more than tracks over the hills. When it snowed, car driving had not always been practical, but the motorbike was different, having the ability to take to the country when roads proved impassable, and sometimes it was the only method of communication when snow brought the wires down and blocked the roads.

Now, Addy knew her motorbike riding had improved considerably through constant practice. At first she had ridden with great caution, slowing to walking pace at every bend and dreading the first snowfall, but she had soon realised that neither her sturdy motorbike nor the jeep she occasionally drove would ever let her down, and she had gradually become comfortably aware that the job held no terrors for her. In fact she had enjoyed work almost as much as she enjoyed play.

The news that she was to be posted to Plymouth, where she and Prue were once so happy, had been a bit of a mixed blessing. The Scots and the people with whom she worked were both courteous and kind. No one had ever commented on her scarred face and Addy herself forgot about it for days, even weeks at a time. Indeed, there were occasions when she had to peer hard at her reflection in order to see the scars at all. After all, the accident had happened nearly seven years ago and now what had once looked like scarlet railway tracks across her brow and upper lip had faded to white and were very much less noticeable. Only in certain lights and at certain angles were they obvious to Addy, and she was beginning to realise that the majority of people, never even noticed them. However, being posted meant she would be meeting new people and new people seeing a stranger in their midst, might identify her by commenting on the scars.

So it had been a real piece of luck to have met Gillian Frobisher so soon after her arrival in Plymouth, and to be greeted like an old friend even better. Gillian had insisted upon taking her to her billet, an old house surrounded by Nissen huts which had seemed to be full of foreign troops, judging by the uniforms she saw as they had made their way between the huts to the large brick-built house.

The place had been full of Wrens, several of whom Addy had recognised, and by the time she had despatched the letter to Prue and received a reply she was very much at home, both in her new job and her new social life.

Everyone knew that an invasion was planned, but the exact date was a closely guarded secret and in the meantime preparations went on which, as Addy and Gillian agreed, must be as obvious to the enemy as they were to the troops themselves, massing as they were all along the coast.

Forests of tents had sprung up and men with accents not unlike those of the Devonshire folk themselves—Canadian and American—were everywhere. Shipping, too, was coming from all ports, for the troops needed transport across the water; needed, too, equipment to enable them to fight their way ashore, and then deeper and deeper into enemy-occupied territory.

Now, Addy's ability as a motorcycle messenger came into its own. Officers who sent her with important papers containing information labelled *Top Secret* soon realised that, despite only having arrived in Plymouth a few days before, this young Wren knew the countryside like the back of her hand, and she became much in demand.

She learned to tell Canadian accents from American, and how to distinguish the various uniforms. She was aware that she was a tiny cog in the enormous invasion wheel and was proud to think that she was, indeed, doing her bit for her country.

She and Prue telephoned one another whenever they could, Prue announcing excitedly that she meant to come to the West Country just as soon as her factory would allow her to stop packing parachutes and undertake more exciting work. Addy agreed that it would be grand to be together once more, but secretly doubted that Prue would ever be allowed to change her job.

Addy had only the haziest idea of how the invasion force would reach their objective, but memories of the panic at the start of the war came to her mind. Then, they had been warned to watch out for men dressed as nuns floating down on parachutes; such men would rip off their disguise to reveal their steel helmets and Nazi jackboots as soon as the time was ripe. She said none of this to Prue, however, but when she spoke to her mother—Nell always phoned from the public box on the corner of Hornby Street—she warned her not to hold her breath. 'It would be lovely to have Prue here, of course,' she assured Nell. 'But there's so much going on that I can't see them letting one

287

girl transfer when there's no particular need. Perhaps later, when the war's over . . .'

Nell laughed. 'You've not seen your sister for a year, have you?' she asked. 'She's got half the American army queuing up to take her to the flicks because they think she's just the cutest thing, and the other half are senior naval personnel who say she reminds them of their own children whom they hardly ever get to see. She'll wind someone round her little finger and be with you in Plymouth before you know it.'

'That would be lovely,' Addy said, rather insincerely. Although Prue could now walk, dance and even run, old habits die hard and she still expected her family to jump when she said so. However, she knew it would not be politic to make such a remark, so she merely pretended to agree and changed the subject.

*   *   *

'Fairweather! You're wanted down in the front hall. Do get a move on, it might be important.'

Addy, who had just come off duty and was sitting on the edge of her bed, wondering whether to write a letter home or to go down to the kitchen and see if anyone had a brew on the go, sighed and got to her feet. She went to the doorway and was about to shout that she was on her way when she heard a murmur of voices and then the sharp, impatient step of someone ascending the stairs. It wasn't likely to be work, then, because messages were usually handed out by men and no man, no matter how important, would dream of coming up the stairs at the Wrennery; could probably be court-martialled for even contemplating such a thing.

Addy went to the head of the stairs, then beamed at her visitor. It was Gillian Frobisher. The older girl was in shirtsleeve order, for it was a hot day, and when she saw Addy at the top of the flight she grinned and said somewhat breathlessly: 'So you *did* hear! Shall I come up or will you come down? There's something I want to talk to you about.'

'I'll come to you,' Addy said readily, and both girls went down to the hall and let themselves out into the sunshine. Here they paused. 'Where shall we go?' Addy asked. 'I'm finished for the day, unless an emergency comes in of course, and if I'm out when it does Pam Symonds will have to take it.'

'We'll walk down to Betty's and see if she's got any homemade cakes left,' Gillian said, clapping her hat on her head and then tilting it forward at a jaunty angle. 'Oh, I'm so excited; I can't wait to tell you . . . but let's get ourselves sat down at Betty's first.'

Betty, a fat and motherly woman in her late fifties, greeted them with the wonderful news that she had just taken a batch of scones out of the oven and would be serving them as soon as they had cooled. 'They'm plain, mind, 'cos us can't get sultanas for love nor money,' she said. 'An' of course I can't spread 'em with butter or cream, but I dare say if I use some of my homemade jam you'll scarce notice the margarine. And I take it you'd like a pot of tea for two?'

The girls agreed and presently were sitting down at a window table, the tea poured and in Addy's case at least the first bite taken from one of Betty's wonderfully light scones.

Gillian took a quick sip of her own tea, then plonked her cup down on its saucer, put both elbows on the table and leaned across it. 'Addy, you know I'm engaged, don't you? Well, I've just had a telephone message to say that Dominic, my fiancé, will be in Plymouth at about five o'clock, and wants to see me!'

'Lucky old you,' Addy said rather indistinctly, through a mouthful of scone. 'I wish I had a regular boyfriend . . . no I don't, though. My life's quite full enough without any added complications. Your Dominic's a soldier, isn't he? You've told me that much, but not much more.' She giggled. 'He's Captain Cranshaw, isn't he? So I suppose you have to salute him every time you meet.'

Gillian laughed too. 'Yes, he's a captain, but he's a war artist. He goes into battle with a pistol in one pocket and a sketchpad in the other. I think "Captain" is a sort of honorary title because he doesn't command any men, or anything like that, but of course he has to have a rank and a uniform to match, or the Jerries could shoot him as a spy.'

'First they have to catch him,' Addy observed, taking a sip of her tea. 'I take it he's going to be part of the invasion fleet when it sets out.'

'That's right,' Gillian said. She looked rather shyly across at Addy. 'Are you busy this evening? I mean, do you have a date?'

Addy gave a contemptuous snort. 'Chance would be a fine thing,' she said. 'But actually I'm not on duty. Why?'

'Well, as I said, Dominic will be in Plymouth this evening and wants to take me out. You're my best friend and I'd like you to meet him. He's most awfully nice; you'd like him, I'm sure.'

'It would be nice to meet him,' Addy said, rather cautiously. 'But I don't want to spend the evening playing gooseberry. Or did you just mean me to meet him and then buzz off on my own affairs? If so, I'd be delighted to shake his hand and wish him luck.' She lowered her voice. 'I know we aren't supposed to talk about it—the invasion, I mean—but everyone must realise it's any day now. The port's so full of shipping I should think the men could almost walk across to the Continent from deck to deck. And if the invasion is going to happen soon, then you and your Dominic won't want me hanging around all evening.'

'What's the invasion got to do with anything?' Gillian said impatiently. 'And I wasn't suggesting you should play gooseberry. What I was going to suggest was—'

'Hey, hold on a minute,' Addy said. 'I meant that if it is going to happen very soon, then you and your Dominic may only have this one date before he's sent off to do whatever it is he does—draw things, I suppose. So did you just mean me to meet him and then go, as I said before? If so, that's all right by me—'

'Will you shut up, you wretched girl, and let me get a word in edgeways?' Gillian interrupted. 'I was about to tell you that my brother's in port as well and wants to meet me this evening. He's in the Royal Naval Air Service and aboard an aircraft carrier, which means I can't get in touch with him. And as you so brilliantly remark, playing gooseberry isn't much fun, but a foursome would be grand, don't you think? That, Wren Fairweather, was what I was about to suggest, only

291

you would keep interrupting.'

'Oh!' Addy said, taken aback. It was one thing to be friendly with a girl who also happened to be the daughter of someone who had risen to the dizzy heights of Rear Admiral before he had retired from the Navy, but going out with her brother was a different kettle of fish. Gillian was lovely, but suppose her brother was a snob and looked down his aristocratic nose at a mere messenger? Suppose the first thing he noticed about her were the scars on her face and he was embarrassed to be seen with her? But if she let Gillian down, it might destroy their friendly relationship, and that was the last thing Addy wanted. When Foliat Manor was no longer occupied by the army, Gillian had promised to use her influence to make sure that Addy was amongst the Wrens who would be billeted there, and Addy longed to return and claim the little bedroom overlooking the rose garden once more.

'Well? Are you on? You'll like my brother, truly you will. He's a grand chap.'

'All right, all right, I'm on. Thanks very much for the invitation, only what are your plans for the evening? Cinema? A meal out? Or just a wander round the town?'

'I don't know. I thought I'd leave it up to the chaps,' Gillian said. 'But it's such a brilliant evening that at a guess I'd say it would be something out of doors. Poor old Giles is either in the cockpit of his beloved stringbag or in his stuffy little quarters below decks on his aircraft carrier. I guess he'll want a meal at some stage or other though—I think the food aboard ship is pretty boring—so if their pockets can run to it we'll go

292

somewhere nice, the sort of place fellows took one in the good old days before the war.'

'That would be lovely,' Addy said appreciatively. 'The food in the Wrennery is pretty basic; a change would be grand. But one thing, Gill: I must pay for my own meal. It's not fair on the men to make them pay all the time, especially on a blind date.'

'Oh, don't be so daft,' Gillian said. 'A pilot in the RNAS gets paid a good deal more than a Wren messenger, and anyway Giles wouldn't like playing gooseberry any more than you would, so he'll be happy to repay you for your company by giving you a meal . . . if that's what the fellows choose to do, of course.'

'Well, we'll see,' Addy said diplomatically. 'Where are we meeting them, incidentally? And when?'

Gillian took a long pull at her tea and then began to eat her scone, speaking with her mouth full. 'On the Hoe. Then if they're late we'll have something nice to look at.' She giggled. 'Dominic sees life through his work; he has a pocket-sized sketchbook and he's always whipping it out and jotting down faces or scenery which he finds interesting.'

The two girls finished their tea and made their way to the Hoe, and before they had been there more than a couple of minutes a voice hailed them and someone came towards them at a fast stride. He was tall and dark and dressed in officer's khaki, and wore his cap at a rakish angle. Addy had expected him to be outstandingly good-looking, and so he was, she thought. He had brown eyes under delicately arched brows, a straight nose and a cleft chin, and very soon Addy saw that her friend had fallen for more than looks. He had a great deal of charm and when he spoke his voice was lovely: deep and pleasant. As they met, he looked round quickly to make sure there were no interested onlookers, then bent and kissed Gillian with a gentle fondness which, Addy thought, spoke volumes.

Gillian turned towards her friend, very rosy-cheeked and bright-eyed. 'Sorry, Addy. This is my fiancé, Captain Dominic Cranshaw. Dominic, this is Addy Fairweather, my best friend.'

Addy went to salute, then realised that Dominic had removed his cap. While she hesitated, his hand shot out and took hers. 'Nice to meet you, Addy; I've heard a lot about you,' he said. 'I was just about to tell you . . .'

He stopped speaking as a tall man in naval uniform joined them. The stranger's eyes passed quickly over Dominic and Addy and fastened on Gillian. 'How ya doin', sis?' he asked in a fake American accent. He bent and kissed his sister's cheek. 'I know we've never met,' he said next, addressing Dominic, 'but I've seen a photograph.' He held out a hand and gripped the other man's. 'You're my sister's fiancé, of course; how do you do, Dominic?'

The other man grinned. 'I'm fine. Nice to meet you having heard so much about you,' he said. 'But I'm forgetting my manners; I take it you've not met Miss Fairweather? Or are you old friends?'

'Oh, Addy, I'm so sorry,' Gillian said quickly, a flush rising to her cheeks. 'This is my brother, Sub-Lieutenant Giles Frobisher. Giles, this is my best friend, Addy Fairweather. I brought her along to keep you company, because three is such an awkward number.'

But Addy was staring at Giles, conscious suddenly that his face was not unfamiliar to her. She knew him! Gillian's twin brother Giles was the man who had rescued Prue and herself when they had had the accident on the swings. They shook hands. 'Don't you remember me?' she said. 'We've met before, though it was a long while ago.'

She waited for him to recognise her, but he was still regarding her with a puzzled frown. 'Have we?' he said. 'I don't recall . . .' He pinched the bridge of his nose between finger and thumb, staring very hard into Addy's upturned face. 'You *do* look familiar, come to think . . . give me a clue!' He grinned; a flash of white teeth in his sunburned face.

'OK,' Addy said rather stiffly, 'I'll give you a clue. Scotland Road, would that help?'

'Scotland Road is what we call the main corridor in all British ships,' Giles said, his frown deepening. 'But Wrens aren't allowed aboard our ships . . .' He paused for a moment. 'Give me another clue,' he demanded.

'I were a lot younger, chuck, and I were wi' me little sister,' she said in the broad Scouse accent which she had had when she lived in Liverpool, but which she had cast aside long ago. 'Do you remember now, Mr Giles? Eh, la', if you don't place me soon I'll say you're thick as a tram driver's glove.'

Addy was feeling rather injured because Gillian's brother had not recognised her, but then she remembered how much she must have changed. She had been a child when they had last met; now she was a young woman, and a young woman in uniform furthermore. Nevertheless, when she saw comprehension dawn on his face, together with a delighted smile, she knew that an answering smile curved her own lips.

'You've remembered!' she said. 'I guess I must have changed more than I realised, but you're exactly the same. Six or seven years don't mean much when you're in your twenties, but when you're twelve . . .'

Her words were cut off as Giles seized her hand and pumped it vigorously, then turned to his sister and her fiancé, standing watching them in complete astonishment. 'It's the kid I found unconscious in a playground, after she and her sister had collided on the swings,' he explained swiftly. He turned back to Addy. 'Well met, Miss Fairweather—or may I call you Prue? And how are the rest of your family?'

'No you may not—call me Prue, I mean,' she snapped. 'Didn't you hear Gillian introduce me? I'm Addy—Prue's my little sister.' Quickly, she outlined what had happened to the Fairweathers and Nonny since she had last seen Giles. He was sad over the loss of the shop, and shocked to hear of Prue's paralysis, reminding Addy that he had left the city before Prue's condition had been diagnosed. But he was delighted to hear that Prue was now fit and well and that Addy's mother had married the new tenant of the Vines and was blissfully happy.

'Though of course I haven't been back to Liverpool much since joining the Wrens,' Addy told him. 'But when I do go back, I'm welcomed with open arms. Mam—she's now Mrs Finch—and Jamie are so happy that they make everyone round them happy too.'

Gillian and Dominic had listened, wide-eyed, as Addy talked, but now Dominic interrupted. 'Well, talk about coincidence!' he exclaimed. 'Fancy you two already knowing each other. But we're wasting valuable time; I only arrived a few minutes before you did yourself, Giles, and I bring glad tidings. I've borrowed a car from a pal so we can go places and don't need to stay in Plymouth.' He gestured ahead. 'See the Austin, parked by the kerb? That's her.'

'Who's a clever fellow, then?' Gillian said admiringly. 'Oh, but what about petrol? Much though I love you, Dominic, I don't fancy getting miles away from HQ and then having to walk home.'

Dominic tutted. 'As if I'd not thought of that! They're economical little beasts, baby Austins, and she's got a full tank. We could run over to a beach I know, go for a walk along the sands and then have supper at the Smugglers' Rest.'

This idea proved popular and presently Addy found herself sitting on the back seat of the small car, her thigh pressed against Giles's, watching the road unwind slowly ahead. When they left the town behind them, Dominic slid an arm round Gillian and after a few moments she snuggled closer, resting her head in the hollow of his shoulder. Beside her, Addy felt Giles stiffen and an extraordinary thing happened. As though he had spoken the words, though in fact he had not so much as opened his mouth, Giles's voice said inside her head: *Bloody cheek! That's my twin sister you're mauling, not some girl you've just picked up.*

Before she had had time to consider, Addy

turned to him. 'You shouldn't say that. They've known each other for ages and are actually engaged, but don't often get the chance to be together,' she said reproachfully. 'And I wouldn't call it mauling to put an arm round someone's shoulders.'

Addy had spoken quietly, but Giles did not bother to keep his voice down when he replied. 'What the devil . . .? Either I'm going mad or you read my thoughts. Unless it was bloody clever guesswork, of course, and if so I'll thank you not to jump to conclusions.'

As he spoke he was moving away from her, almost as though he thought their physical closeness might have been responsible for her words. Addy felt thoroughly foolish. 'I'm very sorry,' she said. 'I don't know what made me say what I did . . . yes I do, though. I actually heard the words; you must have muttered them beneath your breath. But I didn't mean any harm when I spoke to you. I'm truly sorry if I embarrassed you.'

Beside her Addy felt Giles relax, and when she turned her head to look at him he gave her a smile that was almost friendly. 'I'm sorry too; I shouldn't have jumped down your throat when you were defending my sister in a perfectly acceptable way,' he said. To Addy's surprise, he took her hand and wagged it gently to and fro. 'Of course I must have spoken the words aloud and you must have heard me. So let's forget it and begin all over again. I approve of Dominic; he's a really nice bloke. It's just that twins are possessive towards each other sometimes, and I felt a real pang; Gill's found someone she loves more than she loves me, and I wasn't prepared for it.'

Addy glanced sideways at him and saw that he was smiling. 'Tell me, Addy, what do you think of blind dates? Have you been on many or is this your first? Only since we've met before, I don't know whether it qualifies.'

'This is my first,' Addy confessed. 'And boy oh boy, didn't we get off to a bad start! How about you?'

'I've been on one or two blind dates,' Giles admitted. 'So this is your first? Well, I shall do my best to make it memorable. I do trust Dominic can drive with only one hand on the wheel, incidentally—please note, I said it aloud—since I don't fancy ending up in the ditch.'

'No, nor me,' Addy said. 'Can you drive, Giles? I'm a motorbike messenger, but I can drive a car too.'

'Yup, and I suspect I may be asked to do so when we turn for home,' Giles said. 'That's usual. It gives the driver and his girl the freedom of the back seat, so to speak.'

Addy, who had been inexpertly kissed in the back seat of a naval Land Rover several times, gave a smothered giggle. She was about to say that he had best keep his eyes on the road when it was his turn to drive, or his thoughts might come flying her way once more, when to her complete astonishment she felt his arm encircle her shoulders and found herself pulled gently against him. 'We're wasting valuable time,' he murmured into her ear. 'One has to skip the preliminaries on a first date these days, but I must tell you that you've improved no end since I saw you last. Then, dear little Addy, you were a scrubby schoolgirl with a front tooth missing and a face so full of stitches that you looked like Crewe railway junction. And now you're downright gorgeous.'

'No I'm not; you can still see the scars if you look closely, only they're smooth and white now instead of all red and puckered,' Addy said, trying not to sound as pleased as she felt. Such compliments had not often come her way. 'And my tooth wasn't missing; it was just chipped. Mam took me to one of the best dentists in Liverpool and he did such a good job that folk never notice it.' She giggled. 'But I'm always careful never to bite an apple with that particular tooth,' she ended.

By this time they had reached their destination, parked the car and set out to walk along the beach, but when Addy would have followed the other two Giles grabbed her arm and pulled her back. 'You are clearly a beginner in the art of blind dating,' he said reprovingly. 'The whole point is to get separated into pairs, so that you can . . .'

'Only you can't,' Addy said firmly, though with fast-beating heart, as Giles first tried to put his arm round her shoulders and then, when she pulled back, tucked her hand into the crook of his elbow. 'I didn't know the RNAS were so—so forward,' she told him. She put on a prim voice. 'Sir! You must remember that we are hardly acquainted!'

'If you'll just relax a bit, we can remedy that,' Giles said, patting her hand. 'Do remember, Addy Fairweather, that we're old friends. I've met your mother and your grandmother, admired your little sister, visited you in your hospital bed . . . I could go on all night. You really should allow me the odd kiss and cuddle!'

'No doubt,' Addy said drily. 'But for now, arm in arm is quite sufficient.'

'So tell me a bit more about living in the pub. I've never been a publican's daughter, so everything you tell me will be news to me,' Giles said complacently.

'I trust you've never been anyone's daughter,' Addy said with a giggle. 'Well, when the shop was bombed and we moved to the Vines, I was working in a factory making radio parts for Spitfires. When Prue was old enough, she got a job packing parachutes. It's a waste of her talent—she designs and makes all her own clothes—but of course war work takes priority over everything else. When the war's over, she talks about starting a shop and making really gorgeous baby clothes. Mind you, she's still only a kid herself, really, and may change her mind half a dozen times before peace breaks out. She'd like to join the Wrens when she's old enough, but that won't be for a bit yet. What about you then, Giles? Do you have plans for the peace?'

'My parents own a big old house just outside Plymouth, and when the war is over Gill and I intend to go back there, kick out the army and put it to rights,' Giles said, gently disengaging her hand and slipping his arm round her waist, which he gave a totally unnecessary squeeze as he steered her round a great limpet-covered rock. As he was speaking, he guided her to a dry ledge above the tide line, dusted the sand off it, and pulled her down to sit on it beside him. 'It'll cost every penny of our savings, no doubt, but that's what we'd both like to do; Gill thinks it would make a wonderful hotel, but I rather tend towards a sports centre where we could teach holidaymakers swimming, diving, surfing and so on. Some day—maybe on my next leave ashore—I'll take you up to Foliat Manor and you'll understand why it means so much to us.'

'Hasn't Gillian told you that in the early days of the war I was evacuated there?' Addy asked, and was surprised when her companion shook his head and blew out his cheeks in a soundless whistle.

'Well I never did,' he said. 'Was Gillian there at the same time as you? Is that where you first met?'

'Not exactly, though we did meet whilst Prue and I were living at the manor.'

She was beginning to explain about their need to get down to the shore when Giles snapped his fingers. 'Of course! Gill wrote and told me that there was a kid in a wheelchair who had been advised that sea bathing would increase her muscle strength, so she had told her and her sister about our secret path. And it was *you*! But I never dreamed that you were the children I'd met in Liverpool before the war. Well, well, well! Wonders will never cease! But I interrupted you; sorry, what were you about to say?'

'Oh, just that Prue and I both believe that her cure began with the sea bathing and the work we did at Foliat Manor. We loved it so much that we spent time weeding the garden and gathering the crops and so on, so you can imagine how I felt when Gillian said that when the army goes off to free Europe, the house will become a Wrennery and she'll do her best to see that I get my old room back . . . or rather *your* old room,' she continued, suddenly remembering that the room she and Prue had occupied for so long had actually belonged to the son of the house. 'Truly, I loved every inch of the place and must know it almost as well as you do!' Abruptly, she turned against his arm, staring up into his face. 'Giles, did you ever come back to

302

take a look at the manor whilst we were there? Only your room overlooks the rose garden and once, when the moon was shining full on my face, I went to the window to draw down the blind and there was a young man standing in the garden, looking up at the house.'

'Well, it wasn't me,' Giles said at once. 'I thought of taking a look a couple of times but decided it would be too painful, so it's a good thing you knew the manor before the army arrived. As for the bloke you saw, it was probably some fellow from the village. Unless he was wearing doublet and hose, in which case you'll have set eyes on our family ghost,' he ended, giving her waist another squeeze.

Addy sighed but did not, this time, pull away. 'Of course he wasn't wearing doublet and hose, you fool,' she said, unable to suppress a giggle. 'I couldn't really see what he was wearing, but it was something dark and modern . . . trousers and jacket, I'd guess. However, before you start scoffing, do you remember my grandmother? Well, Nonny always told us she has the second sight and can tell the future and so on. She swears she has gypsy blood and said she wouldn't be surprised if I had inherited her gift.'

'Gift! Of course, if you can foretell the winner of the National the day before the race is run, then that could be described as a gift,' Giles said, then gave a gasp as Addy, exasperated, elbowed him sharply in the stomach. 'Now what did you do that for? I'm treating you with great respect, bringing you to my favourite part of this undeniably gorgeous beach, and you damn near knock the breath out of me merely for saying I'd like to know the name of the winner of the National before it's actually run.'

Addy shook her head. 'It doesn't work like that,' she objected. 'And anyway, if I do have second sight it hasn't done me much good. I mean if I knew Prue and I were going to crash on the swings, you wouldn't have got me on one for a fortune.'

'Let's give this second sight a go, then,' Giles said. He turned her in his arms and drew her gradually closer. 'Look into my eyes,' he intoned in a deep, hypnotic voice. 'Look into my eyes, beautiful Adelaide Fairweather, and tell me what I'm thinking.'

Addy giggled, trying to pull back when their noses actually touched, but before she could do so she found herself being soundly kissed. For a moment she attempted to push him away, then suddenly all desire to escape left her. She allowed her mouth to soften beneath his, and felt her body relax too, so that for a moment she was totally absorbed in their lovemaking.

'Coo-ee! Where the devil have the pair of you got to? If we don't get a move on we'll be driving home in the dark and that's no joke when you're on narrow country lanes. Where d'you reckon they've gone, Gilly?'

Dominic and Gillian appeared round one of the tall rocks and Addy, pulling herself together with an effort and moving abruptly away from the circle of Giles's arm, was grateful for the long shadows which must, she hoped, have hidden their occupation from the other couple.

She and Giles got to their feet, straightening their uniforms and dusting sand from their persons. Addy looked a trifle apprehensively at

Gillian, fearing to see censure on the older girl's face, but Gillian was straightening her own smart Navy jacket and beckoning to them to follow as she and Dominic turned and began to retrace their steps, heading for the car once more. 'Good thing we found you when we did,' she said briskly, as Giles and Addy caught them up. 'Did you go up to the headland to watch the sun setting? We did, which was why we realised how late it was getting. We'll have to head for Plymouth now, because we're supposed to be in our billet by midnight.'

'What about food?' Giles said plaintively. 'I thought we were going to the Smugglers' Rest. Mrs Jolly does the best crab suppers in the whole of Devonshire.'

'Trust you to be thinking about your stomach,' Gillian said reprovingly, but when they reached the car and she and Dominic were ensconced in the back seat whilst Giles and Addy occupied the front, she switched on her little pocket torch and examined her wristwatch by its somewhat dim light. 'We *can* go to the Smugglers' Rest if we make it snappy,' she said. 'Only we'll have to eat up and hurry home afterwards.' She leaned over and tapped her brother's shoulder. 'You're the driver— you make the decision.'

Giles sighed. 'We'd best go straight home,' he said reluctantly. 'I don't want to be responsible for getting anyone into trouble and I dare say the owner of this nice little car might agree to lend it again if we take it back in good time.' He started the engine and selected the gear, and the car moved forward. Under the racket of its engine, he spoke softly to Addy. 'I'll be back in Plymouth in a couple of days; I'll give you a ring and maybe we

305

can continue where we left off.'

Addy shot a quick sideways glance at him, under her lashes. If he meant what she thought he did, she ought to object, yet how could she? She was aware that their lovemaking had changed her whole perspective on relationships. She had been kissed and cuddled before, but had never found the experience exciting, had never in fact wanted it to continue. With Giles it had been very different. Just sitting beside him and glancing quickly at his profile, the memory of his kisses caused a tingle to run from the top of her head to the tips of her toes. She thought she had never felt so alive and was not at all surprised when she heard her own voice saying demurely: 'That would be lovely. I've really enjoyed this evening, Giles. I'd—I'd like to do it again.'

Giles took her hand and squeezed it. 'You are a darling,' he said. 'I'll ring as soon as I get ashore; I take it you're on the same extension as Gill?'

Addy laughed and returned the pressure of his fingers. 'It depends whether you ring when we're working or in our billet,' she said. 'As you know, I'm a messenger, so mostly I'm not available during daylight hours, but if I'm out you can leave a message and a number for me to ring.'

It was Giles's turn to laugh. 'I'm aboard the aircraft carrier and don't have a telephone number ashore,' he explained. 'I'll be ringing from a public call box, so if I leave a message I'm afraid it will have to be simply that I'm ashore and will be at a certain spot at, say, seven o'clock in the evening.' He sighed deeply. 'Dear me, this courtship is not going to be straightforward. But I'm certain sure that it will be worth any trouble if it gets you and me together.'

Addy felt the hot blood flood her cheeks and was glad of the dark. 'Courtship? Just what do you mean by that?' she asked. 'This is our very first meeting since I was a scrubby schoolgirl—wasn't that what you called me?—and you're talking as if—as if . . .'

Giles disengaged his hand from hers as he slowed for a T-junction and turned left. Then, as the car picked up speed once more, he put his hand round her neck and drew her towards him until her head rested in the hollow of his shoulder. Addy would have liked to remind him of his disapproval when his sister and Dominic had occupied the same position, but when she opened her mouth to say so, Giles forestalled her. 'I know what you're thinking; you aren't the only one with second sight. You're thinking that I didn't like it when Gill and Dominic cuddled up and now I'm doing exactly the same myself. I'm afraid that was the possessiveness that one twin feels for the other and I was ashamed as soon as you pointed it out, because I knew you were right. But this—oh, this is different! You're special to me in a way no girl has ever been. If Gillian were to object, I should be outraged.' He had been speaking quietly, but now he raised his voice and addressed the couple on the back seat. 'Gillian, I've fallen for your friend and I mean to meet her every time I come ashore. I'm trying to convince her that I'm not one of those Navy types who have a girl in every port. In fact I want you to assure her that I've never had a regular girlfriend until now. Will you do that, sweet sister?'

There was a slight pause before Gillian answered, and her voice was slow and dreamy.

'He's had a great many casual girlfriends but has always made it plain he wasn't serious. Of course, I can only talk about his leaves in Plymouth. For all I know, he might have a wife in every other port.'

'Oh, thank you very much, sister dear,' Giles said, his voice heavy with sarcasm. 'But I don't think it really matters what anyone says because Addy and I are on the same wavelength and I'm telling you, Gill, that I've never been more serious about anything in my whole life. It's Addy or no one.'

'If you say so, brother dear,' Gillian said. 'Though why you want my approval, I can't imagine.' Addy heard her friend sigh, and then the sounds of someone sitting up came to her ears and she knew that Gillian was about to give a considered answer to her brother's remarks. 'Actions speak louder than words, Giles, and none of us know what tomorrow may bring. That's why Dominic and I thought very seriously before getting engaged and didn't do so for two whole years, though we mean to marry as soon as the war's over. The future is so uncertain that a promise of permanence is unfair to both parties. You've only just met Addy, so your rose-coloured spectacles are still firmly in place, but Dominic and I go through all the hell of worrying about what might happen every time we're apart, and I don't mind telling you that if you really love one another, you'll be treading a dark path.'

There was a moment of uneasy silence before Giles spoke again, but when he did his voice was firm and determined. 'Yes, I know what you mean, Gill. I've seen the faces of some of the men when they find that someone they love has been killed in an air raid, or even when they hear their home town has been targeted and many people killed. But fear of what might happen won't stop it, if you see what I mean. Addy and I could go our separate ways, but that wouldn't prevent either of us from meeting whatever fate has in store. So if Addy's agreeable, we'll go on meeting whenever the opportunity arises and get to know each other better each time.' He ran his hand round the side of Addy's face. 'Agreed, little Addy?'

'Agreed,' Addy said quietly. She nuzzled her face into the hollow of his shoulder. 'I shall hate the worrying, of course I shall, but until the war's over I can't have you without it, and I already know I'd rather be with you than with anyone else I've ever met.'

'That's how I feel,' Giles said contentedly. 'And the war's coming to an end, everyone knows it, though it's bound to drag on for a bit whilst our troops free the occupied countries from the Nazi jackboot. Both Dominic and myself will be a part of it, of course, but you'll be at risk, too, because the Jerries will try to put the ports out of action and Plymouth Sound is crammed with landing craft. But what's the point of talking? We'll live one day at a time and meet as often as possible. And now let's concentrate on not having an accident in these narrow lanes.'

For a while they drove in silence, and presently Giles drew up beside the house in which the two Wrens were billeted. Addy got out and to her surprise so did Giles. He took her hand and led her round the side of the house, and when she pulled back she saw the flash of his teeth in the faint moonlight and knew he was grinning. 'Time for our

309

goodnight kiss,' he said. 'You really *are* inexperienced, my little love. Gill gets kissed in the back seat of the car, whilst you and I have to make do with the deep shadow round the side of the house, and hope that no interfering officer comes by.'

'Perhaps we should just shake hands . . .' Addy was beginning, when Giles took her in his arms and began to kiss her, beginning gently, then giving a sound that was very like a moan and gripping her so tightly that she gasped for breath.

'Oh, Addy, if it wasn't for this bloody war I'd . . . oh, I'd . . .'

'No you wouldn't,' Addy said breathlessly, 'Because you're a perfect gentleman. Oh, Giles, are we mad? The invasion of the Continent is about to start and all I can think about is you! When I was a kid I longed to know what you were doing, where you were, whether you ever thought about Prue and me, but in my heart I never expected to see you again. And now it looks as though our lives are bound up with one another, if that makes sense. Just wait until I tell Mam and Nonny—and Prue of course—that I went on a blind date and it turned out to be you!'

Giles was beginning to reply when someone came crunching up the gravel drive. Quickly, he kissed Addy's forehead, nose and chin, then gave her a little push towards the front door. 'Off with you,' he whispered. 'See you soon, my dearest love!'

*   *   *

Curled up in Dominic's arms in the back of the

310

little car, Gillian sighed and put up a hand to smooth the cheek she could not see through the darkness. 'Darling, wasn't that the strangest thing? That Addy and Giles actually knew each other from way back, I mean. She's a super girl, too, bright and sweet-tempered. I don't imagine she's ever considered being a career-Wren, but she'd make a go of it if she did apply.' In the car's dark, leather-scented interior, she snuggled closer to Dominic. 'You like her, don't you? She liked you, but then, as I said, she's bright, and only an idiot could fail to succumb to your charms!'

'Yes, she's a nice kid,' Dominic said. 'Tactful, too—I mean she went off with your brother and didn't stick to you like glue. I feared she might, being clearly inexperienced in the art of blind dates; you did say it was her first, didn't you? But stop talking, sweetheart; we're wasting valuable loving time!'

CHAPTER THIRTEEN

Addy and Giles met three times more before the invasion began. The first time they went to the cinema and on the next two occasions Giles borrowed a car and they drove to what Addy thought she would always consider 'their' beach. The tide was well out on their second visit and deep pools had formed around the base of each of the big rocks. 'I wish I'd thought to bring a bathing suit,' Addy said longingly, for the day was warm, the sun shone and the pools looked most inviting. 'It's awful to be billeted so close to the sea yet

311

unable to use the beaches.'

'Take your uniform off—no, don't hit me, I only mean your skirt and jacket and that—and I'll do the same. Some of these pools are deep enough for a little swim. Thank God they haven't mined this beach; they wouldn't, because it's far too rocky for an invasion fleet to land or depart from. Oh, come on, Addy, be a sport! I'm hot and sticky and could just do with a quick plunge in the briny.'

'I know I shouldn't, but I will,' Addy said, beginning to unbutton her jacket. She laid it neatly on the nearest rock, then turned her back on Giles whilst she unhooked her suspenders and removed her long black stockings. Then she took off her skirt and began to unbutton her white shirt. She had removed it and was folding it up when an awful thought struck her. 'Giles, we've not got a towel and don't even suggest I remove any more clothing because I won't do it and I don't fancy driving to the Smugglers' Rest with this hideous brassiere and my bloomers dripping with sea water.'

Giles, already stripped down to regulation naval underpants, laughed and pointed to the car parked up on the headland. 'There's a rug on the back seat, but it's so nice and warm that if we lie on the rocks after our dip we'll probably dry off without having recourse to it.' He eyed her speculatively. 'Of course it would be far easier to get dry if we took everything off, but I can tell by the look in your eye that you'd feel bathing in the buff is unacceptable to a nicely brought up little Wren, so I won't suggest it.'

'You'd better not,' Addy said severely, but with a fast-beating heart. It would have been so nice to agree, to remove her naval issue underwear and feel the cool water on her hot skin, but she knew it would be foolish, so she trotted across the wet sand and threw herself into the deepest pool, and presently Giles joined her. They frolicked in the water for half an hour, then got reluctantly out on to the sand and lay on the rocks, because Giles pointed out that they needed time in the sun to dry off and already its golden orb was beginning to sink in the west.

After twenty minutes, they both felt able to don their outer clothing, though Addy grumbled that her underwear was still not completely dry. But Giles assured her that no one would ever know it and they returned to the car and made their way to the Smugglers' Rest, where they enjoyed a meal before setting out to return home.

Giles parked in deep shadow just short of the Wrennery and Addy jumped out of her seat. Giles followed suit, but to her surprise did not make for the house, but jerked a thumb at the car. 'Just time for a little cuddle before you go in,' he said. 'No, silly, don't get into the front again. There's more room in the back.'

'That depends on what you mean to do,' Addy said primly. 'For what *I* mean to do, the front passenger seat will suffice.'

Nevertheless, she opened the door, tipped the seat forward and got into the back, sinking into Giles's arms as he joined her. They kissed, but after a moment Addy pulled herself free and twisted in Giles's arms to look up into his face. 'You know when the invasion is going to start, don't you?' she said quietly. 'It's tomorrow, isn't it?'

'We've not been told officially, but the ship's due to sail at dawn,' Giles said. 'I suppose this is another instance of you reading my mind!'

'No one has to be a mind reader to tell that something really big is about to happen,' Addy said. 'And then, although we've only known each other for a few days, I've noticed that when you are excited or anxious a little muscle beside your mouth jumps. It's been doing it today.'

'That was seeing you in your undies,' Giles said with a wicked grin. 'Believe me, woman, if you can look so sexy in those dreadful things my imagination assures me that without them you'd look like the Venus de Milo.'

'If she's the one with no arms, then I'll thank you not to make odious comparisons,' Addy said. 'Oh, Giles, I know it's only been a few days, but I shall miss you so much. I suppose you won't come back to port for weeks because you'll be over-flying enemy territory in support of our troops, but will you be able to send messages back home? I *wish* they'd let us accompany the invasion force, but they won't let girls do anything exciting.'

'Thank God for that,' Giles said fervently. 'I shall have worries enough without adding that one.'

He began to kiss her and Addy, for the first time, longed to give him the intimacy that she knew he wanted, but she knew also that she simply could not do it. At this stage of the war, every single member of the armed forces was needed. And it would be just my luck, she thought miserably as he began to kiss and murmur, to find that I was pregnant. He would marry her like a shot, she knew that, but she also knew, with a shudder of real despair, that he might be unable to do so. His

314

job was a dangerous one. If he were badly injured, he might be in no position to marry anyone; and obviously if the worst happened and he was killed . . . her mind shied away from even the thought.

'Darling Addy,' Giles was murmuring in her ear. 'If you wanted me the way I want you, you'd just pretend to go into the Wrennery and nip out again and we could drive somewhere quiet and private and—and get to know one another better.'

'Oh, darling Giles, I wish we could, but it's too soon, you know. When all this is over, though, I promise you we'll do whatever you want.'

Giles sighed, but released her. 'You're right, of course, and I'm a thoughtless, selfish blighter,' he muttered. 'I shouldn't have asked it of you. Can you forget I ever said anything? Because if we had become lovers, the worry and the waiting would be worse.'

He sighed again and gave her a kiss so light and loving that for a moment she was tempted to change her mind, offer him the only gift it was in her power to give. But before she could say a word, Giles had straightened, got out of the car and walked round to help her to alight. 'I don't imagine there will be much opportunity for fellows to get in touch with their girls during the battles that will take place on such a wide front,' he told her, 'but I've had an idea; maybe it's a stupid one but I think it may comfort both of us. Every night, wherever we are, when the clock strikes eight, we'll try to find somewhere quiet. Then we'll think of each other and try to open a sort of channel between our minds. Oh, damn, I'm not putting this very well, but with your ability as a mind reader I guess you can understand. What d'you think? Are you on?'

'Yes, of course I know what you mean and of course I'll do it,' Addy said, and even as she spoke a picture flashed into her mind—the confined space of the interior of an aircraft, the grey sea and its white-topped waves beneath and somewhere, far ahead, a British battleship. Addy glanced uneasily at her companion, but already the picture was fading and, telling herself that it had been the product of an over-imaginative mind, she stood on tiptoe, flung her arms round Giles's neck and muttered that it would not be only at eight that his image would fill her head. Then she broke away from him and ran up the steps, remaining on the topmost one and waving until the little car rounded the bend in the drive and could be seen no more. Only then did she open the front door, close it carefully behind her and pass through the blackout curtain and into the hallway. A guilty glance at the clock told her that most of the girls would be asleep in bed, so she headed quietly for the stairs and mounted them. Before she had reached the half-landing, however, someone below hissed her name, and looking down she saw Gillian framed in the soft light from the kitchen. 'Addy Fairweather, you're jolly late! Fancy a chat and a cup of cocoa? The kettle's just boiled.'

'Oh, that would be grand,' Addy said gratefully, descending the stairs once more and entering the warm kitchen. Gillian was pouring water into two mugs and presently the girls settled down at the big kitchen table with the drinks in front of them.

'Did you and Giles have a good evening?' Gillian asked, looking rather shyly at the younger girl across the top of her steaming mug. 'Dominic

316

borrowed a jeep. It was the most uncomfortable vehicle, but the tank was full of juice and we went miles. Deep into the Devonshire countryside, not down to the coast. We took a picnic and went for a long walk. We found a little mossy hollow and ate our food there. You know, I fell for Dominic the very first time I met him, back in '42, but he's been sent all over the place—North Africa, Egypt and Italy—so we haven't seen nearly as much of one another as we would have liked. It wasn't until he was posted to Northern Ireland that we began to meet more regularly, but by then we were already in love and planning our future together. Only— only now he's off on the most dangerous posting of all and I'm sick with apprehension. He says there'll be no way he can get in touch until communications are secure between wherever he's posted and Britain.' She took a sip of her cocoa, then stood the mug down carefully. 'Giles and I have never kept secrets from one another, but suddenly there are things I can't bring myself to tell him. Is—is it the same for him, do you suppose?'

Addy was watching her friend's face and realised, suddenly, that it had changed since they had last met. She opened her mouth to say *You and Dominic have become lovers*, then changed her mind. If it was true, then it was none of her business, and if it was not true, or Gillian did not wish it to be known, then she had still better keep her mouth shut. But she thought, a little wistfully, that Gillian had done the right thing. Her relationship with Dominic was of long standing; their love for each other had withstood the lengthy periods of being apart and also the test of time.

317

But she must not continue to stare at her companion, for her eyes might well say what her lips could not. 'Sorry, I was thinking,' she said. 'What did you just ask me?'

'I asked you if you thought Giles might keep a secret from me, now that he has you to confide in,' Gillian said in a small voice. 'But I don't suppose ... I mean, you've only known him for a few days ...'

Addy decided that the time for some straight talking had arrived. She leaned across the table and took Gillian's hand in hers. 'I think you're trying to ask me whether Giles and I are lovers and the answer is no,' she said. 'We both want to, but as you say we haven't known each other long and God alone knows whether either of us will be alive in a few weeks. I'm not saying it would be tempting fate, but if I were to have a baby ...'

'Don't even suggest it,' Gillian said quickly. 'But I know Dominic so well that he's almost a part of me. If something horrible were to happen to him, so that we couldn't marry, a baby would be a consolation. But whatever am I doing, talking to you like this? Nothing will happen to Dominic, and how could I have a baby unless we'd become lovers? It's madness even talking about it.' She lowered her voice. 'You know the powers that be have been trying to make the Germans believe that the assault would be centred on Norway in the north and Pas-de-Calais in the south? Of course we all know differently, but one of the American flyers told a Wren he took dancing last night that the troops are being brought down to the coast tomorrow. He said it was for manoeuvres, but my friend said he winked as he spoke, so I reckon Dominic and I won't be seeing one another for a good while.'

'I think you're right,' Addy said ruefully. She hesitated, then took the plunge. 'I think you and Dominic *are* lovers, Gill, and you feel guilty because it's a secret you can't share with Giles. But I'm sure Giles will guess the first time he sets eyes on you, because I noticed a change the moment I saw you this evening.'

She half expected Gillian to get angry, to deny the truth of what she had just voiced, but instead Gillian nodded. 'Yes, I've heard people say that a girl's expression changes when she's been with a man. I thought it was just something people said to frighten girls into good behaviour—not that I'm a girl at twenty-seven—but now I see that it's true. Oh, Addy, I'm so glad that you know. I suppose it would have been easier to admit if you had told me that you and Giles were lovers. In fact I'd already decided I would tell you my own secret if that had been the case, but now I realise that it really isn't important. What *is* important is Dominic. Of course I want Giles's understanding, but I suppose I can't expect his approval. Giles is quite strait-laced, you know.'

'Is he? I suppose I haven't known him long enough to notice,' Addy said. 'But I don't think I'll be breaking any confidences if I tell you that he sort of suggested we might make love. When I said it was too soon, he asked me to forget he'd ever mentioned it though, so perhaps I should have kept my big mouth shut. Only it seemed mean, when you'd confided in me.'

'I'll not say a word to anyone, not even Dominic,' Gillian promised. 'But I honestly don't think Giles would mind me knowing that he had suggested it,

319

because it must mean he loves you.' She met Addy's gaze and held it, her own eyes very bright. 'Do you love *him*, Addy? I realise you've only known him for a few days, but I fell for Dominic the first time we met, so now I know, if you're right for one another, love can happen in the blink of an eye. Was it like that for you?'

Addy thought, then nodded her head slowly. 'Yes, it was like that for me, though I didn't realise it at the time. I was cross with him because he'd not recognised me as the child he had rescued all those years ago. Then he called me Prue, which is my sister's name, and of course I was jealous because already I felt Giles would always be special to me. And to tell you the truth, when we were kissing good night, for two pins I would have changed my mind, only he went all brisk on me, said goodbye and drove off. I thought then that I'd never forgive myself if something—something bad . . .'

'Stop it, don't say it, it's bad luck,' Gillian said quickly. 'There'll be other chances, I'm sure of it, and the next time Giles suggests it you'll say yes, and we'll all be in the same boat.'

Addy nodded and got to her feet, then carried the two empty cocoa mugs over to the sink, rinsed them and stood them on the draining board. 'You're right; when you love someone, you want to be together all the time,' she said. 'Oh, Gill, won't it be good when this wretched war is over and we can start planning the peace!'

*   *   *

The invasion fleet set out as quietly as was

possible, as soon as dawn began to grey the sky. Dominic was with all the others. He wore his uniform but had a pistol in its holster on his belt since he was an officer and did not have the long-barrelled rifle carried by the troops. He also had upon his person a selection of pencils, charcoal and chalk, and a thick sketchpad, tucked into a special pocket.

The weather was propitious for the Channel crossing; the lightest of breezes scarcely rippled the waves, and Dominic took his place on the landing craft to which he had been assigned, aware that excitement and apprehension warred within him and that at this stage, at any rate, excitement was the stronger emotion.

The breeze smelt of the sea and the shore, and all around him men were talking in hushed voices. They had been informed as they boarded their craft that this was not an exercise but the real thing at last, and that they were headed for the long, white Normandy beaches. Hopefully, they had been told, the enemy would be chiefly congregated in Norway and Pas-de-Calais, but no one believed that the Germans would have been fooled for more than five minutes. It would have been madness to try to invade Norway, with its numerous fjords and rocky shores, when the Normandy beaches, backed by great sand dunes, awaited them.

The light strengthened as they approached the shore and Dominic, sitting with his sketchpad on his knee, began to work. The faces of men about to go into battle are very revealing and Dominic knew it was his job to capture the expressions of the men around him. In doing so, he forgot everything but his pencil moving across the paper, though he grinned appreciatively at some of the remarks he overheard. Everyone was excited; glad, even, that the moment they had waited for was about to arrive. Invasion!

They had guessed that the beaches would be well defended, but not that they would meet a hail of withering gunfire almost as soon as they disembarked in shallow water and began to slog up the srand, the objective of everyone but Dominic being to take out the artillery which was strewing the beach with the dead. Dominic, keeping his head down, continued to draw with quick, confident strokes. Horrible pictures now; the sort the War Office should have expected. Dominic's pencil drew on.

*   *   *

In the sky above the beaches, Giles and Neville had a bird's eye view of the bloody battle taking place below them and did their best to annihilate the German guns and the men firing them. Giles took their stringbag as low as he dared, and went as slowly as he dared, with the result that almost every bomb Neville released hit its target. After the bombs had all gone they went lower still, and very soon they began to see their troops approach the enemy and begin hand-to-hand fighting.

At last Giles turned for home, calling to Neville to guide them back to their aircraft carrier. Both men were exhausted, and Giles was secretly relieved, and guessed that Neville felt the same, when they touched down lightly on deck, with the fuel gauge on empty and their stomachs grumbling, for they had not eaten since a hasty sandwich at breakfast time. They went down the companionway and into the mess, and were soon tackling large plates of stew and potato and talking animatedly to other pilots who had been active that day. Halfway through his meal, Giles glanced at his watch. The planes had taken off at two-hour intervals and Giles and Neville, along with the rest of their flight, had departed from the ship at noon. Now, seeing that it was five to eight, he realised with some dismay that his promise to think of Addy at exactly eight o'clock would be difficult to manage, for he could scarcely get up and leave his dinner—there was apple crumble and custard for pudding—and he did not think he could concentrate on Addy whilst eating and chatting. However, he supposed that the exact time might be impossible for both of them sometimes, so he settled down to eat as quickly as he could, then made his way on to the deck at a quarter past eight. Out here all was bustle, with another flight coming in and personnel everywhere, but he managed to find a quiet corner where he could pretend to be looking down at the calm sea beneath.

Then he began to think of Addy. He thought of her small face with the wide brown eyes fringed with dark curling lashes. He thought of her fall of shining black hair, straight as rain and smelling of primroses, and of her slender strong body pressed against him. He thought of the way her mouth shaped itself almost into a V when she smiled, showing the chipped tooth which she thought no one would notice; perhaps it was only noticeable to the eye of love, he told himself now. Oh, Addy

Fairweather, how I love you and how I hope we'll be together soon, when this wretched war is over.

He waited for quite five minutes, half expecting to hear her voice, but nothing happened and presently, with a sigh, he returned to the mess deck where he was greeted with a punch on the shoulder from Neville. 'What a moment to need a pee, old chap,' Neville said genially. 'Just after you left, Cook announced that there were seconds of the apple crumble, but don't worry, I managed to bag two, so you won't lose out. I've eaten mine already, 'cos I was perishin' starving, and as soon as you've finished yours we'd best get to our hammocks because I've looked on the board—bet you forgot—and we're the first flight off tomorrow, so we might as well grab whatever sleep we can get.'

'I s'pose it's fair enough, and thanks very much for the extra pud,' Giles said, eating it as fast as he could. 'There's only one good thing about a hammock—if you manage to get into the bloody thing—it moves with the motion of the ship so it's like being a baby in a cradle.'

'Aye, unless the sea's really rough,' Neville reminded him. 'Finished? C'mon on then, let's get some shut-eye.'

The two men made their way to their sleeping quarters, took off their outer clothing and climbed into their hammocks. Giles had just cocooned himself into his blankets and was in that comfortable state between waking and sleeping when a voice he knew stole into his head. 'Never mind; you couldn't help it,' Addy said. 'Good night, sweetheart.'

Giles grinned to himself and hunched the covers up round his ears. My imagination's working

324

overtime, hearing what it wants to hear, he told himself. C'mon, Addy, if you're really out there, tell me where you were at a quarter past eight, when I was trying so desperately to get in touch with you. He was not surprised when no answer came, and he slept.

*   *   *

Addy had done her best to 'get through' to Giles when she heard eight o'clock chime as she was riding her motorbike through a small and sleepy village. She had drawn up alongside a mossy field gate and gazed over it at the sheep, placidly grazing in the evening sun. She had concentrated really hard and was able to bring to mind a mental picture of Giles as she had last seen him. He was not handsome, as Dominic was, but nevertheless she knew she would always consider Giles to be the more attractive of the two. He had a bony face, a rather knobbly nose and a very determined chin; his dark hair flopped over a tanned brow and in her mental picture of him his expressive eyes, full of rueful affection, seemed to be smiling into hers.

Addy had tried to link minds with him for ten whole minutes, then had started her engine and set off for her destination once more. Perhaps it took time and patience to get on the same wavelength with someone miles away, or perhaps it was just impossible; anyway, she had work to do. Resolutely, she banished Giles from her mind and concentrated on finding her way through the winding Devonshire lanes to the little port and the officer into whose charge she would deliver the papers in her knapsack.

On her way home, she stopped once more, close by the field gate where she had tried in vain to contact Giles. It was a beautiful spot, so gentle and peaceful that the war seemed a thousand miles away. The setting sun had gilded the fleeces of the sheep and had traced a path, straight as an arrow, across the distant sea. Overhead, the sky was still blue, though it was darkening towards sunset, and Addy allowed the picture of Giles to creep back into her mind. She smiled, half mockingly, remembering her attempt—and presumably his— to get in touch. 'Never mind; you couldn't help it,' Addy murmured, turning the motorbike's wheel towards Plymouth once more. 'Good night, sweetheart.'

*   *   *

The June days passed with the Allies moving ever deeper into occupied territory. Dominic was with his unit, sketching the countryside, and the men who fought to free the French from the hated Nazi regime. The German prisoners of war were given the task of burying the dead. It would have been madness to leave the corpses lying where they fell, for not only would it have been bad for morale but such a quantity of dead men posed a serious health threat. Besides, it was better to give the Germans work which freed the Allied soldiers to press on. Some of the prisoners were cowed in defeat, others defiant, but Dominic simply drew them and neither hated nor loved those he depicted. It was his work and he adored it and thought, when he had time to think, that he was doing a good job and that he was a lucky dog to have been given the opportunity.

In the main, they pushed ahead during the day and bivouacked at night, wherever they could find some sort of shelter. Food was scarce, for the locals had been forced to hand over most of what they produced to the Germans. The Allied troops, however, received rations brought in by transport ships, and when supplies failed to keep up with their rapid advance Dominic would draw a farmer's pretty little girl or handsome, wide-eyed little boy, and be grateful to receive a bowl of oatmeal or vegetable soup in exchange. Other troops used cigarettes as currency, for they were unavailable for the most part, or so expensive as to put them out of reach of the local populace.

Dominic thought about Gillian a great deal, and also about her brother. He wondered how he was getting on, for as they advanced they met pilots who had had to parachute into occupied France when their aircraft were hit, and every time he met one of these fliers he was glad that it was not Giles.

He had hoped that communication between the invading forces and England might be good, but found it not to be so, though he did manage to send a couple of messages to Gillian to say that he was all right and enjoying his work, and hoped she received them. He knew he could tell her very little without falling foul of the censor, so kept his messages brief, did not describe the countryside through which they advanced, and only mentioned that the weather had been kind to them so far, thinking that this was a fact which the Jerries would know as much about as the English.

He wrote to Giles a couple of times, and once received a reply, simply saying that the other man was well and enjoying a bird's eye view of the battle on the ground. Dominic knew that the air force were destroying factories and ammunition dumps but did not expect Giles to mention such things. Instead, Dominic concentrated on his own job, wondering how long it would be before they could take Paris; only then could Operation Overlord be deemed a success.

*   *   *

It was the wind that woke Addy. At first she was only aware of a moaning sound, penetrating her dreams, but then the moaning turned into a shrieking, and she found herself sitting upright and staring, wide-eyed, towards the window, with its rattling panes and rain-streaked glass.

The Wrens had taken over Foliat Manor after the army's departure and she and Gillian were billeted in Giles's old room, since it was impossible for the girls to have a room each with so many people needing accommodation.

Addy waited for a few minutes to see if the storm would ease and allow her to go back to sleep, but instead it grew more violent still, so she slipped out of bed and padded over to the window. Outside, in the faint light from the clouded sky, she could see the trees lashing themselves into a frenzy, and the rain pelting down and puddling the paths which surrounded the rose garden. A crack of thunder accompanied a fork of lightning which lit up the whole scene. Gillian joined her at the window, pressing her nose to the glass and saying excitedly: 'Glory be, what a storm! What a good thing our transport and troop reinforcements travel by day.

328

Have you ever seen anything like it, Addy? I spent my whole childhood at Foliat Manor and I've watched some pretty fierce storms, but nothing to rival this one. Storms are always worse in the Channel because there's nowhere for the waves to go. I hope the *Sparrowhawk* is anchored well away from here or Giles will be in a sorry state by morning.'

'I hope so too,' Addy said fervently. 'He told me that though he had largely conquered it, rough seas had always made him throw up.'

Gillian laughed. 'He's got over that now, thank God,' she said. 'But he still has the devil of a job to get in to his hammock when there are big seas running. I say, what was that? Oh, look, that huge pine over where the tennis court used to be has been struck! Addy, it's on fire! Whatever should we do?'

In the brilliant light from the blazing pine, for one moment Addy saw a man's tall figure, the pale oval of his face turned towards the house. She grabbed her friend's arm and shook it impatiently. 'See that man?' she shouted above the roll of thunder. 'If the pine falls . . .'

'What man? Good God, girl, as if anyone would be wandering round the grounds in weather like this! Oh, I suppose you mean that rose bush; it does look a bit like a man, particularly when the wind bends it right over so it seems to be bowing. But shouldn't we *do* something? The pine is too far away from the house to cause damage here, but if it falls and sets fire to other trees . . .'

'We'd best wake the others, if any of them are still asleep, that is,' Addy said, struggling into her sweater and trousers. 'And you're right, of course, there's no one in the gardens. It must have been the rose bush and the shadows.'

Gillian, pulling on her own clothes, simply nodded, and as they ran along the passage shouting to the other girls she pointed out breathlessly that with luck the rain would douse the fire before it reached the other trees.

This, however, did not prove to be the case and most of the girls spent the night fighting the fire in the underbrush surrounding the great pine. 'We're lighting up a wonderful target for the Luftwaffe,' Gillian remarked to Addy at one point, as they formed a bucket chain and did their best to quench the flames. 'But of course they won't be flying on a night like this, and Doodlebugs, though they may take no notice of the weather, can't see any target, no matter how well lit.'

'That's true. I know it's awful of me, but I thank God when they buzz overhead without their engines cutting out,' Addy said. She put a hand to the small of her back and straightened with some difficulty as the rain, which had eased, began to fall again so heavily that they could not see the manor from where they stood. Addy gestured to the burnt-out undergrowth and the faint curls of smoke arising from it. 'We've done all we can here, Gill, and I think we ought to get back to the house and try to have at least some sleep. Oh, how I pray the boys are safe!'

*   *   *

Giles's ship had been off Land's End when the storm had struck in the Channel, so the men aboard the *Sparrowhawk* had had an excellent view of what Neville had described as the best firework display he had ever watched.

Next morning, however, by the time Giles and Neville took to the air, the storm had gone muttering and grumbling off, leaving clear skies and sunshine to help them on their way. As they flew up the Channel, they began to see signs of the damage that the storm had wrought. They had been told, on this occasion, to take out a bridge that the Germans were using to ferry food and ammunition to their troops north of Paris, but as they neared the French coast Neville spoke. 'Look!' he shouted. 'Can you see the Mulberry Harbours? They were just below us and a bit to the left yesterday but today there's no sign of them. Don't say Jerry has actually managed to destroy them totally.'

'Dunno; but I'll take the old girl lower so we can have a proper butcher's,' Giles said. 'I reckon, myself, that it was a really bad storm . . . yes, look! I believe I can see part of a Mulberry Harbour jutting up over there. If you ask me, the waves sank them. The ships that were moored alongside must have had to get clear or been dragged down too.'

He laughed grimly when Neville said: 'Just goes to show that the weather can do what the Jerries can't. But they'll refloat the harbours, just see if they don't. They're too useful to be allowed to remain on the seabed.'

'Yes, they're bound to,' Giles agreed, turning his aircraft's nose towards the French coast. He thought the Mulberry Harbours a brilliant idea and was sure that the Allies would not let this wonderful invention go to waste. They had been made somewhere in North Wales, when the idea of

331

the invasion had first been mooted. Then, when it was safe to do so, they had been towed across the Channel and anchored at intervals along the Normandy beaches, to provide secure moorings for the transports and troop carriers bringing supplies and reinforcements across to France.

Neville grunted. 'Wonder who invented them?' he said idly. 'The chap deserves a medal, whoever he was. And now let's find this perishin' bridge.'

*   *   *

In July Addy was called to her CO's office and told that she might take a week's leave. 'Are you sure, ma'am?' she said anxiously. She had had to work twelve, fourteen and even sixteen hour days, and was looking forward to getting some rest, but did not want to leave her fellow messengers in the lurch.

However, the CO nodded confidently. 'Most of the damage done by the storm has been put right and we can cope without you for a few days,' she assured Addy. 'You've worked extremely hard without a word of complaint so make the most of it. I know you come from Liverpool, so I've signed your rail pass and the galley will provide you with a packed lunch. Because of troop movements and so on, the railways are pretty busy, so it may take you most of your first day's leave simply to reach your destination. But I know you won't mind that. You should try to sleep en route—if you can get a seat, that is—and remember you have to be back before midnight next week. It makes you sound a bit like Cinderella, but you know how important it is, so give yourself plenty of time for your return journey.'

Addy thanked her, saluted, and early next morning cadged a lift from one of the drivers and arrived at the station before the sun was up. The previous evening, at eight o'clock, she had thought very hard about Giles, telling him that she was about to take a spot of leave and wishing that she could share it with him. She often imagined that he replied to such messages, but she acknowledged ruefully to herself that this was only wishful thinking and that Nonny's much vaunted second sight had not been passed on to her. She had mentioned her efforts, rather shyly, to other girls whose men were away, and found that such attempts to get in touch with a loved one at a certain time were not uncommon. Even though they were largely unsuccessful, those who tried to communicate in this way seemed to find comfort in the endeavour, as Addy herself did.

As the CO had predicted, Addy's journey was a nightmare. She did not manage to get a seat and was crammed in with the service personnel who filled every single carriage. She missed connections, twice caught buses and once hitched a lift, but fortunately she had set out so early that she still arrived in the city of her birth the same day, though it was midnight and raining steadily when she finally banged on the front door of the Vines public house.

She had sent a telegram, so the family knew what day she would be arriving, but of course she had not been able to advise them of the exact hour. Nevertheless, the door was flung open within seconds of her knock and Prue catapulted into her arms. 'Addy, oh, Addy, it's good to see you,' she cried. 'I was on night shift last night so after I'd had a quick zizz I went along to Lime Street, hoping to be lucky enough to meet you off your train. Only then I got chatting with a pal, and he said you might come in at Central . . . oh, Addy, it's so good to see you. You look ever so well.'

'I'm fine,' Addy said as they entered the kitchen. 'I say, what a wonderful smell! Has Nonny made one of her famous casseroles?'

Prue nodded and extracted a dish from the oven as Addy slung her kitbag on a chair, took off her coat and began to make a pot of tea. She poured the brew into two mugs and the sisters settled down at the table to eat.

Presently, their first hunger sated, they began to catch up with each other's news. 'You first, because you're the eldest,' Prue said, reaching for her mug of tea. 'You'd better start with being posted to Plymouth and meeting up with Gillian and Giles again, as you mentioned in one of your letters. Off you go!'

Addy was tired and had secretly hoped that Prue would leave conversation until the morrow, but once she got started she quite enjoyed reliving the experiences of the past few weeks. Normally she and Prue wrote to one another regularly, but they had both been rushed off their feet recently and had only exchanged scrappy notes, so it was news to Prue that Addy and Giles had fallen deeply in love and meant to marry when the war was over.

'Oh, Addy, I'm so happy for you,' she said, when Addy leaned back in her chair and indicated that her narrative was now up to date. 'It makes my own story seem pretty dull, though.'

'It won't be dull to me,' Addy promised her.

'Only I'm jolly tired, so start at once, if you please!'

'I've got a regular boyfriend, too; you'll never guess who it is.'

'Is it someone I know?' Addy asked, surprised. 'Your letters are always full of names, but I can't say I've noticed one in particular . . . yes I have, though. For the past few months you've written a lot about a chap called Nick.'

Prue gave a crow of laughter. 'Oh, Addy, it's Nick Bentley! He's the tail gunner in a Lancaster. Why on earth didn't you guess? You and I have both known Nick for years.'

'Nick Bentley? Well, I'm blowed! I often wondered what had happened to those two after they joined up and left home,' Addy said. 'But you never showed much interest in either him or Paul, or you never mentioned them to me, at any rate. So you're going out with him, are you? How come you met up?'

'Oh, I went to a dance given by the air force at one of the airfields near here,' Prue said airily. 'They send a gharry—that's what they call a lorry—to pick up the girls from the factories and then deliver us to our homes when the dance is over. Nick and I took one look at each other and more or less fell into each other's arms. We danced every single dance together and talked and talked. When the dance finished, he asked if he could meet me somewhere next time he got leave, even if it was only a forty-eight. I explained to Mam how we'd met up again and she agreed that he was welcome to stay at the Vines. Apparently, Mr and Mrs Bentley aren't in the catering trade any more. They keep a small shop in a village in the wilds of Wales somewhere, and have no room for the boys.

So Nick and I have been going steady for over a year and we mean to marry when the war's over.' She fished in her blouse and produced a thin gold chain, upon which hung a small diamond ring. 'Mam thinks I'm too young to wear it on my finger, but when the war's over we'll get engaged properly. And I produce it if someone comes on too strong and pretend I'm practically a married woman!'

Addy laughed. 'You're quite mad,' she said affectionately. 'Any chance of me seeing Nick whilst I'm home? And you must know what's happened to Paul. Is he in the air force, too?'

'No, he's with the army in India,' Prue told her. 'As for seeing Nick, you could probably do that more easily than me, because he's been posted down to the south coast with the rest of his crew. You said your Giles is in the RNAS and flies a Swordfish with only one other crew member, but Nick's Lanc has a crew of six or seven. I tell myself they're safer in the air than on the ground, but even so I worry a lot.'

'Yes, of course you do,' Addy said. 'Be thankful that Nick's aircraft lands on solid ground, though, and not on a tilting deck which bounces up and down every time a wave hits the ship.'

Prue leaned across the table and squeezed her sister's hand. 'Oh poor Addy,' she said sincerely. 'And I don't suppose it's easy to get in touch with Giles by telephone, or letter. I ring Nick's mess two or three times a week and he rings me as well. It's a great comfort.'

'I envy you that,' Addy admitted. 'I think wearing the ring the way you do is brilliant and I wish I could do the same, but Giles and I never really had time to even consider buying one. We went out twice in a car he borrowed, and once to the flicks. As for someone coming on too strong, I'm not a pretty young blonde, so I don't need the protection of an engagement ring.'

Addy had only been joking, but Prue jumped in at once. 'Oh, Addy, you are pretty . . . no, you're beautiful,' she assured her sister. 'You've got a lovely, unusual sort of face and your hair is so dark and shiny—'

'And so straight and gypsyish,' Addy cut in, grinning. 'But in fact I'm generally too tired when I come off duty to want to go out again. Being a messenger is hard work, Prue. My motorbike is heavy and I have to do all my own maintenance. So one way and another I'm kept pretty busy, which is a good thing because it's hard to work and worry at the same time. Now tell me about Mam and Nonny, and Jamie of course. How are they getting on?'

'You've only just missed them; Mam and Jamie had a busy night in the pub and went to bed about ten minutes before you got home,' Prue said. 'And Nonny went off early, after she'd made our supper. Oh, Addy, I think Mam and Jamie are the perfect couple and an example of how I'd like my marriage to be. Mam's a firewatcher, so sometimes she helps to close the pub and then starts work all over again, patrolling her area. But she and Jamie are so happy that I quite envy them. They work together and even when they're not in the pub they're seldom apart. When Mam's firewatching, Jamie sets the alarm and takes her a flask of hot tea halfway through her shift, and when he's doing his ARP work she does the same for him, and never a word of complaint from either of them.

337

'But I've not told you about the plans for tomorrow. It's my day off, so Mam thought you and I might go shopping. We can have our lunch out at a British Restaurant—they're really good, and cheap too—and then, if it's a sunny day, we might take a tram up to Prince's Park. I'm afraid Nonny won't be coming with us, though she loves an outing, because it's her day for helping at one of the local shops. And Mam and Jamie are always busy, so it will be just you and me.'

'That'll be lovely,' Addy said. 'How is Nonny, though, Prue? She always sounds brisk and happy in her letters, but is she just putting a good face on things? And what's this about helping in a local shop? I thought she worked in the bar when they're busy.'

'She used to, but Mam and Jamie don't really need any help now, what with the shortage of drink and all the young men away fighting. However, some small shopkeepers find the amount of extra paperwork which rationing has caused almost impossible to tackle, so Nonny goes round to Mr Robertson's—if you remember, they were always pals—and counts coupons, fills in forms, makes sure that his books are up to date and so on. She goes in two days a week and he pays her ten bob a day, which is good money, but you know Nonny—she'd never let him down even if he didn't pay her a penny.'

'And it's not too much for her?' Addy asked rather anxiously. 'She's an old lady, though she doesn't act like one.'

'She copes extremely well, all things considered,' Prue said. 'But we've done enough talking for one night. Goodness, it's past one o'clock. Let's leave the washing up till morning and try to get some sleep before breakfast!'

CHAPTER FOURTEEN

Despite her intention to get up betimes so as not to lose a moment of her time at home, Addy woke late. When she reached the kitchen, only Nonny was present, placidly stirring porridge and sipping a large mug of tea. She beamed at her granddaughter and came across the kitchen to give her a kiss.

'Hello, Addy,' she said cheerfully. 'Lovely to see you lookin' so well. Your mam and Prue have gone shopping—not the sort of shopping you two girls have planned but food shopping, for the pub this evening—and Jamie's gone off to Seaforth to see if he can get hold of some potted shrimps. But Prue said to tell you she'd not be long, so probably by the time you've ate your breakfast she'll be back and naggin' you to gerra move on.'

'Morning, Nonny. Thanks for hanging about so that I'd have a hot breakfast. Prue told me last night that you're working at Mr Robertson's today.'

'Ah, but I doesn't start till ten,' Nonny explained. She took another drink of tea, then grinned at her granddaughter. 'You were a lie-abed this morning, weren't you? I thought you'd be up with the bleedin' lark.'

Addy laughed. 'I didn't get in till midnight and we talked till almost two o'clock,' she admitted. 'I meant to get up when Prue did but I guess I was so tired I just slept through the alarm and Prue dressing and so on.'

She settled herself at the table and took the bowl of porridge offered with a word of thanks, watching whilst Nonny pottered about the kitchen, cleaned the porridge pan and then began to toast two slices of bread. When they were ready, she buttered one for Addy but chose to cut her own piece into fingers, which she then dipped in her tea.

'Oh, Nonny, how can you?' Addy said, laughing. 'Surely you can eat toast without dunking it.'

Her grandmother laughed too but shook her head. 'It's me gypsy blood,' she said. 'Once they're past seventy, all gypsies soak their toast in their tea to soften it, not that they need to do so any more'n I do, 'cos all gypsies have perfect teeth, as I've told you many a time.'

Addy giggled. She remembered the first occasion when as a child she had popped into Nonny's room with an early morning cup of tea and screamed with terror at the sight of a set of 'perfect teeth' grinning at her from a glass beside the bed. At the time, Nonny had shot upright, grabbed the glass, sending water flying everywhere, and crunched the teeth back into her mouth in one swift movement. Then she had said accusingly: 'Wharrever did you yell like that for, you baggage? You near on give me a heart attack, so you did.' She had stared, challengingly, at the small Addy, who had found herself quite incapable of admitting that it had been the teeth that had scared her so.

Now she hastily banished the recollection. She loved her grandmother far too much to mention either the perfection of her teeth or the blackness

340

of her hair, knowing that the first was thanks to the dentist at Brougham Terrace and the second to the bottle of dye pushed to the back of the kitchen cupboard.

'Well?' Nonny said now. 'What are you grinning for? Are you doubting that I've perfect teeth?'

Addy giggled again, then sobered. 'Of course you have perfect teeth,' she said, knowing that she spoke no more than the truth, for Nonny's false teeth were indeed perfection. 'Nonny, there's something really important I've got to ask you. Is there anyone in the bar likely to overhear, or are we quite alone?'

Nonny, who had been looking pensive, perked up. 'We're quite alone,' she said confidently. 'Your mam employs a cleaner, but she comes in first thing and since it's now twenty to ten she'll have been gone a long while.' She picked up their plates and put them in the sink, then returned to the table. 'I loves giving advice,' she said, beaming at her granddaughter. 'It's something I'm real good at. What's your problem, queen?'

'It's not exactly a problem, it's just that I don't understand something which has happened to me twice,' Addy said slowly, choosing her words with care. 'It's like this, Nonny. When we first moved into Foliat Manor, I was awoken one night by the full moon shining on my face . . .'

Addy told the story as simply and truthfully as she could and was pleased when Nonny heard her out in silence, only nodding occasionally, her bright black eyes never leaving Addy's face.

Addy finished explaining her childhood experience and paused expectantly, but Nonny wagged a reproving finger. 'Twice you said, and

341

that's only once. I want the whole story, if you please.'

Obediently, Addy told her of the night of the storm, and how she had seen the figure again by the light of the fire that had raged at the edge of the pine wood. 'My friend Gillian, who was looking out of the same window, saw nothing,' she finished. 'Well, she pointed out a rose bush which was bending almost to the ground when the wind caught it and asked if that was what I'd seen, but the figure I saw wasn't shadowy or anything like that. I think it might have been the same man I'd seen before, though I couldn't make out his features. Can you explain it, Nonny? At first I simply thought someone had come up from the village to have a snoop round the grounds; a poacher perhaps, though that seemed unlikely. But when it happened again . . . oh, I don't know, I think I had the feeling that it was a bit like watching a film, especially since the figure didn't move but simply disappeared in the blink of an eye.' She gazed seriously at her grandmother. 'You've often talked about second sight but the truth is I never really knew what you meant by it. Would you call seeing that figure second sight? And if so, what does it mean? As you know, we've been back at Foliat Manor for the best part of a month and I'm pretty sure no one else has seen anything untoward. So what d'you think, Nonny?'

'I think you do have second sight, or something very like it,' Nonny said slowly. 'I think you've seen a picture of something which happened long ago or something which is yet to occur. Are you sure you don't know who the man might be? If you've seen him twice you must have some idea, surely?

342

Describe the scene again, first when you were a child and then this latest time.'

Obediently, Addy did so. As she talked, she remembered details about the figure that she had seen without realising that they might help to identify him. 'He was wearing uniform,' she said slowly, pressing her forehead with the tips of her fingers. 'And he's dark-haired. He's tall and quite thin, but broad-shouldered, and he's always looking up at the window of my room.'

Nonny nodded slowly, got up from her place at the table and went to where her hat and coat hung on the back of the kitchen door. 'Doesn't he remind you of anyone?' she asked. 'Though I suppose it's perfectly possible that it's just an imprint on time, if you understand me.'

'No, I don't,' Addy said frankly. 'You mustn't leave me in the lurch, Nonny. I've got to know what it means.'

Her grandmother had been putting on her coat and now she went over to the small mirror and checked that her hair was neatly pinned into its usual bun. With her back to Addy, she said: 'I'm not sure what it means, queen. If you'd only seen the feller once, I'd have said to forget it. It would be something that had happened in the past, maybe long ago. The feller might have been in love with a gal what occupied your room and mebbe he'd left a sort of image on the air. I dunno as I understand it meself, but you've seen him twice, which I tell you straight ain't commonplace by any means. I'll have a think, and if I come up with an explanation I'll let you know.'

She was heading for the back door when Addy shot out a hand and stopped her. 'Nonny, could it

343

mean something bad? Or something sad, perhaps? I've not explained that the bedroom the fellow was staring at belonged to Giles Frobisher until the house was requisitioned. Giles is in the RNAS, so of course he wears a dark uniform, and he and I are pretty close.'

Nonny paused. 'D'you think it's him?' she asked, her tone incredulous. 'The feller who rescued you and Prue that time? You could have knocked me and your mam down with a feather when you wrote and told us you'd met up with him again. But think on, chuck, why should he be starin' up at his own bedroom window? And why didn't you recognise him straight off, if you're such good pals?'

'Yes, I suppose I ought to have known him, if it was really Giles,' Addy said slowly, by no means reassured; the figure had been too far away for her to see his features. 'Then you think I'm simply seeing something that has happened, or will happen? You don't think it's a sign that someone— someone I know and love—is going to be killed?'

Nonny tutted. 'I told you, I don't know what it means, not really,' she said rather crossly. 'Second sight's a peculiar thing an' I don't reckon anyone can explain it. But I'm off now; I don't mean to be late for me work. We'll talk about it later, when I've had a think.' She snatched the back door open, then turned to grin at her granddaughter. 'Just you enjoy yourself wi' young Prue, and stop worryin'.'

Addy grinned back. 'I shan't worry, not now I've passed the buck to you,' she said. 'Have a good day yourself, Nonny, and give Mr Robertson my regards.'

Nonny had been about to close the door, but turned back to wag a reproving finger at Addy.

344

'You've not passed me nothin', but a trouble shared is a trouble halved,' she said rather obscurely. 'If you remember anything else, though . . .'

Addy was about to say she was sure she had told Nonny everything when she gasped, a hand flying to her mouth. Her grandmother, already poised to close the back door, stopped in her tracks.

'Wharris it?' she demanded. 'You've remembered something else, haven't you?'

'Yes,' Addy said slowly, suddenly reluctant to pass on what had just occurred to her. 'Oh, Nonny, on the night of the storm, with the big pine on fire and the whole garden lit up, he—he cast no shadow!'

*   *   *

It was a warm August evening and Prue was out with her friend Maisie from the factory. They had meant to go to the Grafton Ballroom but when they reached it the length of the queue waiting to enter changed their minds. 'There will be five girls for every fellow, which means we'll have to dance with each other, and it's too perishin' hot,' Prue grumbled. 'What would you like to do instead?'

'I dunno; I've got me best dress on and I do love to dance,' Maisie said discontentedly. Then she brightened. 'Tell you what, why don't we go along to Lime Street Station, to the buffet—it'll still be open—and get ourselves a cup of tea and a currant bun? Then we can go back to the Grafton when most of the queue will have gone in and we won't have to hang about.'

Prue agreed with this scheme, the only caveat

from her point of view being that she preferred lemonade to tea on such a warm evening, and presently the two girls were seated in the station buffet with glasses of lemonade before them, though Prue had taken one look at the solid currant buns crouched beneath a fly-repelling glass cover and said that if they ate them they would unlikely to be able to dance a step.

They enjoyed watching the passing crowds and were twice propositioned, once by two aircraftmen and once by a couple of matelots, who claimed to recognise them from a previous visit to the city. The cheekier of the two actually greeted Prue by name, but since the girls had noticed him sitting at a nearby table and straining his ears to hear their conversation, they told him politely, but firmly, to buzz off. 'My feller's six foot four and weighs twelve stone, and he don't like sailors what chance their arm with young ladies like me and my pal here,' Prue said repressively. She finished her lemonade, then pulled Maisie to her feet as a train drew up alongside the platform. 'Ah, there he is; me feller! You can see him over the heads of the crowd.' She turned to grin at the two crestfallen sailors. 'Cheerio, fellers; better luck next time!'

Giggling, the two girls joined the jostling crowd, and Maisie had just remarked that it was a good thing the matelots had accepted the rebuff when Prue gave a squeak. A strong arm had encircled her waist, and now a voice said in her ear: 'Prue! Oh, Prue, I've searched everywhere, I've written . . . oh, my dear girl, I thought . . . I thought . . .'

'Nick!' Prue gasped. 'Why didn't you let—'

She stopped short. The man who clutched her so tightly was not Nick, and for a moment she did not

346

know who he was or how she knew him. Then he gave her waist a squeeze and turned her to face him. 'Ed!' Prue squeaked. 'Ed Wilkinson! Wharrever are you doing here? And how on earth did you recognise me? It must be more than three years since we were both at Foliat Manor and I was a skinny little schoolgirl in a wheelchair. Don't say I haven't changed or I shall be forced to give you a slap.'

Maisie's hand on her arm reminded her that her friend knew nothing of Edgar Wilkinson. Gently, she detached herself from Ed's grasp, for he still had a hand on her waist, and turned to Maisie. 'I'm so sorry, Maisie; how very rude you must think me. This is Ed Wilkinson. Ed and I were both evacuated to a house in Devonshire in the early days of the war. We were there for nearly two years—very happy years—but then Addy and I came back to Liverpool. We wrote for a bit, didn't we, Ed, but then we lost touch.'

'Aye, it happens in wartime,' Maisie said. She shot out a hand. 'How d'you do, Mr Wilkinson? I'm Maisie Finnigan; me and our Prue work alongside each other, packing parachutes. We were on our way to the Grafton Ballroom, but seein' as you two'll have a lot to talk about, I dare say I'd best gerroff home.'

Both Ed and Prue cried out at this, but Maisie was insistent and presently left them, hurrying through the crowd without a backward glance. Prue and Ed followed more slowly and were in time to see Maisie darting across the road heading, Prue was relieved to see, not for her own home but for the Grafton Ballroom. Only then did she turn to Ed and tuck her hand in his arm. 'Let's go back to the station buffet—you wouldn't know, but Maisie and I were in there having a lemonade when your train drew in, though of course we didn't know it was your train,' she said. 'Actually, we only left when we did because two sailors were trying to pick us up.' She giggled. 'Dear Ed, you saved me from being a liar, as we'd just told the fellers that we were meeting my boyfriend. I'd made that up, of course . . . oh, dear, I do hope they aren't still in the buffet. Not that I think they'd try anything on once they see you.'

'They'd better not,' Ed said rather grimly, but presently, comfortably settled at a table at the back of the room, with a ham sandwich apiece and a pot of tea for two, Prue was able to look at her companion properly for the first time. She decided that he had improved greatly. His red hair had deepened to a colour she would have described as dark chestnut, though she imagined that this was probably due to the daily applications of Brylcreem that all young men seemed to favour. But she remembered him as being both pallid and spotty, and though he had a band of freckles across the bridge of his nose his skin was now clear. What was more, his figure showed no trace of adolescent chubbiness and he had grown several inches taller.

'Well? Recognise me again, young lady?'

Prue felt her cheeks grow hot, and said quickly: 'You've changed a lot, Ed, and I suppose I have as well. We've both grown up, and you've done it very nicely, if I may say so! But what was it you said when we met out there?' She jerked a thumb at the busy concourse. 'Something about writing or searching . . . I can't remember your exact words . . .'

'Good,' Ed interrupted fervently. 'The truth is,

348

when I found myself in Liverpool I realised that this was the city you and Addy had come from. I remembered that you'd written to me when you first returned to live at home, so I looked up the letter, found the address and decided to pay you a visit. I reached where the shop should have been, only it wasn't. You can imagine how I felt, Prue— of course I leapt to the conclusion that your family had been wiped out from a direct hit. And yet somewhere in the back of my mind I just couldn't believe you were dead.' He leaned across the table and rumpled her fair curls. 'Several times I've seen girls who might easily have been you, yet somehow, when I got near enough, I knew they were strangers. It's really odd, isn't it, Prue? I mean, I only saw you for a moment just now—and I'd never seen you standing up before!—and yet I never doubted that I'd found my little friend at last.'

'That is *so* romantic,' Prue breathed, very impressed. 'But you haven't explained what you're doing in Liverpool, though I can see you're in the Navy so I gather this is your ship's home port. And if so, I'll take you home and introduce you to my mother and stepfather, and I'm sure they'll ask you to spend your time ashore with us.' She looked at him thoughtfully, memories beginning to flood back into her mind. 'Your parents were killed in a car accident when you were quite young, weren't they? I remember you telling us after we got friendly that your guardians were an old aunt and uncle who lived in London and had no time for the young. Are they still alive? Do you go back there for your leaves?'

Ed nodded. 'Yes, sometimes, but they aren't in

London any more. They're living in a small hotel in Tunbridge Wells. It's mainly occupied by old people like themselves and when I do go there I feel an intruder, so it would be wizard to have somewhere to stay actually in Liverpool. But are you sure your parents wouldn't mind?'

'My mother married the landlord of a pub called the Vines, which they work together,' Prue said. 'My gran lives at the pub as well and of course Addy and I have a room there. But it's a big, rambling old place and they can always find a bed for a friend. Mind you, you'll probably end up behind the bar, or acting as cellar man when Jamie's busy. Jamie's my stepfather; he's ever so nice, and quite young enough to be in the forces, except that he's a chronic asthmatic. But what were you doing on the station, Ed? Don't say your leave is over and you're off back to your ship.'

Ed grinned. 'No, just the opposite. I was about to board a train for London when I saw your blonde head. I've been in hospital, to tell you the truth, and was about to start a couple of weeks' sick leave. Having nowhere else to go, my eventual destination would have been Tunbridge Wells. My guardians simply accept that I'll turn up from time to time, but I always telegraph ahead; so you see if your parents feel they can't cope with a lodger for a couple of weeks, then I'll just catch a train tomorrow instead of today.'

'Can I ask why you were in hospital, or would it be indelicate?' Prue said. Her eyes flickered swiftly across broad shoulders, strong arms and long legs.

Ed shook his head at her. 'I've not explained that I'm in submarines,' he said. 'Our subs aren't like the Americans', nor like the Germans', I'm told;

they're old, ill-equipped and pretty dangerous, to own the truth. We were attacking an enemy convoy when one of the depth charges disabled us. The Jerries knew we were there—they have very sophisticated equipment—but we hoped that if we stayed still they might assume, in the end, that we'd slipped away. I won't go into too much detail, but when you're lying on the ocean bed for a great many hours the air in the sub runs out. One of the crew died, and to be honest, Prue, I passed out before the captain thought it was safe to surface. They got me back to Liverpool and into hospital, but it took time to get me right.'

'Gosh, how perfectly dreadful,' Prue said, round-eyed. 'And are you going back to your sub when your sick leave is up?'

'Probably,' Ed said rather evasively. 'It depends on the state of my lungs, but since I feel fit as a fiddle, I expect the doctors will pass me as A1.'

Prue frowned, dredging up memories of conversations with other men who had served on submarines. 'But someone told me once that submariners were all volunteers. If you volunteered, can't you just—just un-volunteer, if you know what I mean?'

Ed grinned but shook his head. 'I don't think that applies, but in any case I wouldn't let the fellers down. My captain is grand. He's an Irishman called Johnny Mack, and one of the best.' He looked across at Prue and she saw a flush mount to his lean cheeks. 'I don't want to sound conceited but we're proud of what we do in the old *Sunray*. We've got a high score of German shipping destroyed and we've only lost one man so far. We're a good team; there's very little room in a sub, as you can imagine, but each and every member of the crew knows exactly what he must do, from the moment we sight the enemy and submerge to when we're getting the hell out of it in order to surface again.'

Prue nodded slowly. 'Yes. I've heard other submariners talk about the closeness of the crew and how important it is that each man gets on with his neighbour.'

Ed leaned across and picked up the teapot, then lifted the lid and peered inside. 'Want another cup? Only if I'm going to meet your parents, perhaps we ought to leave soon? You didn't say where the Vines was, but I dare say we'll have to catch a tram . . .'

'No we shan't,' Prue said, getting to her feet. 'But on the way I'd better tell you what's been happening to us. To start with, Addy's in the Wrens and has been billeted at Foliat Manor! I explained about my mam . . .'

By the time Prue had faithfully told him everything she could remember that had happened to her over the past couple of years, they were practically at the Vines, and only then did she decide that she must tell him about Nick.

'Ed, you know I told those fellers in the station buffet that I was waiting for me boyfriend? Well, that wasn't true, I said it to put them off, but I do have one—a boyfriend I mean. I've known him since we were just a couple of kids, before I was in the wheelchair. His name's Nick Bentley and his father was landlord of the Vines until he decided to run off, leaving my mam in a very difficult position . . .'

'But you said you go dancing,' Ed pointed out. 'I thought you must be unattached . . . no I didn't, though. Honesty's the best policy and I suppose I knew, in my heart, that a girl as pretty as you would be bound to have a feller. But you can have a good pal as well, can't you? Only if I'm going to be spending my sick leave at your mam's pub, then your feller might get a bit suspicious. What does he do, by the way? I take it he's Navy, coming from Liverpool?'

'Why should he be suspicious? The Vines is a public house with rooms to let on the first floor, which are often occupied by members of the services. And he isn't in the Navy, actually, and neither is his brother, Paul, who's in the army in India. I think Paul trains Indian troops, but Nick is a tail gunner in a Lancaster bomber. He's stationed at an airfield in Norfolk. He told me I won't be seeing much of him now the invasion is under way; but I don't see much of him anyway,' she added ruefully. 'Leave is hard to come by these days.'

'Well, so long as I don't wake up one morning to find your tail gunner's fingers round my throat,' Ed said with a grin.

They had stopped short of entering the pub whilst Prue was explaining, but they could hear the hum of chatter and laughter coming from the bar. Ed turned to her. 'Is there a back way, or do we go in here?'

*   *   *

'Well, what d'you think, Jamie? To hear our Prue talk you'd think that meeting this young feller again was the best thing to happen in her life for a long while, but she says he's just an old pal, so I

353

suppose I've got to believe her.'

Nell and Jamie had closed the bar and seen Edgar Wilkinson of HMS *Sunray* safely ensconced in Paul's bedroom on the second floor. Prue had grinned at her mother's choice of room, however. 'Why didn't you put him on the first floor, next to me?' she had said cheekily. 'Do try and believe me, Mam, Ed an' me are just pals, that's all. Just pals.'

Now that they were alone in the kitchen, Nell repeated the remark to Jamie, adding darkly: 'That's what she said about young Nick; that they were just pals, I mean. Of course Nick's older than this chap, but I wouldn't hesitate to let him have the room next to our Prue. This Ed's different, despite being younger, he's more sophisticated, and, to be honest, a good deal more attractive. Still an' all, he's a submariner and they deserve whatever we can give 'em.' She shuddered. 'Imagine it: shut up in a little tin box at the bottom of the sea, with them depth charge things exploding all around you and the air running out. Remember the *Thetis*? Ever since then I've had the greatest respect for submariners. So even for Nick, I just couldn't deny the boy a room here.'

'I should hope not,' Jamie said rather reproachfully. 'And think on, love. The number of times I've heard you saying that Prue was far too young to start going steady with anyone! And you've encouraged her to go dancing and to parties out at the airfields when they sent a bus in for the factory girls, because you thought she'd not had enough experience of other men. Yet now, when she brings in a nice, upright young feller . . .'

'Do you think he is a threat to Nick?' Nell said, rather doubtfully. 'I feel in a way responsible for

354

Nick, almost as though I were his mother. Maureen was too young to even try to mother the boys, so I did my best by them.' She sighed deeply, fished the last glass out of the washing-up water and handed it to her husband. 'Oh, dear, and he's on sick leave for a whole fortnight! Of course Prue will be working, but she says they aren't nearly as busy as they were, and I know she was hoping to get a week off whilst the weather's so fine. Oh, Jamie, what on earth should I do?'

Jamie chuckled, dried the pint mug she had just handed him and stood it on the tray, ready to be carried back to the bar. 'There's nothing you can do, love,' he told her. 'If you were going to do anything, you should have done it when Prue asked if the lad might spend his leave at the Vines. And remember, it isn't just the fact that he's a submariner which made you offer him our hospitality. He's an orphan, and from what Prue told us earlier his aunt and uncle are too old to have a home of their own but live in a hotel, so in effect he's got nowhere to call his home. What you must tell yourself is that there will always be an element of competition between young men for the attention of the girl they want. And it's the same for girls, of course. Maybe young Ed will find himself pursued by several local girls—perhaps including Prue, perhaps not—and he'll have to make a choice. For all you know, Nick may be dallying after a pretty young WAAF, meaning to tell Prue it's all off, but not quite liking to do so.'

He crossed the kitchen to lower the clothes airer that spanned the ceiling, and spread out the wet tea towels that he had used to dry the glasses on it before pulling on the rope to send it back up to its place. Then he held out his hand and took Nell's in a warm clasp. 'It's been a long day and we're both tired, so let's go to bed,' he said gently. 'And Nell, my dear, you are worrying quite needlessly over Prue and this young fellow, because it's for them to choose, when all's said and done. You could have denied young Ed a room, but what difference do you think that would make in the end? So make Ed as welcome as you have made Nick, and let our Prue make her own decisions. Right?'

He slipped his arm around Nell's waist as he spoke and they began to mount the stairs together. 'Oh, Jamie, you are so wise,' Nell said, snuggling her head against his shoulder. 'And what's more, you're absolutely right. I think of Prue as my baby, but of course she's an independent young woman really.' She chuckled suddenly. 'Wait till Nonny meets him tomorrow morning at breakfast!'

Jamie reached forward and opened their bedroom door, pushing Nell gently before him. 'Shut up and get undressed,' he said. 'It isn't often that neither of us is on duty, so we might as well make the most of it and get a solid night's sleep for once.'

*   *   *

Addy kicked her motorbike stand into position and cast a critical eye over her machine. It was dusty, but, since it had not rained for a couple of days, not muddy. Still, she fished a piece of rag from her pocket and gave it a desultory clean up, then headed for the back door of the manor. She had heard from Prue that their old friend Edgar Wilkinson had turned up in Liverpool; heard with

356

rather mixed feelings that he was staying at the Vines.

Mam was very understanding, Prue had written. *I explained to her that he was just an old friend who had no parents of his own, nor a home to go back to, so she's told him he can stay here. He's in submarines, which is how he came to end up in hospital. I can't say more than that because of the censor, but I guess you can dot the i's and cross the t's.*

Ed's changed a lot, Addy, or maybe change isn't the right word; it's more that he's matured, like cheese! Anyway, it's nice for me to have a fellow to go around with. Of course I'd much rather it was Nick, but no one can have everything and Ed's really good company, only don't worry that I'll fall for him, because I shan't. I'm Nick's girl and wouldn't swap him, not even for Gary Cooper. Well, perhaps I might for Gary Cooper—oh boy, oh boy!—but not for anyone else. I was wondering whether I ought to mention Ed to Nick, but when I asked Nonny she said not. She said it would be a bit like a 'Dear John' letter and blokes who get one of them get miserable and careless and sometimes get killed. I know you don't write to Nick or see him, or anything like that, but if by chance you did come across him, or anyone else who knows us both, then mum's the word, right? I wouldn't have my darling hurt for anything.

The letter had then gone on to talk of how she had enjoyed showing Ed Liverpool, and how he had admired the buildings which had escaped the bombs, and had finally ended with a flourish.

Ed goes back to his sub in a couple of days and then, marvel of marvels, Nick has a forty-eight! I've not seen him for months, so you can imagine how excited I feel. Ed said he wished he could meet this paragon but I don't suppose he meant it. Oh, Addy, I'm up on cloud nine, honest to God I am!

Addy pushed open the kitchen door. The room was full of Wrens, some eating their evening meal, others simply hanging around. The girls looked up as she entered and Gillian, sitting at the table slicing a loaf of bread, jumped to her feet, abandoning her task, and grabbed Addy's arm. 'Where have you been?' she said aggrievedly. 'I've been waiting for you for ages. I've had a message from Dom; it's all in our special code of course because of information falling into enemy hands. Come up to our room, away from all this chatter.'

The two girls left the kitchen, crossed the hall and raced up the great curved staircase, which had once seemed to Addy as close to perfection as a staircase could get but was now scuffed and neglected. They burst into their room and Gillian slammed the door shut and flung herself on to her bed. 'O frabjous day, callooh callay,' she carolled. 'Absolutely splendid news, my dear little Wren. And it wasn't just a message, it was a whole, wonderful letter, full of what he's been doing and how his fellows are getting on. One of the blokes was injured—I think he trod on a landmine—and was invalided back to Portsmouth. I'm awfully grateful to him; he must be a really good bloke because the first thing he did on getting ashore was to despatch Dom's letter and oh, Addy, he says he believes the Allies will take Paris in a couple of days! Imagine, Paris! It's a city Dom knows and loves because he lived there for a couple of years in the late thirties. He's got friends there, people he lodged with, fellow artists, folk he painted, and he can't wait to make sure they're still alive and unhurt. Isn't that wonderful news?'

'Fantastic,' Addy said, sitting down on her bed with a thump. 'But how did he manage to tell you so much? What about the censor? Or didn't the injured soldier actually put the letter in the post at all? Oh, you said it was in your special code, sorry.'

'That's all right,' Gillian said contentedly. 'I've always felt that freeing Paris would be a sign that the war was almost over. Dom's going to write again once the city's in Allied hands because even if there isn't a proper postal service between the two countries there will be constant comings and goings across the Channel. I've written a long letter back to him and of course I'm hoping that we'll be able to keep exchanging news until the Nazi regime collapses and he can come home.'

CHAPTER FIFTEEN

When reveille sounded, Dom struggled out of his sleeping bag and began to dress in his worn and dirty uniform. He wished he had been able to clean it up, for today was to be the sort of day one never forgot; today, if all went according to plan, the Allies would liberate Paris. The troops had been told, some time earlier, that they would not enter the capital because it might mean the destruction of that wonderful city and the deaths of a great many inhabitants, but to everyone's relief and excitement the orders had been changed. Dominic had heard rumours that General de Gaulle had told General Eisenhower that to leave Paris occupied by the Nazis would be a fatal mistake. Ike had clearly bowed to the general's better knowledge of the French people, so today the troops would head for the city, hoping to take it before the enemy realised that the Allies were, so to speak, at the door.

Hastily dressing, Dominic regarded with some distaste his crumpled sketchpad and the few stubs of pencil lying beside his sleeping bag. He was in dire need of fresh materials to do his work, but now that he knew they were to march on Paris this very day, he also hoped that he would be able to buy paper and pencils at one of the many artists' supply shops in the city. He was sure that what awaited them would be worthy of his best efforts and decided that he would ask for more materials. Without them, how could he capture the expressions of relief and joy, or terror and fear, which he was sure would be on every face as the troops marched in? The British army was a pretty weird institution, but since it employed war artists it must surely realise that such men were useless without the tools of their trade.

An hour later, pockets bulging with pencils and a couple of sketchpads, he set off with the rest of his company for Paris. When he had emerged from his tent in the early hours, he had been deeply disappointed to see that the green and gold of the countryside which had met his eyes just before he

360

had entered his tent was now blanketed with a thick white fog. However, within an hour the fog had changed to a faint ethereal mist, and as the sun came up, red as blood, even the mist had disappeared, leaving the sky blue and clear, without a cloud in view. Just the sort of day, in fact, to set off on a great adventure, and Dominic knew that whatever the coming hours might bring, today was the culmination of years of struggle and would be remembered, by himself at any rate, as a milestone.

The British met up with General Patton's American GIs, and as they neared the capital city the steady march with which they had begun their advance turned into something more like a triumphant surging run. Looking up to the top of the Eiffel Tower, which could clearly be seen against the deep blue of the sky, they saw that the Nazi swastika had been replaced by the tricolour of France and knew that one part, at least, of the taking of Paris had gone according to plan. The French Second Armoured Division, under General Jacques Leclerc, must have been the first to enter the city, because had the Americans entered first Dominic suspected that it might have been the Stars and Stripes which fluttered in the breeze.

But very soon, conjecture was replaced by the sheer animal exuberance of the welcome they received. Women threw flowers and sweets, kissed any passing soldier within reach and wept for joy. The crowd consisted mostly of young women, but older ones were there too, clad sombrely in black, though their daughters and granddaughters had clearly dressed in their best and most brilliant raiment. White, scarlet or blue blouses and vividly

361

coloured peasant skirts predominated, giving the impression of a vast flowerbed full of beautiful blossoms.

The roadway was wide, the hum of the crowd loud, yet even so, when the people who had been cheering and throwing flowers suddenly drew back, Dominic heard the firing, the warning screams, then saw someone fall. The Jerries had not just disappeared, then, but were sniping both at the crowds and at the Allies as they marched into the city the enemy had considered their own for so long.

Ahead of him, a couple of soldiers left the marching column unobtrusively and entered a nearby house, and presently the sniping stopped. Then there was the sound of machine gun fire, and once more the cheering, laughing crowd scattered, though not for long. Soon they seemed to either forget the danger or discount it and were back, holding their children up to wave flags. Union Jacks and Stars and Stripes predominated and Dominic found time to wonder where on earth they had got such things on the very day the Allies marched into the city. Then he chided himself for stupidity; they must have known, when the Normandy landings started, that it was only a matter of time before Paris would be liberated, and had acted accordingly, hiding away their brightest clothing and the flags where no prying Nazi was liable to find them.

The columns marched on, Dominic with them, drawing and drawing, knowing that this was a wonderful, unforgettable moment that no one present was ever likely to forget. Beaming women, smiling children, babies who were not as fat as they should have been, were all grist to his mill. Only later did he realise that the happy faces must have hidden minds still torn by fear and pain—anxiety, too, for the Nazis had broadcast that very day, on Paris Radio, that reprisals for the insurrection of the people of the capital would be terrible indeed. After four years of seeing their streets swarming with the steel-helmeted Boche, it could not have been easy to throw off caution and replace it with the joyful acceptance that they were once more free.

Several times, when they were marching through streets Dominic had once known well, tears rose unbidden to his eyes. He had been happy here; so happy! He remembered Michelle, one of the many models who had sat for him. Was she still alive? Still sharing her shabby attic flat with half a dozen other pretty, carefree young girls? He would find out when he was free to wander the streets; but he would have to be careful. Despite the rejoicing, the warmth of their welcome, they had all heard about collaborators and had to accustom themselves to the fact that a smiling face, a welcoming gesture, might turn in a moment to a knife in the back or a bullet in the brain.

They reached the Place de la Concorde and, hearing a muffled explosion, looked to the nearest bystander for an explanation. She was a grey-haired, elderly woman, whose stained black dress was enlivened by the bright red scarf she had tied about her waist. 'Qu'est-ce que c'est?' Dominic asked, and when the woman replied that the Boche, goddamn their eyes, were blowing up the bridges across the Seine, he translated the remark for the men beside him.

As they emerged into the great open space of the Place, the first thing Dominic saw was one of the huge German tiger tanks, its gun turret pointing menacingly straight at the crowd. He was not the only one who hesitated, appalled. Was it about to fire? Or would it simply lumber forward, crushing anyone who could not get out of its path? Of course, it might have broken down and been deserted by its crew. Dominic had heard with horror from a Dutch refugee who had escaped to Britain how these mighty tanks were being manned by members of the Hitler Youth movement, some of them as young as twelve. They were feared, even by other members of the German army, for their ruthlessness and savagery. Whilst the whole crowd hesitated, however, staring at the squat, malignant machine, a group of children broke away from the crowd and raced towards it. One of them held a pistol, a girl of no more than twelve or thirteen. She scrambled on to the tank, stared into the interior for a moment, and then fired repeatedly through the hatch into whatever—or whoever— was inside.

Horrified, Dominic turned away, feeling sick, but the man next to him, seeing his distress, grabbed his arm and pulled him on. 'You don't know what them kids have gone through, sir,' he remarked, as the crowd surged forward once again. 'I've heard stories what'd make your toes curl about the way them Boche behaved towards the French.' He looked curiously down at the sketchpad in Dominic's hand. 'Do you want to get out of the crowd for a minute, sir, so's you can draw them kids?' He added consolingly: 'I reckon there weren't nobody in that there tank; the kid just fired out of devilment. Kids is like that.' He chuckled. 'I've got two of me own; right little hellraisers.'

'Thanks, but I won't stop now, I'll stay with the column,' Dominic said. He knew that the scene would remain vivid in his mind for many a long day and could be committed to paper whenever he had a free moment. 'The Jerries'll have to surrender and my guess is they'll do it officially; I'll probably be there.'

Dominic was right, both that the Germans would surrender and that he would be present to record the event, along with several journalists. They were not present in the left-luggage office on Montparnasse Station, where General von Cholitz surrendered, but went to the Police Préfecture, where the German governor signed the surrender document and ordered a ceasefire.

Dominic was told later, by one of the journalists who spoke German, that von Cholitz had been ordered by Hitler to destroy Paris before surrendering, but had ignored the instruction. 'As well for him,' the journalist had said grimly. 'The French would have lynched him, if the Americans didn't get him first.'

That night, when the rejoicing, the bonfires and the merriment had begun to die down, Dominic slipped out of the hotel in which he had been billeted with a great many other troops, and made his way cautiously to the street where he had once lodged. He had no difficulty in finding the correct house, but knocked very gently on the door, fearing to frighten the inhabitants. Madame Moreau might no longer live here; he knew she had a daughter in Rouen and she might have moved in with her when things in Paris became difficult. Or she might have gone to bed early, worn out by the excitements of the day. He remembered, with wry amusement, how cross she used to get when disturbed by one of her lodgers coming in late, or when one lost his key and was thus forced to rouse her. He refused to allow himself to consider worse scenarios.

However, as he stood at the door, he saw a faint light coming from the window beside him and guessed that Madame was in the kitchen at the back of the house. He knocked again more loudly and was gratified to hear the sound of slippered feet approaching across the small stone-flagged hall. He heard bolts being drawn back and a key grating in the lock. Then the door opened cautiously, only wide enough to allow him to catch a glimpse of a long, thin pink nose and one small, snapping black eye. *'Oui, qui est-ce que?'*

Dominic smiled to himself. He knew very well that Madame both spoke and understood English, but she had probably not done so for four years, and not knowing who was at the door she would naturally have spoken in her own language. But the pink quivering nose and the bright black eye were beginning to withdraw and he spoke hastily. 'Don't close the door; it's me, Dominic Cranshaw. You wouldn't have recognised me in my uniform, of course, but I'd know you anywhere, madame, even though I can only see the tip of your nose. Can I come in?'

Immediately, the door was opened and Madame surged into the street, reached up to seize her visitor's shoulders and kissed him on both cheeks, then gave him a hug for good measure. She was a small, square woman with a deep, rather guttural

366

voice, and like all Frenchwomen of her age and station she always wore black, though in her case this was relieved by white lace collars and cuffs of which she was inordinately proud, since they were of her own making.

Now, however, she was dragging Dominic into the hall, slamming and locking her front door behind him, though she did not draw the bolts across. Then she led him through the hall and into the kitchen. The room was lamplit and there were two young women seated at the table, both of whom jumped to their feet as the oddly assorted couple entered. One was tall and fair, the other much smaller and very dark, and they both knew him at once, as indeed he knew them.

'Dominic!' squeaked the taller of the two. 'Do you remember me? Hélène, who sometimes modelled for you? Ah, but if you don't remember me, I'll wager you remember the *tarte aux pommes* I used to cook. It was your favourite; you used to say you would marry me for my *tarte aux pommes*.'

She spoke in French, for Dominic knew both girls only had a smattering of basic English, so he replied in the same language. 'Of course I remember you, just as I remember Angélique here.' He kissed both girls, noting that they were a good deal thinner than when he had last seen them. 'Tell me, how are all my friends? Jean-Claude, Marianne, little Marie, and the dancer from the Folies Bergères—the American girl whose name I forget? But you'll remember her; she shared a room with a Dutch girl, whose name I also can't recall.'

'Jean-Claude was a member of the Résistance and escaped to England to join General de

Gaulle,' Hélène said. 'Marianne and I lost touch; it happens in wartime. And I'm afraid Marie was killed in a bombing raid, along with several other girls you would have known.'

Dominic stared across at Hélène. 'I'm so sorry,' he said quietly. 'Because I guess it was British bombs which killed them.' He snapped his fingers at a sudden recollection. 'Anna, that was the Dutch girl's name, and the American was Betty. They were both friends of mine; I hope to God they're safe.'

He was addressing Hélène, but it was little Angélique who answered, speaking slowly, he thought, and with some embarrassment. 'I know who you mean. Betty disappeared, and soon afterwards Anna went back to Holland, or so we believe.'

'Disappeared? Do you mean she returned to the States?'

'Well, no,' Angélique said, sounding apologetic now. 'She got herself a German admirer, a colonel or some such. For a while she lived in the lap of luxury, in a jewel of a flat overlooking the Seine. She continued to dance at the Folies, although she must have realised what the other dancers thought of her. Then one day she did not attend the rehearsal for a new show. Rumour had it that she had been taken out by the Résistance for collaborating with the enemy. But it's possible that her boyfriend managed to get her back to the States, or maybe even to Germany. At any rate, no one's seen her since then.'

'That's dreadful; she seemed such a delightful, lively girl, not the sort to desert her friends,' Dominic said. 'But of course when I knew her she was just a young girl in love with Paris and having the time of her life.'

At this point, Madame Moreau interrupted. She came bustling over to the table with a bottle of red wine and some glasses. 'No more sad talk of what has happened to any of us,' she said briskly, handing round the glasses and pouring the wine. 'As I've told these girls over and over, there could be many explanations for Betty's disappearance, not all of them sinister. Anna, for instance, is probably in a worse state than us. Someone said the Dutch are eating candles and roasting rats.' She shuddered expressively. 'But soon they will be free, as we are free, so I propose a toast. To the Allies, victory; to the Boche, annihilation!'

*   *   *

It was very late by the time Dominic had said good night to his friends and returned to the hotel. When he reached it, he had to rouse the concierge, for the man had fallen asleep behind his desk. He woke, however, at Dominic's knock, full of apologies for his lapse, but explaining that he had been on duty for thirty hours and was *'très fatigué'*.

Dominic was pretty tired himself, but at least he now knew how to get hold of such friends as were still living in Paris, though he was not sure whether he would have time to contact anyone before the advance continued. He slipped into the room he was sharing with a number of other officers, to be greeted by a voice saying sleepily: 'Where've you been? To the lav? The one on the next landing is a disgrace.'

'All the lavs in France are bloody awful, but I've

not been down there,' Dominic informed the speaker, stepping carefully over the sleeping bodies which lay between the door and his own bed.

'Where have you been, then, if not to the lav?' another voice remarked. 'But this is Paris, and I suppose one shouldn't question a fellow when he sneaks in like a thief in the night! I guess he had an assignation with a beautiful Frenchwoman; am I right?'

Dominic laughed. 'Dead right. She's seventy-eight and built like a Sherman tank,' he said, climbing into his sleeping bag. 'She was my landlady when I lived in Paris before the war; if you want her address, you can have it when morning comes.'

He waited for a moment, expecting the other to reply, and was rewarded by an enormous snore. Chuckling to himself, he snuggled down into his bag, to dream within minutes of old friends and new ones, of attic studios and tiny cramped bedsitters, of beautiful women and plain ones, even of Gillian, smiling her own sweet smile, telling him not to forget her. 'As if I would,' Dominic muttered in his sleep. 'As if I could!'

* * *

It was an icy cold evening. Addy, driving the big old Rover cautiously, for the roads were frosty, turned in to the ancient lodge which stood to the left of the drive, made sure the car was under cover and could not be seen from the lane, locked the doors carefully and turned towards the manor. She wrapped her scarf more securely round her neck

370

and set off, pushing her hands deep into her pockets and admiring the scene before her as she began to walk up the long drive leading to Foliat Manor. On either side of her were trees, every branch, every twig of which was outlined in white frost, as were the bushes, and the big leggy rhododendron leaves looked as though they had been dipped in icing sugar. When she glanced to her left, she saw that the lawn appeared to be covered in snow and she could not stop herself giving an anticipatory shiver as she crunched across the gravel towards her destination.

Usually, of course, she rode her motorcycle up the drive and had she done so today she would scarcely have noticed the beauty of the frost, being intent only on getting her bike round into the shed and herself into the warmth of the house.

However, today was very different, and excitement over the prospect of what was to come kept Addy from feeling as cold as she might otherwise have done. She had had an enormous piece of luck, and at the thought of it she broke into a trot, eager to tell the other girls, especially Gillian, what her superior officer had just said.

She whipped round the corner of the house, pushed open the wooden door which led into the small courtyard and headed for the kitchen. The yard contained a shed for bicycles and motorbikes, another for logs and a third for coal and coke, though coal was in such short supply that the kitchen range mainly ran on wood. Mindful of this, Addy stopped for a moment in her onward rush to grab an armful of logs. It would save someone else from having to leave the kitchen for the icy yard.

She threw open the kitchen door with her free

371

hand and bounced into the room, kicking it shut behind her. Because of fuel shortages, including gas and electricity which were cut off for certain hours on certain days, the girls no longer even attempted to warm any room apart from the kitchen. Fortunately, it was very large, so at the beginning of the cold weather they had dragged in a number of comfortable, saggy old armchairs so that they could relax in the warm when they were free to do so. In fact, apart from when they were in their beds or on duty, they lived in the kitchen. It no longer seemed incongruous to ignore the beautiful drawing room, the elegant dining room or the breakfast parlour. They would revert to them when the warm weather arrived once again, but for now it was the kitchen to which they returned at the end of their working day.

'Good girl, you've brought some logs,' someone said as Addy walked across the room with her burden clutched tightly to her breast. 'Put 'em straight in the range, Addy, and bless you for your thoughtfulness. I was just about to go outside to fetch some, but you've saved me the trouble; it's like plunging into icy water crossing to the woodshed.'

The girl who had spoken lifted the lid of the range and Addy tipped the logs on to the glowing embers. Then she began to unwind her scarf, took off her gloves and coat, kicked off the sturdy boots she wore for work and went to the cupboard under the sink, where she exchanged the boots for an ancient pair of carpet slippers. She went over to the kitchen table, picked up an empty enamel mug which stood upon it, and wrapped sharply on the wood, causing everyone to stop talking and turn enquiringly in her direction. 'I've got some news,' she said excitedly. 'It's good news for me because . . . oh, well, I'll tell you what's happened and you can judge for yourselves.'

Gillian, who had been sitting at the table writing a letter, looked up quickly. 'Have you heard from Giles?' she asked eagerly. 'Is he coming ashore on leave? Gosh, wouldn't it be fantastic if he arrived in time for Christmas!'

Addy reached over and patted her friend's shoulder. 'No, I've not heard, but it's a good thing in a way if he's not coming to Plymouth because I wouldn't be here to greet him,' she said. 'Oh, Gill, the most tremendous piece of luck—well I think so at any rate! I was called into the CO's office today. I thought it was about my forty-eight, because as you know I didn't take the last one. The trains are so dreadful that I can't get home and back in the time, so I elected to save it up until my next leave. Only the CO said that there's an important meeting to be held in Liverpool in a couple of days' time. The girl who usually drives Captain Solomon slipped on the ice this morning and broke her arm. The CO had been casting round for another driver, preferably someone who knew Liverpool, when she remembered that I was due for a forty-eight and guessed that if I had the opportunity I'd go home. She was awfully decent, said she wouldn't dock my leave, but the captain would be in the city for at least two days and during that time he was unlikely to need me. She said I should report to the Liverpool HQ each morning and evening, unless I was on the telephone, which unfortunately the Vines is not. But it's not far from HQ, so I'll be quite happy to

373

trot down there twice a day to check if and when I'm needed.' She grinned around the room. 'What about that, eh? And so near Christmas, too! I don't suppose he'll want to stay up there for the festivities, but you never know, miracles can happen.'

A babble broke out, but the Wren who had thanked Addy for bringing in logs turned to her. 'If you're talking about Ian Solomon, he comes from somewhere called St Helens,' she said. 'I believe St Helens is pretty close to Liverpool, so you might get Christmas at home, unless he's recalled back here, of course.'

'Gosh!' Addy said, awestruck. 'That would be perfect; but I don't mean to count my chickens. Even to have a couple of days in the 'Pool is an unlooked-for treat. In fact the only snag is that the captain wants to leave no later than five o'clock tomorrow morning. That means I've got to be up by four at the latest.' She turned to look apologetically at Gillian. 'I'd like to say I won't set the alarm, but frankly I'd be scared stiff of oversleeping, so I'm afraid we shall both be woken at four.'

Gillian laughed. 'I won't mind since I shan't have to get up, but can cuddle down and think of you making your way into town in the freezing cold,' she said. 'Why didn't they let you bring the car home, though? I imagine it's not parked out the front somewhere since you came in through the back door.'

'I brought it as far as the old lodge and tucked it out of sight. I made sure it was well under cover because I don't fancy having to defrost the windows and struggle to get her started,' Addy explained. 'If I'd brought her right up to the manor, I'd have had to sacrifice at least one of my blankets, if not two, to make sure she started in the morning.'

'Oh, you poor thing!' Gillian said mockingly. 'Would you like me to come down with you in the morning, bearing a kettle of hot water to unthaw the locks if they've frozen? I remember that happening to my father's old Bentley once, and very annoyed he got. In fact he blamed my mother, though of course she had nothing to do with it.'

This caused a good deal of laughter, someone remarking that it was typical of a man to blame the nearest woman when something went wrong. But Addy was looking hopefully at Gillian. 'Would you really come down with me?' she asked. 'I'm going to take a hot water bottle, but I'd be awfully grateful if you'd come as well. The Rover's heaven to drive and it's got what they call a self-starter button, but it's still the crank handle if things go wrong.'

'OK, I'll hold your hand,' Gillian said. 'Just let me finish this letter and then we'd better both go to bed if you're going to set that bloody alarm for four o'clock.'

Before Addy could even consider going to bed, however, she had to brush and press her uniform, iron one of her white shirts and polish her black shoes. Only then did the two girls climb the stairs to their room, each clutching a hot water bottle. They were in their beds in five minutes, worn out and anxious for the sleep they needed in order to work next day. Addy set the alarm, wound the clock and cuddled down, informing her friend that she hoped her bottle would still be warm enough in a few hours to thaw out anything which had set hard on the Rover. 'I suppose I should have checked the car before I came up, just in case it's already freezing up,' she mumbled. 'Then I could have . . . could have . . .'

And Addy slept.

The shrilling of the alarm woke them at four. They both leapt out of bed like a couple of jack-in-the-boxes and dressed without even considering having a wash. 'There's ice on the ewer,' Addy remarked, picking up her flannel and giving her face a quick and extremely cold rub. Then she belaboured her hair with the brush until it shone like silk and perched her cap on at an angle before turning, somewhat guiltily, towards her friend. 'Oh, Gill, you're a girl in a thousand. I keep telling myself the car's bound to start without trouble, but you've been driving much longer than I have, because you told me once you'd had your own car before the war, so if something does go wrong you'll know what I must do to put it right.'

She adjusted her tie, then went to the window and breathed on the frost flowers that covered the pane. Peering out, she announced that the frost was, if anything, worse than before. Then the two girls left the room and padded down the stairs in their stockinged feet. Despite the hour, the kitchen was still slightly warmer than their bedroom, but when Gillian suggested that they should make themselves a hot drink before venturing forth, Addy shook her head. 'I daren't. It's just occurred to me that though I know where Captain Solomon is billeted, it won't be so easy to find him in the dark. And anyway, we don't know how long it's going to take me to get the car started.'

'You're far too anxious; you'll find the house with ease,' Gillian said cheerfully, reaching her greatcoat down from its peg and shrugging it on. 'Never mind, I shan't complain. I'll just pull the kettle over the heat—such as it is—then I'll come down and see you off and get myself a drink on my way back to bed. Incidentally, what will happen to the car when you reach Liverpool?'

'Dunno. The CO didn't tell me, but if they want me to hang on to it, the Vines has a big courtyard at the back,' Addy said, as they crunched down the drive. 'Goodness, it's as light as day out here, and the shadows are so black they could hide a regiment of militia, as they used to say.'

'Thank you for that comforting remark; I've got to come back alone, past all these black shadows,' Gillian said. 'Ah, here's the lodge at last.'

*   *   *

Despite Addy's fears, the car had started without trouble, and after she had found the captain's digs and settled him in the back seat all went according to plan. The captain, in fact, turned out to be a pleasant companion, for as soon as they left Plymouth behind he asked her to stop the car so that he might get into the front passenger seat.

'Easier to hear what one's driver is saying above the engine noise,' he told her. 'I calculate we will easily reach our destination by two in the afternoon, which is when the first meeting starts, if we drive straight through. When you drop me off, someone will tell you where to park the car, and provided you give the keys to a responsible person you'll be free then until eight this evening, when

'I'd be obliged if you would either telephone in or turn up in person to get your orders for tomorrow.'

'Yes, sir,' Addy said. 'My parents run a public house called the Vines, and though they are not on the telephone there is a box at the end of the road. Would it be possible for me to ring HQ from there?'

The captain nodded. 'Certainly. If I need to see you in person, I'll leave a message to that effect with the switchboard. Do you live far from HQ?'

'No, not very far at all, certainly not more than a mile,' Addy said. She looked at her companion. He was a lot younger than she had imagined he would be, probably in his late thirties, with neatly trimmed light brown hair and beard, and a moustache that curved upwards so that he always appeared to be smiling. She had wondered why he was no longer on active service, but later she had realised that his right arm was artificial. She had hesitated to ask him the question that burned on her lips, but as they neared Liverpool and she felt she knew him better, she cleared her throat. 'I understand you live in St Helens, sir. Do you and your wife have a family? If—if so, you'll be able to get home quite easily, and—and . . .'

Captain Solomon laughed. 'I've a wife, three children and a mother-in-law, all living in St Helens,' he said cheerfully. 'My wife teaches mathematics and music at the local grammar school, and my mother-in-law looks after the children and runs the house. I expect you're wondering whether I shall want to spend Christmas with my family. It would be excellent if I could do so, because the children have seen almost nothing of me since the war began, but like you I'm at the mercy of our masters. I've no idea how long this conference will last, or how long it may be before I'm recalled.' He looked sideways and she saw him grin. 'We'll have to see what we can wangle between us,' he announced, then groaned as they rounded a bend to see an enormous army lorry crawling along in the middle of the road. 'Dear God, will these convoys never cease? It's a good job we're in an official car, because if we try to overtake and meet something else coming in the opposite direction, then at least the lorry we're overtaking will slow down and pull over to let us in.'

Addy agreed, but as it happened the enormous lorry either was travelling alone or had dropped a long way behind its companions, so the Rover was able to proceed on its journey.

They reached Liverpool in good time and drove to Naval HQ, where the captain bade her a cheerful farewell and a young officer saluted him smartly, took the keys from Addy and told her she could reclaim them from the Orderly Room when her captain wanted to use the car again.

Thus it was that Addy found herself on the familiar streets of Liverpool, well before two o'clock, and heading for the Vines, her mind filled with delightful anticipation. She had had no time to warn the family that she would be in Liverpool just before Christmas, and as she approached the pub she was already hearing in imagination the exclamations, excitement and surprise which would presently greet her ears.

*   *   *

379

Nell, Nonny and Jamie were gathered round the kitchen table eating their midday meal. Prue was at work, packing parachutes, though would not be for much longer, as she informed her mother.

She intended to apply to join the WRNS as soon as she was old enough, and meant to ask that she might be boat crew, for she knew it was usually girls who manned the boats which ferried the men from ship to shore and shore to ship. She told her family that she had found a nice young man willing to teach her how to handle such craft and she was quite confident that, should the WRNS accept her, she would be able to show them how useful she would be. Friends already in the Navy—such as Ed—had cautioned her, however, that the armed forces had always excelled in the art of putting square pegs into round holes. She also meant to apply to the WAAF, and Nick had reinforced the warning.

'They'll make you a secretary, and I know from your letters that your spelling is appalling,' Ed had written, whilst Nick, reiterating the point, had told her that she would end up in the cookhouse, peeling whole fields of spuds whilst being shouted at by fat and greasy corporals, all of whom, it seemed, disliked WAAFs on principle.

Nell, eating a potato, had thought that if her daughter really ended up peeling mountains of spuds it would be no less than justice, for Prue was seldom to be seen helping out in the kitchen, though she did occasionally work behind the bar. It's my fault, I've spoilt the child, Nell told herself now. But everyone has to grow up some time, and if the war lasts long enough for Prue to join the Wrens or the WAAF, she'll find it's not so easy to get out of tasks which she dislikes.

However, though Nell was well aware that Prue did not pull her weight at the Vines, she could not help remembering that her younger daughter had spent a long time in a wheelchair through no fault of her own, and perhaps her unwillingness to undertake any sort of domestic chores was her daughter's way of compensating for that wearisome period. When she had suggested this to Jamie, however, he had laughed and said that all the teenagers he knew would have behaved exactly as Prue did unless firmly checked. 'Prue would help you in the kitchen, give Nonny a hand with the washing up and clearing away, probably even make her own bed if you cracked the whip from time to time,' he had said.

'But remember, she does a full day's work packing parachutes and she's off most evenings at dances or parties, so you can't expect her to volunteer to help in the pub as well,' Nell had said rather lamely. 'I don't know why I'm grumbling except that I get rather tired. I did ask Prue to make up the beds last night's lodgers had used with clean linen and to empty the slop buckets, but she hadn't realised we had a full house last night so had arranged to meet a pal. They both want to go shopping for silk stockings and any make-up they can find, so I suppose it was asking too much to expect her to work as a chambermaid on her day off.'

Nonny had been present at the time, her bright eyes going from face to face as Nell and Jamie had talked, but then she broke in, wagging a reproving finger at her daughter. 'Addy done it when she was at home,' she had said reproachfully. 'She worked

381

eight hours assembling them radios, then she come home, took a list of any messages you wanted and went round half Liverpool searching for anything off ration. When she came back you'd send her up to do the bedrooms, or get a meal, and when that was done she'd come through to help me make the sandwiches for the customers or wash up quantities of glasses, or mop the kitchen floor. She was never idle, but small thanks she got for it, my girl.'

Nell had felt a hot flush invade her cheeks and said feebly: 'But that was different. Addy's two years older than Prue and it wasn't she who was paralysed all that time. And I'm sure I did thank her, only—only it would have sounded silly to thank her over and over. Besides, she wouldn't have expected it. She'd have thought I'd run mad, thanking her for what was the—the duty of my eldest daughter.'

Nonny had snorted. 'You never appreciated our Addy, that was the trouble,' she had said. 'But you make every excuse under the sun for Prue, when the truth is she's a lazy little madam what never gives a thought to anyone but herself. You think you're doin' her a favour by lettin' her off helping at home, but I tell you to your face, our Nell, that you ain't. She's become real flighty, what's more. You'd soon have put your foot down if our Addy had brought a fellow home and expected you to feed him, do his washin' and darn his socks, but Prue brings two fellers back and—'

'I don't mend their socks, nor I don't iron shirts and that,' Nell had protested. 'And our Prue is not flighty, she's just lively. But I suppose you may be in the right of it because I do let her get away with

382

rather a lot. Only—only she does so hate housework and I can't help wanting to make up to her for all the time she spent in that wheelchair, unable to run or dance or even walk without help. But I'll try to be a bit stricter in future.'

The night after this conversation had taken place, Nell waited until Jamie had curled round her for sleep and then spoke, her voice troubled. 'Jamie, Nonny was right, wasn't she? I do spoil Prue, but I don't see how I am to stop, not without upsetting her dreadfully.'

Jamie had chuckled sleepily. 'You may not have to, love,' he had said. 'She keeps saying she's going to apply to join one of the services and I see no reason why they shouldn't accept her when she's old enough. After all, now that the invasion is over the need for parachutes is not so desperate. Believe me, whether she becomes a Wren or a WAAF, they'll lick her into shape. I agree you can't do much, having spoilt the kid all her life, but when she finds herself doing punishment drill, running round the perimeter of the parade ground with a haversack full of bricks on her back and her fellow trainees jeering at her, she'll soon change her ways.'

'Anyone want any more potatoes?'

Nell was brought abruptly back to the present by her mother's voice. She jumped, refused more potatoes, and seeing that Jamie, too, was putting his knife and fork together got to her feet. She was just beginning to say that she had a good few messages still to do, so must go out as soon as the washing up was finished, when someone knocked very hard indeed upon the back door. Sighing, she went towards it. Probably it would be someone wanting an out-of-hours drink, or a friend who had not liked to knock on the door to the public bar, knowing they would be having their midday meal. Nell drew back the bolts and flung it open . . . then gasped. 'Addy! Oh, Addy, my love, whatever are you doing here? You're just in time for a bite to eat . . . but why didn't you let us know you were coming? Oh, my dearest child, you don't know how good it is to see you after so long!'

Addy bounced forward, straight into Nell's arms, and the two hugged unashamedly whilst Nell felt tears rise in her eyes and trickle down her cheeks. Odd that she had been thinking of her eldest only moments before, but now was her chance to show Addy that she loved her every bit as much as she loved Prue. She kissed her on her cold cheek, gave her a final hug, then turned away for a moment to close and lock the back door.

This made Addy raise her brows. 'Why did you lock the door, Mam?' she asked. 'You never used to do so before.'

Nell, ushering her into the warm kitchen, sighed. 'Spivs,' she said briefly. 'They've got the cheek of the devil and would think nothing of marching into the kitchen and making free with our storeroom if it was left unlocked. Then you'd find them on the corner, hissing that they'd sell you whatever they'd stolen for only two or three times its true value.' She turned from her daughter to her mother, who was standing by the sink, up to her elbows in hot water, whilst Jamie dried the crocks. They both turned. 'Nonny, Jamie, look who's here!'

Jamie, smiling broadly in welcome, started across the room, but Nonny was before him. She fairly ran to Addy, arms held out. 'Eh, queen, I dreamed of you last night,' she said, enveloping Addy in a warm embrace. 'Mind you, it were probably because young Prue says she's goin' to apply to join the Wrens, but it was you I dreamed of, not her.'

Jamie grinned at his mother-in-law. 'Trust you to know what's going to happen, even before it does,' he said, reaching across her to give Addy a kiss on the forehead. 'Well, my love, you've arrived just in time to take over drying the dishes, 'cos your mam and myself need to get out to buy bread an' that for the bar. Nonny'll look after you an' get you something to eat. That is, if your mam can tear herself away from you for an hour or so.'

Nonny shook her head chidingly at Jamie. 'She's not been home two minutes and you're already putting her to work,' she said. 'Just you go off and do the messages alone for once. Nell and meself will want to hear all Addy's news—and get a meal inside her before any of us are much older. Now, Addy, let's have a look at you.'

She held Addy away from her, gazing critically at her granddaughter, and Nell thought, with a surge of pride, that no one could have looked smarter or prettier. Addy's neat little sailor hat was tipped forward over one eye, her shirt was crisp and white and her uniform was spotless. Yes, Addy was a daughter of whom she could be truly proud.

But Nonny, staring at her, had clearly been speaking and she had not heard a word. 'Sorry, Nonny,' she said apologetically. 'I'm afraid I missed that; I was too busy admiring my beautiful daughter.'

'I said there were a slice of that meat and potato pie we didn't manage to eat on the cold slab in the pantry, and a few spuds—well, four or five anyway—in the blue tureen,' Nonny said. 'Of course, if you don't think Jamie will bring home the right messages, then you'll have to go with him, but . . .'

'Of course he will. Pub landlords have to be able to do all sorts these days,' Nell said and giggled when Jamie broke in.

'Thank you for that vote of confidence,' he said drily, getting his overcoat down from its hook. 'Actually, there isn't an awful lot I can't get in the markets, so I'll be back in no time.' He turned to Addy. 'Whilst your mam puts the pie in the oven and your grandmother slices and fries the leftover potatoes, you can fill me in on how you got here and why you didn't let us know.'

Addy quickly complied, then took Jamie's tea towel and finished off drying and putting away the crocks whilst her stepfather, a canvas marketing bag slung over his shoulder, left the warm kitchen and headed for the markets.

Nell fried the potatoes, jumping as the fat spat, and Nonny popped the wedge of pie into the oven. When the potatoes were cooked to a golden brown, she served up the pie beside them and poured three cups of tea, remarking as she did so that it was made with dried milk, but none the worse for that. Then, rather to Addy's surprise, she got her coat and sat with it across her lap, drinking the scalding tea and watching, with approval as her granddaughter ate. As soon as her mug of tea was emptied, however, she put on her coat, tied her headscarf under her chin and bent to give Addy a kiss. 'You and your mam will have a great deal of catching up to do,' she said. 'Of course I want to hear your news an' all, but I promised Mr

Robertson that I'd go round this afternoon and sort out his points and coupons, so you'll have to tell me all over again what you've been up to when I gerrin this evening.'

'Oh, come on, Ma, surely Mr Robertson can wait . . .' Nell was beginning, but Nonny shook her head.

'It'll be nice for Addy to have you to herself for once,' she said, a hand already on the back door. 'Ta-ra both.'

'Oh! See you later, then,' Nell said. She realised that her mother thought it was time she let Addy see how she was appreciated and made up for her attitude in the past. And it would be easy now, with Addy so bright and cheerful and tucking into the makeshift meal with evident enjoyment. 'I expect the food is pretty good down in Plymouth; they tell us the best must be saved for the armed forces,' Nell hazarded, and was surprised when Addy gave a snort of amusement.

'We make our own meals when we're off duty with whatever we can get hold of,' she said. 'The Navy holds our ration cards, so we are entitled to eat in the galley, only since I'm a messenger I usually take main meals in the form of what they call a packed lunch, which is normally Spam sandwiches and a rather wrinkled apple. But we survive.' She beamed at her mother, popping the last piece of pie into her mouth and speaking rather thickly through it. 'This is a rare treat, I promise you.'

'Good,' Nell said, and could not help remembering that her darling Prue ate everything that was put before her but rarely remarked on it, preferring to eat up and get off than to risk

387

lingering. 'What would you like to do this afternoon? If there are any little bits of shopping . . .'

'Oh, no, Mam. I'll give you a hand with whatever you and Nonny would have done and we can talk as we work. I take it you're still letting rooms? Have the beds been changed yet, or have you got lodgers who are in for more than one night?' She turned to smile at Nell. 'I expect I'll be in my old room, sharing with Prue?'

'That's right; we'll start in there,' Nell said, feeling her cheeks grow hot, for it would be obvious as soon as they entered the room the girls had shared that it was exactly as Prue had left it that morning, her bed unmade, the slop bucket unemptied and Addy's own bed covered in the cast-off clothing Prue had worn to whichever dance or party she had gone the evening before. However, there was no help for it, so as she and her daughter mounted the stairs she told Addy that it was unlikely Prue would have had a chance to do her room before leaving for work that morning.

Addy said nothing, but when she entered the room and looked swiftly round at the chaos she tutted disapprovingly and began to pick up garments from the floor, putting them on hangers and tidying them away in the rickety old wardrobe, which was already crammed with Prue's work clothes and finery.

'As you can see, your sister left in a hurry this morning,' Nell said apologetically, beginning to make the bed. Then, abruptly, she decided she might as well tell Addy how things stood, since if her daughter spent much time at home she would see for herself. So Nell straightened, a hand to the small of her back, and grimaced at her daughter, who was sorting clean linen from dirty with a somewhat set look on her face.

'Addy, my love, I'm that ashamed of the way I've behaved, because this awful mess is mainly down to me,' she said. 'I've let Prue get away with blue murder ever since she started work. The truth is, she's never lifted a finger to help out since you left to join the Wrens, and I reckon that before that it was you who made beds, scrubbed floors and emptied slop buckets. I'm afraid I was a bad mother to you, expecting you to do all the work while your sister idled her time away.'

'Oh, Mam, you shouldn't blame yourself. I always thought you were trying to make up to Prue for being paralysed,' Addy said quickly. She looked shyly at her mother. 'I know you didn't blame me for the accident, not in your heart; you just made me work harder because someone had to do it, and Prue was two years younger than me . . .'

For a moment, Nell was tempted to accept this explanation, but then she shook her head. 'No. The truth is I was so wrapped up in Prue that even when the paralysis went and she could have done small tasks about the house, I told myself that making her do anything she didn't want to do would slow her recovery. And I know I was unfair to you, Addy, but I hope I will never be so again.' She laughed suddenly, pointing to the pile of Prue's clothing that Addy was clutching. 'And look at what I'm making you do now! The pair of us are doing Prue's work, and though she may thank us very prettily because she yearns for your good opinion, as a rule she simply accepts that it's my job to clean up after her. I've talked it over with Jamie and Nonny and I know myself I've done

389

poor Prue no favours by spoiling her rotten. But they say the forces will sort her out and she's goin' to apply to join the Wrens, you know.' She reached across and gave her daughter a quick hug. 'Will you ever forgive me for being so unfair?' she asked. 'You're such a good girl and you were wonderful to Prue when she was ill.'

'Oh, Mam, don't be so daft,' Addy said warmly, returning the hug. She giggled. 'And she's applying to join the WAAF too, isn't she? She said so in her last letter. Well, neither will stand for a mess like this, and anyway, I'll have a word before I go back to Plymouth. After all, this is my room as well as hers whilst I'm at home, and I don't mean to live in squalor or to clear up someone else's muddle.'

'Thank you, darling,' Nell said warmly. 'And now I'll fetch clean sheets from the chest of drawers on the landing and we'll make up your bed. I expect you'll be glad to climb into it when supper's over, after the day you've had.'

*　　*　　*

Addy thoroughly enjoyed her afternoon with Nell. She heard all about the lodgers who came and went according to which ships were in dock and how long the crew would be ashore, and about Mr Fleming, who was almost permanent since he had retired from the Navy on a pension and had, as he put it, 'dropped his hook at a grand safe haven' which was how he referred to the Vines. He was an independent old fellow and made most of his meals on a Primus stove in his room, though he came down each evening to share in the Finches' dinner.

Nell went on to explain that Prue loved to dance, so they did not see much of her in the evenings. But sometimes she brought friends home and they would all gather round the kitchen table after closing time, and play Monopoly or have a game of cards. Then they would enjoy some of Nell's homemade shortbread with a cup of cocoa before going their separate ways.

She and Nonny still went to the whist drives when they were held, to the cinema or the theatre whenever possible, and of course there was firewatching, ARP duties and Nonny's regular shift behind the counter in the NAAFI.

Addy said laughingly that they made her life as a Wren at Foliat Manor seem downright dull. 'It's been too cold lately to do anything in the garden, but we help on the local farms when we're not needed elsewhere,' she said. 'I've fed pigs, searched for eggs when the hens have laid astray, and harvested sprouts when the icicles were hanging on every plant—I got soaked to the thighs, despite my wellington boots. I can't tell you about the messages I've taken because for one thing I never know the contents of the documents I carry and for another we aren't allowed. But I've had some pretty hair-raising rides when the snow has blown across the lanes to form great towering drifts and I've had to lift my machine over them or tried to blast my way through, which isn't always easy. But we have our fun too, of course. When Giles is ashore—you'll remember him, Mam—we go dancing or to the flicks, or he comes up to the manor and we light a tiny fire in the breakfast parlour so that we can be alone, and toast slices of bread over the flames, and talk and talk.'

'It sounds idyllic, queen. I'm so glad you're happy,' Nell said. 'But what about his sister? You said they are twins; surely she'll want to see him as well—and he her?'

'She does, of course, but she's very understanding. If she's not on duty, she'll come in to the parlour for twenty or thirty minutes and then make an excuse to go off and leave us alone. Her boyfriend—fiancé I should say—is a captain in the army. I think his division is spearheading the advance, so though she gets letters, meetings are out of the question. But you've not told me about Nick. Last time I was home, Prue could talk of nothing but Nick.'

'Oh yes, dear Nick. He's had one forty-eight, though we didn't see much of him,' Nell admitted. 'He and Prue were off out most of the time, but they came in for meals, of course. He hasn't changed much, though I suppose he's taller and a bit broader than he was when you lived at home, and he's mad about your sister. I expect he misses her dreadfully, but it's not so bad for Prue. She has heaps of friends, including the young fellow who was evacuated to Foliat Manor with you. Do you remember him, Edgar Wilkinson?'

Prue's letters had mentioned Ed, so Addy just nodded. 'We didn't like him at first; in fact I positively hated him,' she admitted. 'But then we got to know him better and thought he was really nice. He taught Prue to swim, you know, but he never found it easy to make friends. However, Prue said in her letter that he's changed; apparently he and his mates are really close.'

Nell agreed. 'That's right, they would be. We've had other blokes from submarines in the bar from

392

time to time and they all sing the same tune,' she said, 'if the crew aren't looking out for each other, then they don't last long. I reckon it's the most horrible, dangerous job of any in the Navy. Prue once told me Edgar had fearful nightmares, and when you think of being locked inside a sardine tin at the bottom of the ocean for hours on end, with the enemy dropping depth charges, it's no wonder he has bad dreams. Why, I can't even think of it without feeling sick.'

Addy thought that taking off from a small deck and flying miles to your objective before having to find that small deck again, perhaps in ferocious weather conditions, was pretty bad, but knew her mother was right. Submarine crews faced a far worse death than the quick one which would be the lot of Giles and Neville, if they were shot down, or missed their way and ran out of fuel, and had to ditch. However, it did not do to dwell on such unpleasant possibilities, so she turned the subject, asking what was on at the Empire at the moment.

'It'll be a panto from Boxing Day, if not before. I think it's Jack and the Beanstalk,' Nell told her. 'Any chance of you still being here for Christmas? That would be so wonderful, darling Addy.'

'I wish I knew,' Addy said wistfully. 'But Captain Solomon is as keen as I am to spend Christmas here. After all, today's Wednesday and the captain will have meetings Thursday and Friday. Then it's the weekend, when nobody will plan meetings I shouldn't think, and Monday's Christmas Day! Even more to the point, his wife and three children live in St Helen's, so you never know; he might be able to wangle it.'

Nell was beginning to reply when someone

knocked on the back door. Addy jumped to her feet and unlocked it, flinging the door wide.

The figure standing outside bounced into the storeroom and then gave a shriek. 'Addy! Oh, Addy, Addy, Addy!' Prue said, her voice rising with each reiteration of her sister's name. 'Oh, it's wonderful to see you; why didn't you tell us you were coming? Are you here for long? Oh, Addy, I need you so; I've got meself in such a fix. Oh, Addy, you'll tell me what to do for the best, I know you will!'

CHAPTER SIXTEEN

'Oh, Prue, it's lovely to see you as well,' Addy said, giving her little sister a hug. Not that she was a 'little sister' any longer, for she was almost as tall as Addy herself now, with a curvaceous figure which showed to good effect in the tightly belted Burberry she wore. As soon as she was inside she pulled off her scarlet beret and shook out the froth of blonde curls which Addy remembered so well. Clearly, working in the factory had not affected Prue's dress sense, nor caused her to braid or roll or make a French pleat of her abundant locks. Neither had it stopped her bubbling over with enthusiasm, positively gabbling as she seized her sister's hand.

Only when they were in the kitchen did she hiss in Addy's ear, 'Not a word to our mam or Nonny, though, 'cos I'm sure you'll sort me problem out, no trouble, and I don't want them to worry.'

Addy hoped that Prue might suggest the two of

them went for a walk, or to one of the cinemas, or even to a dance, for she was very curious as to what problem Prue could want to share. Her sister had never been secretive; it had been Addy herself who had not always wanted to talk of her doings with the family. She thought that in those days she had probably anticipated Nell's sharp remarks or Prue's indifference, but it made her all the keener to discover just what was worrying her sister now. All the while they were eating dinner and discussing the possibility of Nell and Addy's going shopping next day in the hope of persuading their butcher to sell them sausages or liver, Addy was wondering just what Prue had been up to.

When she suggested, however, that Prue might go with her down to the phone box on the corner to ring Naval HQ, Prue refused, shuddering expressively. 'I'm a working girl now, remember, and I've been at me bench all day, packing bleedin' parachutes,' she said reproachfully. 'And when I gorrout of there I missed me tram and had to walk. Me feet were like blocks of ice, I've got chilblains the size of pennies all up the backs of me legs, and I've been and gone and left me mittens in me other coat, so there's no way I'm venturing out again tonight.'

So Addy went alone and spent the first five minutes in the box thinking of Giles, because it was eight o'clock. She sometimes saw pictures of his face in her mind but tonight she just thought of him and was content with that. Then she returned to the Vines, feeling a warm glow, because the captain had left a message with the switchboard to say he would not be needing her the next day, but would be grateful if she came to HQ in person on

Friday morning, at around nine.

When she got back, Addy offered to go through to help in the bar, but Prue frowned and shook her head. 'That's not on; I reckon we should go early to bed, 'cos tomorrer's me day off, so we can go shoppin' in the mornin' an' see a flick later. With Christmas only a few days off, the shops will pretty empty, and I still haven't bought all my presents.' She turned to her mother. 'You can manage without me just for once, can't you, Mam?' she asked hopefully. 'I'm dying for me bed; I'm wore out, honest to God I am.'

Addy was unable to stop herself giving a snort of disbelief. 'Prudence Fairweather, you're a lazy little tyke!' she said roundly. 'I saw our bedroom before our mam had had a chance to tidy it. I bet you never help with any household chores, nor behind the bar if you can avoid it.'

She half expected Prue to deny this hotly, but with Nonny's and Nell's eyes upon her it appeared her sister had decided not to defend herself. Instead she gave a sheepish smile and pointed out that she did occasionally work behind the bar, though only when the pub had plenty of supplies and was consequently busy.

It was now Jamie's turn to snort, but Nonny, getting up from the table and donning her coat, winked at Addy. 'I'm servin' behind the counter at the NAAFI in twenty minutes, so you two girls can wash up and clear away and then go off to bed,' she said. 'I'll warrant you've a deal of talking to do.'

Addy, who was longing to cross-question Prue, hurried to the sink and began washing up whilst Prue made their hot water bottles. Nell popped in from the bar to ask if they wanted a mug of cocoa to take up to bed with them.

Addy began to say that that would be lovely, but Prue interrupted. 'No thanks, Mam,' she said briskly. 'Or if we do, I'll make 'em with the water left in the kettle after I've filled both bottles.'

Nell, looking rather surprised, disappeared back into the bar and presently Addy and Prue climbed the stairs, entered their bedroom and began to undress. 'It's lovely to be home,' Addy said contentedly, snuggling down, 'but I'm longing to hear your great secret, Prue. I gather you're extremely keen that no one else should overhear it. Why wouldn't you come down to the phone box with me? You could have told me then.'

'I couldn't risk it; we might have been interrupted. And anyway, I know so many people round here that we might easily have had company both going to and comin' from the telephone box. In fact the only really safe place to talk, where you know you won't be interrupted, is in your own bed.'

'True,' Addy said. 'So carry on then; tell me everything!'

There was a long silence whilst Prue apparently tried to find the right words for what she wanted to say. Addy, growing impatient, began to ask if this great secret was connected with work or with Prue's social life, but Prue suddenly sat up in bed and flapped a hand at her. 'Shurrup, Addy Fairweather,' she said crossly. 'And stay shurrup, but keep your lugs a-flappin' an' don't say nothin' once I start. Oh, dear me, you'll tell me I've been a fool, and I know it, but . . . remember me telling you last time you were home that Nick and I were more or less engaged?'

'Yes, of course I—' Addy began, but was

interrupted at once.

'If you want to hear what I've got to say, you mustn't keep puttin' your spoke in,' Prue said severely. She ignored her sister's smothered giggle and after a moment continued, 'I told you then I'd agreed to marry Nick as soon as the war were over. Only—only then I met Ed. I was real sorry for him and of course I saw an awful lot of him when he stayed with us during his sick leave. So when Ed asked me if I'd marry him as soon as the war was over—well, I didn't have the heart to say no.' She stared at her sister across the small space which separated their beds. 'I didn't *mean* to be wicked, but I kept thinkin' if one of them was to be killed . . .'

'Prue, how could you say such a thing?' Addy asked, really shocked. 'It's almost as though you *want* one of them to be killed to get you out of an embarrassing situation. And what do you expect *me* to do about it . . .'

'Addy, will you shurrup,' Prue hissed. 'You said you wouldn't keep interruptin' but you've done nothin' else! Just listen, will you?'

'Sorry,' Addy muttered, repressing an urge to giggle. 'Carry on, Casanova.'

'I don't know what you mean by that, but . . . oh, dammit, did I ever mention a Yank called Oke? Well, his name isn't Oke, it's Oklahoma . . . Oklahoma Verinski. No, no, you needn't answer, I'm pretty sure I never mentioned him in my letters. Well, he's stationed not far from here and comes down pretty often and when he asked me to go steady, and I'd not seen Nick for months, and Ed was off accompanying convoys across the Atlantic . . . well, I said I would. Go steady, I mean, which is an American expression I'd not come across before. Then Oke said he wanted to marry me after the war and take me to his ranch, and he went on about how I'd love the life and how there was no rationing in the States and no bombs . . . certainly no doodlebugs . . . and, well, I said I would; marry him after the war, I mean.'

'Prue, how *could* you?' Addy asked again, trying to stop her voice from trembling. 'Well, go on; what do you expect me to do about it? Surely you can make up your own mind? Which one of them do you love?'

'Whichever one I'm with at the time,' Prue said with devastating honesty. 'I haven't seen Nick for absolutely ages and for all I know he may have got himself another girlfriend by now. He don't write nearly as often as he used to. Oh, and I suppose I didn't mention Patrick, did I? He's the turret gunner in one of them huge flying fortresses. He's ever so nice and you'll never guess what he does in the peace, Addy.'

'I don't think I want to know,' Addy said hollowly. 'Except I suppose I can guess: he's asked you to marry him when the war's over and you've said yes.'

'No, you're wrong there,' Prue said, and Addy could almost hear a tinge of regret in her voice. 'It's made me wonder if he's married already, because the Yanks all seem very keen on marriage and they're all so rich and handsome, and they give the girls they go with lovely things: nylons and boxes of chocolates and packets of gum and bags of sweeties. But this one, Patrick, he's a film star, when he isn't being a gunner. He took me to see a film at the Forum and there he were on the screen,

399

lookin' ever so handsome, and when the credits came up, there was his name, Patrick O'Halloran. He's really nice. So you see, if I play my cards right, I could end up married to a film star.'

Addy sighed. How on earth was she to advise her sister? But of course there was only one solution really: she must persuade, bribe or force Prue to write 'Dear John' letters to all four young men. She hoped very much that, when the chips were down, Prue would realise that she really did love one or other of her unofficial fiancés. She also hoped her sister's true love would turn out to be an Englishman, because already there were stories circulating about how boys from the slums of the big cities in the United States were passing themselves off as rich ranchers, film stars and the like.

'Addy? You haven't gone to sleep, have you?' Prue's voice sounded indignant, and once again Addy had to fight the desire to giggle. As if she could possibly fall asleep when Prue was telling her what she had been up to!

So to prove she was still wide awake she sat up, reached for her dressing gown which lay on the foot of her bed, and wrapped it round her shoulders. 'Of course I haven't fallen asleep,' she said, trying to keep her voice level. 'Prue, you do know that what you've done is very wrong, don't you? No one can marry three young men at once, let alone four. And knowing you, the moment you get your uniform—if you do—and leave home, you'll meet other blokes and make promises that you must know in your heart you can't possibly keep. Look, I'm here all day tomorrow, so that will give us a chance to talk things through and hopefully to come to a decision. Then you will have to write truly apologetic letters to all the young men, except the one you've decided you really do love, telling them that your feelings have changed and that they must not visit you again.'

Prue gave a wail, hastily muffling it, her hands flying to her mouth. Then she dropped them and looked pleadingly across at her sister. 'I can't do that,' she said. 'You must know, Addy, that men in the forces are leading terribly dangerous lives. If someone they love is killed, or a girl gives them the go-by, it takes their concentration away from the job in hand and they can die, and kill their crew as well.'

'And just now you were talking quite placidly about Nick or Ed being killed,' Addy said reproachfully. 'Prue Fairweather, it's time you grew up! A kid of fourteen might behave the way you've done, but you're a young woman now and not a child. If you ask me, the Americans won't break their hearts over losing you; it's just Ed and Nick you should worry about. Why, you accepted Nick's ring, and wear it on a chain round your neck! How did you explain that away to these other admirers of yours?'

Prue tossed her head. 'What do you think I am?' she squeaked. 'I didn't show it to anyone.' She looked discontentedly across at her sister. 'An' I thought that you, being so much older than me, would know exactly what I should do,' she said. 'But all you've suggested is "Dear John" letters and I don't want to break Nick's heart, nor Ed's, particularly as Ed occasionally stays at the Vines. I'd rather not break Oke's or Patrick's hearts either, of course, but I'm sure they'll both find someone else pretty quickly.'

'Well, tomorrow you and I will go off shopping. Mam and Nonny will think we're searching for Christmas presents and of course we'll have to do so, but we'll buy a pad of paper, a bottle of ink and a fountain pen, and we'll write the letters together. As you say, the American ones will be easy, but Nick truly believes the pair of you are going to marry and I suppose Ed believes the same, so, much though you'll hate it, now is decision time. Which of them do you like best?'

'Nick—no, Ed—no, Nick,' Prue said in quick succession. 'Nick's the better looking, but Ed's taller and I do like tall men. On the other hand, though, Ed's got red hair and freckles and I've never liked red hair.'

'What the devil does the colour of his hair, or his height, matter?' Addy said quite angrily. 'Don't you ever give a thought to character, kindness or honesty? When he was just a boy, Ed wasn't kind or honest, as I remember. But Nick was always a decent bloke and very fond of you. Good to you as well. He never grumbled about taking you out in your wheelchair, or carrying you up the stairs. But I shouldn't try to influence you. Just you lie there and think about the pair of them and make a decision. And if your mind isn't made up by tomorrow morning, I wash my hands of you.'

Prue sighed and slid down the bed again. 'All right, all right; I might have guessed I'd end up having to decide for myself,' she said crossly. 'I'll do my best, Addy, honest to God I will, but just bear in mind that I could end up with nobody and I don't want to be a spinster! I want a good-looking, rich husband, a lovely home in the country like

Foliat Manor, and several good little children who always do as they're told and will give me lots of love.'

This time Addy did not attempt to suppress her laughter. 'You are an idiot, Prue,' she said between giggles. 'That's what everyone wants, or every woman at any rate. But it's just a dream, queen, just a dream. Life simply isn't like that. Have you ever heard the expression: "Take the rough with the smooth"? Well, apply it to yourself and your fellers and you'll probably find not one of them will fit the bill. There are always advantages and disadvantages, and you can be cold-blooded if you like and weigh them up before deciding which you really want to marry—if you really want to marry either of them—but remember marriage is for life. Honestly, Prue, it's love that counts. If you love a man enough, then you'd go with him to the ends of the earth, and suffer all sorts of deprivation. There's a quotation . . . Shakespeare . . . hang on while I try to remember it . . . oh, I've got it: *And all my fortunes at thy foot I'll lay / And follow thee, my lord, throughout the world.*'

There was a short silence from the other bed, then Prue sniffed and Addy saw her knuckle her eyes, very much as a young child would have done. 'That's beautiful,' Prue said, her voice husky. 'It'll help me to make up my mind, honest to God it will.'

'Good. Old Shakespeare knew a thing or two, didn't he?' Addy said. 'And now let's get some sleep or we'll be a couple of wrecks tomorrow.'

*   *   *

403

Prue did not wake until Addy began washing, then she opened her eyes reluctantly and scowled at her sister's back view. 'Oh, Addy, it's my day off,' she said plaintively. 'I always have a lie-in on my day off, but you've been crashing about since dawn, so I haven't been able to sleep.' She sat up, rubbing her eyes, then shivered and glanced towards the window, giving a moan as she did so. 'Bloody fog! I thought you said your captain had give you the day off. Why . . . oh, damn and blast, I remember. We're goin' shoppin'.'

Addy rinsed her face and rubbed it dry, then turned to her sister. '*And* we're going to write those letters,' she said, not bothering to keep her voice down though Prue scowled at her and hissed 'Hush!' beneath her breath.

Addy hung her towel over the rail and began to get dressed. 'Don't you hush me,' she said severely. 'And don't forget the rules; I'll do my share of keeping our room decent, but you can jolly well do yours. So you'd better get up and start as we mean to go on.'

Prue sighed. It was clear that whilst Addy remained at home she would have to pull her socks up, as Nonny would say. She remembered, balefully, that in the days before Addy joined the Wrens, she had insisted on Prue's making her own bed and keeping her half of the room clean, so now she climbed from between the sheets, wincing as her feet hit the cold lino, and scuttled over to the washstand. She seized the ewer, meaning to go downstairs and refill it, for Addy had already emptied her washing water into the slop bucket, but to her pleasure, the jug was still half full and the water hot. She poured it into the basin and began to wash, whilst behind her Addy, already neatly uniformed save for her jacket, was vigorously brushing her gleaming hair into the popular pageboy style.

'Why are you wearing your uniform?' Prue asked presently, dressing in a blue tweed skirt and her thickest jumper, for she guessed that it would be cold outside. 'I put all your ordinary clothes—the ones you had before you joined the WRNS—in the chest of drawers on the landing. They may be a bit creased, but—'

Addy turned to stare at her. 'And you intend to join one of the services,' she said in a wondering tone. 'Unless you get special permish—like for a wedding or something—you have to wear your uniform at all times. Oh, Prue, are you sure you wouldn't be happier sticking to your factory? Once you're in the Wrens at any rate, you're there for the duration.'

'The duration?' Prue squeaked. 'Does that mean for ever? No one told me that when I went to the recruiting office.'

Addy laughed. 'No, you idiot, for the duration of hostilities; in other words, until the end of the war, and no one can tell how long that will be, though with the troops pushing across the Continent and liberating all the countries which Hitler annexed, it probably won't be that long.'

'Oh,' Prue said, giving her sister the benefit of her sunniest smile. 'That's all right then. If you're ready, let's go down and grab some breakfast before we set off on our shopping expedition.'

As she spoke, she seized the slop bucket and went to head for the stairs, but was stopped by a wrathful hand grabbing her shoulder. 'Put that down!' Addy said sternly. 'Make your bed, then pick up the clothes you flung down on the floor last night, and *then* we'll go down and get some breakfast.'

Prue's lower lip jutted but a glance showed her that Addy's bed was neatly made and that no clothing lay on either the floor or the chair on her sister's side of the room. So she stood the slop bucket down, hung up the clothing which she had cast aside the night before, and began to make her bed whilst Addy picked up the slop bucket and headed for the stairs.

After a good breakfast, the girls set off on their shopping expedition, though, as Prue told her sister bitterly, on a day of freezing fog such as this everyone with any sense would be indoors. Addy, however, merely grinned at her and continued to walk at a smart pace, her footsteps ringing on the icy pavements. 'Then it's all the better, because we'll have the shops to ourselves,' she said. 'Come *on*, Prue; best foot forward!'

And despite Prue's fears that she would have a horrid time, she soon realised that Addy was not going to criticise or scold and settled down to enjoy her sister's company. She had friends in the factory, of course, scores of them, but now she thought that she and Addy had always been close, and she found it easy to confide in her, knowing that the older girl would not laugh or scoff at her questions and fears.

As Addy had promised, they bought paper, pen and ink in a small stationer's shop halfway through the morning and retired to Fuller's, where they ordered a pot of tea for two and a plate of fancy cakes. Then they settled down to the difficult task of writing the letters. By the time all four were finished, they had drunk two pots of tea and eaten every cake on the plate.

Prue had wept over the letters to Ed and Nick, for the girls had decided that it would be best not to send either of these old friends the sort of 'Dear John' letter that had gone to the American servicemen. Instead, Prue had said she had decided she was too young for a definite commitment. She said they might continue to write but until she was sure of her own mind it was best that they should not meet.

Prue had wanted to give them hope, had actually suggested that she should tell Ed he was still welcome at the Vines whenever he was in the city, but Addy had vetoed this idea. 'It makes a nonsense of the main body of the letter,' she had pointed out. 'You say you're too young to think of marriage, too young for a permanent relationship, but he can come and stay at your home whenever he wishes. Be sensible, Prue. Just *think*, queen. If you give Ed an open invitation, suppose he turns up on the same day as Nick comes home, having been granted a forty-eight? How will you explain that away? Will you expect them to Box and Cox it?'

'I don't know what Box and Cox means,' Prue said. She was aware that she sounded sulky, but no longer cared. As she had been writing the letters to her sister's dictation, she had been realising more and more how much she enjoyed her double life and how flat things would seem without love letters plopping through the letterbox and young men forever at the door.

But Addy was explaining Box and Cox, telling

407

her that it was from a play in which two young men, one working nights and the other days, had shared a bed without each other's knowledge. 'So you see, you might find yourself with some very awkward explaining to do,' Addy ended. 'Honesty is the best policy. Can you imagine how very much more upset Ed and Nick would be if both believed you were going to marry them and they met in the kitchen at the Vines?'

'All right, all right, I know what you mean and I won't add a PS and thank you very much, Addy, for helping me,' Prue said sincerely. 'And now let's finish our shopping because I've still got your present to buy and you've still got mine, so we'd better separate.' She had addressed all four envelopes, licked down the flaps, put on the stamps and tucked them into her shoulder bag. 'Which way are you going? I'm not going to tell you where I'm going because you might guess what I'm trying to buy for you. But I mean to turn to the right. You?'

'Then I'll go left,' Addy said equably. 'And we'll meet back here, right outside Fuller's, in half an hour. Will that suit you?'

'That'll be fine,' Prue said absently, gazing across the road to where a large red pillar box stood. 'I'll just post these . . .' she fished a couple of the letters out of her bag and flourished them under Addy's nose, 'then I'll be on my way.'

Prue crossed the road and pushed the letters through the slit, then set off towards the store that she had in mind. Once out of sight of her sister, however, she dived round the corner and into an alley that housed the back yards of the shops, including their large dustbins. Prue looked back guiltily, but though there were plenty of people passing along the pavements of the main road no one turned into the alley. She waited a moment longer, then fished the two remaining letters out of her bag and proceeded to tear them both into small shreds. Box and Cox it indeed, she thought wrathfully, pushing the fragments of the ruined correspondence well down into the nearest dustbin. If Nick and Ed turned up at the Vines on the same day, she would think of something which both parties would believe; why should she not? She had often gone to the Grafton Ballroom with one young man and returned, after the dance was over, with another. The girls at the factory giggled and said she was a shocking flirt, but several of them behaved just as she did and no one seemed to mind. Addy was an old woman and had not been at all impressed when Prue had told her how receiving such a cruel letter could ruin a man's life. Besides, she *did* intend to marry either Nick or Ed; it was just that she couldn't choose between them. And now that the horrid letters had been destroyed, she would have plenty of time in which to make up her mind. Indeed, as Addy had implied, she might meet someone she preferred to either of them, once she was in the WRNS or the air force.

Humming a cheerful—and rather rude—little ditty beneath her breath, Prue hurried out of the alley and headed for Elliot Street and Blackler's.

*   *   *

Half an hour later, Addy was also humming to herself as she waited for her sister outside Fuller's.

409

Her shopping spree had been successful. Knowing Nonny's love of bright colours, she had bought her a red headscarf, ornamented with pictures of lemons and bunches of purple grapes. She had got Prue a pair of blue woollen gloves, which she had bought in Plymouth, and had just added some tiny blue earrings. And for her mother she had managed to acquire talcum powder and scented soap.

Now, waiting on the pavement, she saw Prue trotting towards her, a broad smile on her face. Addy, who had felt rather mean after making Prue write her four letters, realised that she had done the right thing. It had been hard for Prue to make up her mind to put off both her young men, but now that she had done it, look how happy she was! Addy went towards her, returning her smile. 'Got everything you need for Christmas Day? I managed to get Jamie half a dozen rolls of Life Savers—you know, the mints with the hole in the middle—because Mam told me once he liked to suck them when working behind the bar. She said he doesn't smoke or drink because of his asthma and he can't stand chewing gum because people think he's eating whilst serving his customers. But those Life Savers are what he likes most.'

'Where did you get them?' Prue asked curiously. 'They're American sweets, aren't they?'

'I dunno, but I bought them at a sweet shop in Plymouth and I had to part with coupons,' Addy said. 'Is there a British Restaurant round here? If so, let's make for it; they're marvellous value and the food's really good if you steer clear of snoek.'

* * *

410

Despite Addy's fears that Captain Solomon might be recalled to Plymouth before Christmas, the powers that be must have decided that it was too cruel to despatch them on the long journey on Christmas Day, for the meetings finished at six in the evening on the twenty-fourth. Addy had been hanging around headquarters, hoping desperately that orders might come to remain in Liverpool over the holiday and as soon as she saw the captain's expression she knew that her hopes had not been groundless.

'Any luck, sir?' Addy said as soon as he reached her side. 'Only you look pretty pleased with yourself; is that a good sign?'

'The best,' Captain Solomon said, grinning from ear to ear. 'We leave at the crack of dawn on the twenty-seventh and as long as we're in before midnight all will be well.'

'That's great. If we leave at five, we can do it easily,' Addy said joyfully. 'The roads may be pretty icy, and if we run into freezing fog it will slow us down, but unless the car develops some major mechanical fault which I can't deal with by the roadside, we'll be back in Plymouth in time for supper.'

Returning to the Vines, Addy gave them the good news and everyone immediately began to plan extra surprises. Jamie set off on some mysterious errand, riding his old push bike, and returned an hour later with a large chicken, plucked, dressed and ready for the oven. Meanwhile, Nell hurried off to St John's Market, returning with her shopping bag full of fruit and vegetables, including two oranges which she must have bought on the black market, since only blue ration books were entitled to such exotic fruit.

'And don't you go imagining that we wouldn't have bought extra grub even if you'd not managed to stay over,' Nell told her daughter severely. 'Of course we want to make your Christmas special, but I don't want you feeling guilty because we've splashed out a bit. Now can you give me a hand with the vegetables, because I'll have to be up betimes to cook the bird Jamie just carried in. It's a whopper and will need a fair old time in the oven. We still have gas and electric cuts, and of course on Christmas Day everyone's using gas so the the pressure will be down, so you can't rely on getting the dinner cooked in the usual time.'

'Why don't you use the range?' Addy asked.

Nell heaved a sigh and passed a hand across her forehead. 'Almost no fuel,' she said. 'And the range was never meant for burning wood, because it goes too quickly.'

The women of the family were all in the kitchen performing various tasks. Prue was preparing sprouts, Nonny was peeling potatoes, Addy had just finished scraping carrots and was about to start on the parsnips, and Nell was making stuffing with breadcrumbs, chopped onions and sage, whilst Jamie was serving those customers who had come out to enjoy a pre-Christmas drink.

Prue was the first to finish her work and announced firmly that she was for bed. 'I've not wrapped all me presents yet, so I'll do that before our Addy comes up,' she said, and disappeared up the flight whilst Addy was still beginning to suggest that her sister might make a start on the washing up.

Nell smiled across at Addy but shook her head. 'Let her get her sleep,' she said tolerantly. 'After all, she's worked harder than ever before since you came home. I don't know quite what you told her, queen, but whatever it was, it's worked wonders.'

'Oh, she ain't a bad kid, not when it's pointed out to her that we need a bit of a hand from time to time,' Nonny observed. She looked at her daughter's pale and weary face. 'If you've done with that stuffing, then I'll put it in the bird. You and Jamie will be busy enough tomorrow, so get some rest while you can.' She leaned over and pinched Addy's flushed cheek. 'Me and me granddaughter will have a nice chat.'

Addy could see that her mother was happy to obey, for she and Jamie had had an extremely busy week and must be longing for their bed. Nell, however, lingered for a moment and came across to give Addy a kiss. 'You are such a good girl; if I'm honest, you're twice the girl Prue is, and why I didn't realise it when you lived at home, I can't imagine,' she said. 'But it's never too late to mend. Good night, queen, and God bless. It'll be grand to have you home for Christmas.'

CHAPTER SEVENTEEN

1945

Spring had come, but the weather remained cold. Dominic groaned with the rest, but reflected that, in a way, it could have been worse. Rain in this cold would have fallen as snow, and the frosts and bitter winds were bad enough. If they had been forced to contend with snow, their casualties—probably deaths—would have mounted horrifyingly. As it was, they often awoke to find their blankets stiff with frost.

They had slogged on, however, because of course there was no alternative, and anyway the enemy, though still fighting, were retreating before them. They knew that very soon now the German army would have to surrender, but until then the soldiers, bayonets fixed, rifles at the ready, pressed on.

When the command to bivouac for the night came, Dominic's small party were glad to obey. They had been in deeply forested country, well inside the borders of Germany, for some considerable while, and though he knew they were heading for the Rhine Dominic had no idea of their precise position. So far as he knew, there were no villages, let alone towns, anywhere in the vicinity, just miles and miles of trees, the occasional frozen lake—frozen in April!—and one or two woodman's huts, from the window of which a disgruntled face would sometimes peer out at them. The Germans might have had to accept defeat, but they did not do so with a good grace; quite the opposite. They resented every khaki uniform they saw and made things as difficult as possible, pretending not to understand Dominic's careful German, hiding any food away from the troops, and telling their children dreadful—and untrue—stories of what would happen to them should they so much as smile at an Allied soldier.

In France and other occupied countries they had met with great friendliness and help, even though

414

it usually meant their hosts going without, but here it was different. Sometimes they lay up for the night in a farm where the farmer and his wife would regard them with loathing, especially when their family were turned out of all but one bedroom, so that there might be accommodation for the victorious troops. Most farms had vast larders, filled with sides of bacon, smoked sausage and bottled fruit, and yet they begrudged the troops every mouthful of the food they ate. Sometimes the men put up their tiny tents in the shelter of a hedge or inside a barn, sometimes they lay on soft hay and blessed their good luck, or cursed as they spread blankets on the frost-hardened ground and shivered the dark hours away. Whichever it was, the men accepted it and rarely grumbled. They were in Germany and soon, oh, God, let it be soon, the enemy would see the futility of continuing to fight and would surrender.

'Dig in, chaps,' the command had been given, and Dominic and his friend Connor, who led their section, began to look about them for a suitable spot. It was a beautiful forest, there was no gainsaying that, but the roots of trees spread wide, which made digging doubly difficult. When their trench was about three feet deep it began to fill with water and the two men moved to another position, only to be sent back by a major from another group. 'No use digging to that depth; to find dry soil you'll have to go at least another couple of feet,' the man told them. Both Dominic and Connor knew that the deeper they dug the more water would seep into the trench, but the major, clearly a city man, stood over them until they had dug what looked suspiciously like a water-filled grave, and then, rather than admit his mistake, he marched off, swinging his swagger stick. 'The perfect picture of an ignorant fool,' Dominic whispered to his friend, as soon as the major was out of hearing.

'Shall we try somewhere else?' Connor said, viewing the water-filled trench with deep distaste. 'If we could find some rising ground . . .'

'We'll try until the light fails, which won't be long now,' Dominic said. He straightened his aching back—digging was hard and painful work—and looked around him. 'Isn't this a glorious forest though, Con? When the ferns come out and the buds on the trees burst, which they're beginning to already, it'll be idyllic.'

'Maybe,' Connor said rather gloomily. He brightened. 'Oh, look over there! The chaps have lit a fire, so the grub must have arrived. Let's go and join them.'

The food varied; sometimes it was good, sometimes poor, but tonight they were in luck. Some sort of stew was ladled out of a large tin container into each man's billycan, and was accompanied by thick slices of the black German bread to which the men were gradually becoming accustomed. The food was washed down with large tin mugs of tea and then, as evening drew on, everyone settled down for the night.

Dominic had sketched the faces of the men as they ate their meal in the flickering firelight and then he had torn off a sheet of paper from his pad and in tiny, neat writing finished the letter which he had been writing to his beloved Gillian. He ended his missive with words of hope that the war would soon be over, but warned her that they would have to occupy Germany for many months, maybe years, since the German army could not be allowed to re-form. After that, he ordered himself to go to sleep and presently obeyed his own command and slept deeply until reveille.

Sunlight slanting through the almost leafless branches greeted the men as they struggled out of their blankets, and after a somewhat sparse breakfast and a wash in the icy waters of a nearby stream they collected their gear and set off once more. Because of the difficulties of the terrain, it was not exactly a steady march, for they had to avoid obstacles such as brooks, fallen branches and thickets of undergrowth, too dense to be easily penetrated.

Now, they were traversing a reasonable path, where the trees were thinner and let through more sunshine. Dominic and Connor were in the lead and Dominic, remembering his sketchpad, told Connor that he would hurry ahead since, if he could find a clearing, he would like a sketch of it.

He saw the fallen branch across the way—there had been many such—and bent over it in order to clear it out of the path of the troops coming on behind him. Even as he grasped it, two things occurred to him. This branch had not fallen; there had been no wind strong enough to tear down such a limb for several days. It had been recently cut; he could see the marks of the axe. His hand was already on the wood and the message to let go of it had not reached from his brain to his fingers when there was a tremendous explosion. He heard his own warning shriek, saw, for a second, orange and yellow flames, then he was plunging into a pit of blackness in which he knew only pain, before the

417

dark overcame him.

* * *

'Have you heard! Oh, girls, have you had the wireless on? The BBC have just given it out that German radio has announced that Hitler's dead!' It was breakfast time and the kitchen of Foliat Manor was crowded, but every face turned towards Gillian as she shot into the room, her hands full of letters. 'What do you think of that, girls?'

Immediately, a babble of sound broke out; laughter, tears and exclamations, and Addy, toasting bread, dropped her fork and ran across the kitchen, grinning from ear to ear. 'If that murdering monster is dead, then the Jerries will have to surrender,' she said joyfully. 'And if they do that, our boys will be coming home.' She seized Gillian and twirled her round. 'It seems a lifetime since I saw Giles last. Did the Germans actually say they would stop fighting, or are they going to carry on despite Hitler's death?'

'I don't know, but I imagine they'll surrender soon, surely,' Gillian said. She tossed the letters on to the table and eyed them wistfully. 'I mustn't be greedy, as I had that lovely long letter from Dominic a few days ago. I don't know exactly where he is, I don't think he knows himself, but I *do* know, from listening to the news, that the Allies, which includes the Russians of course, have surrounded Berlin. When they march into the city, it will surely be to receive the Nazi surrender, especially now that Hitler's dead.'

'But who will sign the papers if he's really dead?' Addy asked. 'Himmler? Goebbels? Or someone

418

else?' She pulled a face. 'I bet there are dozens of generals and admirals still alive, no matter how many of the German people are dead; the high-ups manage to keep out of trouble by one means or another.' She glanced at the pile of letters on the table. 'Is there anything for me in that little lot? If so, hand it over, though I guess it won't be from Giles; I had a letter from him quite recently. But it's about time Prue wrote again . . . yes, there's one for me and it *is* from Prue. I say, Hitler dead and a letter from home! Not bad, eh?' She took her letter, went to slit the envelope, then paused as her eye caught the one beneath. 'There is one for you, Gill.'

Gillian took the letter, frowning. 'It's probably from one of my cousins, though I don't recognise the writing. My goodness, what a din! Let's find ourselves somewhere quiet.' She glanced around her. One half of the room seemed to be singing a very rude song about Hitler whilst the other half were hanging out their washing on the Siegfried Line. The two girls grinned at one another and turned with one accord to leave the kitchen, bound for the sunny rose garden where the singing would not interrupt their reading.

There was a bench in a little arbour which was a popular spot on a fine day. Addy and Gillian headed for it, glad though not surprised to find it vacant, since it was still far too early for most of the girls to be out of doors.

'You read yours first, then I'll open mine,' Gillian said. 'I like your sister's letters; they're always amusing, especially the spelling, and she's so frank! I swear I'd recognise the boys she talks about even though I've never met any of them, because she paints such good word pictures.'

Addy immediately opened her envelope, scanned the contents quickly and then informed her friend that the letter contained only one rather startling piece of news:

'Just what you warned me about has happened,' Addy read aloud. *'Nick and Ed came to the Vines at the same time!!! I think those letters we wrote must have gone astray, Addy . . .*

'Ha ha, very likely I don't think,' Addy said sarcastically. 'Young Prue probably destroyed them. I saw her go to the pillar box and put something in, but I didn't question what. Oh well.' She read on.

As you can imagine, I was pretty flummoxed, but in a way it was a good thing, because Ed and Nick really took to one another, so the three of us went out together and got on very well. I had to tell them that I'd decided I was too young to marry anyone because the war would very soon be over and I'm only just seventeen.

We laughed a lot and Nick said when peace came he would take me to Paris and propose on top of the Eiffel Tower and Ed said that was nothing; he would bring me rich jewels from the Orient and cream cakes from Samples, and win me by foul means if fair wouldn't do it. Nick reminded me that he had known me since I was just a scruffy kid and Ed capped it by saying he had known me since we were both scruffy kids. That made me laugh so much that I nearly decided there and then that it was Ed I liked best.

It's odd really, the way things have turned out; I used to think you and Nick would make a go of it, but you've got Giles now; I'm looking forward to meeting him properly once the war's over.

Please don't be cross, dear Addy. It's better to make two men happy than one miserable, don't you think?

Mam and Nonny send love, and so do I,
Prue.

PS Ever since writing this letter, I've been thinking hard about Ed and Nick and I've actually decided, at last, which one I'm going to marry. Nick is better-looking and very probably better-tempered too, but Ed can always make me laugh. He's gentle and kind, and even though he's not handsome, he's very attractive.

So at the moment I think it'll be Ed; only I don't intend to tell either of them. You know me, Addy, I might easily change my mind—only I don't think I shall!

More love, P.

Addy laid down the letter with a sigh. How typical of Prue to say she had made up her mind and then to back-pedal, thus keeping all her options open. But maybe she really does think Ed's the man for her, Addy thought. For better for worse, for richer for poorer, Prue will cleave unto Ed.

She grinned at her companion. 'And now you'd best open yours.'

'Right,' Gillian said briskly, slitting open her envelope. 'Oh, it's not from my cousin, it's from . . .

oh, my God!'

And before Addy's horrified eyes, Gillian pitched forward in a dead faint.

*   *   *

Nick had never liked heights, but somehow, when he was in position in his Lancaster, the ground below was so far away as to seem unreal. Like most tail gunners, he did not wear his parachute, but kept it close at hand and hoped, fervently, never to have to use it.

When they had first begun the big bombing offensives over Germany, there had been a good deal of resistance. Searchlights had followed them relentlessly, enabling the ack-ack batteries to find them, and enemy aircraft had done their best to blast the Allied planes out of the sky. In the early days, the crew had been constantly alert as flak exploded around them and the Luftwaffe pursued them, guns spitting. But gradually the resistance had become less aggressive as the Allies' bombing raids grew more intense.

So when the Lancaster suddenly shuddered and an orange glow lit up the fuselage, it took the men a moment to realise their aircraft had been hit. Seconds later, the skipper's voice shouted at them to jump, since it was clear that the blow had been mortal.

Yet there was no panic. Nick wriggled out of the tail, grabbed his parachute and fastened the buckles with steady fingers, saw the open hatch, felt the up-draught and was awaiting his turn to jump, suddenly aware of sick apprehension and a desire to stay where he was, when a hand thrust him, willy-nilly, through the hatch and he found himself falling, falling . . .

Below him—or was it above?—he saw the burning aircraft, nose-diving towards the earth, and remembered that he must pull the rip cord or the 'chute would not open. He also remembered that, since they had laid their eggs and had turned for home, with luck what lay below them was more likely to be open country than the sprawl of the great city they had been attacking.

For one awful moment, after pulling the cord, he thought that the bloody thing was a duff one, but then he felt the tremendous jerk as his freefall was halted by the billowing opening of the great silken canopy above him, and he found himself floating gently earthwards. At this height, he could even see the sky growing lighter in the east, and looking down he saw between his booted feet fields, hills and what he took to be a village; at any rate, a cluster of buildings.

He was just wondering how long it would be before he reached the comparative safety of the ground when two things happened almost simultaneously. The Lancaster ploughed into the earth, already more than half consumed by flames, and whilst he was still praying that the crew had all got out something struck him a hard blow on his left shoulder, the gentle, easy motion which he had been enjoying became a horrid sideways swing and a voice spoke almost in his ear.

'Gerrout o' me way, you horrible little man. Didn't no one ever teach you to steer the bloody thing?'

'Ralph!' Nick shouted, looking upwards. Both 'chutes were open, but the canopies had somehow become entangled, as a result of which the two men were swinging like a pendulum and descending a good deal faster than was safe. 'I don't know about me steering, but what about you? Couldn't you see me below you?'

'No. Here, I say . . . hang on, Nick, we're going to . . .'

There was a wrenching thud, a sickening moment when the pendulum effect seemed to redouble, and then a gradual cessation. Nick, hating heights more than ever, had kept his eyes shut, but now he opened them and stared straight at a pair of flying boots and the trouser legs tucked into them. And then he looked up . . . up . . . up . . . and saw Ralph's familiar face. His friend was not grinning but looking down and then up, then down again, his expression awed.

'Where are we?' Nick asked faintly. 'It's gettin' light; I can see your ugly mug, but I don't want to look down. Ralph . . . I've gorra feelin' we're not at ground level yet.'

'You're right there. We've got snagged on a very tall pine tree,' Ralph said. 'I don't think we ought to move, old pal. We're still the devil of a long way from terra firma.'

Unwisely, Nick looked down, and promptly recoiled with a shudder. The ground was indeed a hell of a long way off—but his involuntary movement caused their harnesses to creak and shift. There was a tearing sound as the silk of the canopies began to split . . . and Nick began to pray.

*　　　*　　　*

It was a fine evening towards the end of May and

424

Addy and Gillian were working in the kitchen garden of the manor, weeding and hoeing between the lines of peas, beans and potatoes which they would harvest, with luck and good weather, in a few weeks.

Addy had hoped that Giles might somehow manage to get home for the VE celebrations on 8 May, but this had not been possible, and since the army were occupying Germany many of the troops might not get back to Britain for months. To Addy's dismay Giles and his aircraft carrier were bound for the war in the Far East, since Japan had refused to surrender when the Germans did.

Gillian had faced up to the fact that Dominic had been badly injured by the booby-trap bomb weeks before. He was in hospital in Germany but would be sent back to a hospital in England as soon as he was fit enough to travel. His friends had assured Gillian that her fiancé's wounds were not life threatening and that he would make a good recovery, but Addy knew the other girl worried constantly beneath her cheerful façade. For her part, Addy was just happy to have received a letter only the previous day, in which Giles had said he had very real hopes that he would be back in Britain in time for Christmas.

The Japs must realise they're beat, he had written exuberantly. *After all, they've been at war with the Chinese for years and years, so they must be thoroughly fed up with fighting. I tell myself I'll be seeing you, my darling, quite soon and oh, how I long for us to get married so we can kick the Navy out of Foliat Manor and begin on the reconstruction work.*

At eight o'clock every evening, if I'm free to do so of course, I imagine that I take your hand and we wander round the rose garden, across the lawns and through the woods, until we reach the shore. Sometimes, though not nearly so often, we go through the house, planning how beautiful we will make it once it is our own again. Not that it will ever be ours precisely, because we shall share it with Gill and Dominic, but my parents are quite definite that they never want to live at the manor again and have already made it over to Gill and myself.

So roll on peace in the Far East! Once that comes then I'm pretty sure my demob papers will follow and we will be able to start work on our new home.

'Hey, Addy, stop dreaming! That was a perfectly good hogweed you've thrown on the rubbish tip and you know the rabbits adore hogweed.'

Addy came back to the present with a start. 'Sorry. You were quite right, I was working on automatic pilot,' she said apologetically. 'I tell you what, Gill, I've only got one more row to do and then I'm finished. When we've emptied out the weeds into the rabbits' pen—the weeds they like, I mean—we can take the trug and wander down the lane, picking dandelion leaves as we go. Or do you feel we ought to do a bit of weeding in the soft fruit pen?'

'We'll leave the soft fruit for tomorrow night,' Gillian decided. 'I take it you're as thirsty as I am and mean to go right along the lane to the Boar's Head? Even if they've got no beer, after all the

426

VE celebrations, they're bound to have lemonade or something. The landlord's wife was telling me she makes some stuff called raspberry vinegar, which sounds horrid but she says is really delicious. We could try a glass of that; or of course there's almost always cider.'

Both girls laughed. Devonshire cider, so cool and palatable, had not seemed like an alcoholic drink to Addy when she had first sampled it. She had accepted a pint mug, brimming over, then another, and on her return to the manor had fallen down the stairs, not realising that the drink she had thought of as apple juice could have a kick like a mule.

'Well, weeding and hoeing is pretty dusty work,' Addy replied. 'So I see no harm in going to the pub when we've got the rabbit food. And you know the Boar's Head is always full of locals and sailors home on leave; in fact I often think their customers and staff know more about naval matters than the Admiralty itself, so if there is any gossip going, they'll be the first to know.'

The girls were in working overalls but had no intention of changing into proper uniform just to squeeze into the Boar's public bar, and presently they were ensconced on a saggy old settle, each with half a pint of cider in one hand. Around them, conversations whirled and swirled. A couple of soldiers talked about receiving their demob papers, said Winnie was keen to get as many out of uniform as he could. One of them turned to the nearest sailor, asking when the other man thought he would be back in civvie street.

The sailor guffawed. 'Who d'you think's ferrying you lot across from the Continong?' he asked. 'It's us poor bloody sailors what always get the rough end of the stick. Still, I oughtn't to grumble. At least we're in port every few weeks, whereas you poor buggers might not get home for months.'

'Months? It'll be more like years for the fellers in Burma or India,' the other soldier said. 'They're the ones Winnie wants to see back home, but it'll take a deal of organising.' His eye fell on the two girls in their working overalls, quietly sipping their cider, and he grinned down at them and patted Gillian's shoulder. 'Got a feller in the army or the Navy?' he asked. 'Never you mind, miss, Mr Churchill will get things sorted and your blokes will be home before you know it.'

'I'm sure you're right,' Gillian said primly, 'but we're not banking on it.' She drained her glass and she and Addy got to their feet and began to push their way towards the door. Once in the open, they took deep breaths of the sweet fresh air, for it had grown hot and stuffy in the small bar. As they retraced their steps up the lane, Gillian slipped her hand into Addy's arm. 'I feel so mean, because Dominic hasn't been in the forces nearly as long as Giles, but I'm certain he'll get home first,' she said. 'I know Winnie said the plan was to release the men who had been in longest first, but I'm pretty sure it won't be possible. Still, once the Japs throw in the towel . . .'

*   *   *

Back in their small room at the manor, Addy and Gillian collapsed on to their beds, almost too tired to undress, and began to discuss the chances of their menfolk being home for Christmas.

428

They had not turned on the light from force of habit, but sat there in the gentle moonlight, looking out at the dark garden. 'When this is a hotel, or a sports centre, or even if we decide to turn it into flats, I don't suppose it will be us who work in the kitchen garden and tip the tea leaves around the roses,' Gillian said. 'We'll have staff to do it; imagine that, us with staff! Of course we'll keep old Mr Stebbings on, but he's getting a bit past all the stooping and bending, not to say heavy digging, so he will need a boy from the village to do anything he can't tackle.'

'But I love working in the garden,' Addy objected. 'I'd hate to have to give it up altogether. I'd rather we got help in the house, because I don't fancy making beds and scrubbing floors for the rest of me life.'

Gillian laughed. 'One of the plans that Giles and I discussed before the war was turning the west lawn into a really good, deep swimming pool. I know the sea isn't that far away, but folk like the calm water of a swimming pool. And we thought, as the money rolled in—don't laugh, you horrid girl—we might have a sort of Perspex cover, like the ones on aircraft, only much, much bigger, which we could pull over in winter, when the sea would be too rough for swimming and the pool otherwise too cold.'

'That's a lovely idea,' Addy said wistfully. 'But for now, and I suspect for the first few years, we shall have to make do with the sea. Oh, how I love the sea! Next time we've got a few hours of daylight to spare, we really ought to go down to the shore for a swim. The water will be cold, but I reckon we're tough enough to stand it.'

Gillian agreed that this would be a good idea, then stood up and began to shed her clothing. Addy, following suit, remarked that she was due to call in the offices first thing next day to pick up any messages needing delivery. 'So I hope I get to sleep quickly and don't lie here worrying.'

Occasionally, she began the night by thinking cheerful thoughts about the end of the war and Giles's return, then ended up wondering and worrying. She often saw, in her mind's eye, the endless ocean, huge waves, the bodies of great sharks moving beneath the surface, enemy ships firing up at the aircraft above them. But now, she told herself firmly, that part of the war is over. To be sure, Giles was still involved—or soon would be—with the war in the Far East, but that would not, she hoped, put him in quite so much danger. Then she remembered a friend of hers, whose young man was fighting in the Burma campaign. The girl had described the conditions of jungle warfare: the steaming heat, the thick undergrowth through which they had to hack their way with machetes, the natives who did not know friend from foe, and the creatures who lived in the jungle. In Addy's mind now, mosquitoes the size of barn owls, and leeches even bigger, skulking in or around every foetid jungle pool, lay in wait for unwary soldiers. Tigers prowling, regarding everyone as dinners on legs, and snakes descending from the trees—huge boa constrictors which could devour Giles in a couple of swallows, or cobras, whose deadly venom would kill a man seconds after he was bitten.

Addy sighed; she could see a sleepless night coming up, or dreadful nightmares if she persisted in imagining horrors. She turned over so that her back was to the window, for the moon, though only just peeping between the branches of the walnut tree, might also cause her to stay awake. Then abruptly, she was asleep and dreaming.

In her dream, she was floating above a great ocean. She could see a couple of tiny islands, green as emeralds and fringed with golden sands. There were palm trees, and each island had its own coral reef against which the great waves, white-topped and translucent, beat endlessly. It was a beautiful scene and Addy was wondering whether she could float gently down and land on one of the islands and explore when, looking about her, she saw the familiar shape of a Swordfish, such as the one Giles piloted. It was in a steep dive, and fearful apprehension tightened her throat so that the warning scream she would have given would not emerge.

Frantic with fear and horror, for she was certain that Giles must be in the plane—why, otherwise, should she dream it?—she managed at last to force out a scream, even as the plane hit the water, causing a huge sea surge to rise up . . . up . . .

'Giles, Giles!' she heard her own sobbing cry. 'Swim to the island, swim to the island!' But even as the words left her lips, she felt a hand on her shoulder and heard Gillian's voice and woke. Sweat was trickling down the sides of her face and she sat up groggily, beginning to shake. 'Oh, my God, what a dreadful dream,' she said. 'But it really was only a dream. Oh, thank you for waking me, Gill; if you hadn't, I think I'd have died of fright.'

Gillian, who had been bending over her, sat

down abruptly on the end of the bed. 'You nearly made *me* die of fright,' she said reproachfully. 'What the devil were you dreaming about, Addy?'

'Can't remember,' Addy mumbled. And it was true; the dream was receding fast. 'I'm awfully sorry I woke you, Gill, and now I'll be too scared to go back to sleep in case I have the same dream again.'

'Dream? It sounded more like a flaming nightmare to me, the way you yelled out,' Gillian said. 'But don't worry, you'll probably sleep like a baby for the rest of the night.'

Accordingly, Addy settled down and presently her heart ceased to thump so frighteningly. A few minutes later it had calmed down to an even beat, and almost before she knew it, she was asleep.

*　　　*　　　*

'Full moon tonight,' Gillian said idly when she and Addy were getting ready for bed a few days later. 'I can never sleep with the moon in my face so we'd better pull the curtains, though I hate doing so on a warm night.'

'After the day I've had, I could sleep on a clothes line with a searchlight battery trained on me,' Addy retorted. When Gillian had mentioned the full moon, her heart had given a most uncomfortable jump. Suppose she looked out and saw . . . oh, dear God, that figure she had seen before. But of course, full moon or no, nobody was going to force her to climb out of her bed and pad across the lino to stare out of the window. This time, if I happen to wake, I'll turn right over and go back to sleep, she told herself. As for closing the curtains, that would be downright stupid. Why, we didn't even pull them across when the weather was so appalling, so why on earth should we do so now? On the thought Addy climbed into bed and Gillian, already beneath the blankets, murmured good night and settled down.

'G'night, old Addy,' she said dreamily.

Addy laughed. 'G'night, even older Gillian,' she said, and presently, exhausted by their hard work, both girls slept.

An hour or so after they had got into bed, the moon's light had moved round so that it fell full on Addy's face, hard and brilliant as the searchlight she had mentioned earlier. She was immediately awake, but lay there without moving, eyes tightly closed, as though the great, round, silver penny of the moon, once it knew it had awakened her, could force her to act against her will.

In the other bed, Gillian's soft even breathing continued, but of course her bed, being the one further from the window, would not be affected by the rising moon.

Addy had been facing the window, but now she began, very stealthily, to change her position and presently had the satisfaction of knowing that, should she open her eyes, she would see only the humped shape of Gillian, curled up beneath her blankets, and the further wall.

Furious with herself for having woken almost at the moon's behest, she lay still for another three or four minutes, then opened her eyes and was astonished and horrified to find herself staring straight into the silver disc which, seconds earlier, had only been visible through the open window behind her. She was so startled and scared that she sat bolt upright, her heart leaping about in her chest like a frightened bird. How the devil had the moon managed to enter their bedroom? She was on the verge of giving a frightened cry when the solution came to her. The moon was reflected in the large round face of her alarm clock, so what she was seeing was not in fact the moon, but merely its reflection.

So I'm not going mad after all, Addy told herself triumphantly, sinking back against her pillow. Nothing unusual has happened. What a fool I was to be frightened; as if the moon could possibly get into the room, let alone force me to go to the window. Though why on earth shouldn't I? All I would see would be moonlight and shadows, the rose garden, and that gorgeous old briar rose in full flower and smelling so delicious that it almost makes you want to cry. How I wish I could capture the scent in a little bottle and send it to Giles.

On the thought, as though it had been waiting in the wings for its cue to re-enter, her bad dream of a few nights before came crystal clear into her mind, smashing her contentment and filling her with dreadful foreboding. Suddenly she knew that there really was something special about tonight. If she went to the window now, she was suddenly certain that she would know who the man was and perhaps even why he was there.

She sat up straight again, hesitated, then swung her legs out of bed. She knew she would never sleep until she had looked out of the window, so she had best get it over with. She padded across the lino, her mind full of dread, suddenly sure that it would be Giles who stood there, looking up at her. For had this not been his childhood home, had

434

he not been happy here?

She walked firmly across the short space that separated her from the window, telling herself that only a coward would shrink from discovering the truth, even if it would break her heart.

She looked through the window and saw the man's figure, and even as she looked he tilted his face so that she could see every feature as clearly as though it had been daylight. She recognised him and held out her hands beseechingly towards him, feeling his love, loneliness and longing as though he had spoken them aloud. Then she was weeping, tears pouring down her face, and the figure was fading . . . fading . . . fading . . . until it had disappeared completely.

Only then did Addy return to her bed, fish out a handkerchief and mop her wet cheeks. She knew that it was over, that the rose garden would no longer be haunted, in any sense of the word. She knew, also, why he had appeared. It was because he loved Foliat Manor, and had been happier here than anywhere else in his whole life.

CHAPTER EIGHTEEN

Perhaps because of her disturbed night, Addy would have slept through the alarm, but Gillian woke her by shouting in her ear. 'Wakey, wakey, Fairweather,' she said briskly, stripping the bedclothes from Addy's curled-up form. 'Don't forget I'm giving you a seater as far as HQ, and I don't intend to be late.'

Addy groaned, but sat up, rubbing her eyes. 'I

435

didn't even hear the alarm; the first thing I knew was when you bellowed in my ear,' she said resentfully. She glanced towards the window and saw the garden flooded with sunshine, and smelt the delicious scent from the climbing rose which grew against the warm stone wall of the manor. The bedroom seemed small and stuffy and she hopped out of bed and went over to the window, suddenly longing to be out of doors, to be enjoying this beautiful day. She thrust her head and shoulders outside and suddenly the events of the night before came flooding back to her, stealing her enjoyment of the morning and turning the blue sky grey.

Behind her, Gillian was washing noisily whilst singing a cheerful little ditty about finding her thrill on Blueberry Hill. Addy, turning away from the window, wondered that her friend could appear so light hearted when she did not know just how badly Dominic was hurt. For a few weeks Gillian had been a shadow of her former self, but then she had told Addy she must look on the bright side and had been determinedly cheerful ever since. Dominic had actually dictated a letter to Gillian from his hospital ward and its effect on her had been electric. All her gloom and misery had disappeared, especially since she had, as she put it, set her spies to work and discovered that her love would be returned to a British hospital just as soon as the necessary arrangements could be made.

Naturally, she was almost as anxious as Addy herself over Giles, though, en route for the Far East. Addy had never confided in Gillian about her dreams and did not intend to do so. There had been no letter or message from Giles for several weeks, but Addy told herself that this meant nothing; if his aircraft carrier had been hit, they would have heard.

Abruptly, she turned away from the window; the sight of the rose garden, even in brilliant sunshine, brought last night's experience too painfully back to her mind and it did not do to dwell on such things. She was telling herself that it might have been a dream, albeit a peculiarly vivid one, when something else struck her with such force that she almost cried out. It had *not* been a dream; she was sure it had not. And if she was right, Prue, who had said she loved Ed and meant to marry him just as soon as he was demobbed, could not possibly know that her young man was dead; next of kin were always informed of fatalities or serious injuries, but Ed had no next of kin. Everything depended, of course, on whether it would have been possible for someone to go through Ed's effects. If they found letters from Prue, then the authorities would inform her of his death, but if they did not it could be weeks—months even—before the news would get round to her sister.

And when it does, Addy told herself fiercely, I've got to be there, because poor little Prue will need all the loving support she can get. But first of all I must do what Gillian did and find out what has happened to the *Sunray* and her crew. If I'm told it's official that Ed is dead, then I'll make them give me leave and go back up to Liverpool to help Prue over the worst.

Now, Gillian emptied her washing water into the slop bucket, poured out fresh and jerked a thumb to it. 'There you are, you lazy good-for-nothing! All you've got to do is wash, which I take it you're

437

as capable of doing as—' She broke off, staring at Addy with rounded eyes, and her voice when she spoke was no longer bright and teasing. 'Oh, my dear, you look quite dreadful. Your eyes are all puffy and you're white as a ghost. What's the matter, love?'

Addy felt a hot flush burn up in her cheeks. 'Nothing, not really,' she mumbled, going over to the washstand and beginning to soap her flannel. 'I had a rotten night; at first I couldn't sleep, but when I did I had awful nightmares.'

'Oh, you poor thing; nightmares twice in one week,' Gillian said with real sympathy. 'I know what it is, though: you're worrying about Giles. But you mustn't make yourself ill, because that won't help anyone. If you like, we'll go along to the MO and get you some sleeping pills. One good night will break the cycle of bad dreams . . .' she grinned at her friend, 'and then we can *all* get some sleep.'

For the rest of that long day, Addy racked her brains as to how she could discover what, if anything, had happened to Ed, for as the hours wore on she became less and less certain that what she had seen—or thought she had seen—in the rose garden had presaged Ed's death and was not simply her over-active imagination.

She did not want to ask outright, however, which made things difficult, and had almost given up when, as so often happens, the information she was searching for came without prompting of any description. In fact she was in the NAAFI, sitting alone at a table near the window and eating a sticky bun, when a crowd of girls from the offices came noisily in and chose the table next to her own. Addy was within an ace of moving when one

438

of the girls said cheerily: 'Heard the latest on that sub that collided with a U-boat? Apparently the German captain said he was close inshore because he wanted to surrender—a likely tale!—and rammed the *Sunray* by accident.'

Addy pricked up her ears—was she going to learn the truth?

'I can't imagine even a Jerry would risk his neck—and his submarine—by deliberately ramming an enemy vessel, though,' another speaker said. 'Didn't the whole crew escape unhurt?'

'That's right,' the original speaker said. 'Oh, all but one. Apparently he got stuck in the escape hatch and drowned. They got him out when they realised but it was too late. The rest of the crew were all OK, though.'

Addy felt her own chest tighten but leaned nearer to the next table and spoke through dry lips. 'I used to know a fellow who sailed on the *Sunray*. Do you know the man's name?'

Even as she said it, she knew what the girl would say, and tried to look only casually interested. 'I'm not sure that I can remember . . . oh, yes, the bloke who told me about the collision called him Wilkie,' the girl said. 'Is that any help?'

'Thanks very much,' Addy said, without answering the other's question, and left, feeling her eyes begin to brim over with forbidden tears. She had wanted to know the truth, and now that she did know it she must go to Prue as soon as possible. She made for the offices.

*   *   *

439

Addy arrived at the Vines when the family were eating breakfast, and was greeted with delight and many exclamations of surprise. Prue bounced up from her place and flung her arms round her sister, whilst Nell kissed Addy warmly and bustled to the stove to cook up more porridge. Nonny began to brew a fresh pot of tea, while Jamie seized the loaf, cut a slice, buttered it, and handed it to Addy.

Addy slung her kitbag on one of the hooks behind the kitchen door, allowed herself to be pushed into a chair, and began to eat, though, as she told them, she had had a cup of char and a wad on Crewe Station.

'But that must have been in the middle of the night,' Prue observed. She waggled a letter under her sister's nose. 'How odd that you should have arrived when you did! I've had the funniest letter from Nick—I'd just finished reading it to the family when in you popped! Honestly, Nick's usually so serious but this one's a scream and he writes lovely letters. I'll tell you right away that his beloved Lanc was shot down over some German village and he and his pal jumped out, only their parachutes got entangled and then they snagged on a very tall pine tree.' She giggled, her eyes sparkling. 'Can you imagine, Addy? The poor chaps hung there, dreading what might happen, because obviously they're none too popular with the civilians they've been bombing. Nick says the silk was tearing, little by little, and the ground was a long way off. He kept remembering that poem— you know the one:

> Oh mother dear, what is that mess
> That looks like strawberry jam?

> Hush, hush, my child, that is Papa
> Run over by a tram.

only of course in his version, it would have been:

> Oh mother dear, what is that mess
> That came down from on high?
> 'Tis two of our country's enemies
> What looks like strawberry pie.'

Prue was still laughing heartily when Nell leaned over and tapped her on the shoulder. 'Tell your sister how they got down, and then I'll warrant she'd like a nice hot wash,' she said reprovingly. She turned to her elder daughter. 'You can have a can of hot water and a wash in your own room, and by the time you've done that the porridge will be ready to eat.'

'Oh, Mam, you are a spoilsport,' Prue grumbled. 'I were going to make a game of it, let Addy have three guesses as to how they got down.' She turned back to her sister. 'The other crew members from the Lanc had landed close by and they flourished their pistols and managed to convince the locals that if the fellers weren't got down all in one piece there would be hell to pay. In the end, they brought ladders that were being used for repairs to the village church spire and got them down to ground level. So all ended happily. You go up, Addy, and I'll bring the can of hot water, then we can have a nice cosy chat whilst you wash. Is Giles OK?' she added, as they ascended the stairs.

'I haven't heard from him for ages. Communications with the Far East are poor,' Addy said.

'I had a letter from Ed only two or three days ago,' Prue went on. 'He's full of plans for the peace, of course, and should be docking any day now.'

Prue opened their bedroom door, ushered her sister inside and began to pour the hot water she had carried up the stairs into the white china basin, decorated with cornflowers and sheaves of wheat, which had stood on the washstand in their room for as long as Addy could remember. Then she turned to her sister as Addy began to take off her uniform. 'You're looking awfully pale and tired,' she observed. 'But I suppose you're worrying about Giles, or is anything else the matter? Your letters are always fun to receive, but I expect you only tell us the good things that happen and keep the worrying things to yourself.'

Addy began to wash, surprised by her sister's shrewdness. Subconsciously she realised she had always thought of Prue as being a lightweight, someone who did not care to be told bad news. She splashed the water into her face and immediately felt less weary. Rubbing herself dry on Prue's towel, she sat down on the end of her bed and then looked straight at her sister. 'You say you heard from Ed a few days ago and from Nick only this morning,' she said. 'Am I right to assume that— that you aren't interested in Nick in a romantic way?'

Prue frowned, puzzled. 'Why on earth should you ask me that? I *told* you ages ago that I'd made up mind to marry Ed when the war's completely over and he's demobbed.' Then, before her sister could speak, Prue shot across the room and grabbed Addy's shoulders, giving her a hard shake. 'Do you

442

know something I don't? What's happened to Ed? The war's over, in Europe at any rate, so he must be all right, he *must* be!'

Once more Addy had to fight back tears, but when at last she answered her voice was steady. She detached herself from her sister's grasp and stood up, seizing both Prue's suddenly unquiet hands. 'The *Sunray* collided with a German U-boat somewhere off the Devonshire coast,' she said quietly. 'Ed got stuck coming out of the escape hatch and he . . . he . . .'

'He's injured,' Prue said, her voice rising. 'Oh, that bloody submarine! He should never have gone back when he came out of hospital. Is it that? Is he badly hurt?'

'Oh, Prue, I came as soon as I heard,' Addy said, feeling her tears begin to brim over. 'I'm afraid— I'm afraid it's worse than that. He's dead.'

She had expected her sister to burst into tears, to rush from the room, to show her feelings in some dramatic way, but Prue simply stood there, the colour draining from her face to leave it deathly white. Her lower lip began to tremble. 'Dead?' she said. 'But he can't possibly be dead. Why, I hadn't even told him . . .'

Addy waited for her sister to complete the sentence and, when she did not do so, sat Prue gently down on her own bed without releasing her hands and knelt on the floor before her. 'Hadn't told him what?' she enquired gently. 'Obviously he knew you loved him and were going to marry him . . . isn't that the most important thing?'

'No, it's not,' Prue said, her voice suddenly sharp. 'What is important is that I'm pregnant. I'm going to have Ed's baby.'

*   *   *

Tears came later of course. Great floods of tears for the loss of the man Addy was sure her sister had truly loved. It would be bad enough having to tell the rest of the family that Ed would never come home, but almost worse for poor Prue to admit that she was expecting his baby. Addy knew that Nell had always looked upon Prue as totally innocent, knew how hard it would be for her mother to face the tittle-tattle, the spiteful remarks, the nudges and winks from neighbours.

Prue told them at lunchtime, first that Ed had died and next that she was expecting his baby. Nell rushed out of the room in tears, and Jamie followed her, but Nonny was sensible and practical, giving her granddaughter a hug and telling her gently that one day she would be glad that she still had something of Ed. 'The baby's a part of you both; it'll be a living reminder of the fellow you loved, even though he's gone,' she said firmly. 'Your mother's upset—well, she would be—but she'll come round once she gets used to the idea. She was truly fond of Ed, you know; used to say that he and Nick were like the sons she had never had, so it's his loss that she's mourning and not the fact that folk will think you're a bad girl.'

'I don't care what they think of me,' Prue said sullenly, after Nonny had disappeared upstairs to comfort Nell. 'Everyone does it—sleeps with the feller they're goin' to marry, I mean—so why should I be different? Oh, if only Ed was still alive, we'd get married and move down to Plymouth, or some other port, and no one would be counting

444

weeks and whispering behind their hands.'

'You and Nick used to be very fond of one another,' Addy said tentatively. 'I suppose there's no chance . . . I mean, he might accept Ed's baby . . .'

'No, it couldn't possibly be Nick's; I've not been with him, though he tried to persuade me to go on a weekend to New Brighton, only I knew where that would lead,' Prue said miserably, clearly not realising that she had completely misunderstood Addy's remark. 'And I've never done it with anyone but Ed.' She sniffed dolorously. 'And I don't want to marry anyone else,' she added, 'so you can forget that.'

Addy caught hold of Prue's arm. 'Believe me, Prue, you won't always feel like that. One day, you'll meet someone else and you'll marry him to give your little boy or a girl a father as well as a mother. Nick liked Ed, didn't he? And I think he'll understand. If you tell him that Ed has died and you're expecting his baby, I think it's quite possible that Nick may offer marriage, and if he does you'd be every sort of fool to refuse him.'

'Then I'll be every sort of fool,' Prue said sulkily. She turned on her sister, bright colour suddenly invading her pale cheeks. 'You don't know *anything*, Addy Fairweather, or not about men at any rate. I bet you've never slept with that Giles of yours, but I'm telling you, when you have, you won't feel the same about other men!'

'You're right, Giles and I aren't lovers,' Addy admitted. 'We've not known each other long enough, I suppose. But that doesn't mean I don't love him with all my heart, because I do. And we're going to marry just as soon as we can, I promise you.'

'If Nick asked me to marry him, it might be from pity, which I'm damned if I want. Or he might hold it against me that I'd foisted another man's child on to him,' Prue said, sniffing. 'I'm only a few weeks months gone; I dare say if I visited that old woman what lives down Primrose Court she'd get rid of it for me.'

Addy turned to her sister, feeling the hot blood rush into her own cheeks and rage begin to mount. 'Prudence Fairweather, if you do any such thing, no one, not Mam or Nonny or Jamie, and certainly not me, will ever speak to you again,' she said roundly. 'You heard what Nonny said: that you're lucky to have the baby because it's something of Ed's for you to remember him by. Would you want . . .'

Prue promptly burst into tears and flung her arms round Addy's neck. 'No, of course I wouldn't,' she sobbed. 'But I'm desperate, Addy, desperate! They're closing the factory next week and though I expect it will reopen making jam or biscuits eventually, there goes my nice job and my nice wages with it. The services won't take me when they find I'm in the puddin' club, and anyway they've stopped recruiting. What'll I do, Addy, what'll I do?'

'I don't know, but I think it might be best if we had a family conference this evening,' Addy said, after a few moments' thought. 'Only I've got to go back tomorrow and I'd like to know what's going to happen to you before I leave. Now dry your eyes and we'll put our heads together. And do stop worrying, Prue. I'm sure we'll find a solution of some description.'

Addy got back to Plymouth in reasonable time and hurried to Foliat Manor, longing to tell Gillian about Prue's dilemma, only to discover that she was not there. In the kitchen, Avril, a pretty dark-haired South African who had come over to Britain at the start of the war with her fiancé, Fred Knowles, was doing her stint as cook. She and Fred had married and then Fred, Leading Seaman on a corvette, had been killed. Despite her friends' expectations, however, Avril had not gone home but had stayed in the country and joined the WRNS. She was at the stove, poking a fork into a pan of boiled potatoes, when Addy burst into the room, demanding to know where Gillian had hidden herself.

Since it would soon be time for the evening meal, the girls had gathered here to gossip, lay the table, listen to the wireless and exchange news, as they did every evening, so it was extremely noisy and Avril had to shout for quiet before turning to answer Addy's question. 'She's hospital visiting,' she said. 'Her feller's been invalided back to Plymouth since it's his home town, so she's gone down there armed with a basket of strawberries as a sort of get well gift. Apparently, his father died some while ago but his mother lives with his sister down in Mevagissey. They'll be visiting as soon as they know he's back in England, so Gillian zoomed off the minute her work finished for the day in order to see him alone first.'

'That's awfully good news; Gillian must be thrilled,' Addy said, though in fact she felt a little disappointed. She had hoped to be able to discuss Prue's problem with her friend, but could scarcely do so on a crowded hospital ward. Still, if she skipped supper and went straight there, she could tell Gillian all that had transpired as they made their way home to the manor.

Addy turned towards the door, checking her watch as she did so. 'If I hurry, I should just catch the ten to, which stops at the end of the lane when the driver sees someone waiting,' she said. 'It'll drop me outside the hospital if I speak nicely to the conductor. TTFN girls!'

Addy caught the bus by the skin of her teeth and flopped into a seat, thanking the conductor for persuading the driver to wait when he saw her flying down the lane. They reached the hospital and Addy jumped down, hurrying towards the entrance. It had occurred to her that Gillian might be on the point of leaving and she was desperate to tell her friend about Prue and to see whether Gillian could think of an answer.

As it happened, she and Gillian met just outside the hospital, and one look at her friend's expression was enough to put Prue's troubles to the back of Addy's mind, for Gillian's face was tear-streaked and her eyes swollen. She saw Addy and muttered something that Addy could not make out.

'Oh, Gill, don't say Dominic's . . . don't say he's—' Addy began, but Gillian cut her short.

'No, no, he's not dead, but his injuries . . . oh, Addy, let's find somewhere quiet where we can talk.'

'We'll go to that bombsite, just down the road. The kids play there during the day, but no one will

448

be about this late,' Addy said decisively, and as soon as they were seated on a part of a broken stone wall she turned to her friend. She saw that Gillian was now in command of herself, but nevertheless, when she spoke, it was gently. 'Oh, Gill, love, tell me what's happened to Dominic. Is he very badly injured? Somehow, I'd got the idea that they wouldn't send him back to England until he was pretty well right. Was I wrong?'

'No, you were spot on,' Gillian admitted. She bit her lower lip and looked at Addy under her lashes for a moment, then turned her head and stared at her feet in their neat black shoes. 'But he's lost three fingers on his left hand, and the thumb on his right. It was a booby-trap which exploded as soon as he touched a branch laid across the track . . . and he's left-handed, you know. Oh, Addy, suppose he can never draw again? He says he'll manage, he's practising all the time, says he's going to learn to play the piano to make his remaining fingers more supple . . . Oh, Addy, it broke my heart to see his poor dear hands so—so ruined.'

'I'm awfully sorry, love,' Addy said, giving Gillian's shoulder a squeeze. 'But at least he's alive and in England.' She looked shrewdly at her friend. 'And that wasn't the only reason you were crying, was it? I think you'd better tell me the whole story.'

Gillian promptly started to cry again, but then she took a deep breath, knuckled her eyes with both hands, and began to speak once more. 'Oh, Addy, I'm sure the Admiralty are wrong, but this morning Father and Mother got a telegram saying that Giles and his navigator were missing. I won't believe it, but I promised them I'd go round after

449

I'd seen Dominic . . . you've met my parents, so it will be all right if we both go. But honestly, I *can't* believe that something awful could happen to Giles and me not know. We're twins, after all. So if you'll come with me, we'll both do our best to persuade the parents that Giles will be found and rescued. Apparently he ditched in an area of small coral islands . . . oh, Addy, don't look like that! I'm sure he's alive!'

Addy drew a deep, shuddering breath and when she spoke her voice was calm, though the news had set her heart fluttering in her breast. 'I'm as sure as you are that I'd know if—if the worst had happened,' she said. 'Giles and I are pretty close.' She looked hard at her friend. 'Did it say in the telegram *when* he ditched? Only remember when I had that awful nightmare and woke half the girls in the manor with my shrieks? I was dreaming that I was looking down on a blue sea, dotted with little islands, when a plane dived past me and went into the sea. Then the crew were in the water and I screamed at them to swim for the island . . . and then you woke me up.'

'Gosh!' Gillian said, round-eyed. 'But it *was* only a dream. If we could find out when he ditched . . . but I'm sure the telegram won't go into detail, so best not to mention it to my parents. Just say that, like myself, you won't give up hope because you are convinced that Giles is still alive.'

Addy looked rather sadly at her friend. 'You don't believe me,' she said. 'You think I'm making it up—wise after the event and all that—but it was truly what I dreamed.'

Gillian grinned, seized Addy's hands and pulled her to her feet. 'What really matters is that we must stop the parents giving way to despair. I think, if you don't mind, we won't mention your dream, just your conviction that Giles will turn up sooner or later. They do acknowledge that twins often know what is happening to the other, but of course when Father telephoned this morning, I could only say I didn't believe a word of it because I was taking the minutes of a very important meeting. Then, when I got out of the committee room, I had to scurry off to see Dominic, so I've not had a chance to pass on the assurance until now. Come on, the house is only a mile away and I bet my mother will be able to get us sandwiches and coffee, if nothing else. I've not had anything to eat since breakfast and I don't suppose you've had much either.'

Addy thought of the neat little house to which Giles had taken her on one of his leaves. She had liked his parents at once, though she knew she still felt very much in awe of them. Rear Admiral Frobisher was tall and solidly built, with a crop of waving white hair, and pale blue eyes set in a deeply tanned face. His wife was considerably younger than he, and was dark-haired, running her house and her various war work with effortless efficiency. But as they approached the front door, Addy braced herself to face two people whose lives would be devastated by the loss they believed they had suffered.

Gillian knocked, and almost before her hand had released its hold on the brass dolphin knocker the door was flung open to reveal both her parents, standing in the narrow hallway—and beaming from ear to ear. Addy gasped, then saw that Mr Frobisher was holding out a buff telegram form.

451

'You were right, Gilly,' he said exultantly. 'Another telegram arrived not more than twenty minutes ago. They've found them, safe and uninjured! Oh, Gilly, the relief!'

* * *

It was mid-December and a cold and frosty day when Giles came home. He had telegraphed with the time of his expected arrival, so the station platform was crowded with a reception committee consisting of the entire Frobisher family—cousins, aunts and uncles and of course Giles's twin and their parents—as well as numerous friends.

Addy felt very shy; very awkward too. She had suddenly realised that she had not actually seen Giles for many months and guessed that what he had experienced in the course of those months would have changed him. He had been amongst the troops who had watched that terrible mushroom cloud from a safe distance, watched with awe as it grew and grew. Later, horrendous stories had come out of Hiroshima and Nagasaki, stories of hideous injuries and of the devastation of whole cities. The death toll had been impossible to calculate and the Japanese surrender had been almost immediate. When it had been safe to do so, Giles and Neville had flown over a part of the devastated area and Giles had told her that, though it had achieved the objective of ending the war, he hoped and prayed that such a weapon would never be employed again.

However, for now she intended to put such things out of her mind so that she might concentrate upon the joy of seeing Giles once

452

more. She just hoped that he would be able to pick her out amongst the crowd of eager friends and relatives waiting to welcome him.

Beside her, Gillian reached out a hand and poked Addy in the ribs. 'Cheer up! This is the happiest day of your life, remember? It must be ages since you and Giles last met, so for goodness' sake stop looking so worried and manufacture the biggest, brightest smile you've ever smiled.'

Dominic, standing on Gillian's other side, with his right arm looped about her waist, peered round his fiancée to add his own two penn'orth to Gillian's good advice. 'You're afraid he won't even notice you in the crowd,' he said understandingly. 'But I guess he will; you'll have a special glow for him, as he will for you.' Dominic was making great strides towards rehabilitation, though he had to strap his pencil on to what remained of his hand with sticky tape before he began, falteringly, to trace the outline of his drawing. Paint, for some reason, he found much easier. But now he was speaking again. 'Chin up, Addy, I can hear a train. Yes, and it's coming in on this platform. Oh, look . . .' He turned to Gillian. 'See the banner your little cousins are holding up? Someone should have told them that Giles begins with a G and not a J.'

Gillian was still laughing and explaining that the cousins had only started school that September when the train drew to a halt with much hissing of escaping steam and the carriage doors flew open. Men, mostly in uniform or in all the glory of their stiff new demob suits, tumbled on to the platform. Forgetting all her doubts, Addy began to push forward through the throng of relatives, looking

453

for the familiar face, and found herself suddenly seized in a crushing embrace. She had almost walked past him, but Giles had clearly recognised her unerringly. Addy flung her arms round his neck and tried to speak through the lump in her throat, but could not force out a single word. But who needed words? He's not changed one bit, she thought exultantly, pulling his head down so that she might return his kisses. He's still my Giles, even in different clothes, with his hair cut shorter than I remember and his skin burnt to a tropical brown. She opened her mouth, meaning to tell him how much she'd missed him, how wonderful it was to see him again, but she had no chance to even start the sentence.

'Hey, hey, hey, don't eat the girl! And what about a kiss for your Aunt Daisy?' a voice boomed close to Addy's ear. Giles's huge aunt seized Addy's shoulder and pulled her out of his grasp. 'There's your mother, young man, crying her eyes out because you've not so much as looked at her, and your father trying to comfort her . . .'

Giles just laughed, but Addy took his hand and towed him across to where his parents and his twin sister waited. Then she stood back and let them get over the tears and exclamations, the hugs and kisses, which were their right.

*   *   *

It was the end of January and the Vines was full to bursting, with Addy and Gill sharing Prue's room, Giles and Dominic with Nick in the attic and various friends rolled up in sleeping bags on every available surface. Nell and Nonny had offered to give up their rooms to the Frobishers and their various relations, but Giles's parents had preferred to book into an hotel, saying that it would be easier all round, and though she had politely protested Nell was secretly very relieved. She did not yet know Giles's parents well enough to be easy in their company, and anyway there was so much to do! The reception for the weddings which were about to take place would be held at the church hall later that day, with Nell, Jamie and Nonny doing the catering, and despite the fact that the war had been over for five months rationing was still in force and shortages of almost everything had made the preparations a nightmare.

However, as soon as Giles had been demobbed, Addy had written to her mother explaining that he and she wanted to be married from her old home, and because they were twins Gillian had set her heart on a double wedding and hoped that Mr and Mrs Finch would not object if the Frobishers came north in force.

Nell had been delighted, especially when it was made clear that the Frobishers would share all the expenses, and from that moment she and Nonny had begun squirrelling away any non-perishable food they could lay their hands on. Both Gillian and Addy had been demobbed before Christmas and had been towers of strength, seeing to all such details as invitation cards and the booking of the church and the church hall, as well as contacting relatives still in foreign parts and persuading them to send food parcels home. Addy would have liked to stay in Plymouth, Nell knew, but she returned to Liverpool for the New Year despite the Navy's releasing Foliat Manor to its owners. She, Giles and Gillian bade each other fond farewells and Addy took heart from Nonny's wise words: 'You'll be all the fonder for a bit of separation,' she had said. 'And try though we might, your mam and meself can't do everything and Prue's too near her time to be relied on. So just you bite on the bullet, queen, and believe me, your marriage will be all the sweeter because you didn't just think of yourselves, but of others as well.'

*   *   *

The day of the weddings dawned bright and clear, though very cold, and Nell was grateful for Addy's unstinting help. Prue had gone off early that morning on her own affairs but not once had Addy complained that her sister might at least give a hand, Nell reflected now, making up dried milk, adding oats and pouring the concoction into her largest saucepan. The weddings were to take place at three that afternoon so she had decided on a late breakfast, but a substantial one, starting with porridge and going on with sausage sandwiches and coffee. She just hoped that this would take the edge off guests' appetites at the reception, since food was so hard to come by.

Stirring porridge, Nell remembered that Prue had told Nick about both Ed's death and her own pregnancy when he had been demobbed in early December and had waited hopefully for a proposal of marriage. Instead, Nick had been shocked; in fact he had said indignantly that she had more or less promised to marry him and sleeping with another man in preference to himself was a betrayal of their old friendship. Prue had been astonished and wrathful and a bitter quarrel had ensued, so bitter in fact that Nick had moved out of the Vines and rented a room in a small lodging house down by the docks. Nell had tried to persuade him to stay but without success, and when she had told her daughter that she really should apologise to Nick for all the things she had said, Prue had screamed that her mother simply didn't understand and had flounced off to her own room, no doubt to indulge in a hearty bout of tears, though she would never have admitted it.

Fortunately, Paul had come home only a few days after that violent quarrel. After returning from India, he had got a job with a car manufacturing firm just outside the city, and had popped into the Vines to see if Nell could let him have his old room just until he found somewhere to rent on a more permanent basis. He had admitted to Nell that he had received a furious and almost incoherent telephone call from his brother and had come to offer congratulations to Addy and commiserations to Prue.

'Oh, Paul, it's lovely to see you, and it's no use saying I'm ashamed of poor little Prue because if only Ed had lived he would have made all respectable and I could have looked forward to the birth of my first grandchild,' Nell had said. 'And it's not as though Prue is the only unmarried mother in the district, because there are a great many poor girls bringing up babies without the help of a husband. But you know, Prue was torn between Ed and Nick right from the start. To tell you the truth, I think what tipped the scales was that she was sorry for Ed. His parents were killed when he was only seven or eight and his guardians were old and—and—indifferent. When Ed was killed, I thought Prue and Nick might get together again, but I reckoned without the baby. Prue's putting a good face on it, but I believe they're both very unhappy. All right, they may not want to marry, but it would be nice if they could be friends again.'

Paul had chuckled. 'I'm going to take Prue dancing this evening,' he had said. 'And I shall make sure that Nick knows it. I'll take her to the flicks tomorrow night and for a day in the country at the weekend. Believe me, I know Nick too well to imagine he'll let me steal Prue from under his nose. When we were kids, he used to go around with Addy and I went around with Prue, but as soon as we grew up he began to edge me out. He wanted to monopolise Prue—she was such a pretty kid—and I didn't blame him. Brothers are like that, you know, a bit like two dogs with a bone. One will only show interest in it when he sees the other about to pick it up.'

Nell had laughed. 'What a horrible way to put it,' she said, but she had heard the approval in her own tone.

'It's life,' Paul had said, grinning. 'But you must make sure as well that Nick knows what I'm doing. I'll see him tonight when he finishes work and I'll maybe hint that I'm sorry for Prue and mean to take her about a bit, but if I say too much he might twig what I'm up to, which would never do.'

Paul had been as good as his word, and before he had even moved out of the Vines the quarrel had been resolved. Nick had even apologised to Prue, explaining that his reaction to her news had been due to the shock, and Prue had graciously forgiven him, admitting that she, too, had said things she later regretted. Nell had been hopeful that the couple would forget their differences and agree to marry, for it soon became clear that Nick was every bit as interested in Prue and her pregnancy as Prue was herself. Together, the two heads—one dark and the other fair—had bent over a book of babies' names, mocking each other's choices and making ever more weird and fanciful suggestions. Nick took Prue to the cinema and for long walks. He read her baby books and suggested that she follow the advice contained therein.

In fact, Nell thought ruefully now, the only suggestion that Nick had not made, was that they might marry. Nell had never heard of a triple wedding, but talked constantly of the event to come, hoping that it would prick her daughter and Nick into suggesting that they, too, might wed. However, though the pair were now good friends, there was never so much as a mention of marriage, so Nell had given up, and concentrated on the weddings which were to take place. She was sorry that the baby would be born without a father, but decided that it was a decision which only the two people involved could make, and put her younger daughter out of her mind. She had too much to do, she told herself severely, to worry over Prue and Nick.

Nell began to dish up as soon as Nonny and Jamie appeared, then everyone else followed in a rush and they were all sitting at the table with bowls of porridge in front of them when Nell sighed and got to her feet. 'Where's Prue?' she demanded. She looked across at Addy. 'Be a dear and go and give her a shake, queen,' she was beginning, when the back door flew open and Prue burst into the room, closely followed by Nick. Prue was holding her left hand out in front of her and her face was almost split in two by the most enormous Cheshire-cat grin.

'See?' she shouted. 'Pipped at the post, Addy Fairweather! Me and Nick's got married this morning!'

CHAPTER NINETEEN

Addy and Giles stood in the window of the small bedroom that overlooked the rose garden. Frost had glazed the trees, the grass and the bushes, and above, in the dark sky, floated a crescent moon, its light seeming to emphasise the starkness of the deep shadows and whitened branches.

They had enjoyed a brief honeymoon in Blackpool and had then set out on the long journey to Plymouth, arriving there to find no one to meet them, since Gillian and Dominic were still on honeymoon, and the newly-weds had not informed anyone of their arrival time. Knowing the manor would be empty and, presumably, the cupboards bare, they had had a hasty meal in a small café opposite the station and caught a taxi home.

Giles had unlocked the door, thrust the suitcases into the wide hall and pounced on Addy, lifting her up and carrying her over the threshold, ignoring her squeaks of protest. 'It's traditional,' he had said, a trifle breathlessly. He had stood Addy down and clicked the switch inside the front door, but had only laughed when no illumination followed.

'It doesn't matter. I expect the mains is switched off, but I don't mean to do anything about it now. Let's go straight to bed.'

They had climbed the stairs, lugging their suitcases, and without having to consult one another had gone straight to the bedroom that overlooked the rose garden. Now, standing close to the glass, Addy reflected how strange it was that they had both slept in this room for several years, but at different times and never together.

So much had happened here, to both of them; Giles had changed from a boy to a youth, and from a youth to a man, and she had slept here in her early teens and returned as a young woman. Now she reached out and took Giles's hand, sitting down on the bed and pulling him down beside her. 'Giles, when you lived here, before the war I mean, did you—did you ever look out of the window and see someone in the rose garden? Someone you didn't recognise?'

'Now you mention it I did see someone once,' Giles said lightly, 'but I reckon it was one of the village lads, doing a bit of poaching and having a look round at the same time. You?'

Addy thought about the figure in the moonlight, which had turned out to be Ed. Should she tell him? But it was pointless; it had happened and would not, she was sure, happen again. 'Yes, I saw a fellow a couple of times and thought he was probably seeing if he could find anything to steal,' she said with equal lightness. 'We'll have to put a stop to that sort of thing, Giles. And now let's make up one of these beds; there are blankets and pillows, but no sheets. Not that it matters; I could sleep on a perishin' clothes line. I don't mean to unpack tonight; I'll sleep in my undies.'

Presently, they were both snuggled down beneath the blankets and Addy was on the very edge of sleep when Giles muttered something. It sounded like 'He cast no shadow', but before she could ask him what he meant she could tell by his even breathing that he had fallen asleep. Addy sighed and turned in his arms to give him a good night kiss. For a moment she wondered whether that muttered remark could mean that Giles, too, had also seen something strange in the rose garden; then she dismissed the thought. We've come full circle, she told herself drowsily, and we are where we both longed to be. When tomorrow comes, we'll start work on the old place and the past will be forgotten. The future is what really matters, when all's said and done.